THE
HORSEMASTERS

THE HORSEMASTERS

Joan Wolf

A DUTTON BOOK

DUTTON
Published by the Penguin Group
Penguin Books USA Inc., 375 Hudson Street, New York, New York 10014, U.S.A.
Penguin Books Ltd, 27 Wrights Lane, London W8 5TZ, England
Penguin Books Australia Ltd, Ringwood, Victoria, Australia
Penguin Books Canada Ltd, 10 Alcorn Avenue, Toronto, Ontario, Canada M4V 3B2
Penguin Books (N.Z.) Ltd, 182–190 Wairau Road, Auckland 10, New Zealand

Penguin Books Ltd, Registered Offices:
Harmondsworth, Middlesex, England

First published by Dutton, an imprint of New American Library,
a division of Penguin Books USA Inc.
Distributed in Canada by McClelland & Stewart Inc.

First Printing, May, 1993

10 9 8 7 6 5 4 3 2 1

REGISTERED TRADEMARK—MARCA REGISTRADA

LIBRARY OF CONGRESS CATALOGING IN PUBLICATION DATA:
Wolf, Joan.
    The horsemasters / Joan Wolf.
      p. cm.
    ISBN 0-525-93589-4
    1. Man, Prehistoric—Europe, Southern—Fiction.   I. Title.
PS3573.O486H66   1993
813'.54—dc20   92–32106
                                                    CIP

Printed in the United States of America
Set in Electra
Designed by Eve L. Kirch

To Patty, best of sisters, best of friends

ACKNOWLEDGMENTS

I would like to express my appreciation to two particular friends who were of invaluable assistance to me in the writing of *The Horsemasters*.

First, thanks to Edith Layton Felber, who helped me sort through a chaos of ideas and characters to come up with the shape of a novel.

And I would also like to acknowledge Elsa, my beautiful bay thoroughbred mare, whose shadow stands behind all of the horses in this book.

FOREWORD

The catalyst for *The Horsemasters* came from Paul Bahn, the English archeologist who has written in several places of his suspicion that humankind's partnership with horses might have begun earlier than most historians presently think. Bahn points out a number of Cro-Magnon engravings and pictures in which the horses appear to be wearing harnesses, as well as some pieces of portable art taken from the cave of Le Mas d'Azil, where there are numerous horseheads that seem to be wearing some kind of a bridle.

One other fascinating piece of evidence Bahn cites to buttress his theory is the fossil of a horse's tooth that he found in the Begouen family collection. This tooth, dating from about thirteen thousand years ago, bears two transverse polished grooves, which seem to represent a variation of normal cribbing wear. As any horseman knows, cribbing (wood chewing combined with sucking air) is a vice peculiar to horses kept in captivity; it never occurs when they are running free.

In the words of Bahn, ". . . there has never been a valid reason for rejecting *a priori* the idea of close animal control in the late Paleolithic, and indeed there is a body of very varied evidence in favour of such a view; on this basis I consider it perfectly feasible—even likely,—that some human groups in the later part of Würm (and possibly even earlier) travelled with pack-animals, on horse-back, or in transport harnessed to horse or reindeer" (*Pyrenean Prehistory* by Paul Bahn).

Throughout history, whole civilizations have changed because of the horse. People who were once sedentary suddenly found themselves masters of space. Distances dwindled, and settlements were perceived not as homes but as springboards for endless plundering.

This particular kind of horse mentality is relentlessly male; the possession of horses conferred power. From the Bronze Age Kassites, to the Hittites, to the Scythians, to the cavalry of Alexander the Great, horsemen rode over the world. Central Asian horsemen called Huns challenged the power of Rome, and Genghis Khan and his Mongol army conquered much of Asia and Europe. In our own country, the introduction of the horse rapidly transformed the Plains Indian from a subsistence farmer into a buffalo-hunting warrior.

The coming of the horsemen, then, is one of the most ancient of themes, and, considering Bahn's evidence, I decided to explore it in this novel.

The setting for *The Horsemasters* is the Pyrenees mountains some thirteen thousand years ago. Anthropologists call the people of this time Cro-Magnon, and their culture is called Magdelenian.

The language used in this book, as in my previous prehistory novel *Daughter of the Red Deer*, is modern English. The characters are supposedly speaking their own language, and rather than attempt some kind of pseudo–Cro-Magnonese, I preferred to "translate" their words into our own speech.

The horses of the Valley of the Wolf are loosely based on the Villano, the Iberian horse of the Pyrenees referred to in ancient books.

The River of Gold is the Garonne, the Atata is the Ariège, and the Greatfish is the Salat. The sacred cave of the Tribe of the Buffalo is the cave of Niaux, the Great Cave is Le Mas d'Azil, and the sacred cave of the Tribe of the Red Deer is Le Tuc d'Audobert. Thorn's cave in the Valley of the Wolf has never been found.

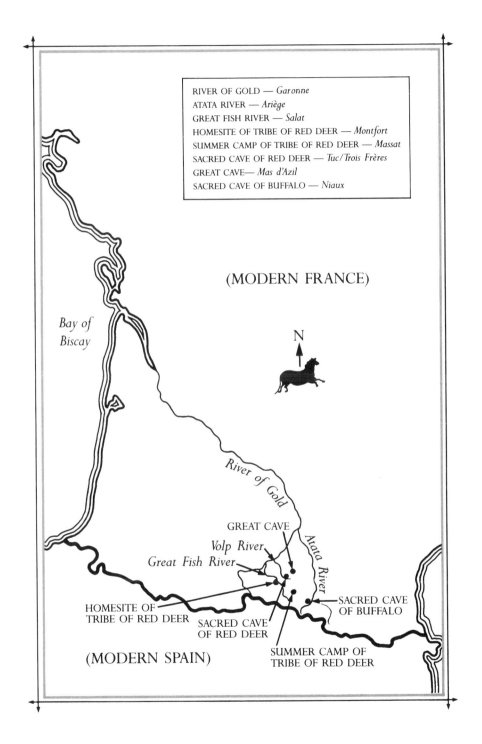

RIVER OF GOLD — *Garonne*
ATATA RIVER — *Ariège*
GREAT FISH RIVER — *Salat*
HOMESITE OF TRIBE OF RED DEER — *Montfort*
SUMMER CAMP OF TRIBE OF RED DEER — *Massat*
SACRED CAVE OF RED DEER — *Tuc/Trois Frères*
GREAT CAVE— *Mas d'Azil*
SACRED CAVE OF BUFFALO — *Niaux*

(MODERN FRANCE)

*Bay of
Biscay*

N

River of Gold

GREAT CAVE
Volp River
Great Fish River

Atata River

SACRED CAVE
OF BUFFALO

HOMESITE OF
TRIBE OF RED DEER

SACRED CAVE
OF RED DEER

SUMMER CAMP OF
TRIBE OF RED DEER

(MODERN SPAIN)

Chapter One

The air in the cave was quiet. That was what awed Ronan most about the initiation cave: it was so quiet. No sound of pine trees stirring in the wind; no dripping of water or rustle of human or animal life. Only silence: deep, profound, endless.

Ronan had been waiting in this cave for a day and a night now. He was alone, with no food or water, and only a single spear for protection in case a cave bear should suddenly decide to invade his solitude. He had no fire, only one small stone lamp to light the thick blackness. His upper torso was naked, save for where it was decorated by the ocher markings painted there yesterday by his uncle.

It was his initiation into manhood, and he must pass the Test of Solitude.

He had been here a day and a night, but shut away from the sky as he was, there was nothing to help him count the passing of time. Ronan himself had no way of knowing if he had been in the cave for a few hours, or for a week. Time here was endless. He only knew that when the men came for him, he must be ready. They must not find him asleep.

The wounds on his upper right arm had long since stopped bleeding, but they still hurt. He thought the arm had swollen. Neihle had cut deep enough to leave scars, though not deep enough to injure the muscle beneath the skin. The scars were an honor, a sign that the man who carried them was an initiated male of the Tribe of the Red Deer. When the rest of the men of the tribe came to get him, and found he had passed the Test of Solitude, Neihle would make two additional cuts on his left arm.

The lamp flickered. The animal fat in which the wick floated was almost burned out. Surely, Ronan thought, that was a sign that the men must come soon.

He was cold. He was hungry. He was exhausted from thirty-two hours without real sleep. But he kept his upright position, seated on the floor with his back propped against the stone wall, his spear held poised in his left hand. When the men came they would find him ready.

They had already made the hunting dance before they left him here alone, initiating him into the male society of tribal hunters. Next after the Test of Solitude would come his initiation into the most important, the most sacred and revered, of all the rites of the Mother.

It would be Borba who would do it; they had settled that between them some time ago. Borba had been initiated when her moon blood began to flow twelve moons past, and so she was well qualified to teach a boy the things he needed to know about mating with a woman.

Ronan had kept himself awake for much of his time in the cave by thinking about what he and Borba would do this night and about what changes it would bring to his life.

He would move out of his stepmother's hut and live in the men's cave with the rest of the initiates. Ronan had long since ceased to listen to Orenda's bitter tongue, but it would be a blessing no longer to be forced to endure her enmity at close quarters. He would marry, of course, but not for a few years yet. Boys of fourteen did not generally marry in the Tribe of the Red Deer.

Freedom. That was what Ronan had thought about all through the long and lonely night of his Test of Solitude. He would live in the men's cave, and hunt every day with his agemates, and lie every night with a different girl. He would no longer be a boy but an initiated man of the tribe.

It would help to make up, a little, for what he had never had.

I will not think of that now, he told himself firmly. It was ill luck to think of angry things during the Test of Solitude.

Ronan's ears, for so long attuned to silence, now caught a faint sound in the distance. A few moments later there was a flicker of light at the end of the tunnel that led into the chamber in which he was waiting.

The men were coming. Ronan got to his feet.

There was a great fire going outside the initiation cave, and after Ronan's maternal uncle had made the cuts on his other arm, the men feasted on the deer they had killed for the occasion. Ronan sat around the fire with the men of his tribe, listening to the laughter and the talking, and helping to pass great pieces of roast deer meat clockwise around the circle. His exhilaration was so great that he did not even feel the pain in his heavily bleeding arm.

The laughter grew uproarious as the talk became bawdier. Ronan's strong white teeth bit into the meat that was handed to him, tearing away a big chunk before passing it along to the man on his other side. He felt the food giving him strength, a strength he would need later, as the men were delightedly pointing out with lavish anatomical detail.

The juice from the meat ran down Ronan's chin, and he wiped it away with his hand. There was blood on his hand, mixing with the red juice of the deer meat. The blood had streamed down his arm from the new ritual wounds. As he listened to the talk, Ronan felt the restless beast of desire rising within him, beating in his blood, hammering in his heart, pulsing in his loins. The meat came around to him again, and he tore off another chunk with his teeth.

"It is time. The women will be waiting." Ronan looked up to see his uncle's tall shape standing before him. The rest of the men were also getting to their feet. It was necessary for them to go to the sacred cave of Earth Mother for the final rite of the initiation ceremony. Borba would be there, with the rest of the tribe's initiated women.

Someone lit a torch from the fire, and then more torches were raised on high. A few men stayed behind to put out the fire, and the rest took to the narrow trail that wound along the river Volp, a trail that would bring them eventually to the place that was the final destination of all initiation ceremonies, both male and female alike.

The women were at the sacred cave already, gathered on the shore of the river that long ago had cut its way directly into the hillside to form a series of underground caverns. For the Tribe of the Red Deer, this seemingly endless, deep, dark cave represented the womb of the

Mother. It was here the tribe brought its young girls when the menstrual blood of life first began to flow; here it brought its young men when they became of an age to worship the Goddess by having intercourse with a woman; here the Mistress of the Tribe twice a year made the Sacred Marriage to ensure the life of the tribe, the life of the herds, the life of the world of men.

No member of the tribe ever approached this place without the hair on the back of the neck rising in awe. And so it was this night for Ronan.

Then he saw his half-sister.

Morna. The Chosen One. The Daughter. The one who would be the tribe's next Mistress after Arika died. She was one year younger than Ronan.

His mouth set in bitterness as he stared at his sister's lovely face. She smiled at him and flung back her red-gold hair. Her eyes glittered in the torchlight.

What was she doing here? he thought angrily. Morna had not yet been initiated. She had no business being here this night.

The Mistress, he saw, glancing around quickly, was not here. Well, he had not expected her to be. Arika had always kept as far from her only son as possible, given the communal nature of the tribe.

Borba was not present, either. She must already be within the cave. Ronan stood in the midst of the men, tense and alert, waiting to be told what to do next. It was Fali, the Old Woman of the Tribe, who approached. In one hand she held a stone saucer filled with red ocher; in the other, she held a brush made out of pine.

"Ronan, son of Arika, grandson of Elen," Fali said clearly as she painted the loop sign of the phallus on his chest between his nipples. "It is your time to learn to know the Goddess as world-maker. It is your time to learn to serve her, as Sky God served her when together they mated to make the world."

The Old Woman finished her work and stepped back. "You may enter the cave," she told him softly. "Your mate awaits you in the first chamber."

Ronan bent his black head and looked down into the bright brown eyes of the Old Woman. Fali, one of the girls kidnapped so many years before by the men of the Horse, was now the only survivor of that fateful event. The Tribe of the Red Deer had changed since then, Ronan had been told. Principally, it had come to recognize more fully the religious needs of its men. His initiation was one of those changes.

The Old Woman had handed him a stone lamp, and slowly he started along the river, following the stream as it wound into the depths of the mountain. Earlier in the spring, Ronan would have needed to take a boat, but it had been dry this year, the river was not as swollen as usual, and it was possible to walk along the gravel at the outermost sides of the cave.

The men of the tribe came to this cave only twice a year, at Spring and Winter Fires, and then they came but to the first chamber. Only the man chosen to make the Sacred Marriage with the tribe's Mistress was ever taken into the sanctuary.

Ronan knew he would never be one of the men to see that sanctuary. His mother was Mistress, and his sister would follow her. As it was taboo for him to lie with either of them, he was fated to remain ignorant of the mysteries that lay beyond the first chamber.

He was not sorry for that, Ronan thought, as he made his way carefully along the shore of the river, lit only by his single stone lamp. The cave was thick with the Mother's presence, thick with the smells of the earth, of the river, thick with Mystery.

Ronan shivered in the chill damp. I have had enough of caves, he thought suddenly, remembering his solitary dark vigil of the night before. Then he shivered again, this time with fear. That was blasphemy!

He made his mind a blank, willing out dangerous thoughts. He looked ahead, his eyes striving to pierce through the darkness, to find the woman he was seeking.

After what seemed to him a long time, the passage widened, and Ronan found himself in the first chamber of the cave. The walls in here were decorated with engravings of animals: buffalo, reindeer, and horses. Most important to the cave's purpose, however, was the sign of the Mother, the P, which was chiseled again and again into the limestone walls.

The river passed through this chamber and then disappeared out of sight into the profound darkness of the depths of the hill. Ronan did not follow the river; instead, he stopped and looked at the girl who was waiting for him.

The women had made a small fire in the center of the chamber

and arranged a bedplace of leaves and grasses covered over by deerskin
rugs. Kneeling upright on the bedplace was Borba, naked save for the
necklace of pointed deer teeth that hung around her neck and the belt
of similar teeth that encircled her slender hips. Her hair had been washed
and left unbraided, and it flowed around her shoulders, bright as sunshine in the dimness of the cave. Upon each high firm breast was painted
a red ocher triangle, symbol of the female.

Ronan halted. He flicked a quick look at the golden triangle that
lay below her belt and felt a vibration beginning within him, low and
dark, thrilling all through his blood and his bones and his muscles. But
he forced himself to stand still and wait. It was for her to show him
what he should do.

"Ronan," she said. Her face was lit by the firelight, and he saw the
flash of her smile. He thought it looked oddly triumphant.

"I am here." He began to walk toward her.

Borba's laugh held a strange, wild note. "You look like a cave
panther, stalking toward me like that," she said. She stretched out her
hands to him, and he came and took them. She tugged him downward
toward her, and he knelt facing her. She had not released his hands,
and now she raised them and put them on her bare young breasts. His
phallus was perfectly erect.

Her wide eyes gazed up at him. "That is good," she whispered. "A
woman likes to have her breasts caressed, Ronan." And then she reached
out and began to untie the leather thong that belted his deerskin trousers.

Nel was coming home from collecting berries with her agemates
and some of the tribe's old women, when she heard the baby crying
from within the forest of evergreens and birch that surrounded the trail.
She halted.

The child walking behind her on the narrow path bumped into her,
and some of the berries in the basket she was carrying spilled.

"Nel!" Rena said with intense annoyance. "Don't stop so suddenly!
You made me spill my berries." And she dropped to her knees to retrieve
what had been lost.

"Didn't you hear the baby?" Nel asked.

"Sa," Rena returned. She looked up. The two children were alone
for the moment; they had been at the end of the line of returning

gatherers, and those in front had not yet realized they had fallen behind. "It is one of Mira's twins. They must have brought it out to the woods while we were at the meadow picking berries."

The sound came again, a thin, fretful wailing. The baby sounded as if it had been crying for some time.

Nel clenched her fists. "I am going to find it," she said.

"You can't!" Rena dropped her basket and reached out to grab Nel's arm. "That twin is dangerous."

"I can," Nel said stubbornly. "How can it be dangerous, Rena? It is only a baby!"

"It is the dark twin, the second one born," Rena said. "When the Mother bore twins at the beginning of the world, one became the God of Light and the other became the God of the Underworld. Now, when twins are born to the world of men, it is necessary to send the dark twin back to the Underworld before it can spread its darkness in the world of light. You know that, Nel. Everyone knows that!"

Nel's face was white and set. Her thin-bridged nose and sharp cheek-bones looked even more prominent than usual, and her glittering green stare was desperate. "Then why does the Mother *make* twins, if one is evil?"

"No one knows why the Mother does as she does," the other child returned impatiently. "She is the Goddess. She does not have to explain herself to us."

The cry came again. "I'll find the baby and hide him away some-where safe," Nel said. "No one will ever know."

Rena's fingers tightened on Nel's arm. "How will you feed it?" she asked practically. "You are but nine winters old. You have no milk to give an infant." Rena loosened her grip somewhat as she saw that her words had made an impact on Nel. She added, in a gentler voice, "It is in my heart that you are more upset about this child than Mira is. After all, she still has one child left to care for, and that is more than enough." Then, when Nel did not respond, Rena said, "My mother told me that in the tribes that follow Sky God, both twins are exposed. At least we do not do that."

"Nel! Rena! What is keeping you?" From a little way up the trail came the voice of one of the old women who had accompanied them. She sounded cross.

"Go on," Rena said, giving Nel a push, and after a minute, Nel went.

Supper was ready when Nel returned to her father's hut, but she could not eat. Her stepmother nagged and scolded and made remarks about ungrateful children, but Nel scarcely heard her. All she could hear, echoing again and again through her mind, was the desolate sound of the baby crying in the forest.

There was no one in the whole tribe who would understand how she felt, she thought despairingly. No one except Ronan, of course, and since his initiation she had scarcely seen him. Now that he was a man, obviously he had no time for the small cousin who was still a child.

"I told the Old Woman I would bring her some of the berries I picked today," Nel said, lying with swift inspiration. She could not bear to stay one more minute within this hut, and she knew a promise made to the Old Woman would be respected even by her stepmother.

Olma frowned, muttered something about needing Nel's help herself, but did not try to stop the child as she left the hut. Nel did not go toward Fali's hut, however, but turned instead toward the river on whose shores the main homesite of the Red Deer was located.

The Tribe of the Red Deer had dwelled in the area of the Greatfish River for as long as anyone could remember. The location was ideal for the exploitation of the reindeer and red deer which formed the chief staple of the tribe's diet. The caves and huts faced east toward the river, in a place that was dry and sheltered from the wind, and on the opposite bank the heights of Deer Hill afforded excellent views of the surrounding territory. The river at this point ran in a series of fords and rapids, and immediately upstream from the homesite it converged with the Leza in a marshy area that was rich in both fish and fowl.

Located thus, at the point where two rivers emerged from their narrow upland valleys into the foothills, the tribe was in excellent position to prey upon the herds of deer as they ascended into the upland pastures for summer feeding and then returned to the lowland pastures for the winter.

This evening, however, Nel was not thinking of deer. She was thinking of the abandoned baby in the forest. Behind her, cookfires were burning cheerfully in front of all the huts, and the tribe was at supper. Only the baby in the forest would not be fed this night, Nel thought. She stared at the swiftly running water of the Greatfish River, and then, abruptly, she began to cry.

A large wolf emerged from the forest upstream and began to lope with long loose strides toward the solitary child. Nel did not see him, and she remained in her place by the shore, weeping inconsolably. The wolf reached her, halted, and began to make small inquiring noises in the back of his throat.

"It's all right, Nigak," Nel said in a voice that shook with grief. "I'm all right."

"What's the matter, minnow?" The voice was familiar, and deeply loved, and, hearing it, Nel struggled to get herself under control. "N-nothing," she gulped.

"I am thinking it must be a very big nothing to make you cry like this," Ronan said. He sat beside her and put an arm around her narrow shoulders. "What is it, Nel?" he asked. "You can tell me."

Nigak switched his attention to Ronan, extending his white muzzle to sniff at the boy's clothes. Nel turned her head and buried her face in Ronan's shoulder. "I h-heard the baby," she said. "C-crying in the forest. Oh Ronan!" Her skinny body was wracked with grief.

"One of Mira's twins," he said softly.

"S-sa."

"It will be dead by now, Nel," he said. "It isn't suffering any longer."

"Do you think an animal got it?" she sobbed.

"Sa."

She continued to sob, and he continued to hold her. Finally, he said, "Come. You are soaking my shirt. You will have to re-scrape it for me, the buckskin will be so stiff."

She shuddered. "I don't understand why they did it," she said. "I will never understand why they did it. They say it is the will of the Mother, but how do they know that, Ronan? How do they know that the Mother wanted them to kill that baby?"

"The Mistress told them so," he said. His face was impassive.

"Suppose she is wrong?" Nel said defiantly. "Suppose the baby was not a dark twin? Suppose the baby they kept is the dark twin, and they have killed the light one?"

A little silence fell. Then Ronan said, "You are a dangerous thinker, Nel."

"So are you," she flashed back.

They looked at each other. After a minute, Ronan grinned. It transformed his face, that smile, transmuting all the dark arrogance into brilliant, beguiling charm. Nel smiled tremulously back.

"I'm sorry about the baby, minnow," he said. "It's why I was looking for you. I knew you would take it hard."

It made her feel better to know he had been looking for her. "Are you sure it is dead, Ronan?"

"I am sure."

She let out her breath in a long, uneven sigh.

"You can't rescue all the outcasts of the world like you rescued Nigak, you know," he said.

The wolf, who had lain down before Nel's feet, lifted his head when he heard his name. He was a magnificent animal, silver gray except for four white legs, a white chest and white muzzle. His clear yellow-brown eyes looked from Nel to Ronan, his ears folded back in friendliness, and his tail wagged.

"Nigak was able to eat meat when I found him," Nel said. "I was going to look for the baby this afternoon, but then Rena said I wouldn't be able to feed him and I knew she was right."

Ronan closed his hand gently around her braid. "You need to toughen up that soft heart of yours, Nel."

"I *am* tough," Nel said indignantly.

"About yourself you are," he agreed. "I don't ever remember seeing you cry for yourself."

"Once I did," she said. Her voice was low. "Don't you remember?"

He gave a tug to the long fawn-colored braid. "Sa," he said. "I remember."

Silence fell between them. Then Nel said, "I didn't think you cared about me anymore. Ever since you moved into the men's cave, I have scarcely seen you."

"Of course I care about you." He sounded surprised. Then he quirked one slim black eyebrow. "We are bound together by blood. Don't you remember?"

In answer she stretched out her right arm, with the white skin of the inner side exposed. They both regarded it with interest. On the fine skin near the wrist there was a small half-moon–shaped scar, a memento of the ceremony Ronan had performed when he was ten and she was five. He stretched out his own arm, which showed a similar mark.

Ronan laughed. "You were so brave," he said, "letting me slice away at your wrist like that. Brave or stupid. I was never certain which."

"Both, I am thinking," she retorted, and they laughed together.

"So this is where you are, Ronan. I have been looking for you." Nel turned to see Borba making her way toward them from the cluster of pines behind. The setting sun haloed the girl's hair with gold, and she was smiling at Ronan.

"Run along now, minnow," Ronan said into her ear.

I was here first. Nel almost said it, looked into Ronan's face, and then did not.

Chapter Two

The following day, as if to atone for the lie to her stepmother, Nel brought some berries to the Old Woman.

The day was warm, and Fali was sitting in the sun in front of her hut, scraping a deerskin and basking in the welcome summer warmth.

"Good afternoon, my Mother," Nel said politely. "I have brought you some of the hawthorn berries I picked."

The Old Woman squinted a little to see who it was. "Nel?"

"Sa. It is Nel."

"Sit down, child."

Nel sat and looked with a child's unwinking stare into the Old Woman's massively wrinkled face. Fali's white hair was scraped back into a short, thin braid, and her smile showed more gums than teeth, but her brown eyes were still bright and alert. She looked back at Nel with the fearlessness of the very old to the very young and said, "Nel, daughter of Tana, granddaughter of Meli, great-granddaughter of Elen."

"Sa." Nel showed no surprise at the extensive naming. It was one of the Old Woman's responsibilities to keep the family lines of all the tribe. "That is who I am."

Fali's next words did surprise her, however. "After Morna," the Old Woman stated, "it is you who would be our next Mistress."

Nel blinked. "I suppose so," she said.

The Old Woman sighed. "Morna looks like her grandmother," she told Nel, "but I fear she is not like Elen in other ways."

Since Elen had died long before Nel was born, she had no reply to this observation.

The Old Woman was going on softly. "It has not been the same in the tribe since Alin left."

This delving into the past was confusing to Nel. "Alin?" She frowned, trying to remember. "My Mother, do you mean the Chosen One who long ago deserted the tribe to go and live with a man of the Horse?"

Fali's eyes flashed, a strangely vivid look in that withered old face. "Alin did what she had to do." The white head bowed. "Elen was a good Mistress," she said. "Arika is a good Mistress. But neither of them could equal Alin."

Prudently, Nel did not reply.

"You have her blood, Nel" was Fali's next remark. "You have the blood of Tor in your line, the blood of Alin's father."

Nel nodded. She knew the name of Tor. Like all members of the tribe, she had been required to memorize her own blood lines.

"I have been watching you," Fali said now, and Nel's head lifted in sudden alarm. Fali went on: "I am thinking that you may have the Mother's healing touch."

"It is only that I do not like to watch anything suffer," Nel answered softly. "I have no special touch."

"If you would like to learn more about the use of herbs to heal," Fali said, "I will teach you."

Nel's green eyes glowed. "I would like that very much, my Mother."

The Old Woman nodded. "Arika has some of the skill, but Morna shows no inclination toward the healing arts. You, Nel"—the bright brown eyes regarded her shrewdly—"you, I think, may be my heir." Before Nel could reply, Fali's eyes closed, and she fell into the light doze of the very old. Nel sat quietly, her thoughts going from Fali's words to the other concerns that had brought her here.

At last Fali's eyes opened. She picked up one of the scrapers and began to rub the deerskin that was stretched out on the ground before the hut. Nel watched for a moment in silence, and then she spoke what was on her mind. "My Mother," she said, "I understand that it is not permissible for hearth-cousins to marry . . ."

Fali looked up from her scraping. "Of course it is not permissible," she said. "Cousins whose mothers were sisters are too closely bound to marry."

"Yet it is acceptable for cousins whose parents were sister and brother to marry," said Nel.

Fali began to rub her scraper over the skin once more. "Sister and brother, that is different. The children of brother and sister are cross-cousins, not hearth-cousins."

"But what . . ." Nel inhaled and bravely brought it forth: "What if a girl wants to marry a boy who was hearth-cousin to her mother? Would that be permissible?"

There was a long silence. Fali's arm had ceased all motion. "Ronan," she said.

Nel felt the heat come into her cheeks. "I was just wondering."

Fali's look was piercing. "Does Ronan wish to marry you, Nel?"

Nel's cheeks flushed hotter. "Na," she answered gruffly.

"Then why ask such a question?"

Nel did not answer.

The Old Woman put down her scraper and folded her withered hands. To Nel's great relief, she gazed away toward Deer Hill. "What are the family lines here?" Fali asked herself thoughtfully. "Ronan is the son of Arika. Arika and your grandmother were sisters; therefore Ronan and your mother were hearth-cousins."

"Sa," Nel said a little breathlessly. "So doesn't that make Ronan and me cross-cousins?"

Fali removed her gaze from the looming hill and turned to Nel. "I am thinking, Nel, that it would not be wise of you to set your mind on Ronan," she said slowly.

"Why is that, my Mother?"

"It would be dangerous." Fali frowned, making even more wrinkles in her face. She repeated, her voice stronger, "Do not set your mind on Ronan."

"The blood ties are too close?"

Fali shook her head. "It is not the blood ties."

"Then I do not understand you, My Mother," Nel said patiently. "If it is not the blood ties, then what is dangerous?"

"You and Ronan together—that is dangerous." Fali reached out and took Nel's chin in her hand. The Old Woman's grip was surprisingly strong. "This is your idea, Nel? Ronan has not mentioned marriage to you?"

Nel shook her head, to indicate a negative reply and to free her chin from that grip. "But I still do not understand you," she cried, retreating beyond Fali's grasp. "If our marriage would break no taboo, then why is it dangerous?" Her voice echoed with frustration and bewilderment. "What have we done?"

"It is not what you have done," said the Old Woman somberly. "It is what you are."

Then as Nel sat, mute and defiant, the Old Woman explained. "Your grandmother was Arika's elder sister, was Mistress before her. You are the next in line after Morna. Arika will never let you marry Ronan, Nel. Put it out of your mind, my child."

Nel bowed her head, to hide the rebellion in her eyes.

During the warm weather the hunters of the tribe moved to their summer camp, which lay in the high country to the south and east of their permanent home. This was a move that was necessitated by the migration of the herds, which ascended during the summer into the pastures of the higher country to feed on the rich, snow-fed grass that could be found there.

The Red Deer summer camp lay at the apex of an elongated triangular basin at the point where the Narrow River suddenly entered a narrow and winding gorge. The basin was bound on all sides by steep slopes formed by the confluence of several small valleys. All of these valleys were cul-de-sacs except the one that led up into the high pass which opened into the country of the Tribe of the Buffalo.

The two large caves which formed the summer home of the Tribe of the Red Deer overlooked the river, and the men of the tribe had also pitched hide tents to extend the amount of shelter.

Life was easy in summer camp. The very old and the very young had been left behind at the Greatfish River; only the initiated males and the women who were not encumbered with small children moved to summer camp. The purpose of the move was to hunt the reindeer and the red deer in order to feed not only themselves but also those who had been left at home. Hunting was not difficult, however, and the living was free and pleasant.

It was Ronan's first season in summer camp, and he found it fine.

By day he and his agemates would roam the mountains, hunting in total freedom, wrestling with each other in the warm sunlight, singing the tribe's hunting songs, holding spear-throwing contests when there was no animal within their weapon's reach.

The nights were for girls. Red Deer girls, with sweet seductive smiles and soft willing bodies.

Ronan had heard from his fellows that in the other Kindred tribes, which followed the male god of the Sky, the unmarried women did not have the same freedom as did the girls of the Red Deer. That was certainly one thing about the Way of Sky God with which Ronan did not agree.

The boy is looking happy, Neihle thought when he came up to the initiates' cookfire one evening to find Ronan eating a supper of stewed deer meat in the company of his agemates. Ronan respectfully rose to his feet when he saw his uncle, and offered him some food.

"Na, I have eaten," the man replied. He looked into the dark eyes of his nephew and saw with some surprise that they were on a slightly higher level than his own. "You have grown two fingers since your initiation," Neihle said. "Something must be agreeing with you."

Ronan grinned.

"Borba is agreeing with him," Tyr, one of the boys at the cookfire, said. "And Iva and Tosa and Lula and . . ."

"That is enough," Ronan said, but a faint smile still lingered on his lips.

"We all have to wait until Ronan makes his choice," another boy complained humorously to Neihle. "The girls will not go with us until he has chosen. Even the older initiates have to wait."

"I am thinking they don't like that," Neihle said, lifting his brows in inquiry.

"They wouldn't put up with it from anyone else," Tyr said matter-of-factly. "For some reason, however, they put up with it from Ronan."

"The reason is perfectly simple," Adun put in. "Ronan can out-wrestle and outfight every one of them."

"A potent reason indeed," Neihle murmured. Then he asked his nephew, "Would you like to come walking with me?"

"Of course." Ronan lifted his spear from the stack piled beside the fire and followed Neihle to the path along the river.

"It is beginning to grow cold in the evenings," Ronan remarked, courteously waiting for the older man to broach his reason for seeking Ronan out. "The summer weather is ending."

"Sa," Neihle agreed. He drew a deep breath, not yet ready to broach a topic of whose reception he was unsure. He said instead, "You like living in the men's cave, I think."

Ronan blew out through his nose. "Sa," he answered shortly.

Of course he likes living in the men's cave, Neihle thought to himself. After years of living with that shrew of a stepmother, the men's cave must seem like paradise.

In the Tribe of the Red Deer, as in all matrilineal societies, a boy's closest male relative was not his father but his mother's brother. Even had Ronan's father not died, Neihle would have had responsibilities toward Ronan. They were responsibilities he always felt guilty he had not sufficiently fulfilled.

Neihle looked down at the ground, stabbing his spear into the dirt as he walked. "Ronan," he said, his voice a little muffled, "I hope you know that if it had been in my power, I would have taken you to live in my own hut. But my wife had so many of our own children to see to . . . She could not cope with my sister's child as well." Unspoken, although well-understood between the two of them, was the fact that Arika would have opposed such an arrangement, and it was his sister's opposition more than his wife's that had weighed with Neihle.

Ronan did not answer right away, and after a moment Neihle turned to look at him. The boy's face was unreadable. Neihle thought painfully that Ronan had learned at much too early an age how to keep his feelings from his face.

"I know that," Ronan said finally. He shifted his spear from his right hand to his left. "You have always done your best for me, Uncle. Be sure I know that."

His best had not been good enough, Neihle thought now, as he walked through the cool evening at the side of his tall young nephew. Ronan's father had died when the boy was but six winters old, leaving him in the hut of a resentful stepmother. Then Orenda had remarried, and more children had come along. Neither she nor her husband had wanted Ronan. They had kept him only at the Mistress's command.

The Mistress, Neihle thought. Arika. In most things, Neihle found his sister to be both just and wise, but he had never understood her in the matter of Ronan.

Arika had lain with Neihle's heart-friend, Iun, at Spring Fires, and had borne Ronan, her first, long-awaited child. But a boy was of no use to the Mistress of the Tribe of the Red Deer, and Arika had not even suckled him, had immediately given him over to Iun's wife, who also had a child at the breast. Orenda's child had died shortly thereafter, and she had blamed Ronan for taking too much of her milk. The boy had never known a happy moment under Orenda's roof.

Arika knew that, yet she had commanded Orenda to keep the boy and made it clear that Neihle was to leave him under his stepmother's care. Neihle had never understood why, until this summer.

He heard Ronan saying, "I bear no ill will toward you, Uncle." There was a faintly sinister emphasis upon that "you," and a shiver ran up and down Neihle's spine.

He sought to change the subject. "Erek brought back word from home that at the full of the moon, Morna is to be initiated."

The men looked at each other. It was always an important moment in the world of the Red Deer when a girl first showed the moon blood that would guarantee the future life of the tribe. When that girl was the future Mistress, the occasion was one for great rejoicing. Yet neither man looked at all elated.

"She has become a woman, then," Ronan said, his voice curiously flat.

"Sa. She has become a woman."

"If Morna will ever be a woman."

Neihle pulled his upper lip. "She is . . . thoughtless . . . sometimes, but she will grow up. Now that her moon blood is flowing, she will grow up."

Ronan snorted. "Nel has more sense in the nail of her little finger than Morna has in her whole head."

"Do not say that to anyone besides me!" Neihle said warningly. "If such words should come to the Mistress's ears . . ."

"I am not a fool. I know how blind she is when it comes to the Chosen One."

The bitterness in Ronan's voice was deep. Neihle understood, but it was dangerous. Ronan's growing reputation among the initiates was dangerous also. Arika did not like it. Neihle frowned worriedly at the hawklike profile of his nephew and finally brought up the subject that was on his mind.

"I have been thinking, Ronan, to take you with me to the Autumn Gathering this year to find you a wife."

"What?" Ronan swung around to face his uncle. His eyes were wide with surprise. "I do not understand you, Uncle," he said.

Neihle was not surprised by Ronan's reaction. It was certainly Neihle's place as the boy's maternal uncle to make his marriage arrangements, and the boys of the Red Deer often left their home when they wed, but Ronan was still young for marriage. As he said now to Neihle, "It is not yet time for me to take a wife."

"Morna is young for her years, but you, sister's son, are old for yours," Neihle returned. "Nor are you the man ever to be happy living under Morna's rule. Even though it seems you could certainly find a girl of the Red Deer to take you"—here Neihle smiled briefly, then sobered—"I have been thinking it would be well for you to consider making your home in another tribe."

Ronan's expressionless mask was not, after all, impenetrable, and Neihle saw the flash of hurt. "It is not that I wish to lose you," the older man said gently. "It is that . . . I fear for you in this tribe, Ronan."

Now Ronan looked astonished. "Fear for me? Why should you fear for me, Uncle?"

Neihle shrugged and answered obliquely, "I have long thought you would be happier in a tribe that followed the Way of Sky God."

Ronan's astonished expression faded, and he looked away.

"I know you listen to stories of such tribes from the men who were born to them," Neihle said. "I have seen your face when Midac tells tales of the Tribe of the Horse and Azur tells tales of the Tribe of the Buffalo."

Ronan did not answer.

"Of all the tribes of the Kindred, only the Tribe of the Red Deer yet follows the Way of the Mother," Neihle said. "They follow the Mother in other places, this I know from the traders, but among the Kindred it is only the Tribe of the Red Deer. That is why Arika is so careful to keep us pure, Ronan. That is why when a young man marries into another tribe, she will not allow him to return here. She does not want the ways of Sky God creeping in." Neihle put his hand on his nephew's arm. "If I have noticed how you listen to the tales of Sky God, then be sure that she has noticed also."

PART
ONE

THE TRIBE
OF THE
RED DEER

Ronan's chin came up. "Noticed *me?* The Mistress? You are think-ing of someone else, Uncle."

Neihle winced, the bitterness in that young voice was so raw. "She knows everything about you, Ronan," he answered. "She knows you are becoming a leader among the boys. She knows the girls are hot to lie with you. She knows you are interested in the Way of Sky God. And even if she never shows it, she knows you are her son."

Neihle's hand on Ronan's arm tightened. "All of these things are dangerous, sister's son. You already have cause to know how ruthless the Mistress can be. If she thinks you may be a threat to her rule . . ."

"A threat to her rule," Ronan repeated. Once more he looked as-tonished. "Can Arika really imagine that?"

"I think so," said Neihle. The two men stood there, facing each other under the darkening sky. "That is why I wish to take you to the Autumn Gathering to find a wife. I wish you would consider it."

There was a long silence. Then Ronan answered, "Perhaps I will, one day. But not this year, Uncle."

Neihle dropped his hand. Trying to throw off his sense of foreboding, he made himself say humorously, "You are having too good a time, I see."

Ronan's dark face lit with its irresistible smile. "Sa," he said. "I am."

The summer weather faded, and Leaf Fall Moon rose in the night sky. In the highest passes of the mountains, snow fell. The deer began their annual trek back to the lower-altitude grazing around the Greatfish River, followed by the hunters of the Tribe of the Red Deer.

As Leaf Fall Moon waned, preparations began for the great semi-annual fertility rite of the tribe, Winter Fires.

It would be the first Fires ceremony Ronan had ever attended, and he looked forward to it with enthusiasm. Not even the news that his half-sister Morna was to make the Sacred Marriage this year could dim his anticipation.

The three girls who had been initiated since Spring Fires were awaiting the coming ceremony with scarcely less anticipation than Ronan. A girl of the Red Deer tribe was not introduced to sex at her initiation rite as was a boy. The girls waited until the next cere-mony of the Fires, when the pounding drums and unrestrained dancing brought heat to the blood and fire to the loins. Then they had their first mating, and the pain was muted by the sweet urgency of the need.

Morna had been pleased when Arika told her she would be the one to make the Sacred Marriage this year. According to ritual, at each Fires the Goddess mated with the god and their joining was what brought fertility to the tribe and to the herds the tribe depended upon for survival. The Goddess's role was usually taken by the Mistress, but this year the role would be played by the Mistress's daughter.

"It makes for a powerful ritual when the Goddess is played by a maiden," Arika explained to Morna. "That is why I will allow you to make the Sacred Marriage this year, at your first mating." The Mistress smiled at Morna's expression. "You must name the man, my daughter. It is always the prerogative of the Goddess to name the man who will play the god."

Morna said, "I know who would be named if the choice were offered to any other of the Red Deer girls. I am thinking it is a pity that Ronan is my brother."

Arika stared in appalled silence at her daughter's faintly flushed cheeks and parted lips. Morna seemed utterly unaware of the consternation her words had produced in her mother.

"Do not ever say such a thing to me again," Arika said in an unusually harsh voice.

Finally Morna realized that her words had upset Arika. "It is not my fault if I do not think of him as a brother," she said defensively. "After all, we have never lived together in one family as brothers and sisters normally do."

Arika was very pale. "Nevertheless, the blood tie is there." She drew a long, calming breath. "Remember, you are not just any girl, Morna. You are the Chosen One of the tribe. You must think always of the tribe, my daughter, and of what is good for the tribe. Not of yourself."

Morna said sulkily, "Sa, Mother. So you are always telling me."

Arika's beautiful mouth set in a grim line. "You need not name the man right now. There is time for you to think about your choice."

Morna tilted her head a little and ran her eyes speculatively up and down Arika's figure. "I hope I am a better breeder than you, Mother," she said. "How many Sacred Marriages did you make before you bore Ronan?"

"Many," Arika said. Her face was like stone. "I also hope that your womb is more fertile than was mine."

"Was?" Morna's perfectly arched brows rose.

She could be clever enough when her interest was involved, Arika thought heavily as she looked into her daughter's lovely face. The problem with Morna was that her interest seemed always limited to herself.

"My moon blood still flows if that is what you mean," Arika answered quietly. "But I do not think that I will ever bear another child."

Morna wound the tip of her long red-gold braid around her forefinger. She looked up at Arika from under her lashes. "Then perhaps it will fall to me to make the Sacred Marriage from now on," she said.

The line of the Mistress's mouth became even grimmer. "I will only give over the ritual to you, Morna, if I am convinced you understand what the responsibility of playing the Goddess entails."

Morna's lips curled in an enchanting smile. She was so beautiful, Arika thought despairingly. Much more beautiful than Nel. Surely the Mother meant Morna to be her Chosen One . . .

"When the responsibility is so pleasant, Mother," Morna was saying, "you can be sure that I will undertake it willingly."

"I am not talking about the pleasure of the mating," Arika snapped.

"I know. I know." Morna wrinkled her small straight nose. "I must think of the tribe. I know that, Mother. How could I not know it when you are always telling me?"

"When you choose the man," Arika said shortly, "come to me."

"Sa." Once more came that curling smile. "I will."

Arika sighed.

Chapter Three

In the Tribe of the Red Deer the winter was never as carefree a time as the summer, but this particular winter proved full of discontent for Ronan. Neihle had voiced out loud thoughts that Ronan had never quite dared to consider, and now they clamored in his mind. As a result, his distaste for Morna became ever more adamant, and more serious.

Ronan was well acquainted with his sister. In the Tribe of the Red Deer, the tie between brother and sister, children of the same womb, was considered closer even than the tie between husband and wife. It was a woman's brother who was responsible for instructing her sons in the skills of hunting and for guiding him through the rites of initiation into manhood. Husbands might come and go, the women of the Red Deer always said, but your brother is your brother forever.

This belief held true for the Mistress of the tribe as well; certainly the man who had always been closest to Arika was her brother, Neihle. So it was that no one in the tribe had found it odd when the child Morna began to seek out the company of her brother, Ronan. Even though Arika had disowned her son, still the idea of the brother-sister blood bond was so strong in the tribe that Morna had managed to spend many more hours with Ronan than anyone had felt it necessary to report to Arika.

For many years Ronan had made an effort to be agreeable to his sister. He understood the sacredness of the sibling bond, and he was intuitive enough to realize that he resented Morna for being their mother's favored child. "It is not Morna's fault she is who she is" was a phrase he had repeated to himself like a charm during all the years of their childhood. It was only within the last few years that he had allowed himself to admit that his dislike of Morna was based on more than mere jealousy.

She had no touch of the Goddess about her. She was selfish, and shallow, and, once her sexuality had been tapped, thoughtlessly promiscuous. During the course of the winter Ronan came to the conclusion that she would make a disastrous leader for the tribe.

Ronan might hate his mother, but never, during all the years of his growing up, had he thought to question her right to rule. The matriarchy of the Tribe of the Red Deer was well-established and, in general, functioned beautifully. "No one has a greater care for her children than a mother does," Neihle had once explained to Ronan when the boy had first questioned him about other tribes that followed a male chief. "Look at the animals," Neihle had said. "Is there anywhere among them a mother who will not fight to the death to protect her young? No father will do that for his offspring; only a mother. That is why we follow the Way of Earth Mother in this tribe, Ronan. And to us, the Mistress is her voice, is the Goddess-on-Earth."

It was a great responsibility to be the Goddess-on-Earth, and during the time of that long, bitter winter, Ronan watched his sister and judged her lacking.

It was an accepted fact in the tribe that the Mistress did not tie herself to one man, that she was sexually free. As the Mother was the Giver of Life to the World, so was the Mistress the fount of life to the tribe. Her sexuality was a great and holy thing, demonstrated most powerfully during the two fertility rites of Winter and Spring Fires. There had never been any sexual jealousy manifested among the men of the tribe in regard to the Mistress. It was simply unthinkable.

During that winter, however, it became evident to Ronan that Morna had no feeling for the sacredness of her sexuality to the tribe. Arika had always understood that, while in one way the Mistress was freer than other women, in most ways she was less free. Clearly, Morna did not understand that. Freed at last from the restrictions of maidenhood, Morna went from boy to boy, from married man to married man, encouraging rivalries and then laughing at the often angry results.

She was not fit to lead the tribe, Ronan thought. In anger, in bitterness, in defiance, he thought it. She would never be fit to lead the tribe.

For the first time in his life, Ronan seriously began to consider the possibility that one day a man might lead the Tribe of the Red Deer. In Neihle's anxiety to remove his nephew from harm's way, he had planted the seed of an idea that, over the course of many long cold winter nights, put down roots in Ronan's mind.

Neihle had said that the Mistress feared her son. Surely, Ronan thought, Arika would not harbor such a fear without just cause. Did Arika see what he saw, that Morna was unfit to take her mother's place? Did she fear that perhaps one day the tribe would turn from the daughter to the son?

These were the thoughts occupying Ronan's mind one spring day when he was standing alone at a secluded spot along the Greatfish River a short way downstream from the tribe's homesite. Two of the older initiates had recently gone off to the local Spring Gathering with their fathers and had not come back. As with so many of the boys of the Red Deer, they had found wives in neighboring tribes and gone to live with their wives' kin. It was the way things were done in the tribe; it was the way things had always been done. The boys, not the girls, left their maternal home when they married.

Ronan did not want to leave his home or his tribe. The very thought made him scowl, and to relieve his feelings he picked up a handful of stones and began to throw them forcefully, one after the other, into the rushing water of the flooded river.

"Ronan." It was a feminine voice. He looked over his shoulder and saw Cala approaching. She smiled at him. "You have been so occupied of late that I have scarcely seen you."

He threw the last stone all the way across to the opposite bank, then turned to face her. "It is Ibex Moon," he said. "A good time for hunting." In fact, the sight of Morna's blatant promiscuity had so disgusted Ronan that he had kept away from all girls for a good part of the winter.

Cala nodded. "I have been hunting with the girls," she said. She halted beside him, standing very close.

He turned back to the water. Cala and he had lain together at Winter Fires last year. He had been her first boy, and he liked her. There was a gentleness about her that reminded him of Nel.

"Ronan," she said softly. Now he could feel her leaning against him, could feel the curve of her hip, the length of her thigh. He thought of what lay between those thighs, and he reached an arm around her under her reindeer fur vest, resting his hand upon her breast. Through the deerskin shirt he could feel her nipple stand up against his palm.

The spring sun was delightfully warm. He was a fool to let Morna spoil his fun, he thought. "Come," he said into Cala's pretty pink ear. "Let's go into the woods."

Linked together, the boy and girl made their way into the clump of trees that screened this part of the river from the valley floor.

They parted within the half-hour, Cala returning home while Ronan remained where he was.

Perhaps he could marry Cala, he thought. Their blood lines were not within the forbidden degree of closeness, and if he married her he would not have to leave the tribe.

He heard movement behind him and spun around, frowning. He did not want any more company. His brow smoothed out when he saw who it was. "Nel. What are you doing here?"

She came to sit beside him on the bank, first plunking the basket she had been carrying down under a tree. Nigak bestowed his usual lavish greeting, licking Ronan's face and sniffing him all over. Ronan scratched the wolf's ruff and looked at Nel. "I have been gathering herbs for the Old Woman," she answered. "We are going to make some medicines tomorrow."

He smiled at her and let Nigak continue to sniff him.

"I passed Cala on the path," she said. Nigak finally finished with Ronan and went to curl up beside Nel. She reached out to smooth the silvery fur between the wolf's ears. Her voice was muffled. "Did you lie with her?"

He was staring at her averted face. "Sa." He sounded preoccupied. "What is that bruise on your cheek?"

She shrugged and still did not look at him. He reached out and took her chin in his hand, turning her face so he could see it more clearly. "How did you get it?" His voice was no longer preoccupied but sharp and authoritative.

Her lids were lowered so he could not see into her eyes. "My stepmother was angry with me. It is nothing, Ronan. Truly."

There was a tense silence. Then Ronan said, "I will deal with Olma for you."

"Na!" She pulled her chin away from his hold. "You will only make it worse if you interfere. I have to live with her. Until I am old enough to marry, there is nowhere else for me to go. It is best for me to try to get along with her, Ronan. Believe me."

He shook his head. "There are too many years before you can marry, Nel."

"Not so many. I have two handfuls of years already, remember." She smoothed one of Nigak's ears and added gruffly, "Would you wait for me, Ronan, or is three years too long?"

"Wait for you?" Ronan repeated blankly. His braid had been loosened in his encounter with Cala, and his black hair was blowing in the breeze from the river. "What are you thinking of, minnow? You and I cannot marry—we are hearth-cousins."

"Na," Nel said, "we are not. I asked the Old Woman, Ronan. You were hearth-cousins with my mother. You and I are marriageable."

He put up a hand to push the hair from his face. "Marriageable?" Silence fell. Then he said slowly, "Is it so?"

She nodded.

"I had not considered that." His voice was thoughtful.

She leaned toward him eagerly. "Would you wait for me, Ronan? I promise to grow up very fast."

He smiled. "The moon blood comes when the Mother wills it, Nel. You will have no say in the matter."

Nel's response to this apparent rejection was to fling her arms around Nigak's neck and bury her face in the fur of his ruff. Ronan reached over and rested his hand on her back. She was such a skinny little thing, he thought, feeling the sharp shoulder blade under his palm. He wanted to murder Olma. He felt Nel quiver, and he frowned in concern. She was not crying?

"Nel?" he said.

"Are you going to marry Cala?" she gulped.

He did not even have to consider his reply. "Na. I am not going to marry Cala." Then he added slowly, "Did you really ask the Old Woman if we would be allowed to marry?"

Nel finally lifted her face from Nigak's fur. "She said the blood tie is not within the forbidden closeness, but then she said something else that was very strange, Ronan. She said that, even so, the Mistress would never allow us to wed."

"Did she?"

Nel watched his expression. "I don't understand," she said. "If the blood tie is acceptable, why should Fali think the Mistress would be opposed to a marriage between you and me?"

"Didn't Fali tell you?"

"She said that I am the one next in line to follow Morna, that it would be dangerous because of that. But I still do not understand."

His dark eyes glittered. "Did she say 'dangerous'?"

"Sa." Nel's eyes were huge. "What can she mean, Ronan?"

Ronan scooped up a handful of the small stones upon which they were sitting and began to toss them, one after the other, into the water. "Neihle thinks the Mistress is afraid that I will prove a threat to Morna's leadership of the tribe," he told her as he tossed the rocks.

Nel scowled and chewed worriedly on the end of her braid. At last she said, "The Mistress is afraid the men of the tribe may desert Morna and follow you?"

A small silvery stone arched high, then fell into the water with a splash. "So Neihle seems to think."

Nel continued to chew on her braid. "When I asked Fali what we had done to make a marriage between us impossible, she said, 'It is not what you have done. It is what you are.' "

"Stop that," Ronan said crossly. "I have told you over and over not to chew on your hair."

Nel dropped her braid. "You are Arika's son," she said. And she fell silent as she contemplated her words.

"Sa," Ronan replied at last. "Much as she would like to forget it, I am Arika's son. And you, Nel, are the granddaughter of Arika's elder sister. If your mother had not been just a babe when Meli died, your mother would have become the Mistress, not Arika." Nel began once more to chew worriedly on her braid. "There are some who might say you have more right to be Mistress than Morna, minnow." He reached out and forcibly removed the hair from her mouth. "I am thinking that is why Arika would consider a marriage between us dangerous."

"But I would never want to be Mistress, Ronan!" Nel cried passionately. "It is much too lonely! I want to have a family." Her face was fierce; her long green eyes glittered. "And I would never never give away my children!" she said. "Not even a boy, not even a twin. Never!"

Ronan said, his faint amusement tinged with respect, "Dhu, you can look as dangerous as a cave lioness sometimes, Nel."

She flashed him a look, but did not reply. They sat in silence for some minutes, each thinking their own thoughts. Then Ronan reached out and gently touched the bruise on her cheek. "I will speak to your father," he said. "He should be ashamed to allow his wife to so mistreat his daughter."

Nel did not agree. "Ronan, you know how afraid Father is of Olma. You will only make him feel bad, and you will accomplish nothing. I can handle my stepmother far better than he can. You are making a fuss over nothing."

"That bruise is not 'nothing.' "

Nel shrugged. "She didn't hit me that hard. It is just that my skin marks so easily."

He said wearily, "We neither of us have had much luck in our families, have we, Nel?"

In answer, she leaned her bruised cheek against his shoulder and closed her eyes. His arm slid around her in an accustomed, protective gesture, gathering her to his side. Linked thus, they sat in silence while the sun went down behind their backs.

This was the first year Ronan would be allowed to take part in one of the most important of the men's springtime rites, the Slaying of the Bear. One of the ways of Sky God that had seeped into the Red Deer tribe over the years was a great reverence for the mighty cave bear, and each spring, as the bears returned to the earth from their winter's hibernation, one particular bear was chosen to be a ritual sacrifice.

Only the initiated men of the tribe were allowed to partake in this sacred hunting ceremonial. Although Ronan and his agemates had not yet participated in the rite, they were well versed in its laws. At his initiation, every boy of the Red Deer was taught the secret language of the hunt, the ritual songs, and the great apology.

Lying with girls was all very well, but all boys of the Red Deer knew that the surest sign that one was a man was to be in at the death of the sacred bear.

The Slaying of the Bear was always performed at the dark between Ibex and Salmon Moons, and this year was no different. On the morning they were to make the sacred hunt, Ronan and Tyr and several other initiates clustered together before the river and watched the first light of dawn begin to turn the sky from black to gray.

"Elder Brother," Tyr said exultantly, pumping his fist in the air, "I am hoping you are waiting for us this day."

One of the tribal beliefs about the cave bear was that he could hear everything one said, even from a great distance. He heard, he remembered, and he took revenge. Consequently, it was forbidden to call the bear by his name, lest he divine the tribe's plans and avenge himself for their trying to kill him. "Elder Brother" was the secret phrase used by the men of the Red Deer to denote the prey they would be stalking.

Ronan smiled faintly at the look on Tyr's face; then he once more inspected the tip of his javelin. The bear was supposed to be killed by one single thrust to its heart, so it was vital that one's flint points be strong and sharp.

The men had already spied out the cave in which a particularly big male cave bear had made its home, and their aim was to get there before the bear had left on its daily search for sustenance. Cave bears were almost pure vegetarians, and to maintain their immense size and weight, they had to consume vast amounts of food.

"Are the boys ready?" It was Erek, the tribe's chief hunter, speaking. Two dogs trailed at his heels as he walked around the group of men, checking to see that all were in place.

Ronan answered for the initiates, "We are ready."

"There must be no talking," Erek warned.

Ronan scowled. "Sa," he said shortly. "We know."

Erek glared at this upstart youngster who dared to speak to him with an edge to his voice. The chief hunter was a big, burly man who looked somewhat like a bear himself. He had been the one to slay the bear for the last several years. There were some who said that his glare alone was enough to cow Elder Brother into submission. It did not cow Ronan, however, who lifted his arrogant nose and stared back.

Erek muttered something that sounded like "insolent puppy," before he turned away to signal that the line of men was to move forward.

That was foolish, Ronan thought with irritation as he fell into his place in the hunter's line. Why antagonize Erek?

He answered himself immediately: Because he is stupid, and I don't like taking orders from stupid people.

The path widened and Tyr came up to walk beside Ronan. Neither boy looked at each other.

Well, the other half of Ronan's mind queried ironically, from whom wouldn't you mind taking orders?

Ronan's mouth curled in rueful self-knowledge, and this time he made himself no answer.

It took the hunters almost two hours to reach the cave in the hills where Elder Brother had made his den. The cave had been tunneled into the stone by a stream many years before, but the stream had dried up since and the cave now looked out upon a meadow that would soon be filled with grass and wildflowers. The cave entrance was partially blocked by a boulder, and Ronan stared at it, wondering if the cave bear was still within.

Erek gestured and the men spread out into a large circle in front of the den. Erek, who as last year's bear slayer was to have the honor of making the attempt again, took up his position a few yards in front of the cave entrance. Then he signaled to the dogs.

Both dogs immediately advanced to the opening beside the fallen boulder and began to bark. Minutes passed. What would they do, Ronan wondered, if the bear had already left the cave. Would they go in search of it?

A sharper note came into the dogs' voices, and the men in front of the cave entrance tensed. Coming out of the darkness of the cave, advancing slowly on all four of its feet, was the bear.

Ronan's heart accelerated. It looked big.

The dogs were in a frenzy, growling and making a high whining kind of noise. The bear halted, looked at the dogs, then looked at the men. One of the dogs jumped up to snap at the bear's nose. The bear swatted at it with his paw. The dogs barked and snarled and approached the bear from two different sides. With a roar of fury, the bear rose up on his hind legs.

Dhu! It was enormous. It was more enormous than Ronan had ever imagined a bear could be. Its deafening roars reverberated around the empty meadow. The rank smell of bear filled Ronan's nostrils. A few of the men stepped backward.

Now! Ronan thought. Now was the time for Erek to make his move. The tradition was for the bear slayer to rush forward while the bear was upright and at bay and drive his spear directly into the bear's heart.

Erek was lifting his spear. The watching men ceased to breathe as
their leader rushed forward into that terrible embrace. If the spear found
the right place, the bear would die immediately. If the bear slayer missed,
he would be mauled to death.

The bear moved just before Erek's thrust. There was a deafening
roar of anguished fury. Then the horrified men of the Red Deer saw
Erek's spear fall to the ground as the wounded and infuriated bear
grabbed the man with its immense and deadly claws.

He hit a rib, Ronan thought in horror. *He missed the heart and hit
a rib.*

The next cry of anguish came from Erek.

Dhu, Ronan thought, looking around wildly, were they all to stand
here like stones and watch their leader being mauled to death? He
looked around again. No one was moving. Then Ronan understood.

They could not attack in a group. Only one man could slay the
sacred bear. If they swarmed over Elder Brother in a group, terrible
luck would fall upon the tribe. Understandably, considering what was
happening to Erek, no one seemed prepared to jump in alone.

A blood-curdling scream came from Erek. Before Ronan realized
himself what he was going to do, he had lifted his spear and run forward.

"Ronan!" It was Neihle's voice. "You cannot do anything alone!
Come back or he'll kill you too!"

It was much later that Neihle told Ronan he had called him back.
At the moment, Ronan was aware of nothing but the immense animal
before him. He reached out and pricked the infuriated bear on the chest
with his spear. "So, Elder Brother," he said. "Here is another come to
slay you."

The bear let Erek slip from his claws and turned to Ronan. Erek
moaned and moved feebly.

The bear came for Ronan.

It all happened very quickly. There was the smell, the heavy, pun-
gent, choking smell. There was the sting of claws raking along his back,
the feel of thick rough fur against his face. Then Ronan's left arm
moved, jabbed, and drove the heavy spear home. He felt the bear sag
against him, felt the moment the breath fled from its body. Slowly,
inexorably, it toppled over, almost dragging Ronan down with it. It was
only at the last moment that Ronan managed to disentangle himself
and pull back, breathing hard.

"Good lad." Neihle was beside him, gripping his arm. "Good lad."

"How is Erek?" Ronan panted, looking beyond his uncle to the man lying on the ground.

The man who was bending over Erek looked up. "He is badly hurt, but he lives. We must carry him home so the Old Woman can see to him."

Silence fell. Everyone was looking at Ronan.

"Go ahead, lad," Neihle said into his ear. "You are the slayer. It is for you to make the apology, for you to chant the sacred song."

Ronan swallowed hard, forcibly controlled his breathing, and moved forward until he was standing over the bear. Even fallen, it was a fearsome sight. Ronan stared as if mesmerized at the large barrel-like body, the big head with its prominently domed forehead, the enormous feet, the claws . . .

"Elder Brother," Ronan said, and was thankful to hear that his voice was clear and steady, "I am sorry to have slain you, but I need your skin for my coat and your flesh for my food. Elder Brother, the Tribe of the Red Deer loves you. Do not be angry that we have slain you out of our great need."

A sigh ran around the listening men. The apology had been made; the spirit of the bear would be appeased.

Next Ronan raised his voice in the sacred chant:

> *O most splendid of animals*
> *Man among beasts,*
> *Now my Elder Brother*
> *You lie dead.*
>
> *May your plight make the other animals*
> *Be like women when I hunt them!*
> *May they follow your way*
> *And fall to me*
> *Easy prey!*

It was vital to inject real emotion into the voice when making the sacred chant for the death of the bear, and Ronan did that. It was not difficult; all he had to do was to allow a small amount of what he was really feeling to creep into his voice. When he had finished, he was amazed to see that many of the men behind him were weeping.

"Well done, sister's son," said Neihle. "Very well done." He turned to the other men. "Now we must bring Elder Brother home."

Chapter Four

Arika was furious when she heard that Ronan had been the one to slay the bear.

"What were the men thinking of," she fumed to Pier, the hunter who had brought her the news, "to allow a boy not yet one full year initiated to be the Bear Slayer?"

"Perhaps you did not hear me, Mistress," Pier answered patiently. "The bear had knocked Erek's spear away and was mauling him to death. Erek would be dead now if it were not for Ronan. Give the boy his due, Mistress. He was the only one of us willing to grapple with that bear." Pier's nostrils flared. "Wait until you see it! Never have I seen a cave bear so large."

Arika made a noise that sounded suspiciously like a hiss.

Pier looked faintly disapproving. "Erek is sore wounded. The Old Woman is seeing to him now."

"Erek should have killed the bear," Arika said. "If a boy like Ronan could kill him, there is no excuse for Erek's failing."

Pier said slowly, "Ronan made the prettiest slaying I have ever seen, Mistress, and I have seen many. Do not belittle his accomplishment. All the men who were there know what it was that he did."

Arika turned her face away. "Very well," she said abruptly. "You may go now, Pier."

"I will go to see how Erek is faring," the man said, with the faintest of emphasis on the word *I*, and he turned toward the hut door.

As soon as the hides had swung shut behind him, Arika began to pace restlessly up and down the small section of floor space that was not cluttered with her belongings. She was still pacing when the Old Woman appeared.

"I have tended to Erek," Fali said. "If the wounds do not become poisoned, he will live."

"Good," Arika snapped. Erek had been her lover for the past two years, but she had no sympathy to waste upon him now. He had failed her.

Fali said into the silence, "The men can talk of nothing but Ronan."

Arika swung around and glared.

Fali did not flinch. "He is like you, Mistress," she said. "Fearless. And he is also a leader."

Something besides anger flickered in Arika's face. She raised her hand, as if to rub it away. "Sa," she said then, very low. She dropped to sit on one of the deerskin rugs that lay on the floor of the hut and gestured to Fali to join her. Moving much more slowly than Arika, the Old Woman seated herself.

"He has my strength of will and Iun's charm," Arika said when at last Fali was settled. Then, in a very low voice, she added, "He frightens me." She picked up a stick in her left hand and poked cautiously at the ashes of the dead fire. "He has always frightened me."

Fali was watching Arika's hand on the stick. "He reminds me of Mar," she said.

At that, Arika looked up from her absorbed poking of the ashes. "Mar? The man of the Horse who kidnapped you?"

"Sa. He and Ronan do not look alike, but in other ways they are very much the same."

"He was a chief, this Mar, was he not?"

"Sa."

Arika returned to poking at the fire. "I have never told this to anyone before," she said, "but the night before Ronan was born, I had a dream." A pile of ash collapsed and dust rose into the air over the hearthplace. Arika put down her stick and looked at Fali. "In this dream I saw a herd of red deer browsing peacefully in the forest. A cave panther was stalking them. I saw the sun shining in the sky, reflecting off the panther's black coat . . . burnishing it, making it shine. It shone until its blackness was almost as bright as the sun itself. It was as if the sun caressed it, loved it . . ." Arika's mouth was thin with pain. "I knew as soon as I saw the boy, saw that black hair, those dark eyes, that he was the panther. And I knew I should have him exposed." Her eyes were somber. "It is my weakness that I did not."

"So that is why you turned your back on him," Fali said slowly.

Arika nodded. "I knew it was dangerous to let him think of me as his mother, to let him think he might have any authority at all in this tribe."

Fali made a little noise that may or may not have signified agreement.

Arika continued bleakly, "But these last few years, as I have seen him growing into manhood, I have known that I was wrong to let him live. I was weak, Fali. For so many years I had longed for a child . . . and then he came . . . and I could not do it."

"It is true he is a leader," Fali said. "But the men have always had a hunt leader, Arika. What is the danger in that?"

Arika looked suddenly old. "There is something in Ronan that the other men do not have." She rubbed her temples as if they ached. She said softly, "He has been asking questions about the Way of Sky God."

Fali said nothing.

Arika dropped her hands. Her eyes met Fali's steadily. "I am the Mistress of Earth Mother," she said. "Out of all the tribes of the Kindred, only the Tribe of the Red Deer still follows the Goddess. It is my duty, Old Woman, to hold the tribe to her Way."

"Ronan is left-handed," Fali said. "The left-handed way is the Way of the Goddess. I am thinking that perhaps she has put her mark on him, Arika. Perhaps that was the meaning of your dream."

"I do not think so," Arika said grimly.

There was silence. Then Fali sighed. "The reason the Tribe of the Red Deer has held to the Goddess for so many ages is that we have always had a Mistress strong in wisdom to lead us. In my own lifetime I have known Lana and Elen and Meli, and you. All understood what it meant to be Goddess on Earth to the tribe." Fali's voice changed. "After you, Arika, there will be Morna."

Arika's chin came up. "Morna will be a good Mistress," she said.

Fali's eyebrows, nested in wrinkles, lifted.

"She is young," the Mistress said to that obvious skepticism. "Young, and still a little thoughtless. She will mature."

"Will she?" Fali said.

"She is all the daughter the Mother has given me," Arika said grimly. "She must."

While Erek's wounds were being attended to, the rest of the tribe was busy preparing the feast which formed the second part of the ritual of the Slaying of the Bear. This feast was traditionally held in the men's cave, and there was a strict tribal rule that only initiated men and women were allowed to partake of the meat of the slain bear. Even the dogs were ejected from the cave on this day, lest they lick some of the blood or eat one of the bones. Both the men and the women had to gather the bones up after the feast and bury them.

To Ronan, the bear slayer, fell the honor of removing the bear's head with the whole hide still attached. Once he had finished this amputation, Ronan hung the pelt in a position of honor in the cave, so the bear would be able to watch the tribe as it feasted. The meat was then butchered and the women cooked it, boiling it simultaneously in two large mammoth-skull caldrons.

Neihle took Ronan to his hut so the boy could wash and change out of his blood-stained clothes.

"You will be playing a bigger part in this feast than ever you expected to," Neihle said as the two of them left his family's hut to return to the men's cave. He smiled. "I hope you are hungry."

"I am always hungry," Ronan replied truthfully. He ran his finger under the decorated leather browband he was wearing around his damp black head. The browband was traditionally worn by the bear slayer at this feast.

"Is that too loose?" Neihle asked. "Let me fix it." Then, when the band had been re-tied and they were walking toward the cave once more, Neihle warned, "You must finish all the meat you are given. There cannot be any sacred bear meat left; it must all be eaten at the feast. And the largest portion of all goes to the bear slayer."

"I can eat it," Ronan said, with all the confidence of a still-growing boy.

Neihle looked amused and did not reply.

The men's cave was crowded with people sitting cross-legged around a slow-burning fire upon which simmered the two great caldrons. The men were seated on the right side of the fire, the women on the left.

The first person Ronan saw when he came in was his mother, seated in the place of honor at the point where the men's side joined to the women's. Neihle had told Ronan that, as bear slayer, he was to take the men's place of honor next to her. Never within his memory had Ronan ever been within touching distance of his mother.

Now, watched by the curious eyes of all the tribe, Ronan made his way around the fire until he reached the empty place beside Arika. He sat down.

Only once did she look at him. Her red-brown eyes were perfectly opaque. Then she turned her face away.

Blind fury swept through him. His hands curled into fists. She was so close that if he moved his arm but slightly he would touch her, yet still she would not acknowledge him.

Ronan struggled to keep the anger from his face. He looked around the fire for distraction and met Tyr's worried eyes. He made himself nod reassuringly. Next, he looked at the bear, hanging on a pole near the cave opening.

Dhu, but he was big!

I won't let her spoil this for me, Ronan thought fiercely. I am the bear slayer, and I won't let her spoil it.

A great sheep's horn filled with blackberry wine was being passed around, and when it came to Ronan, he took it from Arika without looking at her and drank deeply. He felt the warmth of it running through him. He felt himself beginning to relax. The next time it came around, he reached for it more eagerly. Inadvertently, his fingers touched his mother's. Their eyes met in shocked surprise.

Suddenly it was as if the cord that had once bound them together had never been cut, so clearly could he read her thoughts and her emotions.

She was not as cold to him as she would have him think, he discovered. He could see her hurried breathing, could almost feel her effort to keep it slow and steady. Most of all, he could sense her fear.

She had turned away from him almost immediately, but he continued to stare at her averted profile. Then he looked at the hands clasped in her lap. The knuckles were white with pressure.

She was afraid of him.

I am glad you are afraid of me, Mother, he thought, staring at those whitened knuckles with cold satisfaction. Very glad.

He raised his head to regard the tribal circle in front of him and saw Adun looking at him with an odd, almost awed expression on his face. Ronan smiled.

Arika thought the feast would never end. The chanting seemed to go on forever. On her lefthand side she could feel Morna's restlessness. There was no conversation allowed at the bear feast, there was only chanting, and eating, and drinking out of the horn. The men and the women sat on opposite sides of the fire. They even ate out of separate caldrons. Morna was bored.

Ronan was not bored. Arika could feel her son's exuberance, could feel it through that connection between them that Ronan had also discovered. It dismayed her, this sudden awareness that had sprung up between her and Ronan. She did not want to know Ronan. That way lay only danger. Danger, and heartache.

The men had been genuinely impressed by the way he had killed the cave bear. It *was* a huge bear. Arika had been impressed herself when she saw it.

A wolfskin drum was beating softly, and now Pier began to chant the story of the kill. All of those gathered in the cave listened to the tale with quickened attention. Even Morna was listening, Arika saw. The Mistress looked again at the immense bear head. She imagined what it must have felt like, to rush forward into that fearsome embrace.

Unbidden, unlooked-for, unwanted, maternal pride swelled in her breast. She turned from the bear to look at Ronan.

He had Iun's smile and Iun's height, but that hawklike profile was all his own. She thought: He is as beautiful in his own masculine way as Morna is beautiful in the way of a woman.

He must have noticed the motion of her head, for his own turned, and for the second time that day, Arika and her son looked into each other's unveiled eyes.

What each saw this time was a mirror image of the other. The same blood ran in their veins, the same strength marked their wills; the same discipline, the same courage, the same cold determination had molded their characters. They were indeed mother and son. And for a brief and fleeting moment, both bitterly regretted that they also must be enemies.

When Ronan's food was placed before him, he understood why Neihle had been amused.

I cannot possibly eat all of this, Ronan thought. He looked up from the enormous hunks of meat. They had given him at least half of the liver!

From beside him Arika's low-pitched voice said, "You must eat it all. And you cannot get sick."

Ronan stared at the amount of meat the Mistress had been given. It was miniscule compared to the hunks that were reposing on the reindeerskin rug in front of him. He gave her an indignant look.

She smiled at him faintly. It was the first smile he had ever had from her. He picked up a hunk of the liver and bit into it.

"Elder Brother had his revenge," Ronan said to Tyr much later when the feast was finally over and both young men were settling themselves for the night.

"I have never eaten so much in all my life," Tyr agreed. "Not even when I was a boy and would stuff myself on the first salmon catch until I was sick."

"I wish I could be sick," Ronan groaned. "Anything to get this stone out of my stomach!"

"That is the price of being a hero," Tyr said piously.

"Remind me to pay you back for that remark," Ronan said. "Someday, if ever I can walk again."

A chuckle was his only response.

The girls also had been impressed by Ronan's deed. A group of them sat gossiping in the women's cave after the feast was over, not ready yet for sleep and unable to pass the time by doing anything else. For three days after the slaying of the bear, the men of the tribe were considered unclean and had to abstain from sexual activity. Consequently, all that was left to the girls was talk, and much of that revolved about Ronan.

Morna listened and said nothing.

"I wonder whom he will wed?" Cala finally said a little wistfully.

"Why should he wed at all?" Borba asked with a laugh. "He is having much too good a time the way he is."

"All initiates must wed," Tosa said. "Just as all girls must." She shrugged. "It is how things are."

"Sa." Borba sighed. "That is so." She herself was to wed at the full of the next moon, and she was feeling nostalgic about giving up her freedom.

"Not all girls must wed." They were almost Morna's first words.

The rest of them stared at her.

"That is true," Tosa replied quietly. "The Mistress does not wed."

Morna looked from one firelit face to the next. "You will just have to share your husbands with me," she said. And smiled.

A tense silence fell. It was evident from their expressions that the girls did not find this thought particularly pleasing.

Suddenly, Borba's eyes widened. Her lips curved in a smile every bit as enchanting as Morna's had been. "What a shame you will never be able to lie with Ronan, Morna," she said. "*That* is an experience, I am telling you . . ." Borba allowed her voice to die away; then she heaved a shivery sigh.

"That is so." Iva was quick to second Borba's effort. She glanced at Morna's face and added with relish, "A woman has not lived who has not lain in Ronan's arms."

Morna's brown eyes were narrow as they flicked from Borba to Iva. "He is a man like other men," she said, her voice hard.

"Na," said Cala with absolute sincerity. "Ronan is not like other men."

"How can you know that?" Tosa said with affectionate amusement. "You have never lain with another man."

"I have never wanted to," Cala replied simply.

"What does he do that makes him so different?" Morna demanded.

It was Borba who answered. "It is not what he does but how he does it. Even that first time, at his initiation . . ." She slanted a look at Morna and smiled with satisfaction at what she saw on the other girl's face.

"I don't believe you," Morna said.

Borba shrugged.

Iva said, "If you cannot eat buffalo meat, Morna, I suppose it's as well to believe that you would not like buffalo meat."

"I do not understand you," Cala said in gentle confusion. "Why are you speaking thus of Ronan to Morna? Ronan is her brother."

"Sa." Borba tossed back her golden braid. She and Morna looked at each other. "So he is."

Chapter Five

The salmon began their yearly run up the Greatfish River, and the men of the tribe devoted almost all their waking hours to fishing. In the deeper water, they used boats made from bark and nets they had woven from branches and vines to bring in the salmon. Where the river was shallow, they speared the fish with three-pronged harpoons.

Fishing was not a sport to the Tribe of the Red Deer; it was a livelihood. The salmon formed an important part of their diet in the spring, and what they did not eat immediately they dried and stored against the time when food was not so plentiful.

A few days after the salmon had been running strongly, Ronan and Tyr decided to try the upland valley where they had previously placed traps. Nel went with them, ostensibly to collect herbs. The river was narrow in the valley, and the fish trap consisted first of a stone dam the boys had built from bank to bank. Then, upstream of the dam, they had laid circular stone traps in the water to catch the fish when they swam through the slits that the builders had left strategically in the dam. Once the fish were in the trap, all Ronan and Tyr had to do was wade in with a harpoon and spear them.

Quickness was the essential skill if one was to be successful in spearing fish. The wooden-handled harpoon with its three points made out of antelope horn was an effective weapon only if one's aim was sure and one's arm was quick. Both Ronan and Tyr were famous for their expertise with the harpoon, and, after she had collected a token number of plants, Nel spent the day sitting on the shore of the river, enjoying the sun and watching the boys wade from trap to trap spearing salmon. Each time a fish was speared, the boys would hook a bone needle through its gill and run it along the sinew cord they had hung at their waists.

The day's catch was a good one, and the baskets Nel had brought were filled with fish when the three of them finally turned toward home. The boys each carried a basket, and Nel carried the harpoons. The three of them were pleased with the catch, and with each other, and they walked along easily, talking softly and occasionally laughing at a joke.

Once they were back home they separated. Tyr took one of the baskets to his mother so she could gut the fish for him, while Ronan and Nel worked together on the other one. It was a tedious and a dirty job; each salmon had to be slit open, its precious oil poured into a reindeer bladder for safekeeping, and then the fish had to be hung to dry.

"Whew," Ronan said when at last they were finished. "I am as oily and as fishy-smelling as those salmon. I'm going down to the river to wash." He looked at Nel critically. "You had better come too."

It was late and cookfires were being lit in all the huts. Nel sniffed the air longingly, but said, "All right. Just let me get Nigak first."

Ronan waited while Nel ran off to where she had tied Nigak to keep him out of their way while they were working on the fish. He crossed his ankles, leaned on his harpoon, and stared assessingly up at the sky. The weather had been clear for several days now, and it looked as if it was going to hold. He thought: Perhaps tomorrow I will hunt that great stag Pier saw yesterday.

Suddenly an enormous weight barreled into him. If he had not been leaning on his harpoon, he would have been knocked over. It was Nigak, standing upright with his great paws on Ronan's shoulders. He began enthusiastically to lick Ronan's face.

"Dhu!" Ronan grunted, as the wolf gave a playful snap at his nose. "All right, fellow. Down. Down!" Then, to Nel, he said, "I wish he would not do that!"

"I cannot train him out of it," she said.

"Why not? The dogs don't do this." Ronan had managed to extricate himself from Nigak's fond embrace.

"It seems to be one of the big differences between a wolf and a dog," Nel said. "Both of them can learn to be fond of humans, but whereas a dog seems to realize that humans are not dogs, Nigak does not seem to know that we are not wolves."

"Is that why he persists in this face licking and muzzle biting of his?"

Nel nodded. "I think so. It is the way wolves greet each other, you see."

"He thinks we are wolves?"

She nodded again.

Ronan grinned. "This is one very confused wolf, Nel."

"Well, we are his family, you and I. We have been since he was but a pup. Why shouldn't he think we are wolves?"

"The dogs don't think we are dogs," Ronan pointed out.

"Dogs have lived with men for a long time. Wolves haven't."

"I suppose that is so," Ronan murmured. He began to walk toward the river, and Nel and Nigak fell in beside him.

"I brought some soapwort," Nel said, and she held up the plant so he could see it. Ronan grunted.

Nel regarded him curiously. After a moment, she asked, "Were you sad when Borba married?"

He looked surprised. "Na. Why should I have been?"

"I thought you liked her."

"I do like her. I like her so much that I hope she is happy in her marriage."

"Oh," said Nel, and her face brightened.

They had reached the river's shore. It was late afternoon, and the water looked gray and cold. The men and the boats had left the river an hour since, and the fishing nets were folded on the shore, ready for the morrow. Ronan raised his hand to his nose, sniffed, and said, "I cannot stand the stink of fish on me any longer. I am going to get into the water."

Nel did not seem surprised by this decision. All she said was, "You did not bring a change of clothes."

He shrugged. "I will just have to put these back on."

"Those clothes will only smell you up again."

He shrugged once more.

"I'll fetch a fresh shirt for you," she offered.

"Will you, minnow? Go to the men's cave and ask whoever is there to give you one. They know where my things are kept. And trousers, too. I have a clean pair."

"All right." Nel handed him the soapwort and ran off, Nigak loping beside her.

Ronan went along the river to a place where the shore was screened from the homesite by a stand of birch and pine trees. Swiftly, he stripped off his clothes and waded into the freezing river. His teeth chattered as he began to work up some suds with the soapwort. He hoped Nel would hurry.

She must have run full speed, for by the time he was ready to come out, she was back with his clothes. She had also brought an old deerskin for him to use as a towel.

"Good girl," he said, taking it from her and beginning to rub himself briskly. When he had finished, she handed him his trousers.

"How come you don't have any hair on your chest?" she asked him when he had tied the leather drawstring around his waist and was reaching for his shirt.

He shrugged. "None ever grew there. I don't know why."

"It grew everywhere else."

He grinned.

"I haven't started to grow hair anywhere," she said sadly. "My stepmother said the other day that I would probably not reach initiation until I was as old as Fali."

"Don't pay her any mind," he advised. He was running his fingers through his newly washed hair to untangle it. Then, as he began to rebraid it, he asked pointedly, "Aren't you going to wash? You were gutting fish too."

She gave him a sunny smile. "I am going right now to wash my hands."

He finished tying the leather thong that fastened his braid and shook his head. She tried another tack. "Ronan, I was nice enough to get your clothes for you . . ." Then, as he began to walk toward her, she wailed, "The water is so cold!"

"You don't have to take off all your clothes. Just roll up your trousers. Here, I'll do it for you." He dropped down onto his heels and began to roll the deerskin trousers up to her knees.

Her legs had lengthened in the last year, but they were still thin as sticks, he thought. Her skin was beautiful, though, creamy white and smooth as ivory. Except for the scar on her right calf. He remembered the day she had got that scar, climbing a sheer rock face after a stranded baby lamb. Nel and her animals! he thought, finished rolling, and stood up. "Come on, in you go."

She cast him a long-suffering look, but took the soapwort from his hand and waded in. "Wash your hair," he said as she bent to wet her face.

"Ronan!" It was a cry of anguish. "I'm cold!"

"Your hair looks almost as black as mine" came the inexorable reply. "Wash it."

"But my shirt will get wet and my stepmother will scold."

"Take it off then. I'll hold it for you."

The sun was setting and the clear air was cold. The river water was very cold. But Nel's hair was very dirty, Ronan thought. That stepmother of hers would never think to wash it for her. If he didn't watch out for her, she would be utterly filthy. Nel herself, unfortunately, placed little value on personal cleanliness.

He watched as she pulled the shirt over her head. Her poor skinny little body was covered in gooseflesh. He caught the shirt she tossed to him, crossed his arms over his own chest for warmth, and watched as she washed her hair. "Come here," he said when she had finished, "and I'll dry it for you."

She splashed through the water to stand in front of him, and he took the deerskin and toweled her head. Suddenly she put her arms around his waist and burrowed against him. "I'm s-so cold," she said.

"Poor little minnow." She was shivering and he rubbed his hands up and down her back to warm her. His hand looked very dark against her ivory skin. "Come on, get into your shirt and you'll feel warmer." She held up her arms and let him pull it over her head. Her damp hair hung down her back, and he raked his fingers through it as he had done with his own and braided it for her.

"Make sure you put a comb through it when you get home," he ordered. "You have very pretty hair, if only you would take care of it."

She looked up at him. Her long dark lashes were stuck together with wet. "Guess what I found yesterday, Ronan. A baby scimitar cat."

He groaned. "Not another orphan, Nel."

"She is very sweet," Nel assured him. Her mouth looked suddenly tragic. "But I am afraid that Olma will not let me bring her home."

Ronan sighed. "I suppose I could fix you some place to keep her."

Her smile was radiant. "*Thank* you, Ronan."

He shook his head, put a hand on the nape of her neck, and walked her back to the camp.

Summer came, the reindeer and red deer migrated into the higher pastures, and the hunters of the tribe moved to their summer camp on the Narrow River the better to hunt them. As usual, the Mistress remained at the tribe's permanent homesite, but for the first time Morna was old enough to accompany the men and the initiated girls.

There was something about the air in the higher altitudes that Ronan particularly loved. It was so clear. One time, during Antelope Moon, he had gone with Neihle through the Buffalo Pass into the valley of the Atata River to trade with the men of the Tribe of the Buffalo, and he had found the heights of the pass wonderfully exhilarating.

The Tribe of the Buffalo followed the Way of Sky God, and Ronan had carefully watched the workings of the tribe during the two days that he and Neihle spent in its caves. Ronan found many of their ways extremely strange. Part of him was excited to see the obvious dominance of the men of the tribe, and part of him was deeply puzzled. Even though the men ruled, he thought they seemed to be missing many of life's greatest pleasures.

The young unmarried girls, the ones Neihle had obviously brought him to see, were kept separated from the men. They did not mate until they were wed, Ronan was told. The reason for this was that the men of the Buffalo wished to ensure the paternity of their children. Ronan held his tongue, but privately he thought that the men of the Buffalo were fools. What did it matter if another man had fathered your wife's first child? What Ronan did not understand was that the men of the Red Deer had a different relationship with their children than did the men of the Buffalo. As in all matrilineal societies, a Red Deer child belonged to its mother, whereas a Buffalo child, coming from a patrilineal society, belonged to its father. These differing outlooks accounted for very different attitudes about the importance of a child's paternity.

Summer passed too quickly. The nights were coming faster, and frost had already descended on the highest pastures, when Neihle sought his nephew out one afternoon to invite him to make a return trip to the Tribe of the Buffalo.

"Haras, the chief, has several girls who will need husbands this year," Neihle said. "I am thinking, Ronan, that you would be happy in the Buffalo tribe."

Ronan looked up from the hare he was skinning. The two men were alone in front of the big upper cave, and when Ronan did not reply, Neihle added, "The Mistress will give you a good bride price."

At that, Ronan's mouth quirked humorlessly. "I am sure of that, Uncle." He put down his flint knife and rose to his feet. "I am not so sure that I wish to leave my own tribe, however."

Neihle's voice was gentle. "I am thinking you will have to, lad. Sooner or later."

Ronan was staring down at his bloody hands. "Why?"

"You know why," Neihle replied. "This is not a tribe for a male chief, Ronan, and you will be happier in a tribe that is."

Ronan did not look up. "I would have no claims to be chief in a different tribe, Neihle. Here . . . here I have claims."

There was a startled silence. Then Neihle spoke: "You have no claims here. You are a man and this is a tribe that follows the Goddess. You have grown up here, Ronan. Surely this is something you understand."

Ronan slowly flexed his bloodstained hands. "If this is so, Neihle, then why do you say the Mistress fears me?"

"She does not fear you for herself," Neihle said. "It is for Morna that she fears."

"Sa. She fears for Morna. The Chosen One." At last Ronan turned to look at Neihle. His mouth was thin. "Wouldn't you rather be led by me, Neihle, than by Morna?"

"Dhu," said Neihle out of a suddenly dry throat.

"You see. Arika is right to be fearful of me," Ronan said.

Silence fell. The day was unusually warm for so late in the year, and Ronan had removed his shirt to save it from the hare's blood. His torso was still tanned a deep summer brown, and Neihle found himself staring at that wide, well-muscled chest and shoulders. Ronan had long since lost his boyish slenderness, though his waist and hips were slim as ever.

His face . . . when he had said, "Arika is right to be fearful of me," there had been such a look on Ronan's face. Ruthless . . . almost cruel.

"I am young," Ronan was saying now, the ruthlessness even more pronounced. "And the Mistress is old." His dark eyes were cold. "I can wait."

Neihle felt a shiver run up his spine. He had always thought that Arika's fear of her son was unreasonable. Never had he imagined that the Mistress might be right, that there might be something in Ronan to fear.

Until now.

"Have you spoken to anyone but me about this?" he asked Ronan sharply.

"Na." Ronan lowered himself to his heels and once more picked up the sharp flint knife.

Well, at least that was something. Neihle watched his nephew working on the hare and thought about what he might say to make Ronan understand the impossibility of his illicit desire.

"It is true you were the bear slayer," he began. "It is true that you killed the biggest great stag anyone in the tribe has ever seen. But in this tribe, Ronan, it is not hunting that makes the chief."

"I know," Ronan said. "The Mistress's man is the chief in this tribe." Neihle stared as if mesmerized at Ronan's skillful fingers wielding the bloody knife. "But what if the Mistress should choose just one man, Neihle? What if the Mistress should wed?"

"You cannot wed Morna," Neihle said in bewilderment.

"Not Morna," Ronan said. "Nel."

Neihle looked stunned. Ronan looked up from the bloody pile of fur in front of him. "Wouldn't you rather see Nel as Mistress than Morna, Uncle?" he asked.

Neihle began urgently, "You must not say . . ."

He was interrupted by a soft feminine voice. "Ronan, I have been waiting for you." Iva came the rest of the way up the steep path that led to the upper cave and gave Neihle a reproachful look. She put a hand on Ronan's bare brown shoulder and said to him, "I thought we were going to go fishing together."

"I have almost finished here," he answered, his hands busy with the hare. "Be a good girl, and wait for me by the river."

She nodded, ran her fingertips caressingly over the skin of his shoulder, and departed, scrambling down the path to the valley floor.

Neihle watched Iva progress toward the river, his somber face in odd contrast to the enticing sight made by her swinging hips. "You cannot marry Nel, Ronan," he said at last. "You are too closely related."

"The Old Woman says not," Ronan replied.

"Nel and you." Neihle was very pale.

Ronan smiled, and suddenly all the ruthless arrogance, all the cruelty, was gone, swallowed up in that beguiling grin.

"I promise you I am not a fool, Uncle," he said. "I know how to bide my time. But do not ask me again to seek a wife from another tribe."

Morna stood in the arch of the lower cave and watched Ronan cross the valley floor, his deerskin shirt slung over his shoulder. She watched as Iva came out from under a tree to join him, watched as the girl slid her arms around the young man's waist and leaned her breasts against his bare chest. His dark head bent. He seemed to be saying something into her ear. Then he separated himself from her and went to rinse his hands in the river. When he came back to Iva, he draped an arm around her shoulders and, thus linked, the two of them began to walk together up the river.

Chapter Six

After a full summer of watching Ronan, Morna had decided that she wanted to lie with him. She wanted to find out for herself if what all the other girls said about him was true.

There could be no harm in it, she told herself. He had never been as a brother to her. They would simply keep it to themselves, and no one would ever know.

It never once occurred to her that Ronan might not be as eager for her embraces as she was for his.

She watched for an opportunity to be alone with him, but the tribe lived too close to each other at summer camp and no opportunity presented itself. She decided she would have to wait until they returned to their home caves.

The first snow fell in the upper pastures, and the deer began their migration back to lower altitudes. The hunters of the Tribe of the Red Deer followed.

Buffalo Moon was almost at its end when Pier spotted a buffalo bull in the forest along one of the tribe's hunting runs. Buffalo were most often found running in great herds on the grass plains to the north of the mountains, but there were a small number of woodland buffalo in the low hills of the Pyrenees, and occasionally they strayed into the territory of the Tribe of the Red Deer. Morna proposed that the initiated boys and girls of the tribe go together the following day to hunt for buffalo.

The opportunity to take a buffalo hide was too good for the tribe to miss, but the Mistress was not pleased with the idea of sending only the youngsters.

"Buffalo are dangerous to hunt," she said to Morna with a frown. "It will be better to send some of the more experienced hunters after them."

"We have spent the entire summer weather hunting, Mother," Morna pointed out. "We are experienced hunters too."

"Buffalo are dangerous," the Mistress repeated.

"Sa." Morna smiled. "That is the fun."

She meant it, Arika saw. Morna, in fact, was an excellent hunter —the best among the girls, as good as most of the boys. She was fearless and swift and strong. Upon their return from summer camp, several of the men had praised her ability to Arika.

It was important for the tribe to see Morna at her best.

"All right," Arika finally agreed. "The young people may hunt the buffalo."

The bull Pier had seen had been in rut, and rutting bulls were easy to locate because of their bellowing, so it was with high hopes of success that the hunting party of twelve young people set off from the Greatfish River in the direction of the Volp. The day was very warm for the season, and the sky was hazy with the unusual heat. The hunters wore their buckskin clothing without the reindeer fur vests that were the usual gear for this time of year.

"Buffalo meat is delicious in the autumn," Tosa said, as she walked behind Morna along the reindeer track that wound up and down the wooded hills. "There is usually lots of fat." Tosa made a slurping noise, indicating her anticipation of this treat.

Morna, who was greedy for many things but not usually for food, wrinkled her small, perfect nose.

When they reached the area where the bull had been sighted, Morna suggested that the hunters split up.

The others stared at her in surprise.

"Na," Ronan said. "That would be dangerous." He looked at her sternly. "A bull in rut is an evil-tempered creature, Morna."

"I thought the initiates of the Red Deer were men, not boys," Morna said. "Are you afraid?" And she let her gaze trail slowly from one young male face to the next. A look of amusement was in her eyes.

"Of course we are not afraid!" Adun blustered. He was seconded loudly by the rest of the boys.

Morna's eyes came to Ronan and stopped. "I have always been told that buffalo bulls travel alone during the rutting season in search of cows unattended by a male," she said. "I am thinking we will have a better chance of finding the bull if we spread out rather than keep together in one pack."

Dana, a pretty blue-eyed girl, reached out to take Tyr's hand. "Perhaps Morna is right," she said softly. "Perhaps we should split up. We can always climb a tree if we get into trouble with the bull."

Tyr looked at her; then he looked at Ronan and raised his eyebrows. Ronan's mouth tightened, but he shrugged his shoulders, effectively leaving the decision up to the group.

They decided to split up into couples, rutting being on the minds of more than the buffalo on this hazy autumn afternoon.

To everyone's surprise, Morna went with Ronan. This she managed by the simple expedient of announcing that she would be his partner, a decision that obviously dismayed Iva and Cala as well as several of the boys who had hoped to go with Morna. Ronan gave his sister a single hard look, but made no comment.

"If you locate the bull, give the tribe's hunting call," he said to the others; then he lifted his spear and turned purposefully into the forest. Morna followed.

She did not try to talk to him. Morna had never been a great one for talking. She followed after him, watching in silence the buckskin-clad back, slim hips, long legs and midnight black braid which were all she could see of him at present. Their footfalls made no noise on the forest path.

The air was heavy, almost sultry. From somewhere deep in the forest a cave hyena screeched. Birds flew up into the air, crying in alarm. Morna saw the shadow of a deer flit through the deeper part of the woods. Ronan continued to push on through the trees until he had reached the game trail he was aiming for.

The hazy sun spilled through the trees onto the beaten dirt of the narrow game trail, and the boy and girl began to walk along it on silent moccasined feet. The smell of pine was heavy in the unusually warm autumn air. Small creatures scurried in the undergrowth, and overhead a golden bird circled lazily above the treetops.

Abruptly, the hazy peace of the afternoon was ripped apart by an angry bellow. Then came crashing noises that sounded alarmingly close. Through the screen of thin birch and oak and pine, Morna suddenly saw a massive black shape . . . saw great curving horns . . . and the smell of buffalo overpowered the fragrant scent of the pines.

"Ronan," Morna said urgently, and bumped into him. He had stopped, turned toward the buffalo, and was lifting his spear. He did not look at her, but said calmly, "Get up a tree, Morna. That bull is too close."

Morna stared toward the bull, who was striding along aggressively at a much faster gait than the normal lazy amble of the buffalo. As she watched, he hooked a small tree with one of his horns, easily breaking its fragile trunk.

Morna's breath caught. Ronan still had his spear in his hand, and she could see that the screen of trees made getting off a clear throw impossible.

"Get up a tree," Ronan repeated.

"Na," Morna said. "I will back you up." She stood by his side and raised her own spear to her shoulder.

As the two hunters watched through the impeding screen of trees, the great bull halted, lowered his head to the ground, and sniffed intently. Then, with great deliberation, he urinated on the spot he had been sniffing. Next he knelt and rubbed his head and horns in the area he had just dampened. Standing upright, he let out a loud bellow and looked in the direction of Ronan and Morna. His tail went up, a certain sign of danger.

There was but one open line in the trees between the buffalo and where the boy and girl stood, and now the bull moved into that opening.

Without hesitation, Ronan stepped in front of Morna and brought back his left arm. The throw was perfect, straight and true. Unfortunately, however, as the spear left Ronan's spearthrower, the bull stepped sideways with frightening quickness to hook a small birch.

Ronan's spear buried itself harmlessly in the trunk of a tree.

The bull looked at them again.

"He is going to charge," Ronan said. He sounded perfectly calm.

"Take my spear," Morna said from behind him, and put her weapon into her brother's hand.

But it seemed that the buffalo had changed his mind. Before Ronan could make another throw, he had turned away from them and plunged off into the woods.

The boy and girl stood for a moment in silence, holding their breaths. They let them out at almost the same moment; then Ronan turned to Morna and said furiously, "I told you to get up a tree. You could have been killed!"

"*You* didn't get up a tree," Morna pointed out. "I am your hunting partner. If you were going to try for the bull, it was my job to stand with you."

Ronan continued to stare into her face. Slowly his fury was replaced by a look of reluctant admiration. At last he nodded. "I'll get my spear and we can go after it again," he said. He began to turn away.

Morna reached out and put a restraining hand on his arm. "Let it go."

He swung back toward her, a line between his slim black brows.

"Ronan," Morna said softly. She smiled into his uncomprehending face.

"We can still get the bull," he said impatiently. "Let's go."

"I can think of something better to do than chasing bulls." Morna stepped very close to him. "Can't you?"

He still did not understand. His dark eyes were wary . . . and bewildered. Her own eyes were wide and dilated. She reached up, swinging her arm, and struck him lightly across the cheek with the back of her hand. "Stupid," she said mockingly.

He recoiled from the blow. His face went very pale under its tan. His eyes began to glitter.

"Let's go," he said. Now his voice was hard.

Morna stared at that tall strong young male body before her. Her voluptuous apprehension of him was so acute that she felt dizzy with it. The hazy autumn heat had brought out perspiration on her upper lip, and she licked the salty beads. "Ronan," she said. "Lie with me."

She heard the harsh intake of his breath. She felt his body begin to vibrate. Once more she stepped close.

"You are my sister!" His voice was scarcely more than a whisper.

"No one will ever know." She reached up to slide her hands around his neck. She leaned against him. "We were not reared as brother and sister, you and I," she said into his ear. She rose up on her toes and, none too gently, took the lobe of his right ear into her mouth and bit it. "No one will ever know," she said again.

He shuddered. She was close enough to him to feel the immediacy of his other reaction too. Her lips parted in a faint smile, her eyes half closed. She rubbed against him.

He shoved her away. Shoved her so roughly that she almost fell. She scrambled for her balance, then looked up at him. The expression in his dark eyes frightened her far more than the buffalo had.

"It is taboo, Morna," he said. His voice was shaking. "Whether anyone knows or not, it is taboo."

He strode to where his spear was stuck in the tree and pulled it out violently. Gripping it tightly, he said to her, "Do not ever touch me like that again." And he plunged off into the forest alone.

Morna stared after him. After a little, the angry line smoothed from between her brows.

He was afraid of the taboo, she thought. She had not thought Ronan would be afraid of anything.

She thought of the way he had looked at her, she remembered the arousal of his body against hers, and once more she smiled.

It would just take a little more time.

A little later in the day, Adun and Tosa sighted the buffalo that had eluded Ronan and Morna earlier and sounded the hunting call of the tribe. Morna and Ronan arrived on the scene just in time to hear the bull's long-drawn-out dying bellow.

Once they were certain it was safely dead, the hunters moved to examine the animal's pelt. Buffalo would not be wearing their full winter's coat for yet another moon, but the heavier, longer, denser hair had begun to grow in and the pelt was well worth the taking. The boys drew their sharp flint knives from their belts and prepared to go to work.

To Adun, who had thrown the killing spear, fell the honor of making the first slash across the belly. This he did, with the appropriate prayer of thanks to the Mother, and as he withdrew his knife, a huge steaming greasy paunch spilled out of the incision onto the forest floor. Then, reciting yet another prayer to Buffalo God, Adun made the second cut, and a dark green stream of half-digested grass and leaves poured out as well.

The girls had made a fire, and as the boys worked at skinning the pelt, they cooked the delicacies of liver, tongue, and tail. Then they all sat down to eat before returning to the butchering of the buffalo, which job they finished before starting on the trail back.

During the whole of the afternoon, Ronan and Morna were noticeably silent.

"We spotted the bull once," Ronan said in answer to a question of Tyr's, "but I couldn't get a decent throw off through the trees." And he fell silent again. After one or two other attempts to draw him into conversation, the others left him to his own thoughts.

They reached home near the time of sunset, and Ronan immediately looked for Nel. He was feeling both shocked and revolted by Morna's proposal, as well as by his own unexpected reaction to it, and he craved the innocence of his small cousin. Nel was not in her father's hut, and Ronan finally came upon her in one of her favorite hideaways, a small clearing in the woods not far from the river. She was playing with her cat.

Ronan watched the two of them for a moment, remembering the time Nel had first showed him the pitiful little starved scimitar cub. He had been certain it could not live.

"You see babies killed every day," he had said to her sternly, trying to prepare her for the inevitable. "Lions and hyenas and wolves and wild dogs . . . they are always preying upon the deer fawns and the newborn antelope calves. The owl will always kill the mouse. You cannot stop that, minnow. In order for some to live, others must die. It is the Way of the Mother. Why must you break your heart trying to save what cannot be saved?"

"I *can* save this cub," she had said to him fiercely. "I know I can."

She had saved it. The starved little orphan had grown into a sleek and beautiful adult, its curved fangs delicately serrated and deadly sharp. The cat, too, must kill to live.

Just now it was playing with Nel's fingers. She would drum them lightly upon the ground, and the cat would pounce. Ronan could see that the cat had its claws retracted. It was being careful not to hurt Nel; it understood they were playing.

The cat's coat was pale brown and glossy, almost the exact same shade as the child's hair. They had the same color eyes too, Ronan thought, and smiled.

"Ronan!" Nel had seen him.

He moved to join her. The cat stopped playing and watched him cautiously. "Greetings, Nel," he said. And to the cat, he added, "Greetings, Sharan." He dropped down to sit beside them.

"Did you get the buffalo?" Nel asked.

"Sa. We got the buffalo."

"Who? You?"

He shook his head. "Adun."

"Oh." Her wide gaze was very grave. "Who was your hunting partner?" she wanted to know next.

"Morna," he answered, his voice flat.

"Oh," she said again. She sounded surprised.

Sharan began to tap gently at Nel's fingers. She drummed them lightly on the ground, and the cat pounced. Nel said to Ronan, "I washed my hair today."

He nodded approvingly. "It looks as sleek as Sharan's coat."

"You didn't even have to tell me. I did it all by myself."

He smiled. "You are growing up, minnow."

She did not smile back. "I am."

"I saved you some of the liver." He took a hunk of meat out of the pouch at his waist.

"Oh . . . Ronan!" Eagerly, she took the proferred morsel. He watched with faint amusement as she ate it greedily. When she had finished, she licked her lips and gave him a grateful grin. "Delicious."

He reached over and wiped a drip of juice from the corner of her mouth with his index finger.

She scanned his face. "What is wrong?" she asked.

He raised his brows. "Wrong? Nothing is wrong."

"Sa, something is wrong. I can always tell when something is wrong with you. What is it?"

He had not sought Nel out with the intention of confiding in her. He smiled faintly and shook his head. "It is not something I can tell you, minnow. You are too young."

"You just said that I was growing up," she pointed out. She rested her fingers lightly yet commandingly on his forearm. "Besides, there is nothing you cannot tell me, Ronan, just as there is nothing I cannot tell you."

He looked at the small hand resting so assuredly on his sleeve. It was rough and chapped and the fingers bore numerous small half-healed cuts. The innocent hand of a child, he thought. Not at all like the hand that had struck him across the face this afternoon.

The mere thought of what had happened this afternoon made him feel contaminated.

"Ronan?" Nel said softly. "Was it something to do with Morna?"

He gazed into her eyes; then he looked away. In a tight, expressionless voice, he began to tell her what had happened between him and Morna on the hunt.

When he had finished, Nel let out a long soft breath. Ronan looked at her. "I am afraid," he said, "that she will try it again."

Nel said, "I am thinking that she probably will."

"Dhu, Nel!"—there was panic now in his voice—"what am I going to do?"

"You cannot give in to her," said Nel.

"I know that!" he responded wildly. "I don't *want* to give in to her. We came from the same womb, Nel! How could she even think . . ." His whole body shuddered.

"You can know something is wrong and still want it," Nel said. "Is that not true?"

There was a vibrating silence.

Nel began to pet her cat. "She wouldn't climb the tree?" she asked after a few moments.

Ronan rubbed his hand across his eyes. "I wish she had." His voice was deeply bitter.

Nel was scratching Sharan's head between the small pointed ears. The cat closed her eyes in blissful pleasure. Ronan watched the motion of that childish hand and felt oddly soothed. "Sa," Nel said somberly, "it would be easier not to think well of Morna in any way."

"But what can have possessed her, Nel?" he asked in genuine bewilderment. "Morna could have any man she wants. I do not understand her at all."

There was the rustle of something small scurrying among the trees, and Sharan opened her eyes. Both youngsters watched as the cat got to her feet and arched her back, which sloped in distinctive scimitar fashion, downward from the high front legs to the shorter legs behind. Sharan trotted off into the trees to investigate. Nel drew up her knees and propped her small pointed chin on them. Ronan noticed a ragged tear in the deerskin trouser that covered her right knee. Nel would be in trouble with Olma again.

"Perhaps Morna has been watching how all the other girls want to lie with you," Nel said slowly. "Morna has never been one to let someone else have what she cannot have."

Ronan stared into his cousin's small sharp-boned face. "She is corrupt," he said, his voice hard.

"It is not corrupt to feel desire for someone who is taboo," Nel said. "It is the giving in to the desire that is corrupt."

"That is so," Ronan said. He let out his breath and realized that the ugly feeling that had been eating away at him all the afternoon was gone. He smiled at Nel. "You are always good medicine for me, minnow." He stretched his arms over his head, then got to his feet and held out his hand. "Come along, there's buffalo meat for supper tonight."

Chapter Seven

Morna sat in the shelter of the cave's opening and watched the ibex resting on the hillside above her. It was Leaf Fall Moon, and the males and females had come together into one herd, as they did for only a few moons out of the entire year.

The sun was very bright; the air was thin and cold. The young ibex, feeling the itch of the rutting season, were playing at butting and sparring with each other. Most of the females were lying down, chewing their cud in the early afternoon sunshine. Three big rams stood at a little distance from the rest. Most of the herd was facing Morna, but she was downwind of them and they betrayed no alarm.

Morna looked away down the valley to the south, which was the direction from which Ronan would be coming. She could see no sign of him as yet. She got to her feet and moved out from the shadow of the cave opening. The ibex watched her. The females got to their feet; the youngsters stopped playing. Slowly the herd began to move higher up the hillside. Morna watched them until they had disappeared over the top of the hill; then she turned once more to look to the south.

She was certain he would come. He had been avoiding her for the whole of the last moon, but this morning Morna had sent him a message saying that the Mistress wished to meet him here, at this small cave which the tribe used for shelter when it was hunting the hills in the area.

Arika was not at home to give the lie to Morna's message. At sunup she had gone with some of the women to the sacred cave to perform a curing ceremony. That was women's business, however, and Ronan would not know about it. He would have no reason to doubt the message; he would come.

He had been avoiding her, but Morna knew what she had seen in his eyes and felt in his body when last they had been together. He wanted her, as she wanted him. She had only to get him alone again, she thought, and then, whether he willed it or no, she would have from him what she wanted.

Morna shivered with voluptuous anticipation and turned to look at the sleeping skins she had spread so invitingly on the floor of the cave. Then she ran her fingers through her loosened red-gold hair.

Would he never come? She sat on a sun-warmed rock and resigned herself to waiting.

It was an hour before he came around the side of the hill and into her sight. She watched him leap with powerful grace over a boulder that stood in his path, and the blood sang dizzily in her veins. What would he do, she wondered, when he realized who was really waiting for him here?

At that moment, Ronan looked up from the path and squinted into the sun in the direction of the cave. He hesitated, as if unsure of his welcome, and then he came on.

Morna stood, the glorious hair she had inherited from her mother floating around her shoulders, and watched him with wide and dilated eyes. She could tell the exact moment at which he realized who she was. He stopped dead. The entire valley was eerily silent as they looked at each other across the distance.

"You!" he said, his voice loud in the quiet afternoon air. "What are you doing here?"

Morna did not answer. At last Ronan began to walk toward her again, scrambling up the small slide of rocks to the flat apron of ground that fronted the cave. When he was standing within a few feet of her, he said, "You sent that message."

From somewhere on the other side of the hill came the bone-chilling howl of a wolf. Morna smiled. "Sa." Her voice was very soft. "I sent that message."

"Where is the Mistress, then?"

"Performing a curing ceremony for Nara at the sacred cave."

"I should have known," he said. "I should have known she would never have sent to me like that."

Morna did not hear, as Nel would have, the ineffable bitterness that underlay those words. She only knew that he was infinitely desirable as he stood there before her, black-haired and tall, with his arrogant, hawklike face. "Come closer," she said.

He did not move. "What do you want?" he asked.

"You know what I want," she answered with a smile.

He took a single step backward. "What you want is taboo." He backed up another step. "I have nothing to give you that you cannot get from any other man in the tribe," he said.

Morna shook her head from side to side, so that her hair floated around her shoulders. "You know you want to, Ronan," she said. "I felt that the last time we were together." She gestured toward the cave behind her. "I have brought sleeping skins for us." She advanced toward him. "No one but us will ever know."

Ronan was quivering like a stag brought to bay, his narrow nostrils flaring below the high-bridged arch of his nose. Sensing that he was about to turn and run, Morna reached up swiftly and caught him around the back of his head. Then, rising up on her toes, she pressed her mouth to his, still holding his head in her hands so he could not pull away. His crisp black hair felt warm under her chilled fingers. His mouth was hard. She thought she felt him beginning to respond to her kiss, and her soul thrilled with a strange violation of feeling. She wanted to touch him and touch him and touch him, till she had all of him in her knowledge, till she had drawn him into her . . .

She felt his body vibrate, felt the power of him as he bent toward her, closed upon her. Triumph mixed with lust in her surging blood.

And then he had gripped her by the shoulders and was shaking her, shaking her so brutally that her very bones seemed to rattle. She thought she would faint, so ferociously was he shaking her.

"Do not ever touch me again." He was saying that over and over as he shook her and shook her. His hard fingers were grinding great purple bruises into the soft white flesh of her shoulders.

"Ronan!" she managed to gasp through chattering teeth, and at last he let her go.

Their faces were still very close. For a moment they stared into each other's eyes, locked in a strange, pitiless kind of intimacy. It was then that Morna understood at last that Ronan would never lie with her.

He dropped his hands and stepped away, breathing like a runner who has reached the end of his endurance. Morna felt within herself a desire for deep violence. She said through stiff lips, "You will be sorry for this, Ronan." Then she pushed past him and ran like a deer to the path which led southward out of the valley. In less than a minute she had disappeared around the bend of the hill.

After a while, so they would not be lost to the tribe, Ronan went to retrieve the sleeping skins she had brought.

This time Ronan wanted to avoid Nel and her too perceptive eyes. He stayed completely away from home for the rest of the day, returning only after dark had begun to fall. He went immediately to the men's cave, where he spent the remainder of a sleepless night.

You will be sorry for this, Ronan.

He thought of Morna's words, he remembered the look on her face when she had said them, and he knew that he must be careful. She would want to punish him for his rejection. He had best keep well out of her way.

Leaf Fall moon died, and Stag Fighting Moon rose in the sky. The tribe celebrated Winter Fires, with Arika and not Morna taking the role of the Goddess. The weather grew steadily colder, and a few dustings of snow fell. Ronan began to hope that he was safe.

It was at the beginning of Reindeer Moon that it happened. Most of the men had gone upriver to hunt reindeer, but Ronan had remained at home to finish rebuilding one of the huts that had burned down when a spark from the hearth fire had ignited the walls. The day was cold and the women were all within the warmth of their own homes, so there was no one to see when Morna walked into Ronan's almost-completed hut.

He was alone. Nel had borne him company the day before, but her stepmother had kept her busy sewing skins this day. As soon as he saw Morna come in the door, Ronan knew that he was trapped.

Morna stared at him, her eyes wide and expressionless. The light from the open door illuminated her face and hair. He dropped the branch he had been about to weave into the wall structure and faced her, hands loose at his sides.

"You should have done what I wanted, Ronan," she said.

He knew how an animal must feel when it is cornered. As he stood before her, watching helplessly, she took off her fur tunic and dropped it on the floor of the hut. Then she put her hands upon the neck of her deerskin shirt and ripped it down its entire front. He could see her miraculously white skin, see the pink nipples of her bare breasts. She tore the leather tie off the end of her braid and shook her hair until it was floating wildly about her face. Then she began to scream.

At that first high piercing shriek, Ronan panicked. He pushed past Morna roughly, bolted out through the doorframe, and ran.

Everywhere women were erupting out of their huts, shouting to each other in confusion and fear. The blood pounded in Ronan's ears as he raced toward the river, seeking only to get away from that high-pitched screaming that was splitting his skull apart, splitting his world apart.

"Ronan!" He thought he could hear Nel's voice crying his name.

And over all the babble of voices, again and again and again, came Morna's high, piercing screams.

In front of him, coming up the river, there appeared a solid phalanx of men. The reindeer hunters had returned.

"Stop him!" It was Arika, calling to the men.

It was the sound of his mother's voice that brought cold sanity back to Ronan. *It is over*, he thought. He slowed his headlong flight. *Better go back and face it.* He stopped, chest heaving. *There is nothing else to be done.*

Arika stood, white-faced in the almost-finished hut, and looked at her sobbing daughter.

"He wanted me to lie with him, Mother," Morna said. "He said he was the son of Sky God just as I was the daughter of the Mother, and we should overthrow you and rule the tribe together." Morna shuddered. "When I said I would not, he . . . he tried to force me."

"Did he enter you?" Arika asked. Her voice seemed to her to be coming from somewhere outside of herself, somewhere a long way away.

Morna sobbed again.

"*Did he?*" Arika asked.

Morna looked up slantwise, quickly—as if, Arika thought, she were trying to make up her mind what to answer. "Na," she said. "I fought him off."

The doorframe of the unfinished hut was not covered yet with skins, but the light from the open door was suddenly blocked by bodies. The men had brought Ronan.

They thrust him roughly into the hut to stand before her. Arika stared at him. Where had he got that proud dark face? Was it Iun who had lain with her the night this boy was conceived, or was it some other power?

The son of Sky God, he had called himself, giving voice to Arika's most profound and unacknowledged fear.

The Mistress's eyes moved over her son. He had been wearing a fur tunic to work in the cold unheated hut, and the tunic had been pulled askew. Morna must have done that, she thought, or perhaps it was from the rough handling of the men.

Why was he still wearing his fur tunic?

He stood before her, his arrogant head held high. His eyes were wide and dark and bitter. He said nothing.

"Did you do this to your sister?" Arika asked.

He did not answer, but looked at Morna. She stared back, and Arika thought she detected a glint of triumph in her daughter's eyes before she broke again into wailing sobs.

Ronan turned away. "Na," he said stonily. "I did not touch my sister."

"He did! He did!" Morna sobbed. "He said that we should mate, that he would rule with me and bring the Way of Sky God to share the Way of the Mother. Then, when I said I would not, he tore my clothes and tried to . . . tried to . . ." Morna broke once more into wild weeping.

"If Morna's tale is true, why is there no mark upon Ronan?" It was Neihle's voice. Arika's brother looked at her. "His clothes were not disordered when we came up with him," Neihle said, "and his hair is tidy. There are no fingernail marks upon him, Mistress. No sign he has been in a struggle." Neihle turned to his nephew. "What happened, Ronan?" he asked.

"Morna wanted to lie with me," Ronan answered. His voice was flat and oddly still. "It was I who refused, not her."

"Liar!" Morna screamed. "He held me down so I could not fight him, then when I started to scream, he ran away!" Her hand was at her breast, holding her torn garment together. She glared defiantly at Neihle. "If he was not guilty, why did he run away?"

"That is so," Arika heard herself saying. "He proved his guilt when he ran away." She looked again at her son. "I should have exposed you when you were born," she said and saw the shock of her words in his eyes. She continued bitterly, "I knew it, yet I was weak. I can afford to be weak no longer." Her gaze moved from Ronan to scan the circle of men who were watching her. She did not like what she saw upon their faces.

Tyr, Ronan's friend, broke the silence. "You cannot have considered Neihle's words, Mistress. If there was an attempt at rape, Ronan should bear the marks of it."

Now Ronan spoke. "Morna lies, Mistress." His eyes burned with a keen cold light. "She lies, and I am thinking that you know it."

"I am not lying!" Morna screamed, sensing that the tide of sympathy was swinging against her. She put her hand upon her mother's arm. "He tried to rape me, Mother. He is not marked because I could not fight him—he is too strong!" She stared furiously around the circle of men's faces. "I am not lying!"

They thought perhaps she was. It was written on every male face there. Arika looked at her brother, looked at her son, and understood the extent of her danger.

I must get rid of him now, Arika thought. If I wait any longer, it will be too late. She looked again at the faces of the men crowded into the hut. It may already be too late.

She closed her eyes briefly, summoning to her aid all the power of the Goddess. She drew herself up, and authority streamed from every inch of her being. "Hear me," she said. "I am the Mistress of this tribe. I am the Voice of the Mother, the Goddess on Earth. This boy has dared to lay an incestuous hand upon my daughter, the Chosen One of the Mother, and he must be cast out."

Her voice deepened, and the power of the Goddess came over her. Arika could feel it, coursing in her veins, throbbing in her voice. She stared at Neihle, forcing his will to bend to hers. She said, "Anyone who disobeys this command will bear my curse."

A shudder ran throughout the men. The hut was deathly silent. Even Morna's weeping had stilled. Arika kept her eyes on Neihle. "This boy is a danger to all the tribe," she said. "An enemy of the Way of the Mother." She saw the faintest flicker of recognition in Neihle's eyes.

He knew, she thought. *He knew she spoke the truth.* "The Mother says he must be cast out."

Some of the men looked to Neihle, but he said nothing. At last Arika turned to Ronan. "You are to leave this place by fall of night. I will send word to the tribes who dwell near us that none of them is to take you in. You bear my curse," Arika said. "My curse and the curse of the Mother."

The silence in the hut was absolute.

Ronan tore his eyes away from the Mistress's, looked around him, and knew that Arika had won. Since birth the men of the Red Deer had been bred to revere the Mistress. They would not go against her now.

Into the silence came the voice of a child, crying from the door opening, "Mistress, do not believe her! She has tried to seduce Ronan before . . ."

It was Nel.

Arika looked at Erek. "Get her out of here," she said.

The big hunter put his hand upon the child's thin shoulder.

"Na!" Nel tried to pull away. "You must listen to me! Ronan is telling the truth!"

"Go outside, Nel," Ronan said. He did not look at his small cousin; his eyes were all for his mother. They looked like black holes in his stark face. He was breathing like a suffering animal.

"It is not finished between us, Mistress," he said.

"Sa," said Arika wearily. There was the taste of sour bile in her mouth. "I am thinking that it is." She said to Pier, "Take him away."

The challenge had come too soon, Ronan thought, as he put together the pack of belongings Arika was allowing him to bring away with him. A little more time, another year perhaps, and the men would have turned against Morna.

Arika had seen that, of course. It was why she had acted so decisively. She knew she had to get rid of Ronan while still she could.

As always with her, the daughter came before the son.

Cast out. He was cast out from his tribe. Cast out from the other tribes in the vicinity as well, for none of them would dare to risk Arika's calling down on them the wrath of the Mother.

He could not quite comprehend it. Every man belonged to a tribe. It was not possible to survive without the companionship of one's own kind . . .

That, of course, was what Arika was counting on. She thought she was sending him to his death. It is finished, she had said.

"Ronan . . ." He looked up. Tyr was coming into the men's cave, and there were tears in his dark blue eyes. "Ronan, I do not believe her," Tyr said. His voice was shaking.

Neither do most of the other men, Ronan thought bitterly. But they will not stand up to her. Not even Neihle . . .

He made himself shrug, as if it did not matter. "The Mistress has spoken, and the tribe will obey."

"I will go with you," Tyr said.

Ronan stared at him, surprised. "Did you not hear? The Mistress said she will curse anyone who comes with me."

"I do not care," Tyr said passionately. "I will go with you anyway."

Ronan thought, Now that he is out from under the Mistress's eye, Tyr can act like a man. But he cannot stand up to her face-to-face. None of them can.

"Na, Tyr," Ronan said. "Stay here where you belong."

"I belong with you!" Tyr cried.

Ronan turned his head away. "I do not want you."

Dusk was falling and the sky over Deer Hill had turned to lavender when Ronan turned his back upon the Tribe of the Red Deer and began his lonely walk down the Greatfish River.

Nel and Nigak were waiting for him around the second bend.

He saw the sleeping skins at her feet and said, "You cannot come with me, minnow." He spoke as he had not spoken to Tyr earlier, gently.

"You cannot stop me," Nel said. He was close enough now to see that her eyes were red and swollen from weeping. "I hate her!" Nel cried. Her small hands were clenched into fists at her sides. "I hate them both! I won't stay here with them, Ronan. I won't!"

Nigak's ears were at half-mast as he looked anxiously from Nel to Ronan and back again. He whined, but neither youngster paid him any mind.

"She has thrown you away the way she throws away a twin," Nel said passionately. "I hate her!"

"I am no helpless babe, Nel," Ronan answered. "Nor do I mean to perish, I promise you that." His face hardened. "I would not give her the satisfaction."

"It's what she wants." Nel began to cry again, her face screwing up with anguish. "She wants you to d-die."

"Listen to me, minnow." He put down his heavy pack, then held out his arms. She flung herself into them. "I cannot take you with me," he said over the small round head that was pressed into his shoulder. "You are too young. You would only tie me down. I will be safer on my own."

"No one would listen to me," she sobbed into the reindeer fur of his shoulder. "I tried to tell them about Morna, about what she had done before, but no one would listen."

"They are afraid of the Mistress," Ronan said grimly. "They did not want to hear what you had to say."

Nel sobbed on, and he held her, wishing that he had not met her like this. Until now his anger had made him strong; he did not want to feel what Nel was making him feel.

"Come," he said bracingly, "it will be growing dark soon. I must go." He placed his hands on her shoulders and pried her away from his chest.

Nel sobbed on.

"I will come back for you, minnow," he heard himself saying. "I promise you I will come back."

"You p-promise?"

"I promise."

Valiantly, she tried to smile. She said, "Well, if you won't take me, Ronan, at least take Nigak."

Hope flickered in the bleakness of Ronan's heart. He looked at the wolf. Nigak's yellow eyes were fixed on Nel's face. The hope died. Ronan shook his head and said, "He would never leave you."

"For you, he would," Nel answered. "If I told him to."

Ronan swallowed. He wanted desperately to have Nigak. "I couldn't take him away from you, Nel," he said. "You love him."

"I have Sharan," she said. "And I would feel better if I knew that he was with you. Please, Ronan, take him."

It was not in him to refuse any longer. "All right," Ronan said, "if he will come." And he reached once more for his pack.

"Where will you go?" Nel asked, watching with great tragic eyes as he shouldered the heavy load.

"To our summer camp for now," Ronan said. "The caves there are not in use during the winter, and there is yet some game in the area. I can fish through the ice on the river, too, and there are always birds."

"That is a good idea." She brightened. "I know, Ronan! You must search out a place that the Mistress does not know about. Then you can come back and get me, and we will start our own tribe away from them all."

He did not smile at her naiveté, but answered gravely, "That is a good idea." He glanced at the sky. "It is growing late, Nel. I must go."

She nodded hard, three times.

He turned away.

"Nigak," he heard Nel saying behind him, "go with Ronan."

The wolf whined in protest. Ronan felt his muscles clench.

"Go with Ronan," Nel said again.

Ronan did not look back. Nigak was not going to come. Desolation, so successfully kept at bay all afternoon by anger, swept through his soul. He made himself continue walking, a solitary figure in the growing dusk, his eyes fixed steadily ahead.

Suddenly, Ronan felt something warm and damp poke into the hollow of his hand. It was Nigak's nose. Tears slid blindly down Ronan's face as his fingers closed gently over that precious black gift of love. He and the wolf walked on.

PART
TWO

THE TRIBE

OF THE

WOLF

(Three years later)

Chapter Eight

T horn stood just beyond the shadow of the cliff, enjoying the thin beginning-of-winter sunshine. He and his father should have been at work in the sacred cave hours ago, finishing the new paintings for the Buffalo Tribe's Winter Ceremony, but Rilik had been called into a meeting with the chief. Haras had summoned the council of nirum to discuss the situation of the three tribal members who had disappeared the night before.

Fara and Crim were gone, as well as Eken, Fara's sister. They had taken with them all their clothing, their cooking gear, and their sleeping skins. No one was in any doubt as to why they had gone, or where. The question Haras wished to discuss was should the tribe go after them and force them to return?

It was the loss of the women that concerned Haras most. Crim was a good man, a good hunter, and well liked by all. The tribe would miss him. But the women were the valuable ones; two young females of child-bearing age were a resource no tribe would want to whistle down the wind.

"All right, lad." It was his father's voice at last, and Thorn turned in time to see Rilik stepping off the cliff path onto the valley floor. "We can go now."

"I am ready, Father." They moved together toward the river, and Thorn asked, "The men are not going after Crim and the women, then?"

"Na." Rilik's voice was clipped. "Haras decided to let them go."

Thorn glanced sideways at his father's face. It was obvious that Rilik did not agree with the chief's decision.

"What did Herok say?" Thorn ventured after they had launched the small bark boat into the water and scrambled in. Herok was Thorn's cousin, whom Eken was to have wed after the Winter Ceremony this year.

Rilik grunted as he pushed off with the oars. "He was not pleased."

A cold wind was coming down the river, and Thorn pulled up the hood of his reindeer fur tunic. "I can understand why Eken would choose to go with Fara," he said as he huddled into the warmth of his hood. "They were always close, even for sisters, and Eken would not want Fara to be without a woman of her blood when her time for childbirth comes again."

Rilik was propelling them through the water with smooth strong strokes. "Sa," he said grimly. "I can understand Eken. The one whom I cannot understand is Crim. He is a man. His loyalty to the tribe should prevail over foolish fondness for a woman."

"It is not just foolish fondness, Father," Thorn said, a little defiantly. "Fara swore she would kill herself if she had twins again and the tribe exposed them. She meant it, Father. I saw her face when they took away the last ones . . ." Thorn stopped talking abruptly, afraid that his voice was going to crack.

"She probably *is* going to have twins again," Rilik said gloomily. "She has done it twice before; why should the third time be different?" He managed to shrug without breaking the smooth rhythm of his strokes. "That is why Haras decided to let them go. He said that the tribe does not need to be cursed with another set of twins."

"And they have gone to the Valley of the Wolf?"

Rilik gave one last shove with his paddle. "It seems likely. Crim was seen talking to the men from Ronan's new tribe at the Autumn Gathering. Probably that is when he got directions from them."

The boat had reached the shore, and both man and boy jumped out to drag it out of the water.

"Father . . ." This was said as the two walked across the rocky shore toward the cliff they would have to climb to reach the sacred cave. "If Fara does have twins, do you think Ronan will let her keep them?"

They had reached the base of the cliff. "That is why Crim has taken her there," Rilik said. "The shaman says that it is the Way of the Mother to keep one twin. And I am certain Ronan will do what he can to make both Fara and Eken happy. The women will be a valuable addition to that tribe of outlaws he has collected." Rilik looked upward toward the cave, squinting into the sun. "Just as they are a sore loss to the Tribe of the Buffalo," he added sourly.

Rilik had reached for the first hand-grip when he heard Thorn say very softly, "I hope that he will let her keep them both."

Rilik dropped his hand and turned. "Why should he do that?"

Thorn's fawnlike face looked unusually sober. "Because Ronan is not one to be overly swayed by taboos he does not see the sense of himself."

"There is great good sense in the taboo against twins." Rilik's tone became distinctly dry. "However, I agree with you that Ronan is not a man with an over-great regard for taboos. That is what got him expelled from the Tribe of the Red Deer in the first place."

"You said yourself that you did not think he was guilty, Father," Thorn said quickly.

Rilik raised his eyebrows. "Let us say rather that there is some doubt as to his guilt." He contemplated his son for a long moment in silence before remarking, "I did not know you had such regard for Ronan, Thorn. From whence did this admiration come?"

Thorn flushed. "I used to bear him company when he was with us recovering from his injury. Don't you remember, Father?"

"I remember how badly he was hurt," Rilik said. "To say true, I have never understood how he managed to make it through the Buffalo Pass on that broken leg. If it had not been for that tame wolf of his, he would most certainly have died before we found him."

"I used to bear him company while he was getting better," Thorn repeated. "I used to draw . . . for him."

The look Rilik gave his son was sharp as a spear point. "Draw *for* him?"

"Sa."

Silence. Finally Rilik asked grimly, "Did you draw his face, Thorn?"

Silence again. "Sa." Thorn's voice was soft yet subtly defiant. "I did."

"Did he know what you were doing?"

"Sa," Thorn said again. He met his father's piercing gaze. "He was not afraid, Father. I told you he does not care about taboos he does not see the sense of."

"They do not draw in the Tribe of the Red Deer." Rilik's voice grew grimmer with each word he spoke. "They do not make the hunting magic in the way of we who follow Sky God. Ronan would not understand the danger that lies in a likeness. It was wrong of you, Thorn, to take advantage of his ignorance. Very wrong." Rilik's eyes bored into his son's face. "What did you do with the drawings?"

"I threw them in the river," Thorn lied.

Now Rilik let his anger loose. "How many times must you be told? To draw something is to capture its spirit! That is why we draw the animals we hunt, so we can gain power over them. But it is taboo to draw the likeness of a man. That kind of power is dangerous, Thorn! No artist should ever so abuse his gift as to use it in such wise. I have told you and told you and told you . . ."

Thorn bowed his head and listened. It was true that he had been told and told and told. He did not understand himself what it was that drove him to draw people's faces. Drawing animals was enough for his father, had been enough for all the other artists who had gone before him. Why was he alone cursed with this unnatural desire?

At last Rilik fell silent. Thorn heard his father sigh. "Come," he said in a quieter voice. "Let us get to our work."

It took them twenty minutes of climbing to reach the hole that marked the opening to the tribe's sacred cave. They retrieved the soapstone lamps filled with animal fat that they kept just inside the entrance, and Rilik lit the wicks with the live coal which he had carried in an antelope horn at his belt. This particular cliffside cave was extremely deep, and the lamps provided only a little light against the gigantic darkness. Rilik knew the way so well, however, that he could travel the narrow galleries with astonishing sureness and speed.

Thorn followed his father along the dark and tortuous underground passages. After about half a mile they passed a black and silent underground lake, and then they were in the first of the cave's large halls. Rilik turned and followed the walls of the hall, Thorn close on his heels.

They had gone but a short way when Thorn felt the floor beginning to rise beneath his feet. He lifted his stone lamp higher, the chamber walls widened, and then they were in yet another gallery.

The thrill of astonishment and awe he felt every time he came into this place jolted through Thorn once again. For here, in this hidden, high-ceilinged rotunda, the Buffalo tribe kept its greatest treasure. Here Rilik had captured for his people the spirits of the animals the tribe hunted in order to live. Upon the smooth and polished wall were painted buffalo and horses and ibexes and red deer. The animals were so vivid with life they seemed almost to leap out from their stone setting.

Thorn slowly turned his reverent eyes from the paintings and looked at his father. For the vast majority of the paintings in this room were Rilik's work. Four separate panels of animal pictures had he done, all marked by the same loose and airy style. Only the buffalo looked a little stiff, a little less fluid and airy than the rest of the animal portraits. When Thorn had asked his father about this, Rilik had replied that as the buffalo was the tribe's totem, and was consequently neither hunted nor eaten by them, it was not proper to call it up in all its naturalistic reality.

There were no humans at all pictured on the rotunda walls.

Although Thorn had been learning the skills of painting for a number of winters, it was only this year that he had been allowed into the sacred cave, after his initiation into tribal manhood. At first he had only watched his father work, awed by the sureness and the skill of the older man. Thorn had been taught by the shaman to outline his drawing first, and then to fill in the body of the picture. The contour lines could be erased after, Jessl had said. But Rilik was so sure of himself, was so excellent a draftsman, that he laid the wet pigment directly upon the rock walls without outlining first.

At present Thorn was working on the picture of an ibex. These mountain goats were an important food source for the Tribe of the Buffalo, and Thorn was concerned to get as accurate a likeness as he possibly could. He was not yet as confident of his technique as Rilik, so he had begun his painting by outlining the picture in black earth pitch, drawing the lines with a finely tipped bird's feather. The ocher colors with which he was filling in the body were also done with feathers, the delicate lines and gradations of shading evoked by tips of varying thicknesses.

Thorn enjoyed the work. He was happy and excited to see the ibex taking shape under his skilled hand. So it was with a pang of sorrowful bewilderment that he wondered, as he stepped back from the wall to see what finishing touches were yet needed on his picture, *Why is this not enough?*

Winter passed in the territory of the Tribe of the Buffalo, and the first moon of spring rose in the sky. "We will learn if Fara had twins again at the Spring Gathering," Rilik said to his son one chill afternoon as he sat in the men's cave engraving the picture of a horse on a reindeer leg bone. "There will probably be someone there from the Tribe of the Wolf to trade reindeer hides."

"Ronan himself does not come?" Thorn asked.

Rilik raised an ironic eyebrow. "I am thinking Ronan would find it somewhat chancy to turn his back upon that bunch of outlaws for any length of time. He sent someone else in the autumn, and he will probably do the same this spring."

Silence fell as Rilik continued to draw with a graver. After a while Thorn asked, "How many men do you think have joined with Ronan, Father?"

Rilik shrugged. "Who knows? That valley of his has become a refuge for every piece of scum who finds himself thrown out of his own tribe." Rilik looked up from his work, a slight frown puckering his brown-skinned forehead. "My concern is how much success someone as young as Ronan will have controlling them. He is not chief by right of blood, as Haras is. He is only chief because he was the first to find this hidden place of refuge he calls the Valley of the Wolf."

Rilik bent once more to his work. Thorn watched the delicate strokes his father was making to indicate the heavy winter coat of the horse. "There are not so many horses in our hunting territory these days," the boy murmured.

Rilik grunted in agreement.

"Father . . ."—Thorn leaned a little forward—"may I come with you to the Spring Gathering this year?"

Rilik nodded. "I have been thinking that perhaps I would take you, Thorn. It will be well for you to see some of the work that is offered there. There was a spearthrower up for trade last year that was one of the finest pieces of carving I have ever seen."

Thorn's pointed, fawnlike face lit as if from within. "Is it true?" he said excitedly. "I can go?"

"If it is all right with your mother."

Thorn sighed with sheer pleasure. Both of them knew it would be all right with his mother. It would never occur to Thorn's mother to gainsay Rilik.

Thorn propped his chin upon his knees. "What tribes are likely to be there, Father?" he asked eagerly.

Rilik put down his carving. "Tribes come from all over to the Great Cave for the Spring Gathering," he answered. "Even more people than you find in the autumn. There are people of the Kindred from the valley of the Snake River and from the valley of the River of Gold. There are always some people from the tribes on the morning side of the mountains, and from the tribes that dwell by the sea. These are like the Tribe of the Red Deer in that they still follow the Way of the Mother." Rilik solemnly nodded his head. "Truly, you will never see such a number of people from so many different tribes as you will see in the Great Cave in the spring."

"And there is trading?" Thorn prompted.

"There is trading: shells from the shores of the sea, the skins of reindeer and buffalo and white fox, and mammoth ivory and musk ox horn from the north. There are needles to be had, and spears and spearthrowers, beautifully carved. The carvers will even make one especially for you, if you tell them exactly what it is you want. There are all kinds of different burins and gravers to be had, and clay pots for the storing of food. You can get engraved armlets and pendants and headbands and belts." Rilik smiled at his son's entranced face. "The commodities of news and gossip are as readily available as goods, and of course one of the main businesses of any gathering is the transacting of marriage contracts."

Thorn heaved a great shivery sigh. "What shall our tribe take to trade, Father?"

"The knapper will take his tools, the hunters will take their skins, and I will take my engravings." Rilik once more picked up the reindeer bone. "There are not many artists among the Kindred who can draw as well as I," he said matter-of-factly. "Only those from the Tribe of the Horse can match my work, and most of the time they do not come as far south as the Great Cave." Rilik picked up his graver and squinted thoughtfully at his bone. He etched a line and regarded it again. After a few minutes, Thorn rose quietly and slipped away.

———

It was a blowy, chilly spring morning, when the traders from the Buffalo tribe moved off northward along the Atata River, beginning the two-day journey that would bring them to the gathering at the Great Cave. The Atata was one of the great north-south valleys that cut through the mountains, and centuries of migrating animals had pounded out tracks which subsequent human use had etched even more solidly into the earth and stone of the hills. Steep cliffs lined the Atata valley on either side, but the tracks of passage lay mainly on the low ground along the river.

"What is the Great Cave like?" Thorn had asked his father weeks before.

"Wait and see with your own eyes," Rilik had replied. It was the same reply he had given his son when as a child Thorn had once questioned him about the sacred cave. The wait to see the cave had been excruciating, but in the end Thorn had been forced to admit that he was glad he had not known what to expect. "It will be the same with the Great Cave," promised his father. "You will see."

Thorn's waiting came to an end late in the second afternoon of their journey. The Buffalo party was following the track along the Pebble River by then, when all of a sudden the steep heights of a cliff rose up before them, seeming to block the road completely. Thorn checked his steps. There must have been a track, however, for the men in the forefront of the party veered abruptly left. Thorn followed, and there before him was the cave.

It was great indeed, an enormous archway of rosy-colored stone that rose at least a hundred feet above the river. In fact, the Great Cave was more a tunnel than a cave, a huge tunnel cut right through the rock of the cliff from one side to the other. The river roared through it in an uninhibited torrent of white foam. People were encamped all over the gravel before the cave's mouth, and Thorn saw a group of children shrieking with delight as they kicked around an inflated horse's stomach. Several of the children were wet from the spray of water that rose up from the racing river.

In all his life Thorn had met but a handful of people who were not of his own tribe. His eyes widened and his heart began to beat with excitement. The load of engraved bones he carried on his back seemed suddenly lighter. He straightened, looked again at the shrieking children, and smiled.

Chapter Nine

The trading party threaded its way in and out among the tents and the people until it had passed under the soaring rocky arch. Thorn stared about in wonder. Never had he thought it possible for a cave to have ceilings as high as this one! Daylight poured in from the large tunnel opening, and further light came from the small scattered fires around which groups of men were sitting, surrounded by their wares. One group immediately caught Thorn's eye; stacked high against the stone wall behind them was an immense pile of reindeer antlers.

"What are those men doing with all those antlers, Father?" he asked Rilik in a low voice.

Rilik glanced at the men. "They make digging sticks with them, Thorn."

The Buffalo party had halted while Rilik was speaking, and Thorn watched Haras take a lamp over to the men with the antlers. One of them courteously lit it for him from their fire. Haras stayed speaking for a few moments, then led the way toward an opening in the rock that Thorn supposed led to the interior galleries. He turned to follow, tripped, and was righted by his father's strong hand on his arm. "Watch where you are walking," Rilik said.

Haras had disappeared, and obediently Thorn followed him into the darkness. "We always camp in the same chamber," Rilik said from behind Thorn. "It is not far."

Thorn stood quietly while the men went about the business of building a fire. As soon as the fire caught and there was light enough to see, Thorn wandered over to inspect the chamber's walls. He saw no paintings.

"Come," Rilik said, "there is time enough for us to take a look around."

Eagerly, Thorn followed his father along the passage and back into the main tunnel of the cave.

The sound of the rushing river was ever-present, magnified by the great stone walls and roof. Rilik and Thorn walked up the steep path beside the booming water, and Thorn could see that every level surface of the tunnel floor was occupied by groups of men with wares to trade. A number of the men wore the long braid that denoted they came from tribes that followed the Way of the Mother, and Thorn's brown eyes were wide with wonder as he trailed along behind his father, his head swiveling from group to group.

Rilik knew many of the men from previous gatherings and paused often to exchange greetings and news. Even those who came from a distance seemed to know a rough form of the language spoken by the tribes of the Kindred. Thorn, however, was more interested in the items offered for barter than in talk, and the wares he found most wonderful were the shells. The Buffalo tribe had shells that had been made into ornaments for both men and women, but never had Thorn seen such an array of beautiful, unset shells. There were golden shells, black shells, and pearly textured shells of pink and white and gray. There was one in particular, a fan-shaped, pure white shell that Thorn coveted. He would try to trade some of his own engravings for it, he decided, and he would make it into a pendant for his mother.

Thorn turned away from the shells and saw that Rilik had sat down on his heels in front of the feather man. Rilik could spend hours choosing feathers. "May I go outside for a little, Father?" Thorn murmured in Rilik's ear.

"Mmmm," Rilik replied absentmindedly, picking up a fine partridge feather and regarding the width of its spread intently. Thorn went.

It was growing dark outside and Thorn was disappointed to see that the children had stopped their play. Only one little boy was left, desultorily kicking the horse-stomach ball back and forth between his moccasined feet. Thorn regarded his face with interest.

All the lines of the child's face went upward except the eyes, which drooped in an intriguing fold at the corners. The nose was particularly delightful, long and thin and outrageously tip-tilted. The mouth was thin-lipped, too, but its irresistible upward quirk made it look both joyous and generous. The hazy blue eyes drooped sleepily, but their expression was not sleepy at all. Thorn smiled. It was impossible not to smile at such a face.

The child noticed him, hesitated, and then approached. "Would you like to play kick ball?" he asked.

Thorn grinned. "Sa," he said. "I would."

The two youngsters played together happily until the dark set in and their annoyed parents came to fetch them. The boy was the son of the shaman of the Tribe of the Leopard, and the shaman and Rilik thought their sons should have had enough sense to return to their campfires at darkfall. Thorn and Kenje exchanged unrepentent grins and trailed off after their respective parents.

Thorn awoke in the middle of the night, sweating heavily. He felt wretched. His nose was so stuffed he couldn't breathe, and his throat hurt. He sat up and strained to find his father by the light of the single lamp, but all he could see of Rilik was a lump under his sleeping skins.

The only sound in the chamber was the sound of snoring. No one stirred. Rilik was a heavy sleeper, and if Thorn tried to wake his father he would wake the others as well. They would think he was a baby, crying over a sore throat. Tears stung his eyes and he blinked them back. He wished fiercely that he had not left his mother. He lay back down and steeled himself to endure the remainder of the night.

Thorn fell back to sleep just before dawn, and he awoke again with the stir of activity around the fire. "I don't feel well," he croaked to his father. "My throat hurts."

Rilik frowned and put a hand upon his forehead. "Your skin is hot."

Haras saw the gesture and approached them. "What is the matter here?" He sat on his heels beside Rilik, and both men frowned at Thorn.

The chief of the Tribe of the Buffalo was an impressive-looking man: tall and broad-shouldered with sand-colored hair and blue-gray eyes. Those eyes were looking at Thorn with a mixture of concern and irritation. Haras did not want a sick boy on his hands during the gathering.

"The boy seems to have a throat sickness," Rilik said. "His skin is hot, too. I will give him some sage tea, and he can stay in his sleeping skin this day."

Thorn groaned in protest.

"That is what the shaman would prescribe," Haras said authoritatively. "If your skin is hot, you must stay quiet and let the angry spirit within become calm. Go back to sleep. Perhaps you will feel better when you awaken." The chief turned to Rilik. "If his skin does not grow cooler, we shall have to find a shaman to take some of his blood to let out the angry spirit."

Rilik brought Thorn the promised tea, and the hot sage-flavored liquid felt good on his swollen throat. Then the men of the tribe hoisted their wares upon their shoulders and went off to bargain for what they needed, leaving Thorn alone. His throat felt a little better from the tea and he went back to sleep.

He had no idea how long he had been asleep when he awoke again. The gallery was still deserted. To his profound relief, he felt much better. He hated having blood drawn, and with their own shaman not here, it would have to be done by a stranger. Thorn lit the fire from the lamp the others had left burning for him and heated himself some more tea. He drank it thirstily, and when he had finished, he picked up the lamp and went to finish exploring the stone walls of the room.

The gallery was largely undecorated, but along one wall Thorn found that someone had once scratched two very poor engravings of buffalo. Thorn examined them and curled his lip in contempt at the ineptitude of the work. He went to his pack, took out a graver, and set about engraving a proper buffalo next to the other drawings. Once that was done, he engraved the figure of a horse. Then, without any volition on the part of his brain, seemingly entirely on their own, his fingers began to draw the profile of a face.

It was a simple sketch, but the long, tip-tilted nose and drooping eyelids made perfectly clear whose face it was: Kenje, the son of the shaman of the Tribe of the Leopard.

Thorn looked at the picture when he had finished, his face bright with pleasure in his own creation. Then he realized what he had done.

He stepped back from the wall in consternation. Dhu! If anyone saw this picture he would be in very big trouble.

Thorn bent to pick up a rock, so he could efface what he had drawn. Then he remembered his father's words. If this picture had indeed captured Kenje's spirit, what would happen to him if Thorn scratched all over him with a rock? Would something terrible happen to Kenje if Thorn destroyed this picture?

For the first time, Thorn truly understood the magnitude of what it meant to draw a human face. He had made Kenje vulnerable. I had no right to do that, Thorn thought in horror. What am I going to do now?

The answer came almost immediately. He would do nothing. He would leave the drawing as it was and trust to the darkness. It was only because he had been confined and bored that he had taken to exploring the walls. Surely no one else would look. Surely no one else would ever find this drawing. Surely Kenje would be safe.

When Rilik arrived back at the gallery an hour later, he found Thorn drinking sage tea and feeling better.

While the rest of the tribe had been trading, Haras had been meeting with the other chiefs. "There is a fearsome tale being told by the tribes of the Kindred who dwell to the north of the mountains," Haras said that night when he sat around the campfire with his nirum. Thorn and the other youngsters who had accompanied the party sat together in a small circle behind the men, listening quietly. Haras frowned. "I know it sounds unbelievable, but it has come from more than one source."

"What is this tale?" Herok asked.

"It is said that there is a tribe of people who come from the lands of the frozen north. It is said that they are not settled people, that they are ever on the move, ever seeking out better pastures and better hunting territories. The men say that they sweep down upon a tribe the way a fire sweeps across a summer pasture, destroying all that lies in its way."

Rilik was rubbing the tip of his nose, a sure sign he was skeptical. "I do not see how this can be true, Haras. Even if these ravagers are large in number, why do not the other tribes unite and put them to flight?"

"They cannot" came the answer. "Men of the Buffalo, this is the strangest thing of all." Haras lifted his leonine head. "It is said that these men sit upon the backs of horses."

Stunned silence. Then came the cries of disbelief:

"Impossible!"

"That is a shaman's dream!"

"I do not believe it!"

Finally Haras held up his hand for silence.

"Has anyone you spoke to actually *seen* these men?" Rilik asked into the sudden quiet.

Haras shook his head. "They are yet to the north of the place where the River of Gold flows to the sea. The tribes who are at this gathering have not seen them, but in the gatherings to the north they have spoken to men of the Kindred who say that they have."

"What are these riders called?" Herok asked.

Haras said, "The tribes are calling them the Horsemasters."

"If they are to the north of the River of Gold, then they are safely distant from us," Herok pointed out.

"That is so," the rest of the men concurred, and after a while the talk turned to other things.

Men sitting on horses? Thorn thought. Can it be possible?

The following morning Thorn was much better, and since the tribe was not leaving the Great Cave until the following day, it seemed he would have time to see the gathering after all. The first person he sought out was the shell trader, whom he asked for the white fan-shaped shell that he had so admired two days before.

The shell trader laughed at his ignorance and told him the white shell was long gone. "Let that be a lesson to you, youngster," the man said officiously. "Do not wait to make up your mind, but take what you want while yet you can."

Shoulders drooping, Thorn was turning away from the trader's buffalo skins, which were considerably less covered with shells than they had been two days before, when he heard a child's voice say, "Thorn! I have been looking for you."

Thorn turned, and at the sight of Kenje's irrepressibly tilted nose, he felt a sharp pang of guilt. "I was sick yesterday."

"I know. I asked your father where you were. Do you mind if I come around with you today?"

The sight of Kenje put Thorn in mind of that other face he had so illicitly drawn. "Do you know if there is anyone here from the Tribe of the Wolf?" he asked the shaman's son.

Kenje looked first startled and then suspicious. "Why do you ask?"

"A friend of mine joined them last year," Thorn said, surprised by the boy's reaction. "I would like to ask after her welfare."

"Oh."

"Is there something wrong?" Thorn asked.

"Na," said Kenje airily. "Nothing is wrong. They are here, as a matter of fact. Five of them. They brought some fine reindeer skins to trade." He gave a pleased smile. "I got a beautiful white belly for my mother."

Thorn immediately became gloomy, remembering the white shell he had not gotten for his mother.

Even though all the tribes in the mountains hunted reindeer, it was not unusual for fine skins to be in demand at a gathering. It took many reindeer skins to provide a sizable family with skins enough for the rugs, bedding, tents, and clothing it needed to survive. Seventeen full reindeer hides, three white bellies, and thirty legs were necessary for a woman to make a fur tunic, boots, and a sleeping skin. This did not count the other fur, like wolverine, which was used for trim. The reindeer skins from the Tribe of the Wolf had been a welcome addition to the gathering, even though the men themselves were regarded somewhat dubiously.

"I can show you where they are," Kenje said to Thorn. "Just don't tell my father I was talking to them. He says the men of the Wolf are all outcasts from other tribes, and he does not want me to associate with them." Kenje's smoky blue eyes were solemn. He lowered his voice. "One of them murdered his own wife."

Thorn's mouth dropped open in shock. "Is it so?"

Kenje nodded. "I heard the men of my tribe talking about it. The man's name is Bror, and he is the one who had the beautiful white belly I traded for."

"He murdered his wife?" Thorn could not take it in. "But why did her relations not kill him if he did such a thing?"

"She was from another tribe, and they did not find out right away. He did not mean to do it. He loved her, the men said, but he became angry with her one day and he struck her on the jaw. She fell down, and then she died."

Thorn thought of his mother and folded his lips.

"He buried her all by himself," Kenje was going on, clearly relishing the bloody tale. "He could not ask her relations to help him; they would have killed him had they known. And his own tribe was horrified by what he had done and would not go near him. So he took a digging stick and a shovel and he worked all day and all night to dig her a grave. He was full of grief and remorse," Kenje said, obviously parroting an adult's words. "Then all alone he buried her and when it was done he took the track up the mountain and there he met and joined with Ronan to form the Tribe of the Wolf."

Thorn let out his breath in a long sigh. It was a tale that held all the terror of true tragedy.

"Come along," said Kenje, "and I will show you where they are."

The men of the Wolf were packing to leave when the boys approached them. "The one in the middle is Bror," Kenje breathed softly.

Thorn looked at the man who was kneeling over his hide sack, working in what looked like somber silence. Bror was black-haired with a strong-boned face and thick, muscular neck. He looked like a man who carried the burden of wife-murder on his shoulders, Thorn thought. Kenje hung back, letting Thorn move closer to the men by himself.

"I am Thorn, son of Rilik of the Tribe of the Buffalo," Thorn said politely. "I wonder if you could tell me if Fara is well?"

One of the men straightened up from the flints he was packing and looked at Thorn. He was a large man, with short brown hair and small pale blue eyes. He said to Thorn with obvious irritation, "Your chief already asked us about her," and turned back to his stones.

Dismissed, Thorn still stood in place, shifting uncomfortably from one foot to the other. He felt Kenje plucking at his shirt, trying to get him to leave. Thorn ignored Kenje and said to the top of the man's head, "Did she have twins again?"

Once more the man looked up. His blue eyes were hard. "Why do you want to know?"

"Fara was a friend of mine," Thorn answered.

"She had twins again," the man said, his voice as hard as his eyes.

Thorn's heart was heavy. Poor Fara, he thought. Six babes had she born, only to see them . . . "Did Ronan let her keep one of them?" he asked anxiously.

This time it was the man Kenje had identified as Bror who answered. "He let her keep them both."

Thorn's heart lightened, lifted. "Oh," he said with soaring joy, "I am so glad!" He smiled all over his face.

Now the five men were looking at him curiously. "Glad?" Bror asked. "Why should you be glad? It was your tribe that exposed her other twins."

Thorn bit his lip. How to explain without seeming disloyal to his tribe? "It is only that it was a terrible thing for Fara, to have her babes taken away," he said. "It is in my heart that it would have killed her to lose them again."

"Twins are evil," the blue-eyed man said flatly.

"Well, if the babes are evil, they are in the right company," the redheaded young man on the giant's left said with a wry smile. "As Ronan pointed out to you when you objected to keeping them, Heno."

"What did he say?" Thorn asked in fascination.

The redhead, who looked to be about Ronan's age, answered with his eyes on the one called Heno. "He said that the evil two small babes could bring to a tribe of rapists and murderers was distinctly negligible, and we might just as well add to the general wickedness and go ahead and keep them."

Thorn and Kenje laughed, then stopped and stared at the rapists and murderers, hoping they had not been offended.

"Not to mention the fact that he wanted to keep the women," the blond-haired young man farthest from the boys murmured.

"He was right," the redhead said firmly. "We need the women."

All of the men grunted their agreement with that statement. Then Kenje surprised Thorn by stepping forward. "Please," Kenje said, addressing himself to Bror, whose bearing subtly indicated that he was the party's leader, "would you give this to my sister for me?" And he held out the exact same white shell that Thorn had wanted for his mother.

Thorn stared at the shell; then he lifted his eyes to stare at Kenje. The boy's eyes were fixed on Bror. The big man nodded to the blond. "Take it from him, Dai."

The blond young man came forward, and Kenje put the shell into his hand. "I wanted to give this to you yesterday," Kenje said, "but my father was always around." He glanced nervously over his shoulder, as if he felt someone watching him even now. "How is she?" he asked.

"Beki is well," the blond young man called Dai replied quietly. "She and Kasar both. She has a child coming."

Kenje smiled and, like Thorn before him, said, "I am glad. Will you tell her that for me? That I am glad she and Kasar are happy."

Dai nodded and turned away, the shell in his hands. Thorn and Kenje exchanged a look and were beginning to turn away themselves, when a young man wearing the signature braid of the Goddess approached and demanded of Bror, "You are Ronan's men?"

"We are Ronan's men." Slowly and deliberately, Bror rose to his feet. The other four men turned to face the newcomer. The air was suddenly full of hostility.

The braided man seemed not to notice the threatening atmosphere. "I am Tyr, of the Tribe of the Red Deer," he said, "and I have a message for Ronan. Will you carry it?"

"The Tribe of the Red Deer cast him out," Bror replied brutally. His heavy face looked as if it had been carved in wood, so still and stern it seemed. "What do you want with him now?"

"This is not a message from the tribe," the Red Deer man said. "It is a message from Tyr, his old agemate."

There was silence. "And what is this message?" Bror asked at last.

"It is this: The temper of the tribe is changing. Have patience. I will send for you when the time is ripe for your return."

The hostility of the men of the Wolf was now so palpable that Thorn could feel the hairs on the back of his neck standing up.

"That is all?" Bror asked deliberately.

"Sa, that is all."

"Ronan has a new tribe," the redhead said. "He does not need the Red Deer any longer."

Bror reached out and put a large hand upon the redhead's arm. "I will tell Ronan," he said to Tyr, his face impassive.

The braided man nodded, and then hesitated, as if he wished to say more. The expression on Bror's face discouraged him, however, and the men of the Wolf stood in silence watching as the Red Deer intruder turned and slowly walked away. Then they went back to their packing.

Thorn and Kenje waited until Tyr was well away before they followed in his steps.

"Your sister is with Ronan?" Thorn demanded when at last he and Kenje were standing by the edge of the rushing river, safe in the midst of the bustle of men packing up their wares.

"Sa," Kenje sighed. "She is."

"You did not tell me." There was reproach in Thorn's voice.

"It is not something that my father wishes to have known."

"She must have done something dreadful," Thorn said. There was a distinct note of admiration in his voice.

But Kenje shook his head. "It was just that she gave her love to the wrong man."

"Kasar?"

"Sa. Kasar."

"Why was he the wrong man?"

"He came of a poor family. His father was not a good hunter, and the family had only the bare necessities of skins and furs. Kasar could not afford Beki's bride price, which was high. In my tribe, you see, the bride price is very important. The rank of a whole family—husband, wife, and children—depends upon how much was paid for the woman. My father did not want his daughter undervalued."

"What of Beki?"

"She said she did not care, that she wanted only Kasar. But my father is the shaman, a man of great importance in the tribe. He would lose face by taking less for Beki than she was worth."

Thorn nodded in understanding.

"My father said that Kasar could marry Beki if he came to live in my father's house and worked for my father. But if Kasar did that, then his children would belong to my father and not to him. Kasar is very proud. He would not become my father's servant, he said, not even for Beki."

"So what did your sister and Kasar do?"

"Beki pretended that her blood was flowing and went to stay at the moon hut," Kenje said matter-of-factly. "She took food and water with her, so it was not until suppertime of the following day that we realized she was no longer there. Of course, the first thing we did was look for Kasar, and he was gone too."

"They ran away together," Thorn said, fascinated.

"Sa. Kasar had heard of Ronan's new tribe, and that was where they went. Beki sent my mother word by a shell trader that she was safe."

"You must miss her," Thorn said, thinking of the shell Kenje had given to Dai.

"She was a good sister," Kenje said simply.

"Your father is still angry?"

"My father says that Kasar kidnapped her from the moon hut. He has named Kasar for rape and says he will never be allowed to return to the Tribe of the Leopard. So I am glad that they have found safety with Ronan. There is no longer a home for them in their own tribe."

"Thorn!" Thorn looked up to see his father signaling to him from the higher ground near the wall.

"I must go," he said to Kenje.

"Don't tell anyone about my sister," the younger boy enjoined quickly.

"I won't," Thorn said. He took a step, stopped, and said over his shoulder, "I promise."

Kenje nodded and watched him walk away.

Chapter Ten

Thorn finally settled for a handful of small golden shells to bring to his mother. One encouraging thing about the trade was that the shell man was willing to accept one of Thorn's own engraved bones in exchange, and he did not have to go and beg one of his father's. It made the golden shells more palatable, as Thorn was not so certain that he would have gotten the white shell in exchange for his own work.

By late in the afternoon, most of the Buffalo tribe were gathered around their campfire, packing for the return trip on the morrow. It had been a good gathering; most of their goods had been traded successfully, and two of the men had made profitable marriage contracts for their daughters. News had been exchanged, and friendships renewed.

The packing was almost finished when one of the men picked up a torch and went to search along the walls to make certain nothing had rolled away. Thorn was busy arranging his mother's shells so they would not get broken, when a startled cry caught his attention. He turned to see Herok holding a torch up to the wall, right by the place where Thorn had done his drawings. His blood froze.

"What is it?" Haras asked.

"Come here and see," Herok replied.

Haras went over to look at the wall. Then he said, "Rilik."

Thorn sat like a stone and waited. "Thorn," his father's voice came next. It sounded very grim. "Did you do this?"

Thorn got to his feet and bravely faced the men at the wall. His heart was hammering within his chest. "Sa," he said. "I did."

"What is it?" the others were asking. "What has Thorn done?"

Haras told them. "He has drawn a picture of the son of the shaman of the Leopard tribe. A picture of his face."

Shocked silence.

Behind him, Thorn heard one of the other boys say softly, "Thorn, how could you?"

"I didn't mean to do it," Thorn tried to explain. In the light of the torch, Rilik's face looked white as death. "I drew the buffalo and the horse, and then . . . before I even knew what my fingers were doing . . . I drew the picture of Kenje." He met his father's eyes. "I am sorry, Father. I knew right away I should not have done it, but I was afraid to scratch it out . . ." He bit his lip. "I was afraid something bad would happen to Kenje."

"What should we do?" It was Haras, his large, genial face looking worried. "Jessl is not with us. You are the artist, Rilik. Do you know what we should do about this?"

Rilik said heavily, "We must show it to the boy's father. He is a shaman. He will know what to do."

Thorn's chin jerked up. He did not want Kenje, or Kenje's father, to know what he had done. Kenje thought that he was a friend.

"Were you just planning to leave this here, Thorn?" his father asked coldly.

Miserably, Thorn nodded. "I did not think anyone would ever find it. I thought it would be safe, that Kenje would be safe." He had to look away from his father's eyes, they were so cold.

"I will get the shaman," Rilik said to Haras. "We will deal with you later, Thorn."

The shaman of the Leopard tribe came and looked at the picture. He was very upset. He did not know what magic was needed to cancel the power of the picture. Finally, after a long talk with Haras and Rilik, he agreed to perform a ceremony. He also agreed to take a large amount of the goods the Buffalo tribe had traded for in payment for the danger to his son's life.

Thorn was not allowed to attend the shaman's ceremony, nor did he get a chance to speak to Kenje. He saw the boy only once, as he came with his father from the inner gallery after the shaman had finished his rite. Kenje gave Thorn one long, reproachful look as he silently followed his father out of the tunnel. It took three men of the Leopard to carry the goods that Haras had been forced to part with.

Thorn was in disgrace. No one spoke to him. *We will deal with you later,* Rilik had said, and evidently "later" meant when they returned home. For two long days, Thorn walked miserably in his tribe's line of march and thought about what he had done.

His mother was not in their hut when he reached home, and the first thing Thorn did was to get out the pictures he had once drawn of Ronan, the ones he had told his father he had thrown in the river. He had done them three years before on smooth oval-shaped stones, and he had hidden them under some old toys in a deerskin bag he kept in a corner of his mother's hut. He took the bag now to a nook in the cliff face and opened it.

Thorn remembered clearly that he had drawn five different pictures of Ronan's face. He reached now into the bag and first lifted out a small bow that he had once played with; next came a set of darts and the rings made of reeds through which the darts were thrown. There was an old bull roarer, and a set of knucklebones. Then an oddly shaped white rock he had once fancied. At last his fingers closed around a smooth oval stone. He lifted it out and laid it carefully on the ground before him. He reached into the bag again and took out another, then a third.

The fourth time his fingers touched a sharp edge. Slowly, fearfully, he removed his hand from the bag and found himself looking at a fragment of one of the smooth oval portrait stones. One of Ronan's pictures had been shattered.

Thorn sat in utter stillness and thought.

Ronan's picture had been destroyed, but Ronan still lived. Ronan was well. Thorn knew that from the men of the Wolf he had spoken to at the gathering. The picture had had no power over Ronan.

And the picture was a good one. Thorn looked now at the three stones that still retained Ronan's image, looked at the high cheekbones, the arrogantly arched nose, the proud mouth. He had even caught the look of shuttered reticence and the faint suggestion of physical pain. Ronan was there.

Thorn reached into the bag and brought out the last stone. There was a great crack all through the middle of it.

Yet Ronan was fine.

After a long time, Thorn put the stones and the fragments back into the bag and returned to his mother's hut. She had come back from her gathering expedition and welcomed him with soft cries and warm hugs. He gave her the shells he had brought for her and watched with pleasure the way her delicate face lit with joy. For a few minutes he almost forgot that he was in disgrace. Then his father came into the hut, and all his pleasure was quenched.

"W-what is wrong?" his mother asked her husband, divining immediately from the look on his face that something was.

Rilik told her what it was that Thorn had done.

"But surely it cannot be so terrible," Thorn's mother said, standing up for her child the way she would never stand up for herself. "Have you not said, my husband, that the shaman made a ceremony to take away the picture's power?"

"The shaman himself was not certain if the ceremony would be effective," Rilik said grimly. "Haras was forced to give over a large amount of our goods in reparation for the damage done to the shaman's son."

In her gentle way Thorn's mother replied, "If that is so, I am thinking that even if the shaman had known the ceremony to be effective he would not have said so."

"Perhaps that is true," her husband agreed. "But it is unarguably true that his son was wronged. Nor was this the first time Thorn has been guilty of drawing human faces. I have warned him before about it."

Siba made a soft noise of disbelief.

"It is true, Mother," Thorn said.

"Oh, my son," his mother said despairingly. "Why?"

"I do not know," Thorn said with almost identical despair. "I cannot seem to help myself, Mother. My fingers just do it."

"I have spoken to Haras about this," Rilik said.

Tense silence fell.

"He has decided that since you cannot control this urge of yours, Thorn, then you cannot be allowed to draw at all."

Thorn stared at his father.

"This is a blow to me. It is a blow to all the tribe," Rilik said. "There is the promise of a great artist in you. But I think Haras is right. If you cannot control your gift, then you cannot be allowed to use it."

Thorn did not speak. Rilik turned his eyes from his son's face as if it hurt him to look at it. After a moment, he left the hut.

Thorn stood it for the length of one moon before the emptiness in his life became unbearable. He had found the taboo against drawing the faces of humans frustrating, but frustration was a mere triviality in comparison to what the prohibition against drawing at all was doing to him.

Since first he had been able to hold a graver, Thorn had drawn pictures. He drew as naturally as he breathed. To give it up was like an amputation.

At first he had thought his father could not mean it. Surely Rilik would relent. He knew the kind of talent his son had in his fingers; the artist in Rilik would not be able to bear seeing that talent go to waste.

The weeks passed, and slowly Thorn began to understand that it was not his father's voice that counted in this. The chief had been furious about having to pay so heavy a fine to the shaman of the Leopard tribe. Haras was normally a genial and generous man, but in this matter of Thorn he had made up his mind. Thorn had clever hands, said Haras. Let him learn to make tools. And he sent Thorn to work with the flint knapper.

When the last sliver of the Moon of the New Year was hanging in the late-spring sky, it was Thorn who made up his mind. He would do as Crim had done before him, and take the track to the high mountains, the Altas, in search of Ronan.

It was a desperate decision for a gentle and well-loved boy to make. It would give great heartache to his mother and his father, whom he loved. But Thorn knew he could not go on living like this.

He had been born to be an artist. If he could not be an artist in his own tribe, then he would have to go to a place where he could. It was as simple, and as fearful, as that.

Thorn had asked Kenje if he knew the location of the Valley of the Wolf, and the boy had replied that all he knew was that you must follow the Atata River up the Altas, go through the pass to the other side, and find the Lake of the Eagle.

If a pregnant Fara could make that trip, Thorn told himself, then he could too.

Once Thorn had made up his mind, he did not tarry. He waited until the Moon of the New Foals had grown bright enough to light his way, and then he left. Beside his sleeping mother he placed one of the stones which bore Ronan's face, so she would know where he had gone. Then he packed his gravers and his paints and his brushes into his sleeping skins and headed south along the river that would lead him up the Altas.

The river track was protected on either side by high sheltering cliffs, but when the stone walls gave way to a steep forest of beech and pine, Thorn's enthusiasm began to ebb. The smells of strong resin and sharp pine from the great evergreens closed around him. Close by, two wolves howled in concert, and there came a wild shrieking of hyenas from the towering forest on the other side of the river. Suddenly Thorn felt very young, very small, and very frightened.

The miles went by very slowly. For centuries the herds had come this way, following ancient tracks to the rich summer grazing in the high pastures of the Altas, and for centuries the Buffalo tribe had traveled in the wake of the herds, to hunt the animals in their summer environs. Thorn had traveled this track before with the men of his tribe, and so he was ready when the mountain began to rise steeply before him.

The Atata had cut a deep gorge, almost a crack, into the limestone rock of the mountain, and Thorn climbed alongside the river. By the time he had scrambled up through the steep rocky chasm and gained the flat, mist-hung pasture where the men of the Buffalo hunted deer in the summer, the first light of morning was in the sky. Guarded by solemn mountain sentinels just beginning to stain red with the rising sun, Thorn lay down to sleep.

He awoke to the splendor of daffodils, pansies, lilies and other colorful spring flowers, blazing everywhere in the thick grass. Antelope and red deer and reindeer flowed across the brilliantly colored pasture peacefully, blending with each other and then disengaging, harmoniously intent upon nature's great gift to the herds: the mountain grass.

Almost reluctantly, Thorn shouldered his pack, crossed the pasture, and once more began to ascend. Up through a second steep and rocky gorge he went, up through a second chasm and into a second, smaller pasture. On the far side of the pasture reared the vast wall of the Altas, and Thorn's heart sank. It seemed as if all his climbing had been for naught!

Dark fell, and with the dark came the cold. Thorn built a fire and went to sleep under a spray of stars.

He arose with the dawn and commenced his journey upward into a cold and remote universe of stone and sky. The trees fell away, and scrub was the only vegetation in sight. The river fell in one waterfall after another, covering Thorn with a continual, freezing spray. It was midday when he finally gained a third gorge, enshrouded in mist from a hundred-foot waterfall. Thorn stood for a while, his ears full of the water's thunder, and then he began to climb again.

An hour later, he was approaching the pass over the summit. A heavy white fog hung over the splashes of snow underfoot, and the wind lashed Thorn's face, chilling him to the bone. It was not until he was through the pass and had begun his descent of the southern side of the mountain that the mist burned off. When he felt the heat of the sun, Thorn halted, lifted his head, and there, spread before him in all its majestic beauty, lay the glorious alpine world that would one day be known as Andorra.

All around Thorn towered the black and somber peaks of the Altas, with snow lying in vast fields within their folds. The river dropped swiftly through a rich green valley toward the trees that Thorn could see growing at a lower altitude. The mountains on either side of the valley were sunlit, all blue and purple, with snow lying in shining patches upon their steep sides. The sky, dotted with small puffy clouds, shone clear and cobalt blue above the serene and majestic landscape.

Lower down the mountain, in the heart of the valley, there browsed a herd of ibex, interspersed here and there with some ewes and their newborn lambs. The sloping pasture blazed with flowers: narcissus and hyacinth, kingcups, buttercups, gentians of the deepest blue, pansies, anemones, and some flowers Thorn had never seen before.

It was so beautiful that Thorn felt lightheaded.

I must find the Valley of the Wolf, he thought dazedly, and repeated to himself the only directions he knew: Follow the valley from the pass until you come to the Lake of the Eagle.

It was not until late the following day that a weary and hungry Thorn found the lake he was seeking. It lay at the foot of a sheer cliff, its water as clear and calm and blue as the sky reflected in its crystalline depths. There were small scrubby pines growing around three-quarters of the rim of the lake, but it was the colossal limestone cliff that caught Thorn's eye. A pair of golden eagles lazily circled overhead, and Thorn walked toward the place where the cliff extended beyond the water.

From close up, Thorn saw that the high cliff face was actually filled with cracks and ridges, where hardy plants had managed to find a foothold, and where birds had made their nests. Near the base of the cliff the sheer rock gave way to scree. Thorn looked up; there were sufficient footholds for him to climb the cliff, he thought. He would camp now, and tomorrow he would see what lay beyond this wall of rock. He was certain it must be the Valley of the Wolf.

There were fish in the lake, and Thorn was cooking one for his supper when a small herd of gray horses came single-file through the trees, passed close by his fire without seeming to notice it, and went to quench their thirst at the lake. Thorn stared in amazement at the seven horses drinking peacefully such a short distance away. They were young horses, he saw, all grays and all males. They finished drinking, turned, and made their way along the shore. Thorn watched them until they were out of sight.

They had to have seen him, he thought. They had to have smelled him. They had to have smelled his fire. Yet they had shown no fear.

Astonishing.

Thorn slept late the following morning, his body still adjusting to the thinner air. When he awoke the sun was bright in the sky, the birds were calling, the squirrels chattering, and coming slowly around the rim of the lake were two men with spears balanced on their shoulders. Thorn swallowed hard and crawled out of his sleeping skins. They did not notice him until he had moved out of the shadow of the trees onto the very edge of the lake. Then they stopped. Heart pounding, Thorn moved to meet them.

Chapter Eleven

When the men were close enough for Thorn to see their faces, he recognized them as part of the group he had met from the Tribe of the Wolf at the gathering this spring. His spirits soared and his eyes sparkled. He had found Ronan!

The men did not appear to be as pleased to see him as he was to see them. "Who are you and what are you doing here?" the blond asked abruptly, giving Thorn a stare in which there was no hint of recognition.

Thorn, a modest boy, was not dismayed. "My name is Thorn," he replied obligingly, "son of Rilik of the Tribe of the Buffalo. I am seeking the Valley of the Wolf and the man called Ronan."

The blond's slate-colored eyes were hard as stones. "And for what reason was a cub like you cast out of the Tribe of the Buffalo?"

"I was not cast out," Thorn said hastily, anxious to reassure the men that he was not a criminal. "I left of my own will."

The blond laughed.

Thorn's temper flared at the mocking sound of that laughter. "It is true!" he said hotly. "I left because I wished to join with Ronan."

The redhead had not shared in his friend's laughter. He said now, "Ronan is very particular about whom he will accept in the Tribe of the Wolf. They have to have a talent." The look he gave Thorn was insulting. "What is your talent, youngster?"

Thorn said furiously, "I draw."

The redhead's eyes narrowed, and the recognition that had been missing earlier slowly dawned upon his face. "Now I know where I have seen you before," he said. "You are the boy who caused all that trouble at the Spring Gathering by drawing the face of the shaman's son."

"Sa," said Thorn defiantly. "I am."

"You asked us about Ronan."

"Sa," said Thorn. "I did."

Silence fell as the two young men, both of them half a head taller than Thorn, regarded him.

Finally the blond said, "I am thinking Ronan will want to see him, Okal."

The redhead grunted in reply. "We'll have to bring him back with us, Dai. We can't leave him here to watch while we use the passage."

"That is so," the blond replied.

Okal turned to Thorn. "Get your things," he commanded, and Thorn trotted off hastily to collect his belongings. When he returned, the men draped his extra shirt over his head, secured it around his neck with its leather neck tie so that he could not see, and led him forward.

"When we are within the passage, we'll remove the blindfold," they assured him.

It seemed to Thorn a terribly long time that he was walking blind-folded in the dark, trusting his feet to the guidance of these strange men. He strained his eyes in vain; he could see nothing through the buckskin blinder. The air under the shirt was hot and stuffy, and Thorn was profoundly thankful when they halted and he felt fingers fumbling at the thong around his neck. The blindfold was lifted, Thorn blinked, and looked around.

He was in a narrow, stone-enclosed passage, and he realized that they must have entered into the very cliff wall he had been planning to climb. So, he thought triumphantly, the valley did lie behind that cliff!

"The path descends just ahead," Dai said. "Watch your feet." With Dai before him and the redhead behind him, Thorn shortly afterward began to scramble down what was a very steep path indeed.

Dhu, Thorn thought. The cliff in the valley must be much higher than it was on the lakeside. Still they went downward, the path zig-zagging now even as it descended. On they went, until at last the sides of the cliff began to open outward and above their head the slit of blue sky turned into a wedge. Dai scrambled down a last rocky slide, Thorn behind him, and then the two of them stepped out from between the passage walls into a bowl of brilliant sunlight.

Thorn stared in wonder at the scene before him. There was a lake on this side of the cliff too, with water as blue as the cobalt sky above. Beyond the lake there stretched a valley, a rich and beautiful valley, brilliantly dyed with the green grass of mountain pasture and dotted everywhere with the rioting colors of thousands of flowers.

Slowly Thorn raised his eyes to survey the enclosing mountain walls. The cliff that rimmed the valley on its northern and eastern side was immense! The level of the valley floor was indeed far below the level of the lake that lay on the other side of the cliff. Thorn scanned the sheer polished stone of the upper cliff. He might have been able to climb to the top of the cliff on the outer side, he thought, but no one would be able to descend into the valley by way of the inner cliff. That climb was simply impossible.

He turned back to look at the valley floor. The faintest of breezes was rustling the deep grass, and butterflies fluttered around the flowers. On the far side of the lake a herd of mostly gray horses was grazing quietly, some of the mares and foals lying down in the warmth of the sun. Antelope grazed along the western wall, and sheep and ibex leaped agilely among the rocks of the western cliff, nibbling idly at the plants that grew in the ridges there.

A golden eagle rose in the sky, wheeling in great graceful arcs above the sunlit valley.

Surely, Thorn thought in awe, this is a land blessed by the gods.

"This is the valley you were seeking," the redhead said to Thorn. "Ronan named it for that wolf of his." For the first time he smiled, "Though there are plenty who think that the wolf is Ronan himself."

"Okal," Dai said to his companion in a low voice, and he gestured to his left.

Thorn swung around, and for the first time he saw the huts that had been built between the lake and the valley's north wall. He had a brief impression of women sitting before one of the huts, but it was the single man walking toward him who immediately absorbed all his attention.

His shoulder-length black hair was bound with a leather headband, not worn in the braid that Thorn remembered. The injury had left the slightest suggestion of a hesitation in his gait, but still he managed to move like a great cat stalking in the high grass.

Ronan.

Thorn began to smile a greeting, but then he saw that Ronan was not looking at him. His dark stare was trained instead on the blond, and his look was not friendly.

"You know you are not supposed to bring anyone in here without my permission," he said.

"We thought you would want to see this one," Dai answered hurriedly. "We found him camping at the Lake of the Eagle when we were on our way to hunt for ibex. We were careful to cover his eyes, Ronan. He did not see where the passage begins." He gestured toward Thorn. "This is the boy who was asking after you at the gathering."

Ronan raised his brows in a gesture that was suddenly very familiar to Thorn. "Beki's brother?" he asked his men.

"Na. This is the boy who drew his face."

There was silence. Both Okal and Dai stood at attention, looking faintly apprehensive. Finally, to the men's obvious relief, Ronan turned his attention to Thorn. As he looked into the hard, hawklike face of the chief of the Wolf tribe, Thorn began to realize that Ronan had changed.

"Don't you remember me, Ronan?" Thorn forced out the words from between suddenly stiff lips. He was no longer smiling. "When you were wounded and staying with the Tribe of the Buffalo, I would sit with you and keep you company. We played Hunt the Buffalo together . . ." Thorn's voice died away. Ronan's dark face had not changed expression.

"And you drew a picture of my face," Ronan said. "Sa. I remember you, Thorn, son of Rilik." Silence fell as Ronan looked Thorn up and down. The Wolf chief did not appear to be impressed by what he saw. Finally he asked, "Why have you left the Buffalo tribe, and what are you doing here?"

Thorn had felt marginally better when Ronan remembered his name, but that cold stare was unnerving. "I am in disgrace with my tribe," he answered honestly. "It is as you have been told. At the Spring Gathering I drew a picture of the Leopard shaman's son, and Haras had to pay a big fine. So he said that since I could not be trusted, I could no longer be an artist, that I must learn to knapp flint instead."

"And knapping flint is not to your liking?" Ronan's voice was pleasant, but there was something in it that made Thorn flush.

"There is nothing wrong with flint knapping if that is your calling," he said defensively. "It is not my calling, however. I am an artist." He flung up his head and a thick shock of brown hair fell on his forehead. "I came to you because I thought you would let me be what I was born to be."

Ronan said, "Whatever made you think that?"

Bravely, Thorn held that dark stare. "You let me draw your face once," he said.

Ronan's lips curled in a sardonic smile. *He has changed*, Thorn thought again, his artist's eye taking in the new hardness in Ronan's face. Once Thorn had thought the finely cut mouth was beautiful. It looked thinner now than it had three years before, all of its sensuous softness had gone. There was nothing at all of boyhood left in that face.

"I am thinking I did not much care what happened to me at the time I let you draw my face," Ronan said. "Things are not the same with me now."

Thorn said, "You let Fara keep her twins."

The dark eyes opened wide in a surprise that was genuine. Then Ronan lowered his lashes. "I remember now," he said. "You were asking after Fara and the twins."

Thorn nodded and watched him silently, his brown eyes huge.

"What use can you be to me?" Ronan asked the boy.

"I am a good flint knapper," Thorn replied promptly. "I can make tools for you." He cast around in his mind for any other talents. "I can hunt," he added, "and skin my kill, and butcher it. I will do all of these things for the Tribe of the Wolf, if you will allow me the freedom to draw."

"Not faces!" Dai said quickly, looking at Ronan.

"There is no power in the drawing of a face," Thorn assured the blond young man earnestly. "The shaman's son was always safe. It was not necessary for Haras to pay a fine."

"In my tribe it is taboo to draw pictures of a man," Okal said. "It is taboo in all the tribes of the Kindred who follow Sky God." He glanced at Ronan. "And so should it be in the Tribe of the Wolf."

Ronan said, in a deceptively pleasant voice, "I am the chief of the Tribe of the Wolf, and I am the one to make the rules."

Both Okal and Dai stared at their feet and did not reply. Ronan turned to Thorn. "How do you know there is no power in a picture?" he asked.

"I kept the pictures I made of you, and when I went to look at them recently I found that one of them had shattered," Thorn replied honestly. "And another one had broken in two. I think it happened a long time ago, when I put them away with my childhood toys. Yet here you are"—Thorn gestured—"healthy and strong. That is why I know that the pictures have no power—or at least not the kind of power men have feared."

"Luckily for me," Ronan said drily. He glanced at his two followers. "As you say, I am still perfectly healthy."

Dai said, "I do not want him to draw me!"

"Or me," Okal agreed.

Ronan nodded. "It is your right to make that choice." He stared at Thorn. "Do you hear me, son of Rilik? You are not to draw a picture of any person without permission."

"Sa," Thorn replied. "I hear you, Ronan." Then he asked breathlessly, "Does this mean that I may join the Tribe of the Wolf?"

"I am thinking we have need of a flint knapper." Thorn's brown eyes were watching him anxiously. "And of an artist," Ronan said.

Ronan told Dai and Okal to bring Thorn to Fara, and the two young men led the boy in the direction of the huts that were clustered along the shore of the lake. The women Thorn had glimpsed earlier had disappeared, and he looked with eager curiosity at the substantial-looking series of huts reposing in the morning shade cast by the cliff. He commented about how well-built they looked.

"They have to be to withstand the winter weather," Okal replied.

"Do you actually spend the winter in this valley?" Thorn asked in amazement.

The two young men nodded.

"But the snow must be very deep here. And the cold . . . Dhu, even the animals don't stay in the Altas for more than six moons out of the year!"

"It is cold," Okal agreed, "but the huts stay warm. The low angle of the winter sun warms them. There is actually little or no snow on the south-facing cliff, so there is grazing for the animals all winter long."

"This valley is better protected than any place I have ever seen," Dai put in. He pointed to the surrounding cliffs. "We are even protected from the winds."

"But that side"—Thorn pointed to the cliff that ran along the whole western side of the valley—"is very low. It may protect you from the wind, but I do not see how it can keep intruders out."

Dai grinned. "Climb it, and look down the other side," he recommended.

"What is on the other side?"

"The mountains here drop down in shelves," Dai explained. "You have seen how much lower this valley is than the land on the other side of the eastern wall?" Thorn nodded. "Well, it is the same on the far side of the western wall. The cliff is a sheer drop. Unclimbable."

Thorn gazed at the deceptively low cliff. Beyond it, all he could see were the distant mountains of the Altas, lifting their lonely peaks to the sun and the clouds and the god of the Sky.

He let his eyes drift slowly southward. "And that way?" he asked, pointing to where the river had cut a passage through the cliffs on its exit from the southern end of the valley.

"A waterfall," Okal said. "Tremendous. Unpassable." He grinned with satisfaction. "The only way into this valley, youngster, is the passageway through which you just came."

Thorn confessed, "I have been thinking that this is a land where even the gods might dwell."

"No god," Okal said drily. "Only Ronan."

Dai laughed.

They stopped before one of the huts, and Dai called into the open door, "Fara! Eken! I have a visitor for you."

"What visitor?" a woman's voice called back.

"It is Thorn, Fara," Thorn said loudly. "Rilik's son."

"Thorn!" A woman carrying a baby came to the door, and Thorn recognized Fara's sister, Eken, the girl who was to have married his cousin. "It is!" Eken called back into the hut.

"Ronan told us to bring him to you," Dai said.

Eken smiled. "We will take care of him, Dai. Thank you." Then to Thorn, she said, "Come in, come in!"

Thorn ducked into the hut and saw Fara sitting on a reindeerskin
beside the hearth, nursing a baby. Thorn smiled all over his face just
to see her so. Her brown eyes looked so happy and serene as she gazed
up at him, her babe at her breast.

"Have you come for me?" Eken had entered behind him, and as
she took a seat next to her sister her pretty face puckered with a frown.
"If you have come to bring me back to wed Herok, I will not go, Thorn.
I am staying here with Fara."

"I have not come for you, Eken," Thorn said. "I have come to join
the Tribe of the Wolf for myself."

The women looked at each other in wonderment, then turned back
to him. Eken waved for him to sit, and demanded, "Why?"

Thorn sighed, sat on his heels, and told them the story of the
shaman's son. While he was speaking Fara finished feeding one babe,
handed it to Eken, and received the second, which she put to her other
breast. Eken expertly cradled the first babe against her shoulder and
began to pat its back.

"And so you came because you thought Ronan would let you continue to draw?" Eken asked when Thorn had finished his tale.

"Sa. And he has agreed that I may join the tribe—as a flint knapper
and as an artist."

"It is in my heart that you came on a fortunate day," Fara said. "He
has turned away two other men since we first arrived."

"I do not understand that," Thorn said in bewilderment. "If he
wants to build a tribe, I should think he would want to increase his
numbers."

"He does, of course, but these two were particularly unsavory characters," Eken said. "The tribe does not need thieves and murderers to
make up its numbers."

Thorn thought of Ronan's comment about rapists and murderers,
but did not know quite how to put his question. "Ah . . ." he said,
"then what kind of people do make up the Tribe of the Wolf?"

Eken's hand was gently massaging the baby's back. "People who
broke the rules of their own tribes," she said. "People who made a
mistake and were made to pay heavily for it. Not bad people, Thorn."

"People like Beki and Kasar?" Thorn asked.

The two women looked at him curiously. "How do you know about
Beki and Kasar?" Fara asked.

"The shaman's son whose face I drew? He is Beki's brother."

"So," said Fara, and she bent her head to rest her lips on the fuzzy baby head nursing at her breast.

"Well, then, sa, people like Beki and Kasar," Eken said. "When I think of it, there are actually a number of people here who were unlucky in love."

Thorn thought of Bror, whose sad story he had heard from Kenje. There was a man who had certainly been unlucky in love. "What of the two men who brought me here?" he asked Eken. "Dai and Okal. Were they unlucky in love also?"

"Okal was. He is of the Tribe of the Bear, and they are a tribe that is very strict with their unmarried girls. Okal lay with one of these girls and got her with child. She tried to rid herself of it and died in the attempt. Her brothers swore to kill Okal, and he fled to Ronan."

"They must be strict indeed if the girl was reduced to such a fearful measure," Thorn said wonderingly. "Why did she not just marry Okal?"

Fara raised her face from her baby's hair. "He was to marry someone else," she said drily.

"Oh." Thorn thought of the redheaded young man whom he had first met at the gathering and slowly shook his head. "He does not look like the sort of man who would play games like that."

Fara took the baby from her breast and lifted it to her shoulder. "It is not always easy to tell a man's heart from his face," she said.

Thorn nodded politely. "That is so." He glanced at the open door and the daylight beyond it. "What of Dai, then?" he asked.

"I am not sure of his story," Eken answered. "It has something to do with the death of his brother. I do know that he has been with Ronan for a long time—for almost as long as Bror."

"How many people are there in the tribe altogether?"

"There are three handfuls of men—plus one, now that you are here. And one handful plus three of women."

"That is a goodly number," Thorn said, impressed.

"There are children also," Fara said. "Three others besides my twins."

Thorn looked from the bundled twin on Fara's shoulder to the one that was reposing upon Eken's. "Are they boys?" he asked.

"Girls," Fara replied proudly.

Thorn smiled at the look on her face. "I am so glad that Ronan let you keep them."

"He was brought up in the Way of the Goddess," Fara said. "The Mother is gentler with children than Sky God is."

"Yet it is my understanding that even the Goddess allows you to keep but one twin," Thorn said. "At least, that is what my father told me."

"Your father was right," Eken said. "We have people here from the tribes of the plains and they are followers of the Mother. Twins, they believe, are really one child that has split in two in the womb. All of the goodness given to that one child goes into the first twin, the twin of lightness, and this twin they keep. The second twin, they believe, is the repository of all the single child's evil, and this twin they expose."

"But the Tribe of the Red Deer keeps them both?"

Fara shook her head. Her face looked strained. "Na. The Tribe of the Red Deer keeps the first twin and exposes the second. It is Ronan who said both babies should stay." Her arms tightened around the precious bundle on her shoulder. "I will call blessings upon him for the rest of my days for that."

Thorn said, "His heart is kind."

Both Fara and Eken gave him identically startled looks. "I do not know if I would say that, precisely," Fara murmured doubtfully.

"Why else would he allow you to keep the twins?"

It was Eken who replied. "I think it is because he is not afraid." She rocked slowly back and forth, her cheek brushing against the baby sleeping so contentedly on her shoulder. "He is not afraid of twins, at least. Nor"—here she smiled faintly at Thorn—"of having pictures painted of his face."

"But it is dangerous not to fear anything," said Thorn, frowning slightly. "A man who has no fear has no reverence."

Both women gave an identical shrug.

"What god does the Tribe of the Wolf worship?" Thorn asked next.

"We are all from different tribes, Thorn," Fara said, "and we have different ways. Ronan's rule is that each person should be free to follow his or her own way, so long as it does not interfere with the way of someone else."

"What god does Ronan worship, then?" Thorn asked.

"Now that," Eken said softly, "is a mystery."

Chapter Twelve

I t was not long before a procession of women began to appear before Fara's tent. Thorn soon found himself at the center of a good-natured and curious group, all drinking Eken's freshly brewed sage tea. Thorn was still young enough to feel perfectly comfortable among women and children, and so he drank his tea and answered their questions readily, and all the time his eyes were flicking from face to face, trying to match individuals to the names and stories Fara and Eken had told him earlier.

He would have known Beki for Kenje's sister anywhere, he thought, looking at the girl's sleepy blue eyes and tip-tilted nose. Seated next to Beki was a woman called Yeba, whose once-pretty face was disfigured by an ugly scar. It was not until afterward that Thorn learned from Eken the story behind that scar: Yeba's husband had caught her in adultery and in punishment she had been expelled from the Tribe of the Squirrel with the tip of her nose cut off.

Thorn was also introduced to two women from the People of the Dawn, one of the tribes that dwelt on the plain to the morning side of the Altas. Thorn had never before met a woman who was not of the Kindred, and he looked at them with wide-eyed curiosity.

Both Berta and Tora had glossy, dark brown hair, which they wore in a single braid that reached to their waist. Their eyes were large and brown, their nosebones and cheekbones broad, their complexions warmly olive. They were sisters, Thorn found out later, who had left their tribe when their brother had been expelled by the healing woman for being possessed of an evil spirit. The girls had refused to desert their young brother and had taken him into the high mountains in a valiant attempt to contact the spirits that would cure him of the sweating sickness that had so terrified their tribe. There they had been discovered by Heno, one of Ronan's men, and he had helped to care for the sick boy. When Mait had recovered, all three siblings had followed Heno to the Valley of the Wolf. Both girls had since married, and both had arrived at Fara's fire with young children in cradleboards upon their backs.

All of the women were politely curious about what had brought Thorn to the Tribe of the Wolf. Reluctantly, he told them his tale, acutely aware of Beki, Kenje's sister, sitting at his side. When he had finished he turned and assured her earnestly, "I am convinced that Kenje was in no danger." And he related the story of Ronan's pictures.

"Ronan was mad to let you draw his picture in the first place," Fara said firmly. "What was he thinking of?"

Before Thorn could reply, Berta spoke. "Ronan was brought up in the Way of the Mother and we do not believe in painted images as do those of you who follow Sky God." Berta spoke the language of the Kindred, but with an accent that proclaimed her outlander origins.

Beki spoke next, her voice bitter. "I see that my father has not changed. You say that he managed to extort a big fine from your chief?"

"Sa," Thorn said. "We lost all the profits of our trading. Haras was furious with me."

"My father has ever been watchful to make a profit from his children," Beki said, even more bitterly than she had spoken before.

"Fathers do not feel for their children the way mothers do," Berta said. Her baby had begun to fuss a few minutes earlier, and she was busy unfastening her from the cradleboard. "It is a constant amazement to me the way the women of the Kindred have allowed the men to usurp their mother-rights."

Everyone watched Berta as she loosened the leather ties that supported her babe on the cradleboard. "That is how things have always been with us," Beki said finally.

The last tie had been unfastened and Berta lifted her whimpering child into her arms. "This child that you carry," she said to Beki, "will you give Kasar the right to make all the decisions as to what will be good for it and what will not?"

Instinctively, Beki placed a hand upon her swelling stomach. "I will not."

Berta undid the thong on her shirt and put her babe to the breast. The fussing immediately ceased. "If Tabara had belonged to the People of the Dawn she would never have had her children taken away from her," Berta said. "That is a barbarous thing to do to a woman, worse even than what was done to Yeba."

"That is so," Berta's sister, Tora, agreed.

Thorn did not remember being introduced to a woman named Tabara, and indeed, from the behavior of the others, it was clear to him that she was not present.

It was Eken who spoke into the suddenly somber silence. "Tabara was found in adultery. For us of the Kindred that is a serious matter. It strikes at the very heart of the family, Berta. It cannot be passed over lightly."

Berta's babe hiccuped loudly, and all the women smiled. "The family is a mother and her children," Berta said, her hand gently patting her child's back. She looked at Thorn, the only male present. "The man is not important."

Thorn looked back into those challenging brown eyes. The women were quiet, waiting to hear what he might say. "It's not true that the man is unimportant to the family," he said indignantly. "My father was very important to me. It was he who taught me all the skills I need in order to be a man. How can that not be important?"

"Any man can teach those things to a child," Berta said dismissively.

"That is so," her sister agreed. "In our tribe that kind of teaching is done by the mother's brother. A father is not necessary."

Thorn stared at the two of them in amazement. So this was the thinking of women who followed the Goddess! Thorn was very glad he himself came from a tribe that understood the importance of men.

"Is your tribe led by a Mistress, like the Tribe of the Red Deer?" Thorn asked.

Berta shook her head. "The People of the Dawn are led by a chief. A woman has too much responsibility at home to have the time to assume responsibility for others who are not of her family. But the matriarchs of each family sit on the chief's council and give him their advice."

Thorn thought of his shy and gentle mother, who would never think of gainsaying a word that dropped from his father's lips. He shook his head in astonishment.

A little silence fell as Eken filled the cups with more tea. Then a very pretty girl named Yoli said to Thorn, "When you were at the Spring Gathering did you hear aught of a marauding tribe from the north that rides upon the backs of horses?"

"Sa," Thorn said, glad to have the subject changed. He was not accustomed to dealing with such forthright women as Berta and Tora. "My chief, Haras, spoke to us about it. It seems that the tribes to the north were spreading this news around the gathering. The men of the Buffalo found it hard to believe."

"Ronan took it seriously enough to send Bror and Lemo north to learn what they could," Fara told Thorn.

"He did?" Thorn looked bewildered. "I do not understand. Even if the story is true, this tribe is from the Land Where the Ground Stays Forever Frozen. They can have nothing to do with us."

"That is what my husband says," Yeba agreed. "Cree told Ronan he was wasting the men's time by sending them on such an errand."

"Ronan knows what he is doing!" Eken glared at Yeba.

Yeba shot a look of amusement around the circle. "Sa," she said with deliberate mildness, "we all know what *you* think of Ronan, Eken."

Several of the women laughed and Eken flushed. Berta got to her feet. "It is growing close to suppertime," she announced. "The men will be returning soon from the hunt. It is time to light the cookfires."

"Sa, sa."

"That is so."

One by one the women arose and began to return to their own huts. Thorn looked with puzzlement toward the peacefully grazing herds and wondered where the men had disappeared to. They did not appear to be hunting in the valley.

The women of the Wolf were certainly a strong-minded lot, he thought a little nervously, as he turned back toward Fara's tent. The conversation he had heard this afternoon was definitely not the sort of idle gossip about children he was accustomed to hearing from his mother's friends at home.

The men had not been hunting in the valley. A half an hour after the cookfires had been lit, a large group of them returned through the

narrow passage carrying three dead reindeer. Thorn wandered down to
the slaughtering grounds, where the men were skinning and butchering
the carcasses.

Crim took Thorn in hand and introduced him to the men he had
not yet met. To Thorn's surprise, about half of the men wore the single
long braid that distinguished the followers of the Goddess. They were
not from the Tribe of the Red Deer, however. Their accents told Thorn
that much.

Mait, the brother of Berta and Tora, grinned at Thorn happily when
Crim introduced them. "I am very glad to see you," he said. "At last
I will have an agemate!"

Thorn smiled back. Mait looked very like his sisters; he had the
same long glossy braid, the same large brown eyes, the same flat nose
and broad cheekbones.

"We must get Ronan to give you boys a hut to yourselves," Crim
said good-naturedly. "It can be our initiates' hut."

Mait's eyes sparkled. "I will ask Ronan tonight if we can do that."

"Where is Ronan?" Thorn asked, looking toward the passage.

"Up the valley, I expect," Crim replied. He squinted against the
rays of the sinking sun. "Sa. Here he comes now."

Thorn followed the direction of Crim's eyes and saw in the distance
what looked like a man and a dog walking together through the thigh-
high grass that grew near the valley wall. "Is that Nigak with him?"
Thorn asked eagerly.

"Sa."

Thorn noticed that the man carried nothing. "They do not look as
if their hunt was successful."

"They have not been hunting." Crim's voice was stolid. He put a
hand upon Thorn's arm. "Come along, youngster. If you are going to
join the Tribe of the Wolf, you are going to have to work for your keep.
You can help me finish butchering the hindquarters of this reindeer."

With a quick smile over his shoulder at Mait, Thorn went.

Thorn ate his supper with Crim's family, but sleeping space was
tight within Crim's hut, which had to accommodate not only his wife
and sister-in-law but the twins as well, so Thorn slept that night in
Bror's vacant place in a hut that also housed Dai and Okal. Both young
men carried a handful more years than Thorn did, and would have
been nirum, or full-fledged hunters, in their own tribes. Thorn treated

them both with respect and had the sense not to ask them too many questions.

One question he did ask, as he was spreading out his sleeping skins. "How long has Bror been gone?"

"Almost one moon now," Dai said. He too was smoothing out his skins. "I am thinking he will be away for another moon, at the least."

"Sa," said Okal. He was already lying down, his arms crossed behind his head. "There will be plenty of time to build a hut for you and Mait."

"Where does Mait sleep now?" Thorn asked.

"He sleeps with the other unmarried men of the Goddess."

Thorn silently noted this segregation along religious lines. "Is it . . . difficult . . . sometimes," he dared to ask, "trying to live in harmony with people whose ways are so different?"

"Sometimes," Dai admitted. "It is the taboos that cause the most trouble. So far, though, Ronan has always managed to smooth things over."

"So far," Okal said.

Dai got into his sleeping skins. "Aren't you ready, yet?" he asked Thorn impatiently.

"Sa," said Thorn. He crawled hurriedly under his buffalo robe and Dai blew out the saucer lamp that had been lighting the tent. Within a short time the breathing of the two older men told Thorn they were asleep, but still he lay awake. His body was tired, but his mind was relentlessly active, going over again and again all of the things that he had heard during the course of the day.

There were so many questions he wanted to ask! Why had the men left this rich, animal-stocked valley to hunt? What terrible deeds had the other men of the tribe done to cause their expulsion from their tribes? Was there discord in the tribe between the followers of Sky God and those of the Goddess? And finally, what was Ronan doing alone up the valley?

The night passed and Thorn was still awake when he heard a sound outside his hut. Very carefully, he got out of his sleeping skins, crawled to the door flap, and peered outside. The moonlit night was bright enough for him to make out the figure of a man leaving the hut area and walking toward the ground-level rock shelter where the tribe's few dogs slept. Thorn immediately recognized the walk as Ronan's.

Slowly and silently, Thorn dropped the flap and returned to his sleeping skins. He closed his eyes and, finally, he slept.

The following morning Thorn learned that Alos, the female dog brought to the tribe by Yoli and bred by Nigak, had had her puppies. Everyone was delighted with the healthy, active litter. Ronan sent the boys up the valley, giving Mait instructions to show Thorn around. Mait was thrilled at the prospect of a holiday, and he was equally pleased to find himself in the role of leader, a position which, as the youngest member of the tribe save for the babies, he rarely achieved.

Thorn added to his feeling of importance by plying him with questions. The first one was "Where do the men of the tribe go to hunt?"

"This time of year the first herds of reindeer have reached the lower pastures of the Altas," Mait said. "That is where the hunters go. You saw how they came back yesterday with three fine kills."

"I saw," Thorn agreed. "Then it was reindeer in particular you wanted? It is true that I have not seen reindeer within the valley."

"We rarely hunt within the valley," Mait said simply.

Thorn stared in astonishment. "Why not?"

"It is Ronan's rule." Mait smiled at the look on Thorn's face. "Ronan says that we cannot afford to frighten away the animals that dwell here. He says that if we hunt them all the time, they will learn to fear us and will leave. It is better to hunt outside the valley and keep friends with the animals within."

"You never hunt in the valley?"

The boys had stopped by the river, and Thorn's eyes were on a mare and her foal drinking peacefully only a few yards from where he and Mait were standing. The mare was almost white; the foal was dark brown.

"We hunt the horses in the autumn," Mait replied, his eyes also on the mare and foal. "We herd the horses into a corral and kill the ones who do not look likely to withstand the winter. That way we have meat for the winter, and, since we do not bother them again, the rest of the horses soon forget their fright. We do the same with the rest of the animals in the valley; we cull the old and the ill and the injured and leave the sound."

"What of the horses I saw outside the walls of the cliff?" Thorn asked. "Where do they come from? They cannot winter on the open slopes, surely?"

"Oh, they are the young males that Impero chased from the herd," Mait explained.

"Impero?"

"Impero is the name Ronan gave to the herd's stallion. There he is now."

Thorn looked at the magnificent white stallion that was moving among the main herd of mares, which was grazing not far from the river. Even at this distance, Thorn could see how thick and muscular was his neck. The valley horses were unlike the horses Thorn was accustomed to seeing portrayed on the walls of caves. These horses had long, arched faces and long, flowing manes and tails. And they were mostly gray.

Mait continued: "Impero will let the yearlings stay within the valley, but the two-year-olds he drives out. The batch you saw were the ones he drove out this spring, when the mares began to drop their new foals. They will move lower as the weather worsens, and by winter they will have left the Altas altogether and gone down to the plain."

"Why doesn't the Tribe of the Wolf go down to the plain in the winter also?" Thorn asked. "It must be bitter here in the valley."

"We are too small a tribe to establish our own hunting grounds on the plain," Mait explained. "There are many tribes dwelling there, and they would not welcome us. We will have to become much larger and more powerful before we can hope to carve out a hunting territory for ourselves on the plain."

The morning slowly advanced as the boys made their way up the valley. By midday they were hungry, and they climbed up to a rocky ledge to dangle their feet, watch the small herd of sheep below them, and eat the food Fara and Berta had packed.

"Are all of the men of the Wolf outcasts from their own tribes?" Thorn asked after they had finished eating. He had one leg drawn up for support and, absentmindedly, he picked up a small flat stone and began to scratch on it with a sharp pebble.

"Sa," Mait said. "They are."

"At the gathering, one of your men said Ronan had called them a tribe of rapists and murderers." Thorn squinted his eyes to look at the sheep.

"He said that when Heno objected to keeping the twins," Mait said immediately and grinned in remembrance.

"Heno is the big man, is he not?" Thorn asked. "The one with the pale blue eyes?"

"Sa."

"What tribe is he from?"

"He is of the Fox tribe, from beside the River of Gold. I know I should like him better," Mait confessed. "He is married to my sister, and if it were not for him, I would probably have died. He was the one who brought us to the valley. But . . . I do not like him. He is always complaining—the twins were just one example."

"Why did the Fox tribe thrust him out?"

"He was blamed for the death of the chief's son," Mait said. "The Fox tribe has a very strict taboo against their hunters having sex for three days before a great hunt. Heno lay with his wife the night before the hunt, and the next day the chief's son was killed by a buffalo. Someone had heard Heno and his wife and accused him of breaking the taboo. The chief expelled him from the tribe."

"Ah . . ." said Thorn in understanding. "We also have such a taboo, but the men of the Buffalo are wise enough to obey it."

"The People of the Dawn do not have such a taboo," Mait said with a shrug, "and our hunting has never suffered." He leaned over to look at what Thorn was drawing. Thorn gave the stone to Mait to look at and let his own eyes rove over the scene before him.

The horse herd had left the river and was grazing at the southern end of the valley. Almost directly below Thorn's feet was a small group of ewes and new lambs. The lambs were lying in the sun, the mothers grazing. As Thorn watched, one lamb was suddenly seized by a desire to nurse. He leaped up and ran toward the ewes, bleating madly. All the rest of the lambs instantly decided that they must nurse too. The peaceful scene was transformed: lambs bleating and seeking mothers, mothers baa-ing and seeking lambs. As the babies found the right mother, they would fall to their knees and begin to nurse ferociously. Finally, silence fell.

The boys were laughing. "I never knew how amusing animals could be until I came here," Mait said. "It gives you a different feeling about them, sharing the valley with them the way we do."

"It is a wonderful chance for an artist," Thorn said, "to be able to get close to them for so long a time." And he took his drawing stone back from Mait.

"We did not have artists in my tribe," Mait said. "I hope you do not mind my watching you?"

Thorn shook his head and began once more to draw.

"Look," said Mait softly, "there is Ronan."

Thorn lifted his head and both boys sat in silence watching Ronan as he came down the valley, Nigak at his heels.

"What is he going to do?" Thorn asked.

"He has been watching the horses."

There was a startled silence. "Watching the horses?" Thorn said. "But why? Ronan is not an artist."

"He started to do it right after the men came back from the gathering with news of that tribe from the north," Mait said.

Thorn drew in a long breath. "The tribe that rides on horses?"

"Sa. The tribe that rides on horses."

"Can he be dreaming . . . ?" Thorn could not even finish the question, so ridiculous did it sound.

"Sa," said Mait, "I am thinking that he is."

Chapter Thirteen

Ronan lay on his back in the grass, his knees bent, one arm behind his head, the other flung across his eyes to shade them from the brightness of the sky. Nigak lay beside him, his long white muzzle resting on Ronan's hip.

"I believe it is possible," Ronan said softly. "I really do believe it is possible."

Nigak made no answer.

"The rest of them think I am mad. Perhaps I am."

Still nothing from Nigak.

"To do it, though, I will need Nel."

Nigak lifted his muzzle. Ronan craned his neck and looked into the wolf's bright yellow-brown eyes. "You think so too, I see."

Nigak pricked his ears.

"You think I should have gone for her sooner. It is not that I forgot my promise," Ronan explained to Nel's wolf. "It is just that I have been reluctant to leave the tribe."

Nigak sat up, ears still pricked, and stared intently at a small, long-legged foal that had wandered away from its mother.

"Na," said Ronan firmly. Nigak whined. "Na," said Ronan again. Nigak got up and padded down to the river for a drink. His manner was dignified. Obviously this was not a wolf that would dream of attacking a defenseless foal.

Ronan sighed. He would have to do something soon. He could not continue to send the others out hunting while he lay around in the grass and watched horses. His position as chief gave him certain privileges, but he knew he was reaching the end of his men's tolerance.

Dhu! When was Bror going to return? So much hinged on that. Bror would have reliable news about this tribe of so-called Horsemasters. And Bror was the only man he would trust to leave in charge of the tribe while he left to fetch Nel.

The first crescent of Antelope Moon had risen over the sunset last night. It was summer. Bror had been gone for two full moons.

Nigak returned from the stream and stood over Ronan, dripping water on his face. Ronan sat up. "Tomorrow," he promised the wolf as he wiped the wet off his cheek, "I will take you hunting. I can see that young Thorn is scandalized by our laziness."

He put his hand upon Nigak's ruff, and the two began to walk together down the valley toward the camp. Ronan wondered resignedly what problem would greet him today. It seemed a day scarcely passed when the belief of one tribe did not come into conflict with the belief of another. This was one of the chief reasons he was loath to absent himself for too long.

He passed the small hut that the women who followed Sky God had erected at a little distance from the camp to serve as their moon hut. In practice, the only woman who ever used it was Eken, as she was the only one who was bleeding. All of the other women of the tribe were either pregnant or nursing.

This custom of isolating a bleeding woman was not something that the Red Deer tribe had ever followed. Nor had the other tribes from the plain that followed the Mother. The men of Sky God, however, had been adamant that a bleeding woman harbored evil powers that could harm their own masculine abilities, and they had insisted on the moon hut. Eken, reared in the Way of Sky God, had been amenable to the isolation, which indeed was what she was accustomed to in her own Tribe of the Buffalo.

Ronan shuddered to think what was going to happen when the moon blood of Berta and Tora once more began to flow. Neither of those strong-minded sisters was likely to want to spend a week sitting alone by herself in the moon hut!

I will think of something, Ronan promised himself. It was a phrase he had comforted himself with often during the past three years.

He looked toward the north wall and saw two slim masculine figures running to meet him. Mait was still at a distance when he cried out his news: "Bror and Lemo are back and they have word of the Horsemasters!"

Thorn and Mait joined the rest of the tribe in the flat, open space before the huts, and Ronan gestured that they were all to be seated. Thorn realized that the two scouts were to be allowed to recite their story in front of everyone, and his heart began to pound with excitement. He took a place in the tribal circle beside Mait and directly across from Ronan, Bror, and Lemo. Once everyone was seated, Bror began to speak.

"We went far north, almost to the end of the lands of the Kindred, to a tribe called the Tribe of the Elk." Bror's stern, strong-boned face was very somber. "They had a terrible tale to tell."

"Sa," Lemo agreed, his own fair-skinned young face almost as grim-looking as Bror's. "Terrible." Lemo's wife, Yoli, looked at him anxiously, then picked up his hand and held it tight in her own.

"What we heard of these Horsemasters at the gathering is true," Bror went on, turning his head a little to look at Ronan. "The tribe is originally from the frozen north, but it seems they have turned their backs upon the steppe forever. At the Spring Gathering it was said that they were well north of the River of Gold, but Lemo and I learned that they have actually entered into the hunting territories of the Kindred."

Questions and exclamations of dismay issued from every mouth. It was Heno who asked the question that Thorn was most eager to have answered, "Is it true that they ride upon the backs of horses?"

"It is true," Bror said. "There were men in the Tribe of the Elk who have seen them."

"How do they guide their horses, then?" This was obviously a problem Ronan had been thinking about.

"They put a rope around the horse's nose, and hold the ends of it in their hands," Bror returned.

"But you did not see this for yourself?"

Bror shook his head regretfully. "The nirum from the Tribe of the Elk would not show us the way. They were too afraid."

Ronan looked disappointed.

"These Horsemasters are a terrible people," Lemo explained. "They descend upon a tribe like a storm sweeping down from the north, leaving only death and destruction in their wake."

"Death and destruction?" Berta said sharply.

Lemo nodded. His young face was white and set. "The men of the Elk told us that the Horsemasters killed all of the men in the Tribe of the Owl, raped the women, and took them for their own."

There was a horrified silence.

"I have heard of conflicts over hunting grounds," Crim said slowly, "but never has there been such a thing as this among the tribes of the Kindred."

"Nor among the tribes of the plain," Cree said.

"Have these Horsemasters established themselves on the hunting grounds of the Tribe of the Owl, then?" Ronan asked.

Bror answered, "For the moment. But that is what is so terrible about them, Ronan. They do not stay in one place. They take what they will, and then they move on." Bror shook his head in bewilderment. "I can understand that to a people of the cold and barren north, the river valleys of the south must seem sweet. But once they have won a good hunting territory for their tribe, why leave it?"

Ronan said slowly, "If they have truly mastered horses, then it would be easy for them to travel." His dark eyes swept around the circle of his own tribe. "Imagine how swiftly and comfortably you could travel if you were sitting upon the back of a horse!"

Thorn smiled as he contemplated this possibility. "It would be splendid," he said softly.

Beki asked, "Where is the Tribe of the Elk located?"

"On the River of Gold, south of where it flows to the sea."

Silence.

Heno said heavily, "If they follow the River of Gold, it will bring them to our mountains."

Beki shivered and Kasar reached a comforting arm around her shoulders.

"What plans have the northern tribes made to combat the Horsemasters?" Ronan asked Bror next.

"No plans that I could discover," Bror replied stolidly. "They are frightened to death, Ronan. All the talk is of fleeing."

"I cannot believe that the men of the Kindred are so weak!" Ronan's arched nostrils were flared with scorn.

"They are afraid of the horses, Ronan," Bror said. "And the Horsemaster tribe is very large, much larger than any single tribe of the Kindred."

"More reason for the tribes of the Kindred to unite," Ronan said tersely.

Bror shrugged.

"Even if these foreigners do come as far south as the mountains, our tribe will be safe," Yeba said stoutly. "Such a large number of people will never attempt the Altas."

"That is so," Berta agreed. "The tribes of the plain will also be protected by the Altas. It is the tribes of the Kindred that are in danger."

All of the braided men nodded their agreement and looked with pity upon the short-haired men who followed a god and not a goddess.

"They may not come down the River of Gold at all," Kasar said.

Heno nodded. "That is true."

"Their pattern," Bror said heavily, "is to come ever south."

"Well, whichever way they come," Mait said, "the Tribe of the Wolf will be safe."

"That is so," said Tora.

"True," said Cree.

The men of the Kindred were silent.

"Even so," Thorn finally murmured, a frown between his brows, "I do not like to think of the Tribe of the Buffalo under the heel of these marauders."

"Nor do I," Crim said emphatically.

Everyone looked at Ronan. He regarded them austerely. "I will be leaving the tribe for a short time," he said, with a dramatic change of subject. "Bror will be in charge while I am gone."

There was a stupefied silence.

It was Mait who asked, "But . . . where are you going?"

"To the Tribe of the Red Deer to fetch my cousin," Ronan replied. His tone made it perfectly clear that he would not welcome any more questions. "I will not be gone for very long."

It was a measure of his authority that not a single other question was raised.

"You cannot go alone," Bror said at last. "Let me come with you. Crim can take charge of the tribe."

The faces of both Heno and Cree darkened at the mention of Crim being placed in authority over them. Ronan gave Bror a warning frown. "I am not going alone, I will have Nigak. You are needed here."

Bror opened his mouth to protest again.

"And that," said Ronan pleasantly, "is an order."

The way was filled with memories. Once he was through the Buffalo Pass and into the hunting territory of the Tribe of the Red Deer, the memories crowded thick and strong. He had been so occupied these past years that he had been able to push his past life to the very bottom of his mind, where it surfaced only occasionally in disturbing dreams.

At his side Nigak whined, as if he could sense the distress within Ronan. As if he shared it.

"Do you remember this place, fellow?" Ronan asked the wolf softly. He buried his left hand in the thick silver fur of Nigak's ruff, and the wolf pretended to grab Ronan's right forearm with his teeth, a game he had always played with Ronan, never with Nel.

Nel. In the last few days, Ronan's thoughts had turned to her as they had not for three long years. Nel was a part of that life he had pushed into the dark recesses of his mind, that life which included his mother, and Morna, and Neihle, and Tyr. His betrayers.

But not Nel. Never Nel. He should not have waited this long to fetch Nel. It had been a shock to him when recently he had calculated her age and realized that by now she was probably a woman. He could not picture it. He did not want to picture it. He did not want Nel to be changed.

"I'll look for her first at summer camp," Ronan informed Nigak now. It was during the first weeks of his lonely exile that he had formed the habit of talking to the wolf as if he were a person. "If she has been initiated, she will be at summer camp."

But there was no sign of Nel at summer camp. Ronan concealed himself in the woods and watched the comings and goings of the tribe for two full days, and there was no sign of Nel.

The girls were different from the ones he had once shared the summers with. Those girls would all be married by now and nursing children, he thought: Borba and Iva and Tosa and Cala. He saw many of his old agemates at camp, however, although not Tyr.

He did not see Morna, for which he was profoundly grateful. He wasn't sure he could trust himself if ever he saw Morna again.

It was so familiar a sight that it cut into his heart: the easy companionship of the men, the braids they wore, the initiation marks on the muscular arms, the beautiful freedom of the young unmarried girls. The rhythm of life here was unlike the rhythm of life in any other tribe. For the first time in years, Ronan felt the desolation of the exile, the poignant ache for home that he thought he had exorcised high in the Altas, in the new home he had made for himself in the hidden Valley of the Wolf.

Nel had been gathering herbs. Under Fali's tutelage, she was learning to become a curing woman. Young as she was, she definitely had the gift for it, and because of Fali's advanced age, it was Nel's task to keep their supply of herbs well stocked. Lately, Nel had even begun to wonder if it might be possible to make some of them grow closer to her hut. Certain plants always grew in the same places; she had noticed that. Perhaps there was a way . . .

There was the faintest sound of cracking branches, and then something exploded out of the woods beside her. Nel gave a sharp cry and tried to retreat, using her basket to protect herself from the attack of what seemed to be an immense dog. Before she could even try to run, however, the dog reared, knocked away her basket, planted its enormous paws on her shoulders, and ecstatically began to lick her face and snap at her nose. Nel staggered back under his weight, righted herself, and saw the white muzzle and bright yellow eyes.

"*Nigak!*"

The wolf pretended once more to snap at her nose. Then he began to sniff her all over. His whole body was quivering with joy, his tail waving so hard it created a breeze.

"*Nigak!*" Nel said again, kicking aside her basket of herbs and reaching out to hug him. "Is it really you?"

The wolf was sniffing blissfully at her hair. Nel laughed unsteadily and staggered again under his weight. She removed his paws from her shoulders and returned them to the ground, knelt beside him and hugged him again. He was still quivering. "But if you are here, where is . . ." She looked up the track in front of her and then down the track behind. There was no sign of any human. Nigak rolled onto his back, stuck his four white feet up into the air, and whined to have his belly scratched.

Nel laughed again, still unsteadily. "Oh, but it is so good to see you!" she said, and buried her fingers in the soft fur of the wolf's exposed belly.

"He has not forgotten you, minnow." The deep voice came from the forest on her right, and Nel's head whipped around. A tall shadowy shape was coming toward her from within the trees.

"Ronan?" She could scarcely recognize her own voice.

"Sa," he said.

Nel was on her feet. *"Ronan!"* And she flung herself at him in much the same headlong way Nigak had flung himself at her.

"Ooof," he said with a laugh, as he caught her. "You have grown bigger, Nel. You almost knocked the breath out of me!"

"I did not," Nel said, still with her arms locked around his neck. She gazed up into his face with eyes like stars. "You are steady as a rock." Her smile was radiant. "I thought you had forgotten me. I should have known . . . Oh, Ronan . . ." And she pressed her forehead into his shoulder as if she could no longer bear to gaze upon his face.

There came a whine from Nigak, as if he wanted to recall her attention. He began once more to sniff at her. Nel lifted her face out of Ronan's shoulder. She was crying.

"Don't cry, minnow," Ronan said. He wiped away two tears with the tip of his left forefinger, and scanned her face. "You have grown up," he said slowly.

She sniffled and swallowed in a manner that was not grown up at all. "I was initiated at the Moon of the New Fawns."

The Moon of the New Fawns was after Spring Fires. "So," he said, "that is why you were not at summer camp. I looked there first before I came here." He took her face between his thin, muscular hands and tilted it up for his scrutiny.

Nel gazed unabashedly back. He had changed, too, she saw, though not so dramatically as she. His face looked sterner than she remembered. The arched nose and high cheekbones seemed more prominent, the line of the mouth harder. His hair was shorter and no longer worn in a braid.

"I have heard about the Tribe of the Wolf," she said softly, still gazing at him with delighted wonder. "You did what I said you should do—you found your own place and made your own tribe." Then, as he looked puzzled, she asked, "Do you not remember, Ronan?"

His eyes suddenly opened wide. "That is right. You did say that . . ." He laughed. "I had forgotten."

"How could you have forgotten?" Nel demanded indignantly. "You did it!"

He smiled, his face blazing into vivid life, and all of a sudden he looked like the Ronan she remembered. "So I did. And now I have come back for you, just as I said I would."

She heaved a great sigh. "I thought you had forgotten me," she confided. "I have been so worried! I should have trusted you to keep your promise."

The shadow of something came and went across his face. "Of course I did not forget you," he said. He looked her over again. "I cannot believe how much you have changed!"

"I've grown taller," she said shyly. "I used to look into your chest; now I look into your chin."

"It is more than that." She realized with shivery delight that he was looking at *her* chest. "It's a good thing Nigak recognized your scent," he said. "I'm not sure I would have known you."

"But I'm still Nel," she said, anxious to reassure him that her feelings for him were the same. "I haven't changed *inside*, Ronan."

"That is good to hear," he said, and did not smile.

"Did you say you were at summer camp?" she asked.

He nodded.

Nel chewed her lower lip. "Have you talked to anyone else from the tribe?"

"Na."

"If Arika should learn that you are so near . . ." Nel gave a quick, hunted look over her shoulder.

All the light left his face. "I am not afraid of the Mistress, Nel."

"She also has learned of the Tribe of the Wolf, and she does not like it."

"Stop chewing your lip," Ronan said. His mouth looked hard. "What the Mistress may like or dislike does not concern me anymore."

Nel stopped chewing her lip. "Where are the rest of your party?" she asked.

"I came alone."

"Alone!" She glared at him, her eyes very green. "You should not have come alone!"

"I have Nigak," Ronan said. On hearing his name, the wolf left Nel and came to thrust his nose into Ronan's hand. With his free hand Ronan smoothed the fur on Nigak's forehead. "Do you still have Sharan?"

Nel's face gave him his answer before she spoke. "Na," she said in a constricted voice. "She went out hunting one day and just never returned."

His hand stilled on Nigak's forehead. "I am sorry, minnow," he said gently.

She was gazing steadily at the leather strings that tied his buckskin shirt at the throat. "Perhaps she found a mate and decided to stay with her own kind. I hope that is what happened."

"I hope so too."

A little silence fell. Then Nel raised her eyes and said, "Were you wanting me to come away with you right now, Ronan?"

"At this very moment, do you mean?"

She nodded seriously.

"I was planning to give you time to collect some of your things, Nel." He sounded amused.

"My things don't matter, but I think it would be better to wait until tomorrow. Fali will miss me if I don't return shortly, and she is sure to send some of the men to look for me. It will be wiser if we give ourselves a good head start."

"I agree," he said.

"I have to help Fali with a curing ceremony tonight, but I will meet you early tomorrow morning in the clearing near the stunted pine," Nel said. "We can make our plans then."

"All right."

She slipped her arms about his waist and gave him another hug. "I have been so lonely without you, Ronan!" She looked up. "I am so glad that you have come."

"Sa," he said, gazing seriously into her eyes. "It is good to be with you again, minnow. Very good."

Chapter Fourteen

Nel did not sleep all night. At the sound of the first bird, she arose without disturbing Fali and made herself tea. One of the chief advantages that had fallen to Nel as Fali's assistant was that the Old Woman had removed her from the hut of her stepmother. Fali was still asleep when Nel left the hut on silent feet and made her way into the forest.

Nigak was not at the clearing when Nel arrived. Ronan was alone, eating the bird he had cooked for breakfast. He looked up as she materialized out of the woods.

"Hungry?" he asked.

"Sa. I only had tea." She crossed the clearing to sit on her heels beside the small cookfire. He handed her some of the partridge he had roasted.

"Where is Nigak?" Nel asked. She pulled off a small piece of roasted bird and put it in her mouth.

"He went hunting. He will be back."

Nel ate the morsel of food, then licked her fingers. Ronan watched with smiling eyes as she pulled off another piece and put it in her mouth. A peaceful silence fell as the two of them ate their breakfast.

"So," Ronan said, when he had thrown the last of the small bones into the fire, "tell me. How does it go with the Tribe of the Red Deer?"

Nel said, "You have cut off your braid."

He looked at her. "Sa, I have cut off my braid. How has Morna been behaving herself?"

"Why?"

He glared in exasperation. "Because I want to know!"

"I mean why did you cut off your braid?"

Ronan gave in. "At the time it seemed the appropriate thing to do."

Nel continued to regard him thoughtfully.

He said, "I cannot believe the way you have changed."

"Surely you did not expect me to be still a child, Ronan?"

He frowned. "But even your face is different, Nel. You used to have a pointy little face, all sharp bones and angles. Now . . ." He shook his head in bewilderment.

"Well, you are different, too," she said. "And it is not just the braid."

His expression hardened. "A lot has happened to me in the last few years."

Nigak came cantering into the clearing. As soon as he saw Nel, he halted, his ears went up, and his tail began to wave. "Nigak!" Nel said, holding out her hand, and the wolf tore across the clearing, stopped, whined, and flipped on his back.

The thin look left Ronan's mouth, and he laughed. "Evidently you don't look different to Nigak at all."

Nel was scratching Nigak's belly, and she bent her head to whisper something in the wolf's ear. Her braid fell forward across her shoulder, exposing the soft, tender skin of her nape.

The only sound in the clearing was the murmur of Nel's voice and Nigak's little whines of pleasure. When finally she raised her head, Ronan was looking at her with an odd expression in his eyes. It disappeared almost as soon as she saw it, and he asked quickly, "Do you still live with your father and stepmother? Or have you moved to the women's cave?"

"I live with Fali," Nel said. Nigak pushed her hand with his head, and she bent once more to bury her face in the wolf's neck. "I missed you too, Nigak," she whispered. "I missed you too."

"Fali?" Ronan said.

"Sa." Nel straightened up and Nigak went to stretch out beside Ronan, his long white muzzle resting with familiar trust on Ronan's thigh. "It happened shortly after you left. Fali began to teach me her skills of curing, and then she took me to live in her hut so that I could learn even more."

"What did Arika say to that?" Ronan asked slowly.

Nel looked surprised by the question. "Nothing."

"And Morna?"

"Oh, Morna did not like it at all, but that is because Morna does not like me. She knows I don't believe her tale about you. In fact, I am thinking there is but a handful of people in the whole tribe who do believe it, Ronan."

"That is not how it seemed to me three years ago," Ronan said bitterly.

"It was Arika's word that prevailed on that day," Nel assured him. "Not Morna's. The Mistress wanted an excuse to send you away."

"But *why?*" For the first time since the day he had walked away from his home, Ronan put the question that had tormented him. "Why did they let her do it if they did not believe it?" Dark shadows stained the skin beneath his eyes. "Why did Neihle not stand up to her?"

"I asked him that once," Nel answered. She paused, her memory summoning up that scene between the nearly hysterical child she had been and the heartbroken man who had been Neihle. "He told me that he understood why Arika had done it, that she had banished you because she feared that when she was dead you would wrest the rule of the tribe from Morna."

Ronan said, "He knows what Morna is. Neihle has no use for Morna!"

Nel sighed. "I am thinking it was not in Neihle to go against his sister. She is sacred to him, Ronan. She is sacred to all the tribe. She is as the Mother to them."

The shadows under his eyes looked like bruises. "In the Tribe of the Wolf I have people from the plain. The tribes there still follow the Way of the Mother, even though they are led by a chief."

"Fali has told me this," Nel said.

He looked surprised. "Has she?"

She nodded. "She says that is why Arika thinks it is so important for the Tribe of the Red Deer to keep its Mistress. Fali says it is the only tribe she knows of that is led by a woman."

Ronan looked broodingly into the low-burning fire. Nel watched him in silence. Finally he asked, "Has Morna borne children?"

Nel shook her head.

The bruised look began to fade from beneath Ronan's eyes. He looked so different without his braid, Nel thought. He did not look like a boy any longer. She asked, "What god do you follow in the Tribe of the Wolf?"

"Most of my people are from tribes of the Kindred and make their prayers to Sky God, but as I said before, there are a number from the plain who follow the Mother."

"And you?"

"I follow the Way of Ronan," he said, dislodged Nigak from his thigh, got to his feet, and began to pace restlessly around the clearing. It was then that she noticed the limp.

"What happened to your leg?" she asked sharply.

He stopped pacing instantly. "I broke it."

"When? How?"

He looked so . . . remote . . . Nel thought, resisting the urge to run to comfort him. Instead, she clasped her hands tightly in her lap and forced herself to remain where she was as he answered with palpable unwillingness. "It happened that first winter, when I was alone at summer camp." He would not look at her. "I was climbing after some sheep when the ground gave way beneath me. I fell down the hillside."

"Dhu," Nel whispered.

His eyes flicked briefly to her face. "I knew immediately that it was broken. I cut some branches and tied them to the leg for support. Then I went to get help from the Tribe of the Buffalo."

Nel contemplated those brief remarks. It had been winter. He had been at summer camp, and to get to the territory of the Buffalo tribe he would have had to climb through that high pass. Nel let out a careful breath. It was a miracle he had not frozen to death.

"How long did it take you to reach the Buffalo tribe?" she asked.

He shrugged. "A handful of days."

"You walked on the broken leg?"

"I leaned on a stick."

"I cannot understand how you did not freeze to death."

At last he looked at her. "If it had not been for Nigak, I would have. You saved my life, Nel, when you gave me Nigak. He fed me. If I had not had food, I would most certainly have frozen."

"He *fed* you?"

"Sa." The taut look on Ronan's face relaxed slightly. "Do you know how wolves feed their pups?" Nel's eyes enlarged noticeably and she nodded. "Well, I could not hunt, and I had no food, and I remembered how wolves feed their pups. I knew Nigak was hunting, and I knew I was in danger of freezing if I did not get some food into me, so when he came back to me once after a hunting expedition, I licked his muzzle the way I once saw a wolf pup do."

"Oh," Nel said, her eyes enormous.

"What came up wasn't overly appetizing," Ronan said ruefully, "but after I cooked it, it was fine. It kept me warm, and it kept me alive."

"Oh Ronan," Nel said, turning to gaze at Nigak, who was lying on his side, snoozing with his four white legs stuck out in front of him. "Isn't Nigak splendid?"

"Sa," Ronan said, grimly serious. "He is. He stuck with me, Nel, all the way, and when finally I went down, he fetched help for me."

Shivers ran up and down Nel's whole body, and she folded her arms tightly across her chest. "How far did you get?" she asked.

He began to pace around once more. The limp was not that bad, she thought. There was just the faintest unevenness in his gait. In a man who had not Ronan's fluid way of moving, it would scarcely have been noticeable. "I made it to the Atata River," he said. "It was lucky for me there were hunters in the area." He paused in his pacing to look at the peacefully sleeping wolf. "Nigak led one of their dogs to me. At least, that's what they told me. I don't remember. I was halfway on my journey to the Land of the Dead."

Nel shivered again to think how close she had come to losing him. "And the men of the Buffalo tribe took care of you?" she asked.

"Sa. I stayed with them for the winter, and in the spring, when my leg was healed, I left."

She said, "The leg healed well. You were fortunate."

"I limp."

She shook her head.

"You noticed it immediately."

"Someone who did not know you would not have noticed it at all."

"Well, it does not matter," he said.

She gave him a beautiful smile. "It does not matter at all."

He stared at her with the odd expression she had surprised in his eyes earlier. Then he blinked twice, rapidly, as if he were banishing a distraction, and said, "Nel, I want to talk to Tyr. Is he at home? I did not see him at summer camp."

"Sa, he is here. Dana is due to give birth very shortly; that is why Tyr did not go to summer camp this year."

"I want to see him. Would it be possible for you to bring him here to me?"

"Of course." She got to her feet. "He will be so glad to see you, Ronan. He has missed you."

"Mmmm," Ronan said noncommittally.

Nel glanced at the sky. "I had better fetch him now, before he leaves camp for the day's hunting."

"Would you mind, minnow?"

"Of course not," Nel said, smiled, whirled, ran lightly toward the surrounding forest, and was gone.

It was after midday when Nel returned, bringing Tyr with her as promised. It was an obviously emotional moment for Tyr when first he laid eyes on his old agemate again.

"Ronan!" He came forward to place his hands upon Ronan's shoulders in the traditional greeting of the tribe's men. "It is so good to see you!"

"Tyr." Ronan was far more composed than Tyr. He looked into his old friend's familiar dark blue eyes and felt surprise that Tyr had changed so little.

A silence fell. Tyr reluctantly dropped his hands. He said, "Did your men give you my message? Is that why you have come?"

"I got your message," Ronan said, "but it was Nel who brought me here."

"Nel?"

The three of them were standing at the edge of the clearing, Tyr in the shade of a tree, Ronan in full sun. Nel stood between them, half in the light and half in the shadow. She said to Tyr, "I am going with Ronan back to the Valley of the Wolf." Happiness rang in her voice.

Tyr's face sharpened, and suddenly Ronan saw that his friend was indeed older than the boy he had left. "Does Fali know this?" Tyr demanded.

"Of course not." Nel frowned. "Nor are you to tell her, Tyr."

Tyr's mouth set. "She must be told," he said.

Ronan's remark, "I did not realize that Fali was so fond of Nel," clashed with her own furious "Na!"

Tyr turned to Ronan. "It is more than Fali's fondness that must be considered here," he said grimly.

"I do not understand you," Ronan returned, his slim arched brows demanding an explanation.

Tyr gave it to him. "You cannot take Nel with you, Ronan. Fali has been training her to be our next Mistress."

"*What?!*" The exclamation came not from Ronan but from Nel. "What are you talking about, Tyr? Morna is to be the next Mistress!"

"Na, Nel," Tyr said, almost wearily. "Fali has been grooming you to become Mistress after Arika."

Nel's face was both angry and bewildered. "Fali has been teaching me the art of curing."

"She has been teaching you more than that. Did you not notice?"

Ronan asked in a hard voice, "Does Arika know what Fali has been doing?"

"Sa." The intake of Nel's breath was audible at Tyr's affirmative.

"Who else knows?" Ronan demanded.

"The council of matriarchs. Neihle. Erek. Me. That was what I meant when I sent to tell you that the temper of the tribe has changed. We will not accept Morna as Mistress, and Arika knows it. She has not yet displaced Morna formally, but . . ."

"What is she waiting for, then?" Ronan interrupted.

"She has been waiting for Nel to become a woman," Tyr said.

At that, both young men turned to look at the girl between them. She was standing still as a stone, the shadow from an overhanging leaf making a mark of shadow, like a moth, upon her sunlit cheek. Tyr said to her, "Nel, Arika is planning to ask you to make the Sacred Marriage at Winter Fires."

A small sound came from Nel, the sound made by a frightened animal when it is finally cornered. Acting from the habit of many years, Ronan held out his arm to her. She moved instantly into his embrace, nestling against his side and shoulder, just as she had when she was a child.

Ronan was immediately and acutely conscious of the fact that it was not a child's body pressing up against him anymore, and he drew a long, careful breath before he spoke. "Nel will not be making the Sacred Marriage this winter," he said. "She is coming with me."

He felt some of the tension drain from the slender young body sheltering against him. "Besides," Nel said from behind the safety of his arm, "Morna would never stand for my making the Sacred Marriage. She hates me."

"Morna will have nothing to say about it," Tyr answered grimly. He looked at Ronan. "All of this happened after you left. Neihle and Arika had a long talk, then Arika and the matriarchs talked, and finally Arika agreed to let Fali take Nel in charge. That is why I sent you the message that I did. Once Nel is Mistress, then will it be safe for you to return home."

"I find it hard to believe that Arika would allow Morna to be supplanted," Ronan said bitterly.

"The Mistress has not been the same, Ronan, since she banished you," Tyr replied.

Ronan laughed.

"Don't," Nel said and turned her face into his shoulder.

A painful silence fell.

"Well, minnow," Ronan said finally, his voice expressionless, "what do you want to do?"

She raised her eyes to him. In the merciless light of the midday sun, her creamy skin was flawless. "I want to come with you," she said.

"You cannot!" Tyr cried.

"My need of Nel is as great as yours, Tyr," Ronan said somberly. "And I am thinking also that my need and yours may one day prove to be the same."

Tyr stared at Ronan with a mixture of anger and curiosity. "What do you mean?" he demanded.

"Have you heard," Ronan asked, "of a tribe called the Horse-masters?"

"Do you really think that the Tribe of the Red Deer may be endangered?" Tyr said. They were sitting now around the remains of Ronan's breakfast fire, Tyr listening to Ronan's tale with ever-increasing horror.

"I think it is possible. If this tribe continues on its southward path and comes down the River of Gold, all of the tribes in these mountains will be endangered."

"We have heard nothing of this," Tyr said. "We went late to the Spring Gathering, and we heard nothing."

"My men heard rumors at the gathering, and so I sent scouts north to search out the truth," Ronan said. "That is how I learned what I have just told you."

"You sent scouts?"

"Sa. Men I could trust not to be swayed by gossip. Men who would see for themselves."

Nel said, "And it is true? This tribe has truly learned to tame and ride horses?"

Ronan nodded. "It is true."

Nel's long green eyes glittered. "How wonderful that must be!"

Ronan's smile was wry. "The Tribe of the Owl would not agree with you, Nel."

Nel bit her lip. "That is true."

"There are horses in the Valley of the Wolf," Ronan said, watching her closely. "One herd of mares with one stallion. We have lived beside them now for three years, Nel." He paused. "It is in my heart that we could tame them."

Nel's eyes widened.

"If anyone can do it, Nel, you can. You have ever had the Mother's understanding of animals."

"Have you tried to tame them?" she asked.

"Na. I decided I would come first for you."

"I see," she said quietly.

Tyr had been listening to this interchange with growing incredulity, and now he said, "You are going to attempt to ride a horse yourself?"

"If these marauders do indeed come south, Tyr, then it will be well for us if we can face them with their own weapons."

"We?" Tyr said.

"We. The Tribe of the Wolf and the Tribe of the Red Deer and the Tribe of the Leopard and the Tribe of the Buffalo, and all the tribes of the Kindred that dwell in these mountains. There are many of these outlanders, Tyr. They are the equal in number of at least a handful of our tribes together."

Tyr pulled on his braid. "Dhu. It is hard to comprehend all that you have said."

"So now you know why I want Nel to come with me," Ronan said.

Both young men looked at Nel. "It is true that she has a way with animals," Tyr said. "She tamed a wolf. She tamed a scimitar cat."

Nel said nothing.

Tyr turned again to Ronan. "But what are we to do, then, for a Mistress? The Old Woman has declared that Nel is truly Chosen. The tribe will accept Nel over Morna. I am not certain they will accept anyone else."

Nel said in a tight little voice, "Fali never said aught of this to me."

"She was waiting to tell you," Tyr said. "She knew you would be . . . reluctant."

"She was right," Nel said. "I am more than reluctant." Her face was set. "I refuse."

Ronan rested his hand upon the back of Nel's neck, a gesture that dated back to their earliest childhood. "Don't fret, minnow," he said grimly. "No one will make you do anything you don't want to do while I am here."

There was a quick flash of green as she glanced sideways at Ronan, and then she was looking again at Tyr.

Ronan said, "I will take Nel back with me to the valley. I will tell you now how to find it, Tyr, and when you know it is time to declare a new Mistress, send to tell us. We can decide then what it is best for us to do."

"I do not want to be Mistress, Ronan," Nel said levelly.

His hand on her neck tightened with reassurance. "I hear you, minnow." Over her head the eyes of the two men met, and slowly, Tyr nodded his head.

Nel told Ronan that it would be better for them to leave at night. "As soon as Fali sees my sleeping skins gone, she will know that something is wrong," she said. "If we travel all night, we will have a good start if there is a pursuit."

He agreed, and since the moon was full, and the sky clear, they decided not to delay but to leave that very night.

Fali was sitting in front of their hut scraping skins when Nel returned.

The girl halted for a moment to compose her face before she approached the Old Woman.

"Good afternoon, my Mother," Nel said. She put down the basket of herbs she had hastily collected as an excuse for her absence. "How are you faring this day?"

"I am well," Fali replied. She squinted up at Nel. Her brown eyes were still amazingly bright in the nest of wrinkles that was her face. "You were gone early, Nel."

"Sa." Nel hoped her smile looked natural. "The day was fine and I could not keep within."

Fali nodded wisely. "You are restless. At your age that is only natural. It is a pity that your moon blood did not begin to flow before Spring Fires instead of after."

"Na!" Nel said quickly. "That is not it at all. I am glad I was not yet a woman at Spring Fires, my Mother. I was not ready then."

Fali regarded her steadily, and Nel sustained that shrewd gaze with fortitude. "It is true that there are some girls who are not ready in their minds even though their bodies say otherwise," Fali said. "I was such a one myself. I did not take a mate for one full year after my moon blood had begun to flow. But I would not have thought that of you, Nel. I have always thought you were old for your years."

Nel shrugged and began to sort through her basket of herbs to escape Fali's scrutiny. "Nevertheless, I was not ready to take a mate at Spring Fires," she said.

"And at Winter Fires?" Fali asked. Her voice was just faintly sharper than it had been.

"I will be ready by Winter Fires," Nel said. She looked up. "Will I be able to choose the man?"

"Of course you can choose the man," Fali said. The sharpness had disappeared from her voice. "There is not a man in the tribe who does not dream of lying with you, Nel."

Nel bent lower over the basket, to hide the resentment she feared must show on her face. Of course she would be able to choose the man if she were the one making the Sacred Marriage, she thought. It was infamous of Fali to be keeping that from her.

"You flatter me," was all she answered.

"Na. I do not flatter you. Unlike Morna, you have no understanding of the power of your own beauty."

At that Nel's head jerked up. "Your fondness blinds you, my Mother. I am not beautiful like Morna."

"That is so," Fali agreed. "You are not beautiful like Morna. You are beautiful like Nel."

Nel smiled and nodded and rose to her feet. "I will brew us some tea," she said, and escaped into the hut.

The Old Woman went to bed early, for which Nel was profoundly grateful. The evening had been difficult. She was very fond of Fali and had always been intensely grateful to the Old Woman for removing her from the custody of her father's shrewish wife. That gratitude was tempered now by the realization that Fali had had an ulterior motive. Nel reminded herself of that motive all evening, hugging her resentment to herself in an effort to blunt the guilt she was feeling at deserting Fali in her extreme old age.

When Fali had been safely asleep for some time, Nel quietly packed up her sleeping skins and other belongings. Moving on silent feet, she crept to the door of the hut and slipped out. Nothing stirred. Cautiously, Nel moved away from the hut. No dogs barked. Like a shadow in the moonlight, scarcely daring even to breathe, Nel slipped through the sleeping camp.

Ronan was waiting for her in their appointed place, standing on the stony beach and gazing out over the moon-silvered water. He had not yet seen her, and Nel stopped for a moment to feast her eyes on him. Then Nigak was loping toward her, his ears pricked forward, and Ronan turned and said her name. Nel walked forward to meet him.

Chapter Fifteen

Ronan and Nel traveled in the moonlight, following the Greatfish River south almost to the point where it branched off east and fed into the Narrow River. It was an hour before dawn when Ronan called a halt. "Let's stop and rest until midday," he said, "and then continue on until supper time."

Nel nodded wearily. She had scarcely slept the previous night she had been so excited about Ronan's return, and she was so tired she could scarcely speak. She let her backpack slide to the ground and collapsed beside it.

"Do you want something to eat?" Ronan asked softly.

"Na," she said. She was resting her forehead on her updrawn knees. "I just want to sleep, Ronan. I am so weary."

"Then sleep." He picked up her pack and began to unroll her sleeping skins. She watched as he spread them out for her. He turned. "A drink?" he asked.

She licked her dry lips. "Sa." She took the deer bladder he offered and drank the lukewarm water. Ronan had chosen a place on the edge of the forest; the trees were behind them, the river before. In the moonlight Nel could see a small herd of antelope drinking daintily from the river. The whoop of a hyena came from the forest. Crickets chirped, frogs croaked, and somewhere a wolf howled.

"Crawl in, minnow," Ronan said, and she did. Within minutes she was deeply asleep.

Fali knew what had happened the moment she awoke and saw that Nel's sleeping skins were gone.

"He has come back," she said out loud. She closed her eyes briefly, then opened them again. Nel's place was still empty. "Goddess," the Old Woman said plaintively, "what are we to do now?"

Slowly, creakingly, Fali got to her feet. Her joints were always so stiff in the morning. "I feared this," she said to the empty air. "I never thought that Arika would be rid of him so easily. Now he has taken our Chosen One." She passed her trembling hand in front of her face. "He always did remind me of Mar."

She would have to tell Arika. They must get Nel back.

Arika will send to the men at summer camp, Fali thought. She will send to Neihle. Neihle will go after her and bring her back.

Fali went to the door of her hut and lifted the skins. Seated outside, and obviously waiting for her to awaken, was Tyr. He stood up when he saw her. "My Mother," he said respectfully. His blue eyes were grave. "I must speak with you."

Fali gestured for him to come in.

"Let me make up your fire," Tyr said as he ducked into the dark hut, which was redolent with the scent of the herbs drying on a rack in the corner. "You have not yet had your tea."

"That would be kind of you, Tyr," Fali said. It was true she had not yet had her tea. Nel had always brewed her morning tea for her. A pang went through Fali as she thought of how she would miss Nel. Slowly she sat down in her accustomed place and watched Tyr as he started the fire with the live coal she kept stored in the hearthplace stones.

"I saw Ronan yesterday," he said, when the fire had caught and the tea was heating.

"I knew it was so," Fali replied. "When I awoke this morning and saw that Nel's sleeping skins were gone, I thought immediately of Ronan."

"You did?" Tyr glanced at her admiringly.

"I have long known Nel's feelings," Fali said. "And I have long suspected that Ronan was not finished with the Tribe of the Red Deer."

"If you think he took her for revenge, my Mother, you are wrong," Tyr said.

Fali handed Tyr two cups made from deer frontal bones, and Tyr dipped them in the tea and filled them. Fali said, "I do not know what to think, Tyr. What did Ronan say to you yesterday?"

Tyr told her about the Horsemasters.

Fali heard him out without interrupting. "If Ronan wishes to try to tame horses, let him do so by himself," she said tartly. "He does not need Nel. You must go after them, Tyr, and persuade her to return."

"She will not return without Ronan," Tyr said.

"She knows nothing of our plans for her," Fali said. "When she learns that she is to be our Mistress . . ."

Tyr shook his head. "She knows," he said. "I told her."

Fali drew her aging, fragile bones into an erect posture. "It was not your place to tell her such a thing, Tyr."

"Perhaps not." Tyr stared down into the clear pale liquid that was his sage tea. "But she was leaving us, My Mother, and I thought to hold her with such a word."

"What did she say?" Fali asked after a moment.

"She does not want it." Tyr drained his cup. "She would not leave Ronan."

Fali muttered something under her breath. Then she said more clearly, "And what did Ronan have to say?"

"He said we should send to him when the time for the choosing of a new Mistress came, and they would decide then what they would do."

"They?" Fali said.

"That was his word."

"I know what is in his mind. He thinks to marry her," Fali said angrily. "He thinks to marry her and rule through her."

Tyr pulled at his braid. "Sa," he said, "I am thinking that is what he will do."

Silence fell within. From outside the hut they could hear the sound of children shouting with excitement as they played a chasing game.

"So," Fali said with great bitterness, "it has come."

Slowly, carefully, Tyr spoke the words he had been formulating in his mind all during the night. "That is the way the tribes of the plain do it, My Mother. The husband of the Mistress is the chief." He picked up his cup and turned it around and around with his fingers, looking at it to keep from having to look at Fali. "After all, it is none so different from our way. The man who plays the god at the Fires is our chief. What is the difference?"

Silence. When Fali spoke her voice was heavy with irony. "There is a great difference, Tyr, between a hunting chief who changes with the seasons and a tribal chief who is permanent."

This time Tyr was silent.

Fali leaned forward. "There is great earth magic in Nel," she said. "She is close to all things beloved by the Mother. I have long felt she was the one Chosen to lead the tribe." Fali's gnarled, almost skeletal hand shook as she set down her cup. "Arika knows this also. But Arika will never allow Nel to succeed her if Nel is married to Ronan."

"I still do not understand why such a marriage is so impossible," Tyr said stubbornly. "Other tribes with a male chief follow the Way of the Mother. The woman is still Mistress of the Mother. No man would be fool enough to think he could intrude on such a sacred thing as that. The chief is not the son of a son, as it is with those who follow Sky God. The chief is the man who marries the Daughter."

"Ronan is too dominant," Fali said.

"I will tell you this, my Mother, and I speak as one who knows him well," Tyr said. "In all his life there has been but one person to whom Ronan would listen, and that person is Nel."

Fali looked skeptical.

"It is true. And if it was true when she was but a child, how much more will it be true now, when she has become such a beautiful young woman?" Tyr nodded. "You underestimate her, my Mother."

Suddenly Fali looked very weary. "I do not know," she said. "I cannot judge. I am old, Tyr. I am old and full of sorrow for the loss of my daughter."

"She told me to ask for your forgiveness," Tyr said. "She hoped you would understand."

"I understand all too well. She has chosen Ronan. Over the tribe, over me, she has chosen Ronan."

Tyr stared at his moccasins and did not reply.

"I must tell Arika." Fali began to rise and Tyr hurried to help her. "Arika will know what to do. Arika will know how to get her back."

Tyr stood watching in silence as the Old Woman walked slowly out of the hut.

———

Arika did not want Nel back. "I will not send after her," the Mistress said after Fali had finished her story. "Above all else, the Mistress must be willing, and today Nel has shown us that she is not."

"It is not that!" Fali said. "It is that her attachment to Ronan is so strong . . ." Her voice trailed off at the look on Arika's face, and Fali bowed her aged head.

"I cannot get free of him," Arika said dully. She was holding a scraper in her hand and now she banged it on the ground in rhythm with her words. "No matter what I do, I cannot get free of him."

"You have always thought of him as an enemy," Fali said. "And I confess that I too have seen in Ronan a resemblance to a man I once knew, a man who once brought much trouble to the Tribe of the Red Deer. But I am thinking now that perhaps we were wrong, Arika. Perhaps Ronan is loved by the Mother. Perhaps that is why he has survived."

"I do not think so," Arika said. Deep lines were carved on either side of her mouth.

Silence fell in the Mistress's hut. Fali was falling into a light doze when Arika finally spoke again. "It is fortunate that I have never formally put aside Morna."

"You are not thinking to have Morna follow you?" Fali asked sharply.

"What choice have I got?" Arika replied.

"Only two children have you borne in your lifetime, Mistress," Fali said bluntly, "and of the two, I prefer your son."

Anger flared in Arika's red-brown eyes. "I will never give him the chance to get his hands upon this tribe! Never while I live will that happen, Old Woman."

"I hear you, Mistress," Fali said heavily. Then, almost as an after-thought, she asked, "What of these Horsemasters?"

"Let my resourceful son deal with them," Arika snapped.

"Sa," said Fali, "sa." She rose slowly and creakingly from her deer-skin rug and passed out of the Mistress's hut.

Arika went to Morna's hut to tell her daughter that Nel was gone.

"Good riddance," Morna said. "The Old Woman has made so much of her of late that she has been acting as if she were a shaman."

"Fali is very fond of Nel," Arika said temperately.

"Where has she gone to?" Morna asked next. She tossed her red-gold head. "Run away with some man, I suppose."

"Sa," said Arika. "She has."

Despite her words, Morna was surprised. "Who?" she demanded. "Not a man of the Red Deer?"

"Not a man of the Red Deer."

"Then who, Mother?" Morna asked impatiently.

"Ronan."

"*Ronan!*"

"Sa. Ronan."

A shifting current of emotions eddied across Morna's face. Finally she said scornfully, "I suppose he has no women in that valley of his, and Ronan is not a man to lie alone. Nel always followed after him like a fawn after its mother. I suppose he thought lying with her would be better than nothing."

Arika turned toward the door. Morna had been jealous of Nel ever since Nel's growing beauty first became apparent. Arika had never suffered from jealousy herself, and she hated to see it in her daughter. "I do not know his reasons," Arika said, "but Nel has gone with him. I thought you should know." She pushed aside the skins and left.

Left alone, Morna frowned and darted restless glances around her hut. At Arika's request she had not gone to summer camp this year, and she was hating the summer, stuck at home with only the old men, the boys, and besotted husbands like Tyr.

The thought of Nel and Ronan together was eating into her. "I'm glad she's gone!" Morna said out loud. And it was true. She was glad. She was not glad, however, that Nel had gone with Ronan.

Morna went to the door of her hut, pushed aside the skins, and looked out at the peaceful camp. The only people visible were women and children. Morna was sick to death of women and children.

I don't care what Mother says, Morna thought defiantly. If I want to go to summer camp, then I will. Her spirits soared. She turned back into her hut and began to put together her hunting things.

The sun was shining brightly when Nel awoke that afternoon. She sat up and saw that Ronan's sleeping skins were empty. There was a roasted hare impaled on a stick over the doused ashes of a cookfire. He had been busy while she slept.

At that moment, Nigak cantered around the bend in the river. His ears pricked as soon as he saw Nel; he raced up to her and enthusiastically began to lick her face.

Ronan's voice said, "I was going to wake you if you were still asleep." Nel raised her head and her heart caught as she saw him following Nigak up from the shore. The ends of his hair were dripping from his wash in the river, and for some reason, the familiar sight brought tears to Nel's eyes. She looked away so he would not see.

"It's growing late," she heard him saying.

"I was tired," Nel murmured apologetically. She sniffed the fragrance from the cooked hare. "The food smells wonderful. I'm starved."

"You have time to wash first," he said austerely.

Nel's head snapped up. "I am not a little girl any longer, Ronan," she informed him. "It is not necessary for you to tell me when I should wash."

"That is nice to hear," he said. He began to remove the hare from the roasting stick. He looked up at her and raised his eyebrows. "It won't take you long."

Nel almost refused. Then she thought that a refusal would only convince him that she was indeed still a child, so she rose with dignity and went down to the river.

Nel's thoughts were in a tumble of confusion; everything had happened so fast, from the time Ronan first showed himself until the time she had left the tribe with him, that she had had no chance to sort her feelings out. At first, she had assumed he had come for her in order to carry her away and marry her, a scenario Nel had dreamed about for years. Then he had said that he wanted her to help him tame the horses.

It had almost sounded as if that was all he wanted her for, she thought, as she picked her way over the stones at the river's edge. And he was still treating her as if she were a child . . . sending her to wash her face and hands! The other men of the Red Deer had certainly noticed that she was no longer a child.

She plunged her hands into the water and bent to splash some on her face. Ronan had noticed the change in her too, she remembered.

"I am still the same inside," she had assured him. But it wasn't true.

A dreadful fear smote Nel. Perhaps he was already married. Dhu, if that were so, then what would she do?

"Nel!" He even sounded as if he were calling a naughty child, Nel thought rebelliously.

"I'm coming," she called back, and waded out of the shallows.

As soon as Nel had gone down to the river, Ronan began to cut up the roasted hare. Whistling between his teeth, he speared the tenderest pieces onto another stick for Nel. He waited, and when she seemed to be making no motion toward returning, he called for her. Without waiting any longer, he began to eat his own portion hungrily.

He chewed slowly as he watched her coming back across the rocky shore to the sheltered place beneath the trees where they had pitched their camp. The afternoon sun played on her soft brown hair. He was finding it increasingly difficult to match this slim and beautiful girl to the skinny child with legs like a newborn foal that had lived all these years in his memory.

He intended to marry her. It was why he had never looked to take a wife from the women who had joined the Tribe of the Wolf. He had always known that one day he would go back for Nel and marry her.

But now that he was with her again, he didn't know how to proceed. Any other Red Deer girl who chose to make this kind of a journey with him would expect to share his sleeping skins. But Nel had always regarded him as her big brother. He might frighten her if he tried to present himself as a lover. He did not want to frighten Nel.

He must give her time, he decided. He must accustom her slowly to the idea of marrying him. The very way she had instantly agreed to come with him demonstrated her innocence. She had never once questioned his intentions, had assumed that all would be between them as it always had been.

He would have to restrain himself, he thought firmly. He would have to give her time.

Nel arrived back at the fire, cast him a reproachful look, accepted her food in dignified silence, and sat down to eat. When she had finished the hare she slipped off one of her moccasins, flexed her foot, and bent forward to rub her instep.

"Are you hurt?" Ronan asked.

"Not really. I stepped on a rock last night and bruised my foot a little, that's all. I shall be fine."

"Let me see." He came to kneel in front of her and she relinquished her foot into his hand.

Her slim, high-arched foot was the color of ivory, clean and cold from standing barefoot in the river. Ronan looked down at the straight toes and healthy pale pink nails. "There," Nel said, pointing to a bluish mark at the highest point of her instep arch.

"I see," he said.

His hand looked very dark against her pale delicate skin. Her head was so close to his that he could smell the fresh scent of her hair. He held her foot almost gingerly and looked up into her eyes. She had very long black eyelashes. He had never before noticed how odd it was that her lashes should be so dark when her hair was so light. She looked back at him and said reproachfully, "My poor feet are freezing. That river water is like ice."

He dropped her foot as if it was burning him. "I know." His voice sounded thick and he cleared his throat. He backed away from her. "I don't think that bruise will hinder your walking."

"I told you it wouldn't," she said impatiently. She threw her empty stick into the trees. "I am ready to leave if you are."

He jumped to his feet. "Pack up your things and we'll go," he replied, and went to collect his own.

They were following the same route Ronan had followed over three years before when he had been expelled from the Tribe of the Red Deer: south along the Greatfish, east along the Narrow River, through the Buffalo Pass, and into the hunting grounds of the Tribe of the Buffalo. Then they would go south along the Atata, following it all the way up the Altas and across to the other side. If the weather held, and they made good time, the whole journey should take them seven days.

"We will have to detour around summer camp," Ronan said, and Nel nodded in agreement.

Ronan left the river track as soon as they turned eastward, choosing instead a series of deer tracks that ran through the thickly forested hills. The afternoon was quiet, but hidden within the protective pine and birch of the forest lurked a plenitude of wild animals, and Ronan's eyes were wary, his large spear grasped firmly in his left hand as he kept a constant lookout for possible danger.

He caught glimpses of deer as they flitted through the forest, the merest tremors of movement at the edge of his vision. Halfway through the afternoon he saw the unmistakable tracks of a bear, and his vigilance increased. But Nigak gave no sign that he scented a bear close by, and the tracks soon disappeared. The afternoon had advanced considerably when Ronan spotted a magnificent red deer stag, with splendid spiraling antlers, lying on a moss-covered rock halfway up the hill to their left.

"Look," Ronan said softly over his shoulder to Nel. The deer blended into rock and hill so well that it was not easy to distinguish.

"He has picked a perfect lookout place," Nel said, and Ronan could tell from her voice that she was smiling.

They had been walking for perhaps five hours when Ronan heard the grunting sound of animals foraging nearby among the trees. He halted and turned to Nel, scanning her face for signs of weariness. "Boar," he said. "Are you ready to stop for the night? Shall I get us one for supper?"

She put down her spear and shifted her backpack. "Are we near the cave you told me of?"

"It is yet another two hours ahead."

"I can go for another two hours," Nel said.

"Are you sure?" He had felt guilty when he had seen her exhaustion at their first stopping place. "We are safely ahead of a messenger, if there is one."

"I am sure," Nel said firmly, and motioned him onward.

An hour later, Ronan saw the leopard spoor. Leopard and bear were what he had principally watched out for all afternoon, as leopards were known to inhabit the territory around the Red Deer summer camp. The tribe had lost more than one man to leopard in Ronan's lifetime. Ronan stopped, bent, and looked closely at the droppings on the track. They were warm.

Nel came up beside him. Ronan looked up. "Leopard," he said.

Instinctively, Nel looked up into the trees.

Ronan shook his head. "It is going along the track." He looked at his spear as if to check it. "We had better proceed carefully." He whistled for Nigak, but there was no response. They walked on.

It was five minutes before they came upon the leopard, crouched in the undergrowth to the right of the track, watching a single young antelope as it grazed in a small forest glade beyond. Ronan and Nel halted, stood in perfect silence, and watched.

The leopard was lying very low to the ground, almost upon its belly. Its lowness and its spotted hide made it virtually invisible to the antelope, which was grazing peacefully. As Ronan and Nel watched, the leopard got to its feet and began to creep slowly forward. Suddenly the antelope looked up. The leopard froze, one paw still suspended. The antelope looked all around the glade, its gaze passing right over the leopard, then once again it lowered its head to graze. The leopard waited, then slowly it crept forward again.

Once more, the antelope looked up. Once more the leopard froze. This time, however, Ronan was sure that the antelope had spotted the predator, for it stared directly at it. The leopard never moved. The antelope continued to stare. Slowly, half-inch by half-inch, the leopard lowered its body toward the ground. Still the antelope looked. The leopard sank downward until its body was flat against the ground. The antelope began to graze once more.

After a short time, the leopard slowly began to creep forward again.

For ten minutes Ronan and Nel stood in fascinated silence and watched the scene being enacted by the leopard and the antelope. Again and again the antelope would look up. Again and again the leopard would freeze and the antelope would apparently see nothing. Finally the leopard was within sure striking distance of the antelope. Ronan felt his own muscles tense as he watched the leopard collect itself. He held his breath.

Nigak's blood-curdling howl ripped through the air. The leopard and the antelope reacted instantly, the antelope running for its life into the forest, the leopard streaking in pursuit. At first the antelope ran straight, but then it started to zigzag among the trees. In so doing it gained ground on the leopard. Within seconds the two animals had passed out of Ronan's sight.

"You certainly spoiled that leopard's afternoon, Nigak," he heard Nel saying beside him.

The wolf was panting, his tongue lolling out, his ears flopping sideways. He looked very pleased with himself. Nel laughed. "Lucky antelope," she said.

"Unlucky us," Ronan returned. "I'm sure that leopard has cubs somewhere to feed. The antelope would have kept them busy until we were out of their territory. Now she will be hunting again."

"How much farther do we have to go?" Nel asked.

"The cave is but an hour ahead," he said. "We will be safer there than we will be camping in the forest with a hungry leopard."

Nel nodded again, shifted her pack to a more comfortable position on her back, and prepared to move.

The cave was one Ronan had found during the second summer he had spent at the Red Deer summer camp. He had taken Cala there once, but as far as he was aware no one else knew of it. It was sufficiently removed from camp, and sufficiently hidden, for him to think that, even if Arika ordered a search, he and Nel would be safe.

They reached it an hour before darkfall.

"I have some fruit and some dried meat in my pack," Nel said as they climbed the last part of the hill that led to the cave. "We can have that for supper. It is too near dark for you to go out hunting."

"All right," he said.

The cave did not go deep into the hill, but the single chamber was of quite a decent size. The first thing Nel saw when she came in was the remains of the fire he and Cala had built. "Ronan," she said. "Someone else has been here."

For some reason he did not understand, Ronan did not want to tell her that he had brought Cala here. "Na," he answered carelessly, "that is just the remains of the fire I built myself when I was here years ago."

Nel was still staring at the hearthstones and the ash. "I had better get some wood for a new fire before it grows too dark," he said to distract her attention. "Can you fetch us some fresh water? There is a stream just yonder," and he pointed.

"All right," Nel said, and turned away from the hearthstones to collect the bladders they used for carrying water.

By the time the dark came, Ronan had a good fire going. They ate, and Nigak left to go hunting for his own supper. Nel began to spread her sleeping skins, and Ronan sat at his place by the fire and watched her as she bent and straightened, bent and straightened.

Her waist was so slim and supple, he thought. He wanted to put his hands around it. He could see the sweet curve of her breasts beneath her buckskin shirt. He wanted to put his hands on them as well.

Dhu, this was torture! She finished with the skins and came to join him at the fire, stretching out her long, slim legs to the warmth. Still without speaking, she untied the leather thong that fastened her braid and began to undo her hair.

Ronan had not lain with a girl in a long, long time. It seemed the men who followed Sky God had different attitudes about women from the tribes who followed the Mother. In fact, the last girl he had lain with had been a girl from one of the Goddess-worshiping tribes of the plain. They had met by chance on one of Ronan's periodic scouting trips, had taken great pleasure in each other, and had said good-bye with smiling goodwill.

That had been last fall. A long time ago. He looked again at Nel, devouring her with his eyes.

She had unwoven her braid and was running a comb made from bone through all the shining length of her hair. He watched her, the tension growing inside of him. Her fawn-colored hair reached to her waist and looked as soft and silky as the inside of an acorn. One strand fell like a streamer across the swell of her breast. Ronan had to restrain himself from reaching out to touch it.

In any other girl, he would have seen the hair combing as an invitation. But this was Nel. Incredibly, this soft and beautiful woman, sitting at his side and rousing his blood with such perfect and inviolable innocence, was Nel.

He had never wondered what Nel would look like when she became a woman. He knew he could never have imagined this.

Nel raised her head and shook back her hair, sending the fragrance of herbs drifting to his nostrils. She saw him watching her and grinned. A little girl's grin in her beautiful woman's face. "See, you did not even have to tell me to comb my hair!" she said.

Ronan concentrated grimly on controlling his arousal. It was not easy. Her narrow nose was a smaller, less arched version of his own. Her high cheekbones were rosy with the firelight. The teeth exposed by that urchin's grin were white and even.

"Nel," he heard himself asking, "if you had stayed to make the Sacred Marriage at Winter Fires, whom would you have chosen as your mate?"

The grin faded. Her face grew almost wary. "I do not know," she said.

He did not like that wary look. She was hiding something. "There was no one boy you particularly liked?" he pressed.

"Of course not." She was looking even warier.

"It is not so foolish a question," he said. Even to himself his voice sounded harsh. He struggled to lighten it. "By the time most girls reach the age of initiation, they have one particular boy that they like."

"You say that because the girls always liked you!" she retorted.

"Not at all," he said.

"It is true, and you know it." She swung all her hair to one side of her shoulder so she could rebraid it.

"We were not talking about me but about you," he said.

"There is nothing to say about me. On the other hand, there is always something interesting to say about you. Half the women of the tribe went into mourning when you left."

"To hear you talk, one would think I never did anything but spend my time with girls," he snapped.

"You certainly spent a *lot* of your time with girls," she replied teasingly. "There was Borba and Iva and Cala . . ."

He was glaring at her now. She had almost finished her braid. He felt savage. "Well, I am telling you now that I have had no time for girls these last three years. I have been too busy trying to keep a tribe together."

She was tying the thong that held the end of her braid, and her head was bent so that he could not see her face. For a moment her fingers stilled. "You are not married, then?" she asked.

Silence. Nel raised her head and looked at him out of shadowed eyes. "Did you think I might be married?" he asked carefully.

"The thought had occurred to me," she admitted.

He stood up. "Well, I am not." And he stalked to the cave door and went outside to look for Nigak.

Chapter Sixteen

Nel was in her sleeping skins pretending to be asleep when Ronan returned. She was not asleep, however, but awake and hugging to herself the news that, after all, Ronan did not have a wife. He might still regard her as a child, but at least now she would have a chance to change his perception.

She kept her eyes closed as he put more wood on the fire, then got into his own sleeping skins. He was annoyed with her for teasing him about all his girls. Strange, she thought sleepily, he had never grown annoyed at that before. She drifted off to sleep.

Shortly after midnight it began to rain. Nel awoke and heard the drops drumming steadily on the limestone rock of the hillside. She had always hated the rain, which was forever associated in her mind with the day her mother had died. She could remember still how wet her father had been when he came into the hut where she was staying while her mother gave birth to the new baby. She could remember still the smell of his wet buckskins. She would remember always the sound of the rain beating steady as a shaman's drum against the skins of the hut. She could not recall what her father's words to her had been, but she would never forget the sound and smell of the rain.

It had been raining on the day she and Ronan had sworn blood kinship. He had found her huddled in the forest crying, and it was then that he had proposed the bond.

A gust of wind blew a spray of rain into the mouth of the cave, dampening the watch fire Ronan had built. There was no sound of any animals outside, only the sound of the rain. As if the dousing of the fire had sounded a silent warning, Ronan sat up.

"I'll get it going again," he said when he saw that Nel was awake also. She crawled out of her sleeping skins, knelt shivering on top of them, and watched as Ronan put on fresh wood and fed what was left of the embers with dry leaves. The leaves caught, and the flaring flame illuminated and bronzed the skin of his face and throat. The thong at the neck of his buckskin shirt had come loose in his sleep, and the shirt hung open, baring his throat and chest. He had taken off his headband earlier, and his black hair was slipping over his forehead. He pushed his fingers through it and looked at Nel. "Are you all right?" he said softly.

Her eyes moved beyond the fire to the arch of the cave's entrance, the darkness, and the rain. "It's raining," she said stupidly. There was the faintest of tremors in her voice.

He grasped his sleeping skins with one hand and dragged them over to where hers were spread. Then he dropped down beside her and reached for her with his left hand as his right hand pulled his skins over the two of them for warmth. He drew her to lie beside him, his arms gathering her close. "It's all right, minnow," he said. His breath was feather soft on her temple. "Nothing bad is going to happen. You're with me now."

The air smelled of smoke and of rain. Nel turned her face into the smooth, bare skin of his throat and breathed deeply the scent that was Ronan. His arms held her fast, secure, safe. She snuggled closer to him, closed her eyes, and went back to sleep.

When Nel awoke the next morning, she was alone. She put her hand on the skins next to her where Ronan had lain, but they were no longer warm from his body. She felt oddly desolate.

It was gloomy outside, but the rain had stopped, and water in a skull container was hung over the fire, heating for morning tea. Ronan had probably gone to check the bird snares he had set last night. Nel sat up slowly, sighed, and set about brewing the tea.

Ronan returned a short time later, pausing for a moment in the frame of the cave opening, two willow grouse in his hands. Nel's head jerked around instantly, and their eyes met. He smiled, but it was not a smile that Nel recognized. It was the sort of smile he would give to a stranger. "Breakfast," he said lightly and came into the cave.

Nel plucked the feathers from the birds in bewildered silence while Ronan collected rocks and arranged them on the fire to heat. When the birds were plucked, she braised them on the hot stones. They were delicious, but the food stuck in her throat.

What was wrong? she wondered, watching Ronan's aloof face from under lowered lashes. He had been so good to her last night, so comforting, and this morning he was behaving as if she were someone he had just met.

"Douse the fire," he said in the cool, efficient voice she was coming to hate. He had not called her "minnow" once all morning, she thought in dismay. Obediently, she doused the fire, shouldered her pack, and trudged behind him down the game track.

The second day of their journey was much like the first. They kept to forest game trails and made camp in the late afternoon in a cave. Ronan got a boar for supper in much less time than he had anticipated, and consequently there were still several hours of daylight left once they had finished their meal.

They sat together around the fire, and for the first time in her life, Nel wondered what she and Ronan could find to talk about. She chewed on her lower lip and watched him out of the corner of her eyes. He was staring into the smoking fire, a thin sharp line between his black brows. He was deeply burned from the sun, and she could see the shadow of a beard under his skin. Like most of the Red Deer men, he shaved his beard with a flint razor every morning, but by nightfall it began to come back.

What was wrong? Nel wondered desperately. Why was he treating her with this distant courtesy? What had she done? Was she sorry that he had come for her? Was he angry because she had been such a baby last night?

The measure of her uneasiness was that she was afraid to ask him what was wrong.

"Tell me about this tribe of yours," she said abruptly. "I know only the little that I have heard from Tyr."

He narrowed his eyes against the smoke and looked at her with surprise, as if he had forgotten she was there. "All right," he said. "But first let's find someplace else to sit."

The cave they were occupying was set midway up a hillside, affording it a good view of the surrounding country. Ronan propped his back against the rocky face of the hill and gestured Nel to sit at a little distance from him. There had been no sign at all of a pursuit, but Ronan's vigilance was for more than the merely human. They had seen more leopard tracks during the course of the day.

Nel sat in the place he had indicated, hurt that it was so far away from him, and drew up her knees. "Tell me first how you found the valley," she said.

Evidently he was as happy to have a topic of conversation as she, for he answered readily. "I found it shortly after I left the Tribe of the Buffalo." As he spoke, his eyes were moving over the scene before them in a hunter's endless vigilance. "The men of the Buffalo told me about the tribes of the Mother that inhabit the plain beyond the Altas," he said, "and I decided I would try to find them. None of the tribes of the Kindred would risk incurring the Mistress's curse, and I thought it would be wisest to go to a place where the Tribe of the Red Deer was unknown. So Nigak and I set off to cross the Altas."

There was a movement among the trees a little way down the hillside, and Ronan stopped talking to watch. When he was certain it was only a deer, he picked up his tale. "I followed the Atata, as the men of the Buffalo had told me to, and, after a two-day climb, we reached the summit."

He paused again, as if reliving in his mind that particular moment. Once he had started speaking the tension between them had disappeared, and he said, now naturally, "It is amazing, Nel, how different the land is on the afternoon side of the mountains. Our side is narrow and steep, with only small pastures for grazing, but the far side is wide and sloping, with great wide valleys that in summer are thick with grass."

"Are there tribes dwelling in the mountains there?" she asked.

He shook his head. "There are summer camps, but no permanent dwelling places. There is snow for seven moons out of the year, and the animals descend into the lower levels once the snow begins to fall. As with us, the men follow the herds."

Ronan was scanning east now, his face turned slightly away from her. "I had decided before I left the Buffalo tribe that it would be better to present myself as a man from one of the other tribes of the Kindred," he said. "I did not think that tribes that follow the Mother would be overly hospitable to one of her castoffs, so I cut off my braid and pretended to be a follower of Sky God."

His rueful voice did not entirely disguise his underlying bitterness. Nel was tensely quiet. "The tribes of the Mother wanted no part of a man of the Kindred," Ronan said. He shrugged. "But they would not have wanted me if I had told them the truth, either, so I really cannot say that I made a mistake."

Nel felt building within her an anger so great that she thought her chest would burst with it. She pictured his rejection, his isolation, and her heart burned with fury. How could Arika have done this to him?

". . . that is when I found the valley," he was saying. "I was so confused, Nel; I did not know where to go." He was talking to her now the way he always had, and Nel blinked back tears. He said, "Nigak and I climbed back up the Altas, and Nigak found it." He turned his head to give her a swift smile. A real smile. "That is why I called it the Valley of the Wolf. Nigak began to chase one of the horses from a herd we came upon, and right before my eyes the horse disappeared into a wall of solid rock! When I investigated, I found the path into the valley."

The light was beginning to grow dim. Night was coming on. Nel said gruffly, "Tyr told me that they said at the gathering you had named the valley for yourself, the lone wolf."

He quirked one black brow. "Did they? Well, they were wrong."

"And what is it like, Ronan, Nigak's valley?"

"It is beautiful, minnow," he replied simply. "I cannot say for certain that no one else has ever been there, but there are no signs of human life, no old shelters or hearthplaces. Only the herds of horse and antelope. The ibex. The sheep. The eagles."

Nel did not speak, only drew in a long slow breath. His teeth looked very white in the slowly gathering dusk. "You will love it," he said.

She nodded.

"When I first saw it I thought: I can survive in such a place. Nigak and I, we can survive."

At the starkness of his words, Nel's nails bit into her palms so deeply they drew blood. Ronan was once more scanning the hillside. "I lived there alone for several moons," he said, "and then I met Bror."

She said through the pain in her chest, "Who is Bror?"

"One of my men. The Ibex tribe had expelled him, and he had

decided to aim for the tribes of the plain. They gave him the same welcome they had given me, however, and, since he did not have a clever wolf with him, he was reduced to wandering the pastures of the high Altas."

"Why did the Ibex tribe expel him?" Nel asked.

She saw the whites of his eyes move as he shot her a sideways look. "He murdered his wife."

"Oh," said Nel.

"It is not as bad as it sounds," Ronan said, and he told her Bror's story. "He was in a pit of despair when I met him," Ronan concluded, "so I brought him back to the valley with me, and we lived together for the rest of the summer."

"You helped each other," Nel said.

In the dusk she saw Ronan's mouth curl with irony. "We were not exactly a happy pair, minnow."

"Who was your next recruit?" she asked.

"Asok. He is from one of the tribes of the plain. They cast him out because he raped a woman."

"That is nice," Nel said.

"Asok says it was not rape, that she was willing. The girl's mother, however, said it was rape." His voice was very dry. "The tribe followed the Goddess, and the woman's word held. Asok was cast out." Ronan's profile was even more hawklike than usual. "I was certainly not in any position to question his story."

Nel said nothing.

"This was in the autumn, during Buffalo Moon," he continued. "At Leaf Fall Moon we added Dai." He glanced her way. "He and his brother were out hunting, and his brother was killed by Dai's spear. Dai swears it was an accident, but his father did not believe him. It seems there was not always good feelings between the two brothers— or between his father and Dai."

Nel nodded and smoothed the tip of her index finger along the buckskin that covered her knee.

"That was the lot of us the first winter," he said. "We stayed in the valley, and the following spring we added more men. Then came the women."

"What could a woman possibly do to cause her tribe to cast her out?" Nel asked in wonder.

"Well," Ronan said with amusement, "actually most of our women were not cast out; they chose to leave on their own. Two of them even brought their husbands along with them."

Nel smiled, more at the amusement in his voice than at his words. "Tell me," she prompted.

So he told her of Beki and Kasar, and of Lemo and Yoli. He told her of Mait's two steadfast sisters. He told her of the two women who had been expelled for adultery.

"Their tribes cast out these women because they slept with a man who was not their husband?" Nel said incredulously.

"Sa." Ronan shrugged. "To my thinking, it is the husband who should be ashamed for not being able to satisfy his wife. But that is the Way of Sky God."

Silence fell. For a little while they had fallen back into the old companionship, but with the mention of sex, the new constraint had come back. "It is growing dark," Ronan said abruptly. "Let's go into the cave and I'll build up the fire."

Nel sat cross-legged on her sleeping skins, Nigak beside her, and watched Ronan out of troubled green eyes. The new fire roared at the cave opening, a ward against night-prowling animals, and its leaping flames clearly illuminated Ronan's tall, lean figure as he came toward her. He halted when he was still at a respectable distance, sat and pulled out his knife and a sharpening stone.

Nel was not ready for sleep as yet, and she sought to restore the comradeship they had briefly known by asking him more questions. "How many of the women in the Tribe of the Wolf follow the Mother?" she began.

"Just two," he answered. "Berta and Tora, Mait's sisters. The others are all from the tribes of the Kindred."

Nel watched the shadows dancing on the planes of his face. He was concentrating on the flint blade of his knife. "The tribes of Sky God are hard on women," she murmured.

For the briefest of moments he lifted his gaze. "I have thought that more than once," he said, then went back to his blade.

What was the matter with him? Nel thought unhappily. Why was he acting so strangely? Why wouldn't he look at her? Most of all, why was she feeling that she could not ask him these questions?

She asked him another kind of a question instead. "What of the men? What god do they worship?"

"The men are more evenly divided."

She thought about this. "How do you keep the peace?" she asked with real curiosity.

His lips curled into a wry smile. "With difficulty."

She would not let him get away with the evasion. "But how do you do it?"

He shrugged. "I am the chief. They do as I say, or they go. That is how I do it."

Nel considered this ruthlessly simple philosophy, her brow furrowed. "Are all of your women married?" she asked next.

He let out his breath in a faint noise of exasperation. "So many questions!"

"I want to know," she said stubbornly.

"All except Eken are married."

"Eken?" Nel said. "Who is Eken?"

Nigak, disturbed by the new note in Nel's voice, got up from beside her and went to lie down next to Ronan, resting his muzzle on Ronan's thigh. Ronan smoothed the wolf's ruff and said calmly, "Eken is Fara's sister," and then he told her the story of Fara's twins.

Nel bent her head in order to conceal the tears that had begun to pour down her face. He had kept the twins, she thought. Her throat ached with the effort of holding back her sobs. She loved him so much. He had kept the twins.

He finished his story. She would not look at him. "And will you marry this Eken?" she managed to get out in a constricted voice.

"Na." She heard him put down his knife. "Are you crying?" he asked suspiciously.

She shook her head in false denial.

"Don't, Nel." His voice was almost desperate. "I hate it when you cry."

"I c-can't help it," she sobbed, giving up her attempt at concealment.

"But why?" He sounded harrassed. "I promise you, the twins are perfectly safe."

"I am c-crying because you k-kept them," she said.

He muttered something she could not understand.

"And I am crying because I love you," she sobbed even harder.

Even through her own distress she could hear the sharp intake of his breath. After a moment she heard him ask, "But why should that make you cry?"

She answered in what could only be called a wail, "Because you don't love me!"

Silence.

"Of course I love you," he said distractedly. "I have always loved you. You know that. Why else would I have come back for you?"

"You hardly talked to me all day!"

He did not come to comfort her. He just said, "I am sorry. I had something on my mind. I did not mean to ignore you, minnow. Now, please stop crying!"

She lifted her face with its streaming eyes. "You think I am still a child," she accused him. "You still tell me to w-wash in the river."

His face was wearing an odd, strained look. "What do you want from me, Nel?" His eyes had shadows under them. "You will have to tell me, because I don't understand."

Nel sniffled and said, "I want you to m-marry me."

He stared at her and did not answer.

"Do you remember how you asked me the other day if there was a man that I liked?" She wiped away her tears with the backs of her hands and sniffled again. She faced him bravely. "Well, if you had not come for me by Winter Fires, I was going to go and look for you. I was not going to take another man."

There was an empty space between them, and they gazed at each other across it. Mixed with the smell of the smoke, there drifted to Nel's nostrils the scent of rain. The fire flared suddenly, exposing clearly the expression on Ronan's face. With a jolt, Nel recognized it as the look she had seen so many times before when she had caught him looking at Borba, or Cala, or one of his other girls. Only now it was for her. She stopped breathing.

"Think, minnow," he said. "Are you sure this is what you want?"

She stared at that hard, intent, hawklike face. He meant now, she realized in astonishment. *Now.* Her eyes stretched wide in amazement. She did not have breath enough to speak, but she managed to nod her head.

Sa, she thought to herself over the thundering of her heart. Sa, Ronan. It is what I want.

Ronan could scarcely believe what had just happened, what Nel had just said. He had thought she would be the one who would find comfort in picking up their old relationship once again. It had been for her sake that he had been treating her like the little girl he had once known.

You think I am still a child, she had said. Dhu, did she think he was blind?

It was true that he had been terse with her all day, but that was because he was finding it so difficult to pretend to be her brother. He had been brotherly last night, and what a mistake that had been! It had been instinct on his part to comfort her. He knew how she dreaded the rain. But then, when she had nestled so trustingly against him, he had thought that he would go mad. She had slept; he had not closed his eyes.

He looked now into her beautiful eyes. He had never seen them so green. Dhu, how he wanted her! It was a pain in him, the wanting. She had nodded in answer to his question, but he thought she looked uncertain. She probably had not expected him to respond as quickly as he had. He moved Nigak's head from his leg, held out his hand to her and said softly, "Come here to me, minnow."

He watched her rise from her skins, her slim young body unfolding with supple grace. She crossed the space that divided them and dropped down beside him on her knees. Nigak got up and went to sleep on the warm spot that Nel had just vacated.

Ronan cupped her face between his hands. "Are you yet a maiden?" he asked, though he was certain he knew the answer.

"Sa," she whispered.

He should be sorry for that. He had been the first man before and he knew that mating was painful for a maiden. He smoothed back the silky hair at her temples. There were little hollows there, delicately scooped in the bone. The firelight accented the faint slant of her eyes, making them look mysterious and exotic. He ran his thumbs along her cheeks, feeling the sharpness of the bones beneath the perfect skin. "We can wait if you like," he heard himself saying. "You don't have to lie with me now if you are not yet ready, Nel. I will wait."

I must be mad, he thought, and waited, hands cupped around her face, for her answer.

She ran her tongue around the inner circle of her lips to wet them. Every part of him was wildly aroused. It had been too long since he had lain with a woman. He would die if she wanted to wait. She gave him a faint, shy smile and said, "Now."

He bent to put his mouth on hers and felt himself rocked by fierce, hot passion. Her lips were so soft. She yielded before him, letting him push her back upon the skins, raising her arms to encircle his neck. So soft, she was. So warm and sweet and soft. He kissed her lips, her cheeks, her throat. Her skin was like new velvet. He stripped off her tunic and buried his face between her breasts.

"Ronan," she said. She reached under his own shirt and ran her hands up and down the bare skin of his back. The touch of her fingers drove him wild. The scent of the herbs with which she washed her hair filled his nostrils. He put his mouth upon one small, perfect breast, and heard her whimper deep in her throat. His blood roared in his ears, and he knew suddenly that he was losing control.

"Minnow," he said in a desperate voice he did not recognize. He put his hand upon the waist of her deerskin trousers and lifted his head to look at her. "Minnow, I cannot wait . . ."

She smiled at him. Through the red mist of desire, he saw that smile.

"It's all right, Ronan," she said. Her small hands touched his, helping him with her clothes. He was sweating all over. "Nel," he groaned, as he drove into the soft and tender bliss of her. "Dhu, Nel . . ."

It was Nel who went to sleep first, nestled in the curve of his body. Ronan lay awake, trying to cope with an unfamiliar storm of emotion.

He looked down at the fawn-colored head that was tucked so trustingly into his shoulder. He had hurt her. He understood that there was no way around that, but he had hurt her more than was necessary. He had been too urgent, too hungry. He, who had always prided himself upon his skill in giving delight. He had been about as skillfull as a bull, he thought. And with Nel! But he had wanted her so badly. He had wanted her more than he ever remembered wanting anything before.

She stirred a little in his arms, and then was quiet again.

Ronan held her, and for the first time in his life he understood the meaning of sexual possessiveness. Nel belonged to him. She always had; she always would. No one else. Him.

He bent his head and buried his mouth in the silky hair that was spread on his shoulder.

She stirred again. "Ronan?" Her voice sounded blurry with sleep.

"Sa." His reply was soft. "Are you all right, minnow?"

"Mmmm." She was drifting back to sleep even as she spoke. After a few minutes his own eyes began to close, and then he too slept.

Chapter Seventeen

Nel awoke to find Nigak licking her face. She saw instantly that Ronan was no longer beside her, and she was pierced by loneliness. Don't be a fool, she scolded herself, as she sat up and patted Nigak vigorously. He has only gone to check the bird traps; he will be back.

When Nigak felt that he had been greeted with sufficient enthusiasm, Nel arose and went to look outside the cave. The sky was gray and overcast. There was still no sign of Ronan, so Nel took a skull container and went to the stream where they had got their water the previous night. She filled the container and washed herself. Then she filled it again and returned to the cave to brew morning tea.

Ronan returned just as the water was beginning to boil. He had two quail in his hand, and suddenly, looking at that splendid, intensely masculine figure outlined against the cave opening, Nel felt shy. He was accustomed to girls who were so much more experienced than she . . . she had not been very adept last night . . . she looked away from him and said stiffly, "The tea is almost ready."

"Good," he said. "I'll pluck the birds."

Nel watched him from under lowered lashes. She knew the look of him so well: the set of his shoulders and collarbone, the arch of his arrogant nose, the black sweep of lashes against the hard line of his cheekbones, his mouth. She thought again of last night, felt her color rise, and jerked her eyes away from his face, to the thin, strong hands that were dealing so competently with the bird. She shivered and looked away.

"Are you too sore to walk today, Nel?" she heard him ask.

The color in her face deepened. She shook her head.

Silence fell, not the uncomfortable silence of the last few days, but not the companionable silence they had always known either. This was a waiting silence. Finally Ronan said, "Is something wrong, minnow?"

She heard the concern in his voice. She shook her head again. She looked at him out of the side of her eyes and said in a small voice, "I am feeling shy."

At first he looked astonished, and then he grinned. Nel looked at that wonderful, familiar smile—so vivid, so beguiling, so ablaze with the sheer joy of living—and she grinned back.

"Finish those birds," she ordered. "I am starving."

He laughed. "Sa, sa, sa. I am trying to hurry."

They cooked and ate their breakfast, shouldered their burdens, and again took up their journey.

Once more they were finding their way along narrow animal tracks, keeping away from the river and the accustomed hunting places of the Tribe of the Red Deer. The overcast day made navigating through the forest more difficult, as they did not have the position of the sun to give them their direction. Ronan was an excellent woodsman, however, and was able to tell their direction from the bark of the forest pine trees. The brightest spot of bark always faced due south. Nel knew this, of course, as did all the members of the Red Deer tribe, but she could not read the trees the way Ronan could. When facing a quadrant of bright-colored trees, an expert was needed to distinguish the exact point at which the bark was brightest and so determine due south from southeast or southwest.

It began to sprinkle rain in the middle of the afternoon. As there was no cave nearby, they decided to set up a tent before they were caught in a downpour. Once Nigak saw the preparations being made for camp, he disappeared into the forest to hunt. Ronan went to cut down some saplings to make a frame for the small tent skin he carried, and Nel built a fire under cover of the trees to cook the partridge Ronan had trapped earlier.

They ate sitting under the canopy of the trees, and when the rain began to drip through, they moved into the small tent. Their sleeping skins covered all the floor space, and they had to crawl as there was not enough headroom in the tent for them to stand.

Outside the night was wet and black, and the scent of pine hung heavy in the air unmixed with the smell of smoke. It was too wet for Ronan to build a fire to keep away animals. The forest rustled restlessly with the falling rain.

"I don't think the rain will ever make me unhappy again," Nel said.

Ronan was half-reclining next to her, propped up on his elbow, watching her with unreadable dark eyes. "Is it so?" he asked softly.

She peered at him by the dim light of their solitary stone lamp. "Let's say the marriage words to each other," she said.

"Now?"

"Sa. Now."

"All right, if that is what you wish." He sat up, frowning slightly. "I am trying to remember them," he confessed.

"I know them," Nel said. "Shall I go first?"

He smiled and held out his hand. "You go first."

Nel put her hand into his and said clearly, "This is Ronan, the man that I take for my husband. I ask the Mother to bind us together for the life of the tribe."

She waited a moment; then she turned her hand and squeezed Ronan's fingers. "Now you," she said.

"This is Nel," he said, repeating her words, the words used by the Tribe of the Red Deer, "the woman that I take for my wife. I ask the Mother to bind us together for the life of the tribe."

They looked at each other, holding hands and listening to the echo of the words still hanging in the pine-scented air.

Ronan said, "I am so sorry I hurt you last night, minnow."

Nel shook her head. "It was not your fault. It is ever that way for a woman. Fali said that it is the Mother's way of reminding us that the pleasure of mating is followed by the pain of childbirth." Her fingers curled within his large hand. "You made me very happy," she said.

He held her hand hard and shook his head. "But I will make you happy tonight," he promised. "I swear it, Nel. You must just trust me . . ."

She was laughing softly. "Na," she said. "You know how impossible it is for me to trust you." She pulled her hand from his grasp and then reached up to cast both her arms around his neck.

"Aieee," he said, pretending to lose his balance and falling forward so that she ended up on the ground with him on top of her. She squeaked in protest, and he lifted his weight, bracing his hands on either side of her shoulders and looking down into her laughter-flushed face. "You are an impudent brat," he said.

"Perhaps," she retorted, "but I am your brat, remember."

The laughter left his eyes to be replaced by a look of intense concentration. "Sa," he said. "You are." And he bent his head to put his mouth on hers.

This was a much longer lovemaking than he had been able to manage the previous night. Tonight there was time for touches, for caresses, for finding out all the secret places of the other's body. When Ronan fumbled at Nel's shirt, she arched her back to help him push it out of his way, then reached up to him, cupping his shadowy face between her hands and drawing him downward. His mouth touched her breast. She buried her fingers in his hair to hold him there.

In the dimness of the tent, they stripped off their clothing and learned each other's bodies entirely by touch. At one point Nigak returned from hunting and tried to join in what he obviously thought was a game. Ronan snarled at him to get away, and he whined and backed out of the tent to go and find himself a dry spot somewhere under a tree.

"Poor Nigak," Nel said with a soft, unsteady laugh.

"He'll be all right," Ronan said. "Nel. Now, Nel. Now."

She tilted her hips upward to meet him, to receive the power of him into her, to rock with him in the passionate, heaving darkness, until the world exploded into ecstasy for them both.

They lay for a long time afterward, locked together, neither of them wanting to separate. Outside the rain poured down, but it no longer had the power to disturb Nel's happiness. She went to sleep.

Shortly after midnight the rain stopped, and the moon was shining brightly when Nel awoke with a start, aware that something had disturbed her. She looked toward the tent opening, expecting to see Nigak, and saw instead a very large cave hyena looking in.

"Ronan," Nel breathed, not taking her eyes off the hyena. It was so close that she could smell its foul breath.

"I see." His voice was as quiet as hers had been.

Nel did not move. Cave hyenas were dangerous predators, and this one was far too interested in the tent and its apparently sleeping inhabitants. There was a sudden flash of movement as Ronan rose to his knees, simultaneously bringing forward his arm. The hyena shrieked as the spear pierced its chest. It staggered back, away from the tent opening, then collapsed in the bright moonlight.

"Hyenas travel in packs. I had better build a fire in case there are any more about," Ronan said, and he crawled out of the tent. Nel watched him bending over the hyena, preparing to drag it away from the tent. Once she saw Nigak join him, she closed her eyes and went back to sleep.

The sun was shining when Nel awoke again, and it shone every day of their journey thereafter. As soon as they were through the Buffalo Pass, Ronan slowed their pace. Nel did not protest. Both of them knew that once they reached the valley they would be surrounded by the demands of other people, and both of them were in a mood to cherish this brief golden time they had to themselves. The summer days were warm, and it was delightful to splash in a stream, to hunt for birds, to gather and eat the ripe summer fruit, to make love endlessly in the glow of the golden summer sun.

They avoided the caves of the Buffalo tribe, as Ronan had no desire to answer questions about its members who had defected to him, and they took their time in reaching the Altas.

Nel felt the change in Ronan on the day they reached the first of the high mountain pastures. He was beginning to turn away from her, she realized. His mind was focusing on things that were not Nel. It was inevitable, she knew. They could not go through life in the kind of glorious isolation they had known these last ten days. She knew that, but the knowledge made her sad.

Her melancholy mood vanished, however, as they began the real upward climb. Nel had lived among mountains all her life, but the Altas were like nothing she had ever known. The deep gorges, the violent torrents, the steep forests—all excited her awe, her delighted wonder. When they reached the tarn at the top of the last valley, and Nel saw the majestic snow-capped peaks looming before her, she was quite simply dazzled.

Nigak led them through the pass; he led them in fact the entire way
to the Lake of the Eagle. Nel was enchanted with how much gentler
the southern side of the mountains was than the northern side. This
time of year, the high mountain pastures were filled with flowers, butterflies, birds, ibex, and sheep.

"When does the snow begin to fall?" she asked Ronan, turning her
face upward, like a flower, to the welcome heat of the sun.

"It can begin as early as Buffalo Moon in the high passes," he
answered. "Our valley is below the treeline, so we don't usually see
snow until the end of Leaf Fall Moon."

When they reached the Lake of the Eagle, Nel looked with amazement at the seemingly impenetrable cliff behind which Ronan had told
her the valley was located. She was even more amazed when Nigak ran
right up to the cliff wall, then disappeared.

"That's how it happened the first time," Ronan said as he followed
the wolf, Nel beside him.

Nel was silent as she entered into the passage behind Ronan, silent
as she scrambled down the steep, rocky path, silent as she stepped at
last from the confines of the wall and saw stretched before her the
hidden, perfect beauty of the valley.

Horses and antelope took mute note of the new arrivals, raising their
heads from grazing to look, then lowering them serenely once again.
The valley grass was even lusher than the grass Nel had seen outside
the walls. Two golden eagles circled in the air, casting their shadow
over the blue waters of the lake. More antelope were lying in the sun
along the eastern wall, and with them were a few mares with their foals.
Posted on high ground above the mares and foals, his splendid head
moving watchfully from side to side, was a magnificent, long-maned
white stallion.

Nel let out her breath slowly and looked at Ronan. He was wearing
his sternest look, which she knew meant he was deeply moved. "It is
beautiful," she said.

He merely nodded. She leaned her head against his arm, and together they gazed out at the Valley of the Wolf.

It was Nigak who alerted the tribe to Ronan's coming. The wolf
came cantering out of the passage and headed straight for the huts in
the northwest corner, eager to see if everything was still as he remem-

bered it. Fara and Eken were there with the twins, and Berta, Tora, and Tabara, who also had small children. Mait and Thorn were at their hut as well, as Thorn was making some new spear points for the men. It was the two boys who were the first to race toward the passage to greet their returning chief.

Thorn was not surprised to see that there was someone with Ronan. After all, Ronan had told the tribe that he was going to fetch his cousin. Thorn's headlong flight checked somewhat, however, when he realized that Ronan's cousin was a girl. Beside him, Mait gave a startled exclamation as he too recognized the sex of Ronan's companion. Both boys slowed their gait to a more dignified speed.

When they were within earshot, Thorn heard Ronan say to his companion, "It's the cubs."

"Ronan!" Thorn said in breathless greeting.

"Why aren't you two out hunting?" Ronan asked.

"I was making some new spear points." Thorn smiled radiantly. "I am so glad you have come home!"

"Sa," said Mait. "I, too, am glad."

"Life under Bror was that bad?" Ronan asked.

"Na!" both boys protested at once.

"That is not what we meant," Mait said.

"Bror is a good leader," Thorn said. "But . . . but he is not the chief."

The girl gave a soft chuckle, and Ronan turned to her. "Nel," he said, "here are Mait and Thorn, the two youngest of the tribe's men."

Thus given permission by a formal introduction, Thorn at last looked at the girl.

She was one of the most beautiful girls that Thorn had ever seen. He stared at her. "I am pleased to meet you, Mait and Thorn," she said. Her voice was deeper than he had expected. She smiled at them. Her eyes were as green as grass.

"W-welcome," Mait said. He was staring at Nel with his mouth slightly ajar.

"Sa," Thorn said, quick to echo Mait's courtesy, "welcome to the Tribe of the Wolf."

Two white-muzzled puppies came rushing up.

Ronan said to the girl, "The pups are Nigak's get."

"I can see that," the girl said. She held out a hand and rubbed her fingers together. "Greetings, little ones," she said. To Thorn's utter astonishment, both puppies bounced right up to her and offered their heads to be scratched.

"They are splendid," Nel told the boys.

Thorn said blankly, "I cannot believe they went to you like that."

"Nel has the Mother's touch with animals," Ronan said with a faint smile. "It was she who trained Nigak. She found him when he was a pup not much older than these two here."

"Is it so?" Mait asked the girl. "You took him from his mother?"

The girl called Nel shook her head. "He was crying over the dead body of his mother when I found him. Her other pups had left her, but not Nigak. It took me one entire day to persuade him to come with me."

Thorn's imaginative mind pictured the scene. His brown eyes brimmed with grief. "Poor Nigak," he said.

"I am thinking it was Nigak's lucky day when Nel found him," Ronan said.

"Yours too," the girl retorted.

Ronan grinned.

Thorn stared at the transformation that grin brought to Ronan's thin-boned, arrogant face. It made him look lit from within. It made him look . . . young.

Mait said diffidently, "Are you Ronan's cousin?"

Without answering, Nel looked toward Ronan. Following her lead, the boys also looked to their chief. Ronan said, "Nel is my cousin." The smile was gone from his face. He was looking at Nel and not at the boys. He said, "And she is my wife."

Chapter Eighteen

The subject of Nel was discussed with varying degrees of enthusiasm in all the tents of the Tribe of the Wolf that night.

Berta and Tora were delighted to have another woman who worshipped the Mother added to the tribe. "It is not that I do not like Fara and Beki and Yoli and the others," Berta confided to her sister as they worked together to clean away the remains of the evening meal. "But their ways are not our ways. It is good that this Nel has come."

"Sa," Tora agreed placidly. The sisters were alone in Berta's tent, where both their families had eaten dinner. Berta's baby began to fuss, and Tora, seeing that Berta was still occupied, went over to the infant, picked her up and began to nurse her. The baby, as accustomed to her aunt's milk as she was to her mother's, fell instantly silent.

"The married men are meeting this night," Berta said, as she finished scouring the pottery vessels in which she had served the venison stew.

"Sa," Tora said again. "So Asok told me."

"What does Asok think of the horse-calling rite?" Berta asked her sister.

Tora shrugged one shoulder carefully, so as not to disturb the nursing baby. "Asok was reared in the worship of the Mother, so the horse calling is not strange to him. But he has been listening to Heno and the other men who follow Sky God, and I am thinking that he likes what he hears."

Berta finished with the pottery and put it away in its proper place. She turned to look at Tora. "Poor Ronan," she said. "It is in my heart almost to feel sorry for him. Some of the men will be angry no matter which way he moves on this."

"We shall see how clever a chief he really is," Tora said, and both women glanced at each other, their brown eyes brimming with secret amusement.

Fara and Crim were not so pleased with the advent of Nel. They had eaten dinner alone in their hut, as Eken was spending the week in the moon hut.

"I had so hoped that he would marry Eken," Fara sighed. "She was hoping also; that is why she refused to wed any of the other men."

"I know," Crim said. He was very fond of his sister-by-marriage. "What did she say when you told her?"

"She did not say much. But she looked . . . stricken."

"Well, there is certainly no lack of men for her to wed in the Tribe of the Wolf!" Crim said bracingly.

"I know. But she had set her heart on Ronan. He should not have done this to her."

"He did nothing to encourage her," Crim pointed out fairly. "The wishing was all on Eken's side."

"He should have told us he was married," Fara said. "Then Eken would not have hoped."

"He wasn't married," Crim said. "I thought the same as you, and so I asked him why he had never mentioned his wife. He said he and Nel had spoken the words of binding only a half-a-moon ago."

"Then he should have told us he planned to marry."

Crim shrugged. "He had not seen Nel for three years, Fara. He probably did not know what would happen between them." He added, as Fara made a discontented face, "You surely did not think a man like Ronan would live forever without a woman."

"Of course I didn't," Fara said irritably. "That is why I was sure he would marry Eken."

"Well, Eken will just have to marry someone else," Crim replied. "Either Dai or Okal would take her in a moment, and they are both brave, well-looking young men."

"They are not Ronan," Fara grumbled.

"Neither am I," pointed out her husband, "and you seem to be content."

"Oh . . ." Fara looked at him, and then she smiled. "But Eken cannot marry you either."

"That is so," Crim said. "Poor girl."

His wife pretended to throw a cookpot at him, and, laughing, he ducked out of the tent to go to the married men's meeting.

Bror had been in Ronan's hut many times, but he entered this time with unusual reluctance. There was a woman in Ronan's hut now, a woman in Ronan's life. Bror's heart was sore as he thought that things between them would never again be the same.

Bror had to duck his head to get under the hut door, and as he straightened he scanned the hut swiftly, searching for the intruder. His tensed muscles relaxed as he realized she was not there. Ronan glanced up from the leather pack strap he was repairing, smiled, and said, "Sit down, Bror," gesturing to Bror's accustomed place at the barely smoldering hearthplace. As Bror advanced, he continued to scan the room for signs of the new occupant.

A row of spare clothes hung on the right wall, all neatly arranged on pegs that had been hammered into the saplings that formed the hut's frame. Bror recognized Ronan's familiar garments, but hanging in company with them today were a smaller fur vest and a deerskin shirt and trousers. Beneath the clothes, Ronan's reindeerskin boots stood in solitary splendor. Bror thought, that girl will have to make herself a fur tunic and some boots if she wants to stay here for the winter.

Standing along the right wall near the clothing pegs were two pottery jars for water and a small stack of wood and kindling to make the fire. Ronan's weapons were propped in the corner as usual, and near them was the heap of deerskins on which Nigak made his bed.

Three long flat table-stones lined the back wall. On them were arranged a familiar assortment of items: sinew, spearheads and arrowheads, leather thongs of differing sizes, eating utensils, a basketful of red berries, a basketful of dried tea, and an extra stone lamp.

Two neatly rolled sleeping skins were lying along the left wall of the hut, and another neat pile of scraped leather waiting to be cut into whatever shape Ronan needed. The empty drying rack was on the left wall as well.

The hearthplace was in the center of the hut, under the hole that had been left for the smoke. The floor around the hearthplace was covered with reindeerskin rugs.

Ronan's wife, Bror thought as he took his place, had not brought much to her new home.

"So," Ronan said. He put down the leather strap. "What were the problems?"

Bror found himself smiling. "You are so sure I had problems?"

"If you didn't, I will pass the leadership to you right now."

Bror laughed. "Most of the problems I managed to solve all right. There are two, however, that require your attention."

"Two," Ronan said, encouraged. "That is not so bad."

"Wait until you hear them," Bror said.

Ronan raised his brows. "I am waiting."

"The men from the tribes of the Goddess are demanding to celebrate a ceremony called the horse-calling rites," Bror began. He saw Ronan's face immediately grow wary, and he nodded ruefully. They both knew how explosive the word *rite* could be in this religiously diversified tribe of theirs. Bror continued, "The tribes of the plain hunt the horse to live, and the purpose of this particular rite is to insure the increase of the horse herds."

"Mmm," said Ronan suspiciously. "What does it entail?"

"The young unmarried men of the tribe impersonate stallions. Each night the young women (both married and unmarried) wrap their nakedness in a horseskin and go to the ceremonial dancing place. After the stallion dance is over, each of the women approaches the horseman of her choice, offers him food, and invites him to walk in the forest with her. You can guess what happens next."

Ronan groaned.

"According to the men of the Goddess, this rite represents the women of the tribe mating with a stallion. This, of course, pleases Horse God, and he sends more foals to the herds as well as making certain the herds come into the hunting grounds of the tribe."

"Do they really mate?" Ronan asked. "Or is it just ceremonial?"

Bror said, "With all those young stallions heated up from a dance? What do you think?"

There was a line, thin and deep as a knife cut, between Ronan's eyebrows. "This was proposed by the men of the Goddess?" he asked.

"The unmarried men of the Goddess—backed up, I might add, by the unmarried men of Sky God. It is a good ritual, they told me with grave faces, because the Tribe of the Wolf also hunts the horse."

"And the married men don't like it."

"The married men will not stand for it. Heno has been quite eloquent on the subject."

"I can imagine," Ronan muttered. "What did you tell them?"

Bror replied promptly, "I told them all that we must wait for your return, that you would decide."

Ronan said, "What do *you* think, Bror? Are they serious?"

"They are serious—all of them. It is the old story, Ronan. Not enough women for too many men."

Ronan grunted. "I am almost afraid to ask you what the next problem is."

"The hunting has not been good these last weeks. We have lost our luck with the reindeer; some one of us must have offended them."

"Who is accusing whom?" Ronan asked resignedly.

"The usual. Cree is accusing the men of Sky God of a lack of reverence. He says they kill female reindeer, and that is why the Mother is angry and has taken away the herds." Bror ran a hand through the curly black hair that hung down across his broad forehead. "On the other hand, Heno is accusing the men of the Goddess of not practicing proper sexual taboos. He says that they are sleeping with their wives before they hunt, and that is why the reindeer have gone away."

"*Heno* was expelled from his tribe for sleeping with his wife before a hunt," Ronan said ironically.

"That is how he knows how powerful the taboo is. So he says."

"Dhu."

"Those are the two problems I could not deal with," Bror said.

Ronan said, "If I understand you correctly, we have one situation which pits the unwed men against the married men, and another situation which pits the men of Sky God against the men of the Goddess."

"Sa."

Ronan said wearily, "I sometimes wonder if it will ever end, Bror."

A new voice, low-pitched yet unmistakably feminine, said, "What don't you think will ever end?" Bror's head snapped around in time to see Ronan's wife coming in the door, two deer bladders filled with water in her hands. Nigak entered on her heels. She smiled at Bror and went to pour the water into the pottery containers along the right wall. Then she sat herself beside Ronan, as naturally, Bror thought with a resentment he tried to conceal, as if she belonged there. Nigak curled up in his accustomed place in the corner.

"It's the same old tale," Ronan answered her. "The customs of the Goddess seem always to be coming in conflict with the customs of Sky God." Briefly he recounted what he had just learned from Bror.

Nel made a sympathetic sound and turned to look at Bror. "What do the women say about this?" she asked.

"About what?" He knew he sounded abrupt, but he could not help himself. Ever since Eda, he was afraid to be around women.

"About the horse-calling ceremony," Nel said patiently.

Bror shook his head and looked desperately toward Ronan.

Ronan took pity on him. "I am thinking that this ceremony sounds somewhat like the Red Deer's ceremony of the fires, Nel," he said.

The long green eyes turned away from Bror. Nel answered her husband slowly, "The fires is more than a prayer to the Mother for good hunting and the fertility of the herds, Ronan. It is for the life of the tribe as well." She turned her disconcerting gaze back to Bror and asked, "Why do only the unmarried men play the stallions?"

Bror addressed his answer to Ronan. "That was my own question. The only answer I got was the usual, 'It was that way from the beginning.' "

There was the sound of feet approaching the hut and a man appeared in the low doorway. It was Heno. "Ronan," he said loudly, "the married men of the tribe wish to speak to you."

Ronan arose without haste, went to the open door and ducked his head to go outside. Sitting in silence within, both Bror and Nel could hear his voice very clearly. "I have been speaking with Bror and he has told me of the differences within the tribe," he said. "I will deal with them tomorrow morning in the hearing of everyone."

"Has Bror told you that the married men of the Goddess are in agreement with the married men of Sky God over this business of the horse-calling?" a nasal-sounding voice asked in tones that were not quite insolent but certainly verging on it.

"He has told me, Cree," Ronan replied.

"Then you must understand . . ."

"*You* understand, Cree," Ronan interrupted with cool authority. "I will deal with this tomorrow, after I have had a chance to reflect. Not tonight. Now you may return to your wives, all of you."

There was the sound of feet. The men were going, Bror thought thankfully. Then came a voice Bror recognized as Heno's. "Remember, Ronan, now you also are a married man. How would you like to see your pretty new wife mating with Bror?"

There was a charged silence, and then the sound of feet moving hastily away. It was not until the men's steps had completely died away that Ronan came back into the tent, his face pale with anger under its dark summer burn. Bror could not bring himself to look at Nel, but clenched his big hands into fists and said to Ronan, "I told you it was serious."

"So you did." A beat of silence, then Ronan added quietly, "I am sorry you had to hear that."

At first Bror assumed that Ronan was speaking to his wife, but then he saw that the chief's dark gaze was fixed on him. He went hot and then cold. He stood up. "It is growing dark. Good night, Ronan." He flicked his eyes in the girl's direction, mumbled something he hoped sounded polite, and fled.

There was silence in the tent for quite a while. Then Nel said softly, "Poor man."

"Sa," Ronan sighed. "He is a good man, minnow." He sighed again. "That, of course, is why he suffers."

It was growing darker in the tent, and Ronan reached for the stone lamp that stood upon a rock at a little distance from the hearthplace. The lamp was similar to those Nel had seen all her life, an open vessel hollowed out of soapstone and filled with animal fat, which melted as the flame heated it. However, instead of the moss the Red Deer tribe used for a wick, this lamp used a long stringlike piece of plant, which was pleated into a sawtooth shape and then floated along the edge of the vessel. The string, Nel found, was very efficient; for more light, you lengthened the wick, for less light you shortened it.

After Ronan had trimmed the wick and lit it with a coal stored in the stones around the smoldering fire, Nel said, "What are you going to do about the disputes?"

"The hunting conflict I can deal with," he answered as he set the lamp on its rock. He turned back to her. "It is this business of the women that is the thorny problem."

"No one appears to have asked the women for their opinion of the horse calling," Nel remarked.

"Bror would not go near the women, Nel. That is the chief difficulty of leaving him in charge of the tribe. The men respect Bror. They are even a little afraid of him, and this is good. Men need to be a little afraid of their leader. But he will not involve himself in anything that has to do with the women."

"You will have to meet with the women yourself, Ronan," Nel said. "You cannot make any decisions until you hear what their wishes are."

He had set the lamp almost directly behind him, and its warm glow was lighting his head and shoulders. He gave her his most beguiling smile. "I have been thinking that now I am a married man, I have someone to help me in this matter of the women."

She did not return his smile. "I do not know these women, Ronan."

He dismissed her words with a casual gesture. "That does not matter. You are my wife, and that makes you the chief woman of the tribe. This will hold sway with the women of Sky God." He leaned a little forward, compelling her with both voice and body. "You were also the Chosen One of the Mother; this will hold sway with Berta and Tora." His eyes were very large and brilliant in the light of the lamp.

"What do you want me to do?" Nel asked.

"What you just said I should do. Talk to them. Discover their thoughts in this matter. They will speak to you more openly than they would ever speak to me."

Nel stared at him, speechless.

He reached toward her and took both her hands between his. His hands were warm and strong around her small, cold fingers. "Minnow," he said coaxingly, "you will not refuse to help me?"

She would never refuse to help him, and he knew it. She sighed. "I am far more skeptical about my effectiveness than you are, Ronan, but I will talk to the women and try to ascertain their feelings about this ceremony."

His arm came around her and drew her to his side. He bent his head and she lifted her mouth to give to him.

In the morning Nel went first to Berta's hut. There she found both sisters busily pegging out a reindeerskin for scraping. They offered Nel tea, and she accepted.

"I have come," she said after the initial courtesies of greeting had been exchanged, "on behalf of the chief. He wishes to know the will of the women of the tribe in regard to this horse-calling ceremony."

Berta and Tora exchanged an enigmatic look. Berta said primly, "We do not speak for the women of the tribe."

"I understand that," Nel said. "I have come to you first, however, because you are followers of the Goddess. This rite is a rite of the Goddess, or so Bror has told the chief."

She paused, and two sleek dark heads nodded agreement. Berta said, "Sa. It is a rite of the People of the Dawn, and of the River People also I think."

"Is it one of your important rites?" Nel asked.

Berta and Tora looked at each other. They shrugged. "There are many rites in our tribe," Tora said. "The horse calling is one of them. It is no more or no less important than any of the others."

"It is not one of the chief rites, then?"

"Na," said Berta. "The chief rites are the rites of the Fires."

Nel nodded in understanding. Then she asked, "Do you know why it is that the stallions must be played by the unmarried men?"

Again the frustrating twin shrugs. "It was that way from the beginning," Tora said unhelpfully.

Nel persisted. "Would it be considered irreverent if the married men played the stallions as well?"

Again the sisters exchanged a look. "It has never been done before," Tora said.

Nel sipped her tea. "I understand that it has never been done before," she said, "but what if it was done now?"

Berta frowned. "There is no power of the unknown if a woman lies with her husband," she said. Her head lifted in a gesture of enlightenment. "Perhaps that is why the unmarried men play the stallions." She looked challengingly at Nel. "If you are of the Goddess, then you will understand that."

"I am of the Goddess," Nel returned. "I understand the things of the Mother. But at our ceremony of the Fires, which is a very powerful fertility rite, a woman may lie with her husband."

Berta smiled back, showing very white, very strong teeth. "May lie? Or must lie?"

Nel raised her delicate brows. "May lie," she said.

Silence fell. Nel sipped her tea. The sisters looked at each other. Finally Tora said, "Ronan wants to let the married men play the stallions?"

"It is a possibility," Nel said.

There was silence as the sisters thought. "Among the People of the Dawn," Berta said at last, "a woman can approach any number of men at the horse calling."

Dhu, Nel thought in dismay.

"Some of the women of our tribe have gone with two handfuls of men in one night," Tora said proudly.

"Dhu," said Nel out loud.

The sisters smiled serenely.

Nel said slowly, "Such a thing is possible in your tribe, Tora. Such a thing is possible in my tribe. But it is not possible in the tribes that follow Sky God."

"The women of those tribes are fools," Berta said scornfully.

"Not fools," Nel said. "It is not their fault if they have been cut off from the Mother."

"They live their lives under the foot of a man," Tora said.

Nel looked surprised. "Beki? Does Beki live her life under the foot of Kasar? Or Yoli under the foot of Lemo?"

"They are different," Berta said with a shrug.

"I am thinking of Yeba and Tabara," Tora said. Her brown eyes flashed. "Do you know what happened to Tabara because she lay with a man who was not her husband?"

"She was cast out," Nel said.

"She was cast out, sa, but her husband kept her children!"

"I did not know that," Nel said softly.

"Can you imagine such a thing? Taking her children away? Did her husband carry those children inside his body? Did he give them his blood? Did he give birth to them in pain and suffering?" Tora looked magnificent in her fury. "Men," she said. "Men know nothing!"

"Poor Tabara," Nel said, her voice filled with pity. "Does she still grieve?"

"Grieve?" It was Berta who answered this time. "Of course she grieves. She carried those children under her heart. They grew into her heart. They will never grow out of it. That is what it means to be a mother." She scowled at Nel. "Does a man know this?"

Nel shook her head.

"All a man knows is one moment. After, his life and his body are the same. It is the woman who carries the fruit of that moment for nine long months in her womb. It is not for a man to make the rules about mating. It is for a woman."

"Ronan thinks this business of the horse calling has come up because the unmarried men want a woman," Nel said.

"Of course that is why it came up," Berta replied.

"If it is not for the men to make the rules, but for the women," Nel said, "what do you think the rule should be about the horse calling?"

Silence.

"You cannot complain about the men making the rules if you allow them to do it," Nel said reasonably.

Still silence.

"Perhaps we should get the other women and discuss it as a group," Nel said.

"Sa," said Berta. She smiled. "That is what we should do."

Chapter Nineteen

The women met. One hour later Nel returned to Ronan to tell him what had been said. After he had finished laughing, he agreed to allow the women to present their decision to the men of the tribe.

It was late morning by the time the tribal members assembled to listen to their chief. They sat outdoors in a great circle, cross-legged, solemn, in the order of their temporary alliances: the married men beside the married men; the unwed men beside the unwed; and the women.

Berta and Tora had their babes in cradleboards upon their backs. Fara held one twin in her lap, and next to her, holding the other twin, sat a pale-faced Eken, returned that morning from her week's stay in the moon hut. Tabara's toddler, the only child her first husband had allowed her to keep, sat between his mother and Beki, his thumb in his mouth.

No one spoke. Even the children were quiet. The only movement came from the birds overhead and the dogs as they wandered between the lake and the tribal circle, occasionally coming to sniff at the clothes of a particular friend. All the heads turned as one when Ronan and Nel and Nigak came out of their hut, approached the circle and took their places at its head. The tribe regarded its chief with varying degrees of expectancy and waited for him to speak.

"There are two things we must discuss in this council today," Ronan began pleasantly. His voice was quiet yet perfectly audible, his face quite unreadable. He sat with one hand resting on his knee and the other on Nigak's head. The soft summer breeze blew his black hair back from his face and ruffled Nigak's fur. Ronan's eyes held Thorn's briefly as he glanced around the circle.

I want to draw this, Thorn thought. Of late he had been drawing scenes of tribal life in a cave he had found in the cliff near the waterfalls at the other end of the valley. He had kept scrupulously to his promise to Ronan, however, and only drew the faces of those who had given him permission. The other figures he left deliberately unclear.

". . . discuss first this business of the offense to the reindeer," Ronan was saying. Thorn wrenched his mind away from thoughts of the cave and focused his attention on his chief.

"We are from different tribes, and we worship our gods in different ways," Ronan continued, "but if you think about it, all of our ways are based on one single belief: that everything in the world has its own spirit." He paused to give them a moment to take in what he had said, then went on: "The trees and the grass, the plants and the berries, the red deer and the reindeer, the people of the Goddess and the people of Sky God—all have their own spirit. And to live our lives rightly, it is required of us that we give reverence to that spirit."

It was very quiet on the floor of the valley that morning. The animals were all grazing on the far side of the lake. Not even a bee buzzed as Ronan went on. "Some things we all understand. All hunters, no matter what their tribe, know enough to give thanks to the animal who has given his life for our food. All of us treat a beast's body with reverence, speak of it respectfully, handle its remains with care, use it thoroughly and avoid waste. All of us understand the necessity of showing appreciation for what is given. All of us understand that a display of arrogance, power, or pride will offend the animal's spirit and anger the gods."

Thorn thought of how his father had told him it was important to honor the animal who had given his life that men might live, and he nodded in agreement. All around him he saw others nodding in the same way.

Ronan was going on, "The hunters of each tribe have their own way of expressing this appreciation for the spirit." He looked at Heno. "The hunters of the Tribe of the Fox do not sleep with their wives for three days before a big hunt, and this is their way of showing their reverence, of asking the animals to grant them the grace of a good kill."

Heno nodded emphatically, and Ronan's gaze moved on to Cree, who looked back sourly. Ronan said, "The hunters of the River People kill only the male animals. This is their way of showing reverence to the Mother, their way of contributing toward the continuation of the herds." He paused. "Is this not so, Cree?"

After a moment, Cree's nasal voice answered shortly, "It is so."

Still watching Cree, Ronan continued, "As you all know, other tribes have other customs than these, and other taboos."

Ronan paused and, reluctantly, Cree nodded. Then Ronan looked slowly around the fire, gathering each man under his power. He said, "Men of Sky God. Have any of you lost your hunting luck because you have killed a female animal?"

"Na."

"Na."

"Never."

"That is what we were saying . . ."

Ronan held up the hand that had been stroking Nigak. Silence fell. He asked next, "Have any of the tribes of the Goddess lost their hunting luck because a man slept with his wife before the hunt?"

The same chorus of negatives rang out.

Crim demanded, "What are you saying, Ronan? Are you saying that none of our tribes follow the right way?"

Ronan smiled faintly. "Na, Crim. What I am saying is that all of our tribes follow the right way."

In the silence, Nigak opened his yellow eyes and peered at the men assembled before him. Finally, Mait said, "I don't understand." A few sympathetic grunts indicated that he was not alone in his bewilderment.

"What I am saying, Mait," Ronan answered, "is that what is important to the gods is not the actual custom, but what is in a man's heart. Some customs we all follow. None of us will let a dog lick the blood of our kill. That would be disrespectful. All of us give thanks to the animal when it falls, asking that we be worthy to share in its life. Is this not so?"

"Sa."

"Sa."

"That is so."

"Then there are different customs. Some of us bury the heart. For us, that is respectful. Some of us burn the heart. For us, that is respectful. What we do does not matter, what matters is what is here," and Ronan knocked his fist against his chest. "It is the spirit of the man that is important to the spirit of the animal." He looked at Mait. "Are you understanding me?" he asked.

"Sa," Mait said. His big brown eyes, so like his sisters', were shining. "I am."

Ronan looked from Mait to Thorn and then around the circle of male faces before him. "We are from different peoples and different tribes," he said. "If we wish to live together, we must understand that there are other ways of doing things, other ways of showing reverence. What is right for Heno to do, because to him it is a way of showing reverence, is not right for Cree. Cree's way is different. All ways are right, if the heart is right.

"The Mother knows this. Sky God knows this. They can see into the heart, and that is what is important to them."

Thorn's puppy came up behind him, pushed his muzzle under Thorn's armpit, and whimpered for attention. Thorn hushed him softly.

Cree was saying, "But the reindeer will not come to us. They are offended."

"This may well be," Ronan said. "Someone in the tribe has perhaps failed to show reverence. Perhaps someone spoke boastfully about his kill. Perhaps someone talked and laughed too loudly while butchering his meat. These things can happen, and the spirit of the reindeer is offended. We must all take great care to be reverent, and they will come back again. They always do."

"Sa," said Dai and Okal and Lemo and Kasar.

"That is so," said Asok and Sim and Mitlik.

"Cree?" Ronan asked. "Heno? Are you understanding me?"

Cree nodded grudgingly. Heno grunted.

"Then let there be no more of these accusations," Ronan said. For the first time a hint of coldness crept into his voice. "It is important that we think of the things that draw us together, not of the things that pull us apart. If there is a man here who cannot bring himself to look with tolerance on the ways of another tribe, then I say now that that man does not belong in the Tribe of the Wolf."

Absolute silence. Heno and Cree were staring intently at their knees. Thorn looked wide-eyed at Ronan. Just as the silence was about to become uncomfortable, Ronan said in a different voice, "We have another matter to discuss today."

All around him Thorn could feel men snapping to attention. Tension thrilled in the air. They had all known in their hearts that Ronan would settle the problem of the hunting luck. It was always like this. The men would quarrel and one tribe would blame another and tempers would flare and they would come to Ronan and he would settle it.

That was how it was for most problems. This matter of the horse calling, however, was something else, and all knew it. This was the first time that an alliance had been made that did not fall along the lines of which tribe a man came from or which god a man worshipped. Some of the men of the tribe had a woman and others did not: that was the crux of this particular problem. It would not be settled easily.

Ronan said, "Hunting is the business of men, and so it is proper for the chief to settle hunting quarrels. The ceremony that has been proposed is not just for the men, however. It is for the women also, and I understand that the women have something to say to the men of the tribe on this matter." He inclined his head toward his wife. "Nel?"

Nel hesitated, then turned to Berta. "I am a newcomer to this tribe," she said with charming diffidence. "It is not yet for me to speak for the women's side."

Berta shook her sleek dark head. "You are the wife of the chief. You have told us you were to be the Chosen One of the Mother. The women of the Wolf feel it is proper that you speak for us."

The other women all nodded, and Beki gave Nel an encouraging smile.

"Very well," Nel said. She folded her hands, rested them upon her crossed ankles, regarded the men before her, and for a moment looked uncannily like Ronan.

How can that be? Thorn thought. But his artist's eye saw the answer almost immediately. The resemblance lay in the tilt of the head, the lift of the chin, in the thin-bridged arrogance of the narrow nose. In that moment, Nel looked like a woman who could rule a tribe.

Nel was speaking. "The women of the tribe have this to say to the men in regard to the ceremony of the horse calling." Her face was grave, almost stern, and she was directing her comments to the unmarried men. "The women say it is a fine ceremony when it is done by the tribes of the plains. It honors the horse; it ensures the fertility of the herds; it gains their cooperation and permission so that hunters can take those that are needed for food and for clothing. It is a fine ceremony."

As Nel was speaking, Thorn could see the single men beginning to perk up. Mitlik, who was from the River People and who had introduced the idea of the horse calling to the Tribe of the Wolf, was grinning.

"However," Nel said, "it seems to the women's side that the men who proposed this ceremony have not taken into consideration the fact that there are no women of the Wolf eligible to participate."

The single men all turned to look at Mitlik. "Why is that?" he demanded indignantly of Nel. "Among my tribe the married women always participate in this ceremony. In fact," he added loudly, "it should please a husband to have his wife join in this rite." Here Mitlik threw a defiant look at the married men, who were glaring at him furiously. "A woman who 'calls the horse' proves to her husband that she seeks his success in hunting," Mitlik stated. "And good hunting leads to a good home, good health, and plenty of food and clothing!" He sat back, and the single men all nodded their vigorous agreement.

Kasar said heatedly, "I have never heard anything so ridiculous . . ."

"Go find your own women and leave ours alone!" said Lemo.

"I have not finished," Nel said, her soft voice somehow managing to make itself heard above the deeper voices of the angry men. Ronan shifted his position slightly, and the men quieted and turned again to Nel.

"Is it not true, Mitlik," Nel asked, "that the women who are with child do not 'call the horse'?"

Once again heads swiveled toward Mitlik. "Is that true?" Okal demanded.

"Well . . ." Mitlik looked uncomfortable. "Sa. I suppose that is true."

"And is it not true also that the women who are yet nursing their babes do not participate?" Nel asked next.

"Dhu," said Dai disgustedly.

Crim was heard to chuckle.

Mitlik was looking distinctly crestfallen. He mumbled, "I never heard of that."

"It is certainly true among the People of the Dawn," Berta snapped. "It is most probably true among the River People as well. You just never noticed."

Mitlik ducked his head.

"There aren't any women left!" Kort said indignantly.

"You are a fool, Mitlik," said Okal.

The married men were grinning at the obvious discomfiture of their rivals.

Nel said, "Yoli and Beki and Yeba are with child. Fara and Berta and Tora and Tabara are nursing children. Eken, in accordance with the traditions of her people, is a maiden, and such a ceremony is not for maidens. This leaves," Nel said gently, "only me."

The men all looked at Ronan.

"I am thinking it is not possible to have a ceremony with only one woman," Nel said.

"That is true," Dai said, hastily averting his eyes from Ronan's face. The rest of the unmarried men signaled their enthusiastic agreement with Dai.

Nel looked at the faces of the single men and bit her lip.

"Why didn't you tell us this before, Berta?" Heno called to his wife. "You let us get into a sweat when all the time you knew you would not participate."

Berta answered sweetly, "I do not recall being asked."

Heno glared. The sweetness of Berta's smile matched her voice.

"*Why* can't a pregnant woman participate in this ceremony?" Dai asked suddenly. "If she can mate with her husband without fear, then why cannot she mate with another man?"

Tora gave him a pitying look. "She would not be mating with another man, but with a stallion. Her baby would be born with hoofs!"

"Sa," Berta agreed. "And nursing mothers cannot take a chance of losing their milk."

The rest of the women nodded their agreement.

Crim's deep, reasonable voice was heard. "This particular issue may have been resolved, but there is yet a problem within the tribe." He was addressing Ronan. "I was not in agreement with the ceremony proposed by the unmarried men," he said. "It is not our way in the tribes of Sky God to share our wives with other men. However, I can understand the thinking of men such as Mitlik and Dai and Okal. They are young, and they have been too long without a woman."

"I understand this too, Crim," Ronan answered. "There is little I can do about it, however. We are not likely to have much success if we try to trade for wives at a Gathering; no father will agree to send his daughter into the outcast Tribe of the Wolf, no matter how high the bride price we offer."

Glum silence greeted this unwelcome, if patently true, observation.

Nel was the one to speak next. "I am not certain of this, because it is not the way of my tribe, but it seems to me from what I see that the girls of Sky God are often given in marriage to men they do not like." A single line creased the smooth skin of her brow, and she turned to Yoli. "Is this not so?"

"Sa." Yoli's voice was bitter. "It is so."

Yoli's story was well known to the tribe, and it was certainly illustrative of Nel's point. Both Yoli and Lemo were from the Tribe of the Fox, where Lemo's father was the chief. Lemo's mother was frail, however, and unable to fulfill the many duties expected of the chief's wife. So the chief had taken Yoli for his second wife in order to keep up his position. Unfortunately, Lemo and Yoli were already in love, but her father, proud of the honor being offered to his daughter, would not listen. Much against her desire, he had married Yoli to Lemo's father.

As the months went by, the two young people had become more and more attached to each other. Yoli was in despair. She hated the embraces of the old chief, but she could not bring herself to wrong him by secretly lying with his son. At last, in utter desperation, Yoli had tried to hang herself. Luckily she had been found while she was yet alive, and then she had been made to confess the cause of her violent action. In response to her confession, Lemo's father had expelled both his son and his wife from the tribe.

"There are many girls who are forced to marry men who are not to their liking," Yoli said now to Nel. "Their fathers don't care. All they are interested in is a good bride price."

"And the older the man, the more likely he is to come up with a good bride price," Beki answered, knowing from bitter experience how important this issue was.

Heno moved restlessly. "There are more important things to do than to sit here and listen to women whimpering," he growled.

"It is you no one wants to listen to," his wife informed him.

"Hold your tongue, woman!" Heno roared.

Berta opened her mouth to reply, but Ronan cut in acidly, "If you have more important things to do, Heno, then you may go and do them." He turned his head. "What are you thinking, Nel? Do you think we could persuade some of these unhappy girls to join the Tribe of the Wolf?"

Nel answered, "Why not?"

"I can name you three girls who would much prefer to marry Dai than the husbands their fathers have picked for them," Beki said promptly.

Dai looked pleased. Kasar scowled. "I did not know you had a fancy for Dai," he said to his wife.

Beki was amused. "I was using Dai as an example, Kasar. Any of our men—Okal or Mitlik or Kort or Altair—are better than the choices of these fathers I speak of."

"This is all very well," Okal said impatiently, "but how do we go about meeting these girls?"

It was Ronan who answered. "At the Spring Gathering. I will take the unmarried men and those of our women who feel able to make the trip."

Beki grinned. "I will talk to the girls from the Tribe of the Leopard."

"And I to those of the Fox," said Yoli.

"And I to those of the Buffalo," said Fara.

"There is little point in our speaking to the women of the Goddess," Tora said. "We marry whom we like."

"The women of the Goddess might be glad of an opportunity to marry with real men," Heno said.

Tora regarded him scornfully. "The women of the Goddess are the only women who bring forth real men," she answered.

Nel once more bit her lip.

Ronan said briskly, "I believe we have resolved the problems we came together to discuss. I have noticed we are growing low on wood. Bror, take the men and bring in a fresh supply." Ronan stood up. "This council is over." As the men and women of the tribe rose to go about their business, Ronan turned to Nel. "You and I, minnow," he said, "are going to look at horses."

PART THREE

THE

HORSEMASTERS

(Two years later)

Chapter Twenty

Fenris, leader of the tribe known to the Kindred as the Horsemasters, sat on the stallion he had named for one of his gods and surveyed the camp spread before him. The women had the cookfires burning, and children prowled from tent to tent in hopes of a stray bit of food. At a little distance up the river from the buffalo-hide tents, the tribe's great horse herd grazed voraciously on the newly burgeoning spring grass.

The day was cold and clear and bright, the scene before him peaceful, but Fenris's brow was furrowed with trouble. The horses had already grazed down their present pasture and would have to be moved again on the morrow. The hunting these last few days had been scarce, and the local tribes long since thoroughly vanquished.

No grass for his horses. No plunder for his restless warriors.

We have been too long in this place, Fenris thought. Winter is finishing, and it is time to move on.

To many chiefs, the prospect of moving so large a group of people and animals would have been daunting in the extreme. It did not daunt Fenris, whose grandfather many years before had collected his people and his herds of short-maned, stocky horses and led them from the freezing open steppes of the north into the rich, temperate river valleys of this southern land.

It was a vagabond life the Horsemasters had led since leaving the steppes, the sort of life attractive to adventurers, to men who were restless and ruthless, wild and brave. Such a people were the men of this tribe, and the chief of them all was their kain, Fenris.

The grass of this river valley was rich and green, Fenris thought now as he surveyed the sunlit scene before him. The River of Gold, the men of the Kindred called it, and the grass it nurtured was more beautiful than gold to the horse herd Fenris and the men of his people held more sacred than they did their own children.

For it was the horse that had made these men what they were: hunters and warriors, fierce and mobile, the nightmare of the peaceful, unmounted tribes over whose lands they so ruthlessly swept. The horse was their chiefest treasure, their greatest wealth, the symbol of their status and their power. They were the Horsemasters, the terror of the world.

The spring grass was growing in the valley of the River of Gold, but in the Valley of the Wolf the snow still lay deep. Ronan, coming into Bror's hut after a day spent outdoors, looked grateful to be met by the warmth of a fire and the cheerful faces of the group of men who were sitting around the hearthplace talking, drinking tea, and chewing on pieces of frozen fish.

Thorn immediately jumped up and went to fetch a bone scraper, saying, "I'll brush your coat for you, Ronan." He met Ronan in the doorway, and the chief stood patiently with his arms extended while Thorn carefully beat the snow out of his reindeerskin tunic. The tribe had long since learned the importance of keeping their clothes as dry as possible, for wet skins became very stiff and had to be rescraped.

When Thorn had finished, he took Ronan's coat and hung it, along with his gloves, on the drying rack that was affixed to the hut's right wall. "What did you find?" Ronan was asking Bror as Thorn returned to his own place by the fire.

Bror replied, "The snow is still very deep in places, but it is possible to get through the pass."

Ronan held out his hands to the warmth of the fire. "Good," he grunted.

Thorn stared at Ronan's face, trying to read the chief's thoughts. Crim, who was sitting on Thorn's left, said, "We need more tea," and busied himself by ladling water into the skull kettle from the large pottery pot that stood close by the fire.

Over the past few years, the Tribe of the Wolf had devised different ways to cope with the bitter winter weather that prevailed at the valley's high altitude. The problem of keeping water available they had solved by cutting blocks of ice from the lake directly after the first freeze. The ice was then piled on trestle tables near the huts, and whenever someone needed water, all he had to do was bring in a block of ice and drop it into the water pot near the fire.

It was killing work, getting the ice out of the lake, but on the whole the tribe had found this to be a much easier way of securing water than the slow and tedious method of collecting and melting snow.

There was silence as everyone watched Crim with an intensity that suggested they had never before seen a man ladle water. The silence at last was broken by a nasal voice that yet bore the distinctive accent of the Goddess-worshipping plains. "I have been wondering, Ronan, why you are so interested in whether or not the pass over the mountain is open," Cree remarked.

Ronan was busy chewing the piece of frozen fish Okal had handed him. Another winter survival trick the tribe had learned during its years in the valley was the value of uncooked frozen fish. About twenty minutes after one had finished it, the fish would begin its warming work, and it would continue to keep one warm for hours. Ronan had been out in the cold for most of the day, and he was chewing now appreciatively. After so many years, he, like the rest of the tribe, had even come to like the taste of it.

Heno answered for his otherwise-engaged chief, his voice faintly belligerent: "You know why he is interested, Cree. He wants to spy once more upon the Horsemasters."

"Of course," Crim said in his calm way. "It will be spring now in the lower altitudes and they will be moving from their winter camp sometime soon. If they follow the River of Gold or the Atata, they will be coming directly into our mountains."

Cree tossed the cold dregs of his tea into the fire, which sizzled when the liquid hit it. He said, looking at Ronan and not at Crim, "I do not see why that should concern us."

Ronan looked thoughtfully at Cree, continued to chew slowly on his fish, and did not reply.

"If the Horsemasters come down the Atata, they will come to the home caves of the tribes of the Squirrel and the Buffalo," explained Crim, who, like Thorn, had been born to the Buffalo tribe.

Kasar said, "If they follow the River of Gold, they will come to the tribes of the Leopard and of the Red Deer." His young jaw was set. "Surely you can see that we have cause, Cree, to be concerned about the movements of these horsemen."

Thorn stared with apprehension at Cree. Over the last three years, the divisions between the men of the Goddess and the men of the Kindred, once so troublesome, had seemed to evaporate. Thorn was perhaps more aware of this change than most, for he had been making a kind of chronicle of tribal life on the walls of a valley cave, and so he had marked the growing sense of comradeship that was by now such a distinguishing feature of the Tribe of the Wolf.

But Thorn had not forgotten that Cree had always been the spokesman for the men of the Goddess, and he waited now in some trepidation for Cree to speak again.

When he did, Cree's voice was gentle, but in the dangerous way that Ronan's could be gentle before he unleashed his temper. Thorn shivered. "It seems to me," Cree said softly, "that the tribes of the Squirrel and the Buffalo and the Leopard and the Red Deer have far more cause to be concerned about the Horsemasters than does the Tribe of the Wolf." He paused to spread his hands in a gesture that encompassed them all. "*We* are in no danger. The horsemen will never find this valley."

The crackling of the fire was the only noise in the hut. Like every other man present, Thorn was well aware that Ronan had made a plea at the last Autumn Gathering for the Kindred chiefs to organize a unified defense against the Horsemasters. Thorn also knew that Ronan's words had fallen on deaf ears.

When Ronan still did not reply, Cree went on. "Surely we have more than done our duty in this matter? If the endangered tribes fail to listen to our warnings, that is their sorrow, not ours."

"Sa," Mitlik agreed. "After your failure at the Autumn Gathering, Ronan, we were certain you would cease to carry on this watch of yours."

Thorn watched as Ronan swallowed the last of his fish. "There is no harm in it," the chief said mildly.

"It takes hunters away from the valley for long periods of time,"

Cree pointed out. "And there is a certain measure of danger involved in all this spying as well."

Heno said hotly, "You are not concerned, Cree, because the tribes of the plain are not yet endangered! We of the Kindred cannot afford to be so disinterested."

Thorn felt his stomach muscles cramp. It was happening again, he thought despairingly; the old division was once more rearing its ugly head. Now Cree was saying, "I think Ronan is right when he says these Horsemasters will come south into the mountains. I think that the tribes of the Kindred are fools not to be preparing to fight to save what is theirs. But I also think that the Tribe of the Wolf has no stake in this fight and that we ought not to involve ourselves in a danger that is not ours."

There was a rustle of movement; then Mitlik spoke again to back up Cree. "It seems to me that the men of the Kindred have forgotten that they are no longer bound to the tribes of their birth." He turned to Heno, demanding, "What concern can it be of yours if the tribe that drove you out is plundered by these Horsemasters?"

For once, Heno's bluster failed him. "It seems senseless, I know . . ." His voice trailed off, and he scowled.

Thorn fixed large, urgent brown eyes on Ronan's face. As if he had heard Thorn's unspoken plea, Ronan finally spoke. "I can understand that the men of the Goddess should feel this way." His voice was quiet. "Indeed, you all have been very patient with what you must regard as my . . . obsession . . . with these Horsemasters."

Cree said, "The tribes of the Kindred have not listened to you, Ronan. You have tried to warn them, but they think they can hide themselves away from these plunderers, can go to earth like the fox and wait for the storm to pass over."

"They cannot," Ronan said.

Cree shrugged.

The water in the kettle began to boil.

"We cannot live in isolation, Cree," Ronan said. "Human life would vanish from the earth if it were not for the fact that people live together in communities." His dark gaze touched face after face around the fire, making each man feel he was being spoken to directly. "It is in my heart that the people of this tribe understand more than most just how vulnerable the solitary individual is," he said.

That is true, Thorn thought with deep emotion.

Asok, another man of the Goddess, said with intense passion, "We have our community, Ronan! It is here in this hut, with the men of the Wolf."

The air in the hut quivered with the power of those words. *The men of the Wolf*, Thorn thought, and looked with something like anguish toward Mait, the friend of his heart. Mait looked gravely back.

It was Kasar who first found the words to answer Asok. "What you say is true, Asok, and, believe me, we men of the Kindred feel as strong a loyalty to this tribe as do the men of the Goddess. But I cannot forget that I have a mother still living in the Tribe of the Leopard. And sisters and brothers as well." Kasar's voice quivered slightly. "I cannot turn my back upon them. It is just not in me to do that."

"I am thinking that is true for all the men of the Kindred," Crim agreed softly.

Thorn thought of his mother. Of Rilik. And bowed his head in agreement.

Some of the water boiled over and steamed on the fire. In silence, Crim lifted the kettle off the fire and dumped in the herbs to steep for tea. Everyone watched him, their faces somber with the recognition that a crisis was upon them.

Bror was the one to drag it out into the open. "Last autumn you asked the tribes of the mountains to join together in defense," he said to Ronan. "Do you plan to ask them again?"

Ronan's face was expressionless, his voice calm. To look at him, Thorn thought, you would never know he was facing the possible disintegration of his tribe. "I do," he replied. "It is true that they did not listen to me in the autumn, but part of the reason was that the chiefs were still angry with the Tribe of the Wolf for luring away some of their girls. If I can bring them news that the Horsemasters are definitely coming south, however, I think they will be forced to listen."

"And if they agree this time?" Bror pursued. "If they do in fact join together to form a defense, then will you expect the Tribe of the Wolf to join with them also?"

Ronan's eyes were brilliant in the light of the fire. "Sa," he said. "I will."

"Even the men of the Goddess?"

Thorn held his breath.

Ronan said, "Even the men of the Goddess."

Cree spoke just one word. "Why?"

Ronan's eyes lifted toward the hole in the roof where the smoke was escaping into the cold clear air of outdoors. When he spoke, his voice was reflective. "In the winter," he said, "when the blizzard comes, we all work together, seeking only the welfare of the tribe. It is the tribe that matters, because only if the tribe survives will the individual members of the tribe survive as well. If a hut is damaged, it is not one man or one family who is responsible to repair it. We all respond together, each forgetting his individual concerns and answering to the common need of the tribe."

Ronan's gaze lowered fractionally. "Is this not so?" he asked.

Nods came from all the men.

The timbre of Ronan's voice changed. "Then understand this. These Horsemasters are like the blizzard. They are the storm that endangers all the people of these mountains. In the face of such a threat, it is no longer possible for a man to say *My tribe* or *My land*." At last Ronan's gaze came to rest upon the men before him. "Do you not see?" he asked them all. "It is *our* world that is threatened. In this, none of us can stand alone."

Thorn felt tears sting behind his eyes, and angrily he blinked them back. Surely, he thought fiercely, surely even Cree would be swayed by such a plea.

He was astonished when Cree shook his head in disagreement. "I am sorry, Ronan," the man of the Goddess said, "but the people of the Kindred tribes are not my people, nor are the mountains beyond the pass my world."

Ronan's left hand moved and was abruptly stilled. His dark eyes watched Cree. How bitter this moment must be for him, Thorn thought. For five long years had Ronan toiled to bring these men of different tribes and different faiths together. Now, just when it seemed that he had succeeded, were they to break apart over the issue of the Horsemasters?

"What I am," Cree went on, "is a man of the Wolf." He looked at Ronan, and his face was very grave. "I have said what I felt had to be said. Now I will tell you this. If it is the decision of my brothers to join in this defense, then I am with you."

Something flashed in Ronan's face, and then he bent his head to peer intently at his trouser leg, apparently concerned with a hair that was clinging to the buckskin.

"I too," said Mitlik.

"And I," said Asok, and Mait, and all the other men of the Goddess.

Thorn was grinning at Mait and Mait was grinning back. Then, like everyone else, the boys looked toward Ronan.

"Dhu," said Ronan, abandoning the phantom hair. In the light of the fire, his skin looked very flushed. His eyes glowed. "It seems we are a wolfpack indeed."

Thorn's throat closed down.

Heno dropped a big hand upon Cree's shoulder. "You are a good man, Cree. We have had our differences, but I have always thought you to be a good man."

Thorn's attention was suddenly arrested. He looked at Heno and Cree and saw a picture.

Ronan said, his voice sounding a trifle breathless, "The first thing we must do is discover in what direction the Horsemasters are going. If they turn back north, or toward the east, then all our plans are unnecessary."

"Do you want me to do the scouting this time?" Bror asked.

Ronan shook his head. "I will go myself, Bror. You and Nel can take charge of the tribe until my return."

Nods all around indicated the general agreement of the men with this arrangement, which had worked satisfactorily before. "The tea is brewed," Crim announced, and Thorn moved to help him fill the cups.

It was an hour later when Ronan finally approached his own hut, the same one he had inhabited two years before when Nel had first come to the valley. He pushed back the skins at the door, ducked in, and was greeted by warmth and brightness, two dogs, one wolf, and his wife.

Nel had been with him all the afternoon, working with the horses, but during the time that he had been in the men's hut she had got the reindeer stew they were to have for dinner heating on the fire. Her own furs were draped on the drying rack, and Ronan went to hang his in the same place.

"The pass is open?" she inquired from where she sat by the fire, surrounded by animals.

"Sa." He balanced his mittens on top of the rack and turned to look at her. "The pass is open."

She nodded. Leir and Sinta, two of last year's puppies, now fully grown, arose from their warm nest near Nel and came with wagging tails to escort Ronan to his own place. Nigak, who was lying with his nose pillowed on Nel's lap, opened his eyes to watch the dogs, then closed them again. Nel had taken the puppies as soon as they were weaned, and Nigak tolerated them.

Ronan sat down.

"When will you go?" Nel asked.

"As soon as I can. I just told the men that I would be leaving Bror and you in charge of the tribe."

Nel nodded again. She and Bror had managed very well last autumn and last spring when Ronan had also left the tribe for a moon in order to spy upon the Horsemasters.

"I wish I could take you, minnow," Ronan was saying now regretfully. "Aside from the fact that I will miss you, it would be good for you to be able to see for yourself how these people manage their horses. But I cannot leave Bror to lead the tribe alone, and he is the only man who can replace me without causing jealousy."

"I understand that, Ronan," Nel said softly.

Ronan stared broodingly into the fire. The two dogs had lain down on either side of him, their white noses propped on their front paws, and they too stared into the fire. Ronan said, "I wonder sometimes if I am deluding myself, Nel, with this watch that I keep on these invaders. We have tamed some horses of our own now, it is true, but ours are a mere handful in comparison to the vast herd kept by the Horsemasters."

"At least you are doing something," Nel pointed out. "The rest of the tribes are just sitting and waiting. Even when you told them at the Autumn Gathering of how close the invaders were, still all the other chiefs could do was hope that the Horsemasters would turn north once more and bother someone else!"

Ronan's expression was grim. "It will not be long now, and we shall all know for certain what it is they are going to do."

Nel reached up to push a loose strand of hair off her forehead. Her movement disturbed Nigak, who raised his head and yawned, his tongue curling over the sharp points and ridges of his teeth. The dogs watched him with respectful fascination.

"Who are you planning to take with you?" Nel asked.

"I am thinking I will take a man from each tribe," Ronan answered slowly. "If the Horsemasters do indeed begin to move south along one of the two rivers, it will be necessary for us to move quickly to organize a defense. If I send a man of their own as messenger, I think the tribes are more likely to listen."

Nigak was treating Leir and Sinta to an unwinking yellow stare. Both dogs dropped their ears a little in submission and glanced anxiously at Nel.

"Nigak," Nel said reprovingly, and the wolf rested his head once more on her lap. She buried her fingers in his ruff.

"Who will you take from the Buffalo tribe?" she asked Ronan.

"Crim." Ronan's voice was muffled, as he was bent over unwrapping the thongs that tied his boots.

"Why do you not take Thorn instead?"

"Thorn?" Ronan's head came up in surprise. "Thorn is just a boy."

"He is older than you were when you were expelled from the Red Deer tribe," Nel pointed out.

Ronan went back to unwrapping his boots. "Thorn is not like me."

"He has an artist's vision," Nel said. "He may see things among the Horsemasters that you have missed."

Ronan snorted with disbelief.

Nel looked with affectionate amusement at his bent black head.

The thongs were untied at last, and Ronan pulled off his boots, flexing his bare feet with obvious relief. Then he began to pull the grass liners out of his boots, so he could dry them before the fire.

Winter boots were a serious thing in the Tribe of the Wolf. Unlike moccasins, which were made from the thin skin of the reindeer's leg, boots were made from the thick skin that was found over the forehead between the antlers. To wear the boots, one lined them first with grass, which the tribe dried and put up in skeins precisely for this purpose. The dried grass kept the feet warm and dry by absorbing the perspiration and passing it through the porous hide so it was evaporated into the cold, dry external air. This was important, as in great cold any moisture left on the skin left it vulnerable to frostbite.

Ronan finished spreading the grass and went to put his boots along the wall near the drying rack, next to Nel's much smaller pair. He picked up his moccasins and came back to the fire. "Why don't you want me to take Crim?" he asked.

"I rely on Crim's level head when you are gone," Nel admitted.

Ronan slid his feet into the moccasins. "I suppose I could take Thorn," he said at last. "His father is a man of some standing in the Buffalo tribe."

There was a pause; then Nel said bitterly, "It was impossible to talk to the chiefs last autumn, Ronan. They none of them would listen to you. Why should it be different this time?"

"They listened," Ronan said. "They just would not believe that they could be in danger. I hope that they were right."

"But you do not think so."

He shook his head. "I do not think so." Then he sniffed. "That stew smells good," he said. "When do we eat?"

At those magic words, Leir and Sinta sat up and barked.

Later that night, Nel lay awake in the dark listening to the sound of the dogs snoring. Ronan's bare shoulder was warm and smooth under her cheek, and their combined body heat made the sleeping skin they shared extremely comfortable. They had not made love earlier, as Nel's moon blood had begun to flow the day before.

Ronan always said he did not mind that they had not yet had a child. In fact, he had said on more than one occasion that perhaps it was for the best, that he did not know what he would do if she were unable to carry on the work that she had undertaken with the horses.

Nel knew there was some truth to his words, but it did not make her feel better about her childlessness.

Every other woman in the tribe had a baby. Only she was barren. Ronan had fathered children before, she knew. Borba's and Cala's sons had both borne unmistakable resemblances to him. But every month her moon blood flowed, and none of the herbs she had brewed and taken had changed that.

The other women would occasionally tell her how fortunate she was to be married to Ronan, who would never put her aside because she was barren. "All can see how much he does love you," Fara had said just yesterday, when she had caught a glimpse of the despair that Nel usually managed to hide.

It was true, Nel thought now, lying safe and cherished within the curve of Ronan's body, he did love her. She was his minnow and he would never do anything to hurt her. Besides, he was so involved just now with the horse training, where he needed her, and with the threat of the potential invasion, that a child simply was not important to him.

She had so much, Nel told herself. It was foolish of her to want more.

But she could not help it. She wanted a baby. She loved her husband. She loved her animals. But with all her heart and soul, she yearned for a baby.

Nel's deepest fear was that she had offended the Mother and her childlessness was her punishment. The Goddess had marked her out to be the next Mistress of the Red Deer, and instead Nel had chosen Ronan. Theirs was not a union that the Mother was likely to bless.

What could she do? Every moon, when her blood flow came, Nel's thoughts traveled along the same familiar track. What could she do to placate the Goddess?

We should go to the sacred cave.

This was the thought that of late had been coming ever more frequently into Nel's mind. If she and Ronan could make the Sacred Marriage together in the Goddess's most holy place, then perhaps the Mother would relent. Then, perhaps, Nel's womb would wake with the life of a child.

Somehow, Nel thought, placing her hand on her flat stomach, somehow she had to get Ronan to the sacred cave.

Chapter Twenty-one

The sun was hot on her head as Nel stood regarding the herd of horses the tribe had penned into the large open space between the cliff, the lake, and a long fence they had built of saplings and tree branches. The horses were all young stallions, taken as yearlings when Impero had driven them forth from the main herd when their dams had dropped a new foal. The three-year-olds were all regularly ridden now by the tribe's men, although the two-year-olds so far had not been ridden by anyone but Nel and Beki and Thorn and Mait, all of whom were lightweight enough for a youngster's back.

The horses saw her and four of them came over to the fence, hopeful of getting a treat. Nel had discovered that most horses loved one in particular of the wild roots that grew in the high mountain forest, and she usually kept a supply on hand to use as bribes and as rewards.

"Sorry, Nettle," she said, showing an empty hand and then patting a pink nose. "Sorry Acorn, Clover, and Nep." The horses snorted and turned away. Nel watched them return to the herd.

These young stallions were dark in color, but if the horses in the main herd were any indication, many of them would turn lighter as they aged. The predominant color in the main herd was gray shading to white, and it was a common sight to see an almost pure white mare with a dark brown foal running by her side.

There was the sound of squeals, and Nel looked toward the cliff wall just as two of the horses reared and struck out at each other with their front hooves. Nel frowned. For about the hundredth time she reflected that mares would be much easier to keep penned up together than stallions were. The Horsemasters rode mares. Ronan said that the only stallion kept by the Horsemasters belonged to their chief.

The problem Nel and the Tribe of the Wolf faced was that if they tried to separate some of the mares out of Impero's herd, the stallion would certainly attack them.

"He has done half our work for us by forcing out the yearling colts," Ronan had said when first they discussed their horse-taming project. "We can drive the colts into the corral and work with them without any fear of Impero trying to liberate them. And if we keep them separated from the main herd, then I do not think that Impero will object to their presence in the valley."

Nel had agreed, and so it had come to pass. In fact, building the corral fence had been much harder work than driving the small band of yearlings into it. Nor had it been difficult for Nel, with her finely tuned instincts, to get close to the animals. As long as she always preserved perfect calm and made no unexpected movements, she had soon been able even to touch them. Nor had the yearlings proved anxious to escape from their confinement, knowing that Impero's bared teeth and lashing heels awaited them on the other side of the fence.

The tribe had watched with fascination as Nel went about the taming of their captured horses. She was infallible when it came to animals, knowing just when a youngster was afraid and when it was merely being cantankerous, when it was necessary to reassure, and when to be stern. The tribe had made nosebands with reins attached, copied from the halters Ronan had seen used by the Horsemasters, and Nel had gotten each yearling accustomed to wearing one.

Then, one momentous day in late fall, shortly before the snow was due to fall, Nel had gotten on the first horse's back. For the experiment she had chosen Sunny, a stocky dark gray youngster with a markedly pleasant disposition. For days she had been accustoming him to her weight, leaning on his furry flank, draping both her arms over his broad back, all the while rewarding him lavishly with treats, and then, finally, Ronan had put his hands about her waist, lifted her high, and plunked her directly onto an agreeable Sunny's back.

It had been surprisingly easy. The colt had stood perfectly still at first, his ears flicking back and forth in surprise. Then he had turned his head to look at her. Nel had patted his neck and talked to him. Then, with little clicking sounds, she urged him on, and the colt had begun to walk. Nel had grasped the long silky mane in one hand and held the rope reins in the other, and the Tribe of the Wolf was horsed.

Of course, it had not always been so easy. Not all the horses were as agreeable as Sunny, and it had taken the tribe some time to learn how to sit on a horse's faster gaits. There was not a one of them who did not have a collection of bruises from falls taken when their mounts had made an unexpected stop or turn. But in this, the second year of their horsekeeping, all the men and women of the tribe could ride. Some were unquestionably better than others, but all could keep their seats on a horse.

There were enough horses to mount all the tribe, not including the next crop of yearlings Impero would drive out when the new foals came this spring.

There were already too many horses for this corral, Nel thought. For the past two winters the tribe had cut the late summer grass from other parts of the valley, dried it, stored it, and fed it to the herd during the winter. It was a tremendous amount of work, and unnecessary if only they could let the horses out of the corral to roam the valley. All they had to do was put a fence in front of the opening to the passage out, and the entire valley would become a corral. But they couldn't do that because of Impero and the mares.

Nel sighed. "Are you worried about Ronan?" Beki asked her, and Nel turned to look at her friend.

Nel shook her head. "In truth, I was wondering where we were going to put the new yearlings."

Beki said, "Perhaps we could drive Impero and the mares out of the valley."

"Perhaps, but if we did that, then we would lose our source of new horses."

"Not if we kept some of the mares," Beki said.

"If we kept some of the mares, the stallions would fight over them." Nel sighed again. "When a stallion sees a mare, he has but one thing on his mind."

"In that they are not so different from the males of humankind," Beki said drily, and both women laughed.

Nel's eyes moved slowly up the cliff, then moved even higher, to where the distant peaks of the Altas towered against the blue sky. "I wonder how they are faring," she said.

Beki's eyes followed Nel's. "I do not have good feelings about what they will find, Nel."

Nel's uplifted face took on an expression that was strangely stern. "Nor do I, Beki." She turned away from the snow-covered peaks. "Nor do I."

Fenris squinted into the sun, watching as the vast train of horses and people wound its way along the river in the direction that he had chosen. His scouts had reported that this river rose in the mountains to the south, that there were many tribes living in these mountains, and that the grazing there was excellent in the spring and summer. Plunder for his men, grazing for his horses: these were the chief conditions sought by the kain of such a tribe as Fenris's, and so south they would go, following this river the local tribes called the River of Gold.

It took less than a day for the tribe to break camp, even a camp that had been home to them for all the winter. The women loaded the tents and household necessities onto sledges, which were harnessed to horses for pulling. The men stacked their treasure onto their packhorses and mounted their steeds. The remainder of the horse herd was driven before them, followed by some of the mounted men, the sledges, then the rest of the mounted men, and finally the women and children on foot. It was a daunting sight, to see the Horsemasters move so large a camp so quickly.

Fenris gazed toward the mountains, and, not for the first time, he contemplated the spinelessness of these people of the south. Life had been too easy for them, the kain thought scornfully. The game here was too plentiful, too easy to hunt; these southern tribes knew nothing of the struggle for life that had toughened his people in the far north. These tribes of the Kindred did nothing but hunt the teeming herds and draw pictures in their caves. Thus far Fenris and his men had swept them away with scarcely a fight.

"Kain," said Surtur, one of his anda, the men who made up his elite fighting circle. Fenris looked and saw that Surtur was pointing to a solitary figure that had separated itself from the slowly moving group of women and children and was standing alone and stationary by the river.

Fenris's thick blond brows drew together.

"Shall I get her?" Surtur asked.

"Na. I will," Fenris said shortly, clapped his heels against his horse's sides and galloped off.

The girl stood still at the water's edge and watched him come, nor did she flinch when he pulled up only inches before her. Instead, she bared her small white teeth at him in a grimace that was not a smile.

"Why have you left the women?" Fenris demanded. His gray eyes, with the white squint lines radiating out from the corners, were dark with temper.

The girl did not seem discomposed by the kain's anger, which would have terrified every other woman and most of the tribe's men. She shrugged. "I do not want to walk," she said.

"You are one of the women, Siguna. You will walk," he said.

She shook her head vehemently, so that the pale silvery hair fanned out around her shoulders. "I said I do not want to walk."

They stared at each other, angry gray eyes into angry gray eyes. "I will tie you to my horse and drag you after me," he said.

"I have been riding all the winter!" she cried passionately. Her fair young skin was flushed with emotion. "I ride as well as any man. You know that! I will not walk."

"Then I will have to drag you."

Her eyes did not waver. He would do it, and she knew it. His men would think well of him for disciplining one of his women in such wise. She set her teeth. "Drag me, then," she said.

A flock of geese rose from the river, honking and calling in the clear, sun-warmed air. Their wings beat between the two humans and the sky.

Fenris's face did not change expression, but of a sudden he reached his big, callused hand down to her. "You may ride with me for a little while," he said. "And then you must walk."

Her face, which had been rigid and shut, flashed open in a brilliant, joyful smile. She reached up her hand, put her foot upon his, and let him pull her onto the horse's back before him. She leaned comfortably against his broad chest and said contentedly, "Thank you, Father."

Thorn watched the big blond man on the brown stallion as he pulled the slim, even fairer young girl onto the horse's back before him. Then the two of them galloped up the valley, with a cloud of other horsemen filling in behind them.

"They can certainly ride," he murmured, knowing from bitter experience just how difficult it was to be so at one with a horse. The big man was holding the girl and guiding his horse with seemingly effortless ease. The girl's hair is the color of moonbeams, he thought.

"Sa, they can ride." It was Ronan who answered. "And, as we feared, they are moving up the River of Gold."

"So they are," said Kasar, his voice very grim. The Tribe of the Leopard, to which he was born, had their dwelling place not far from the intermingling of the Greatfish River with the River of Gold.

"I wish we had come horsed ourselves," Ronan said now. "We could move so much faster!"

"You said yourself it would have been too difficult to get the horses over the Altas in the snow," Kasar replied. "Our horses are young and untried, not like these," and he gestured toward the tribe that was wending its purposeful way along the river.

"We will have to get them over it now," Ronan said. He gestured to his men to retreat within the cover of the forest. "This is what we must do," he resumed when they were once more gathered together. "Kasar, you to go to the Tribe of the Leopard, Thorn to the Tribe of the Buffalo, Mitlik to the Tribe of the Red Deer, Dai to the Tribe of the Squirrel, Heno to the Tribe of the Fox, Okal to the Tribe of the Bear. You are to tell the chiefs and leading men of these tribes to come to the Great Cave at the full of the moon to meet with me there." A nerve flickered along Ronan's lean jaw. "We must unite if these invaders are not to destroy the tribes of the mountains the way they have destroyed the tribes of the plains!"

Grave nods came from the men who were gathered around their chief. "I will return to the Valley of the Wolf and bring the rest of the men and the horses to the Great Cave," Ronan went on. "I am thinking the horses are important; it is they that will put heart into our people and encourage them not to give up."

Again those solemn nods.

"If I am late getting to the Great Cave, you must make the chiefs wait for me."

"Ronan," Mitlik said, "you are sending me to the Tribe of the Red Deer. Do you want me to bring the Mistress?"

In the sudden, tense silence, a squirrel scrambled down the tree beside which they were standing and scurried across the forest floor. "If she wishes to come, then she should come," Ronan replied at last. "If she does not, then you must try to bring some of the men. Speak to Neihle, the Mistress's brother, and to Tyr. They are two who will listen to words of mine."

Mitlik bowed his head.

"Let us go then," Ronan said. "We have no time to waste."

Nel had ridden her favorite horse, a bright copper-colored colt with three white stockings she had named White Foot, toward the narrow southern end of the valley, where the river escaped through a cut in the rampart wall. There was never any ice on the river at this end of the valley, the current moved too rapidly, and here was where the valley animals watered throughout the winter.

Impero and the mares were grazing along the eastern wall when Nel and White Foot came cantering into their vicinity. The cliff wall here was forbiddingly high, its upper part dropping down for hundreds of yards as sheerly as if it had been cut by a knife; but above the floor of the valley it sloped, cracking into fissures and ravines in which were growing clumps of juniper, mountain pine, and alpen rose. There was no snow on these sunny slopes, and the mares and yearlings, intent upon finding forage, paid no attention to Nel and her mount.

Not so the white stallion, who was immediately alarmed by the presence of another male. Impero snorted, dropped his nose, and moved immediately into full gallop, gathering his mares and offspring from their foraging and rounding them up until they formed a tight little band. When they were all securely herded behind him, he trotted out to hurl his defiance at White Foot, raising his head to the heavens and bugling forth a brassy challenge to come forth and do battle.

White Foot was afraid of the stallion, the father and protector who had so inexplicably turned into his implacable enemy. But something in his blood roused at that neighing challenge, and he reared up, snorting, his front hooves pawing the air.

Nel had already twined one hand into the colt's mane for security, and now she used the other to slap him on his shoulder to get his attention. As soon as his front hooves were on the ground, she twisted her own body around, bringing the colt with her; then she drove him with her legs away from the stallion. They galloped along the river toward the extreme southern rim of the valley, not pulling up until they had reached the wall. Then Nel looked around.

Impero was still staring after them, his scarred, muscular white neck raised high, his nostrils distended. Thorn should paint him like that, Nel thought suddenly. He looked magnificent. As she watched, he whirled and plunged straight into the closely bunched herd of mares and yearlings, scattering them and thus giving them his permission to resume their hunt for food. As they broke away and returned to the lower levels of the cliff, the white stallion stood on guard, dividing his attention between his mares and the three-year-old son he perceived as a potential rival for their favors.

Well, thought Nel resignedly, it's pretty clear that I had better give up any ideas of keeping more than one stallion with the mares. If even White Foot wants to fight . . .

White Foot was immune to challenges at the moment, however, for not even Impero's bugle could be heard above the thunder of water as it raced through the ravine in the cliff wall and poured down a sheer two-hundred-foot slide to a great pool of churning white water at the cliff's base outside the valley.

White Foot had grown up with the sound of the waterfall, and it held no fear for him. The young stallion stood quietly under Nel's command, and she patted his neck softly before she turned him and began to go back, this time following the western wall of the valley, where the snow still lay in patches.

Mait met her at the corral with the news that Ronan was back. She left Mait with the task of returning White Foot to the company of his fellows and raced on foot around the lake, moving as fast as she could in her winter boots.

The entire tribe appeared to be gathered in the large open space between the huts and the lake when Nel came racing up. Everyone had turned to look at her, but Nel ignored them all, running like a deer straight into Ronan's arms. They closed around her, lifting her off of her feet.

"You're back," she said breathlessly.

"Sa. I am back." His rough cold cheek was pressed against hers. "You are strangling me, Nel."

Indeed, her arms were clasped so tightly about his neck that she thought she probably was. She never admitted to anyone, and certainly not to him, how terrified she was for him every time he left on one of these expeditions. She loosened her grip a little and leaned her head back so she could look into his face.

He was unshaven and tired-looking, but otherwise she approved of what she saw. She said, "I missed you."

"I missed you too, minnow," he said in her ear and bent to put her back on her feet.

Nel looked around, saw Beki standing there without Kasar, and understood at last that Ronan had returned alone. She waited until she was sure the panic she felt would not show in her voice. Then, she asked, "They are coming south?"

"Sa," Ronan answered her, his voice oddly gentle. "They are coming south."

To Ronan's surprise, and not entirely to his pleasure, all of the tribe's men insisted upon accompanying him to the meeting at the Great Cave.

"You cannot all come," he said immediately, when he realized what was being proposed.

"Why not?" Crim asked.

"We cannot leave the women and children here without any men." His carefully patient voice said that surely they should have been able to see this for themselves.

They were all crammed into Bror's tent, women and children as well as men, and even though no fire was burning, it was hot from so many bodies. The dogs had been sent outside, but the toddlers were crawling busily under everyone's feet. Ronan loosened the thong that tied his shirt at the throat.

"You sent to the Tribe of the Red Deer?" Bror asked.

"Sa."

"We have discussed this while you were gone," Bror said, "and we have decided we cannot send you alone into the hands of your enemies."

Impatience was written clear on Ronan's face. "You are not sending me alone. I will be taking most of the men, as well as the horses. But I cannot take all of the men because of the women and children. There must be someone here to hunt for them."

"Who were you planning to leave in the valley?" It was Cree's nasal voice. "The men of the Goddess?"

"It would seem the reasonable choice," Ronan replied. "By your own admission, you do not have the stake in this fight that we of the Kindred have."

"If you are going to meet with the Tribe of the Red Deer, then you will need your men who worship the Mother behind you," Cree returned.

Ronan's face was beginning to take on what Mait always thought of as its "black look." The chief did not like it when his men tried to overrule him. "Then who have you decided will stay with the women?" Ronan asked in the overly pleasant voice they had all learned to distrust. "You, Bror?"

Bror scowled ferociously and did not reply.

It was Berta who answered the angry chief. "No one will have to stay with the women, Ronan, because the women are coming too."

At that, Ronan's head snapped around. He stared in astonishment at the madonna-calm face of Berta. "You cannot," he said.

"Certainly we can," she replied, not one jot of her serenity ruffled by his glare.

Ronan turned now and looked at Nel. Her face bore the same serene look as Berta's. She met his eyes, but did not speak.

Ina, the two-year-old daughter of Berta and Heno, toddled over and sat on Ronan's foot. "Go with Wonan," she said with satisfaction and gave him a beatific smile.

"The women are determined, Ronan," Crim said with a smile.

"We cannot drag the babies down the Altas!"

"The babies will be easier than this age will be," said Beki ruefully, coming to pick up Berta's daughter. "The babies we can strap on cradleboards to our backs."

For the first time since they had sat down, Nel spoke. "The Horsemasters move their whole tribe," she pointed out gently. "Surely they have women and children too."

Ronan looked from his wife to the faces of the rest of his rebellious followers. Then he thrust his hands into his hair and bent his head so that his face was hidden. They all stared nervously at the long slim fingers that were curved into the thickness of the raven black hair.

Bror drew a determined breath. "We are not trying to undermine your authority or go behind your back," he said. "You are still our chief. That is why we feel that we must come with you."

"I see." Ronan's voice was muffled.

Mait looked anxiously at Nel. She was watching her husband. "Ronan," she said now accusingly. "Stop laughing!"

"Laughing?" said Asok indignantly. "What is funny here?"

Ronan raised his flushed face. "The picture of me, stalking into the Great Cave followed by a train of squawling babies."

"We won't let the babies squawl," Fara promised with a grin.

"That will be a nice change," Crim remarked.

Ronan sobered. "I thank you all. It is nice that you are so concerned for me. But we have never taken these horses out of the valley. I cannot trust them with the children."

"We tried them out while you were gone," Berta volunteered. "They were perfectly fine."

Ronan looked again at Nel. "You took the horses out of the valley?"

"They were very well behaved," she said sedately. "I feel quite confident they will prove to be no trouble."

"Give up," Crim advised him. "We have."

"Go with Wonan!" Ina chanted again, liking the sound of the words.

Once more, Ronan began to laugh. "All right," he said when at last he had caught his breath. "But if I say you must return to the valley, then I will expect to be obeyed. We have no guarantee what the tribes will decide to do."

"That is precisely why we are all going with you," Bror said grimly, to which the rest of the tribe signaled their sober agreement.

Chapter Twenty-two

Of the six tribes Ronan had sent messengers to, three had answered his summons.

From the Tribe of the Leopard came Unwar, the chief; Hamar, the shaman; and eight of the chief nirum.

From the Tribe of the Buffalo came Haras, the chief; Jessl, the shaman; Rilik, Thorn's father; and seven other of the chief nirum.

From the Tribe of the Red Deer came Arika, the Mistress; her brother, Neihle; three matriarchs and five other men. Her daughter, Morna, she had left at home.

Most of these people had been gathered at the cave for several days before Ronan arrived with his following. The chiefs of the Leopard and of the Buffalo, knowing Ronan was coming from the Altas, had been prepared to wait, and they spent the time conferring between themselves. The delegation from the Red Deer arrived only the day before Ronan and the Tribe of the Wolf.

It had been an adventurous journey down the Altas, as the horses had not been quite as placid as Nel had predicted. After the first two days, however, the colts had settled down and proved reasonably obedient.

Never, for as long as he lived, would Thorn forget the moment when the men of the Kindred tribes first saw the Tribe of the Wolf on horseback. He had been standing before the Great Cave with Rilik and Haras, and when the horses rounded the turn and came into sight,

Haras, squinting into the sun, had first mistaken them for a wild herd.

"Horses!" the Buffalo chief cried, with a mixture of alarm and surprise. Then his breath sucked in audibly as he saw the human figures on the horses' backs.

As Thorn watched his tribe approach, fierce pride surged through his heart. Ronan and Nel rode at the tribe's head, Ronan on Cloud, the big gray colt he had tamed himself, and Nel upon White Foot. They rode as well as any of the Horsemasters, those two, Thorn thought: upright and proud, their thighs slanted slightly forward, their knees bent, their lower legs back. Behind them came the rest of the tribe, with some of the men leading packhorses behind them. The dogs ran about between the horses' legs, except for Nigak, who had positioned himself firmly at Ronan's side.

"Dhu!" said Haras. "I cannot believe what I am seeing!"

"Is it possible?" Rilik breathed.

From all around came the sound of running feet as the tribes came racing to see the impossible.

"Men on horses!"

"Not just men—women too!"

"I cannot believe it."

"How did they do it?"

Then, fearfully, a voice asked, "Is it the Horsemasters?"

"Na," came a feminine voice with the accent of the Red Deer. "It is Ronan!"

"Ronan never said aught to us about this," Haras managed to get out at last. He glanced reproachfully at Thorn.

The horses and riders had stopped at a discreet distance from the gawking onlookers.

Thorn's nostrils were flared with pride. "We have been taming horses for two years now," he said to Haras. "This is the first time we have taken them out of the valley."

"You too?" Rilik turned to stare at his son in wonder. "Do you ride too, Thorn?"

"Sa," Thorn replied. "I am one of the first to get on them because I am so light."

Rilik's mouth was open with amazement.

"Stay back everyone!" Thorn called as the crowd began to surge forward. "You will frighten the horses if you get too close."

Everyone took a step backward.

"Father, you and the chiefs may come with me," Thorn said grandly, and he began to walk forward, followed by Rilik, Haras, and Unwar. Arika and Neihle stood a little apart from the others, in the shadow of the enormous tunnel through the hillside that formed the Great Cave.

Ronan flicked his eyes once toward the place where his mother stood before greeting the four men who had joined him. "Thorn," he said. "Rilik." Then, formally, to Unwar and Haras: "I greet the chief of the Leopard and the chief of the Buffalo."

"Arika of the Red Deer is also here," Unwar returned, having seen that glance toward the cave, "but the chiefs of the Squirrel, the Bear, and the Fox declined to come."

"I see," Ronan said expressionlessly.

The chiefs stared with amazement at Cloud, who snorted, rolled his eyes, and danced sideways. Ronan patted his arched neck and the colt quieted.

The chiefs had hastily backed up, nervous around the dancing hooves. "This is astonishing!" Haras said from the safety of his newly gained distance. "You never told us you were riding horses!"

Ronan sat calmly upon his excited colt, replying to their many questions, but all the while Thorn sensed that his real attention was elsewhere, was focused on the red-haired woman who stood with such absolute stillness within the shadow of the cave's opening. Cloud, sensing the tension in his rider, began to swish his tail and trot in place.

"The horses are tired, and so are the children," Nel said to her husband in her soft husky voice. "I am thinking we should get all settled before we talk further."

Ronan looked at her, and for the first time in Thorn's memory, he had the feeling that Ronan didn't know what to do. His face looked strained and taut. Cloud tossed his head up and down, and then he reared. "Get off of him, Ronan," Nel said calmly, and Ronan obediently slid to the ground and once more patted the gray colt's neck. "You said you knew of a fairly enclosed place to pasture the horses," Nel continued, talking to her husband in the same ordinary tone. "Why don't you take the men there, and I will get the women and children into shelter."

Again Ronan nodded. Yet still he remained, irresolute, all of his being taut with his awareness of his mother. Nel said, "Thorn will go with you," and she slid off White Foot and beckoned to Thorn to take the colt's reins. Then she walked over to Ronan.

To Thorn it seemed as if her closeness served to sever the spell that was holding Ronan in thrall. He looked down into his wife's worried eyes and smiled a little crookedly. "All right, minnow," he said. Briefly he touched her cheek with two of his fingers and let out his breath. "I am all right." He said to Thorn, "Come along and we'll pasture the horses."

Nel waited until the two of them had moved off before turning to the chiefs. "You will have to show us where it will be best for our tribe to camp," she said. "We do not know this cave."

"Of course," replied Haras, who was by nature a genial man. "There is plenty of room within the cave itself."

The representatives of the other tribes all watched with awed fascination as the women and children of the Tribe of the Wolf began to stream toward the cave, while the men led the horses away.

"Berta," Nel said as one of the women drew abreast of her, "will you take charge of the camp?"

"Of course." Berta's large brown eyes glanced shrewdly from Nel to the group in the cave's opening. "No need to concern yourself with us, we shall be fine."

Nel gave her a grateful smile and then began to walk toward the group from the Red Deer.

Neihle stood on one side of Arika, and Erek on the other. Tall men both, but the sheer presence generated by the small slender figure between overpowered them. Nel glanced at the rest of the delegation and registered with relief the absence of Morna.

"Mistress," Nel said respectfully and bowed her head.

"Nel," Arika replied. "I did not know if I would see you here."

Nel raised her head. The Mistress looked older, she thought. There was a sprinkle of gray in her hair. Age would never completely dim the beauty of Arika's face, however, nor soften its utter ruthlessness.

"How is Fali?" Nel asked.

"She died shortly after you left us," Arika replied calmly, not at all concerned to soften the blow.

Nel closed her lips to stifle a cry of pain.

It was Arika's turn to ask a question. "Have you married him?"

Nel nodded, her lips still taut.

"Have you a child?"

Nel drew a long breath and gathered all her forces. "Na," she said evenly. "We have not."

Arika frowned.

"I am surprised that you have come yourself to this meeting, Mistress," Nel said next, anxious to steer Arika away from the too-tender subject of children. "It is not usually your way to mingle with those of other tribes."

"It is not a far journey from the home of the Red Deer to the Great Cave," Arika replied. "I thought it would be wise to see for myself what plots Ronan might be spinning." She looked beyond Nel to where the men of the Wolf were leading the horses away. "I must confess, I had not expected this."

"It was Ronan's idea to try to tame our own horses," Nel said.

"I am sure it was," Arika agreed in almost the exact deceptively pleasant voice her son could use. She regarded Nel dispassionately. "Now I understand why he needed you, Nel. You have ever had the Mother's touch with animals."

Nel tasted bitter anger in the back of her throat. Her narrow nostrils quivered. "You have never understood Ronan," she said. "You have not the heart for it."

Arika looked surprised by Nel's reaction, and then she turned thoughtful. "I understand him all too well."

Never had anyone seen Nel's face look so cold. "You understand nothing," she said to the Mistress of the Red Deer, turned her back and walked away.

Ronan pastured the horses in a grassy valley near to the Great Cave and delegated several of the men to remain with them, to keep a watch out for wild animals.

"The Horsemasters keep their horse herd together this way," he explained. "Horses are like men, their instinct is to stay together. The grass is plentiful here and we should have little trouble with strays. However, our horses are accustomed to the valley, where they have few enemies. We must be doubly vigilant to keep them safe."

The men agreed fervently. No one wanted to see the work of the last two years go down under the attack of a lion, or stampede away into the hills.

When Ronan returned with the rest of the men to the Great Cave, Arika was gone from the entrance. Beki and Yoli were there instead, waiting to take them to the place where the women had set up camp and were cooking supper.

The tribes met that night in council at the place in the Great Cave where the chief men usually consulted during a Gathering. It was cold within the tunnel near the river, and they built a fire in the hearthplace and gathered around it, each leader accompanied by his train of followers. Ronan brought to the fire the men who had been with him on his last spying mission as well as Bror, Crim, Berta, Beki, and Nel. Nel sat beside Ronan. Neihle sat beside Arika. The shamans of the Leopard and the Buffalo sat beside their chiefs. The rest of the followers sat slightly behind.

Ronan spoke first, his manner brisk and businesslike. "I thank you for answering so promptly to my call. I had hoped to see the men of the Fox, the Squirrel, and the Bear as well, but I understand they chose not to come."

"Like us, the Tribe of the Squirrel dwells on the Atata," Haras said. "As you reported that the Horsemasters were coming down the River of Gold, they felt they would be safe."

Unwar of the Leopard added, "And the tribes of the Fox and the Bear, which dwell south of us on the River of Gold, feel they also will be out of reach of the invaders."

Ronan's face was somber. "To be frank, I am surprised. I had expected to see the tribes that dwell on the River of Gold before the tribes that dwell on the Atata. Or even the Tribe of the Red Deer." He did not look at Arika when he said this.

Haras said, "Our coming is not a commitment, Ronan. We came to hear you, only." He smiled ruefully. "Thorn was very persuasive that we should at least do that."

Neihle said, "The Tribe of the Red Deer has come to listen also."

"What I have to propose is easily said." Ronan's face went from shadow to clarity in the flickering light of the fire. "I think we should bring all of our tribes into one united group and push these Horsemasters out of our mountains."

"Fight, you mean," Jessl, the shaman of the Buffalo, said in a neutral voice.

Ronan nodded.

Hamer, the bone-thin shaman of the Leopard tribe, directed a glittering look at Ronan. "I am prepared to accept the fact that there is indeed such a tribe as the one you describe. There have been reports of them from other sources. Other *trustworthy* sources," he added with a smile like a knife. "However, I fail to see what we can hope to accomplish by opposing them directly. These horses of yours are impressive"—the shaman's thin nose lifted to indicate that he, for one, was not overwhelmed—"but from what your own man tells us"—a derogatory flapping of his hand here toward Kasar, who had eloped with Beki, the shaman's daughter—"they are only a handful against the large numbers owned by the invaders."

Behind Nel, Beki squeaked with fury. Nel heard Kasar murmur something soothing to her. Ronan's reply to the shaman was quiet and reasonable, "They do not need to know how few our horses are. If we make quick raids upon them, and then withdraw into the hills, how are they to know that we do not have horses in the numbers of their own?"

"That is a good point," Haras said.

"What is to prevent them from spying upon us in the same manner as we have spied upon them?" Jessl asked.

"We know the mountains and they do not," Ronan answered. "We can hide where they cannot find us."

"That is another good point," said Unwar. He thrust forward his chin and demanded of Ronan, "Why do we need to oppose this tribe when we can hide ourselves away and take up what is ours again when this swarm of invaders has gone elsewhere?"

Ronan regarded the chief of the Leopard, a short, bulky man, with flat, forbidding features and heavy-lidded brown eyes. "We can evade them on horseback," Ronan explained, "but not on foot. Other tribes have tried such a strategy and it has not proved successful. For one thing, these Horsemasters are a greedy lot. They do not seek merely the food that they need to live. They seek to take the things that other tribes have, so that they can appear important in each other's eyes. They will not be satisfied with merely using our caves and our huts, with hunting in our forests and our pastures. They will want our furs and our tools, our necklaces and our bracelets." He paused. "They will want our children to serve in their tents, and our women to lie in their sleeping skins. This is what they have exacted from other tribes whose homesites lay in their path, and this is what they will want from us. Trying to hide availed these other tribes nothing. The Horsemasters always found them."

The sound of the river was loud in the sudden quiet. Ronan had not once glanced in the direction of Arika and Neihle, but Nel could feel his awareness of them as they sat quietly, making as yet no attempt to participate in the talk. She thought gratefully that he did not seem as tense as he had been earlier. He could not afford to be distracted now; he needed all his concentration for this discussion.

Haras said determinedly, "It is true that this is the tale we have been hearing at gatherings for the last two years. I will tell you now, Ronan, that before you arrived, Unwar and I, together with our councils of nirum, discussed this situation, and we believe that because of the mountains we are in a better position to keep out of the Horsemaster's way than were the tribes of the plain."

"I do not want them in our mountains at all," Ronan said forcefully. "If we unite, there will be enough of us to drive them out. Why should we run and hide in fear and trembling, like the antelope when it beholds the leopard, when we have it within our power to act like men?"

There was an uncomfortable silence.

"Big words are easily said," Hamer sneered.

Jessl's more conciliatory voice was heard. "Once these Horsemasters realize that the River of Gold is leading them out of the rich river valleys of the north and into high mountains, they may turn back on their own."

"That is so," agreed Unwar, and Haras also nodded his splendid sand-colored head.

"They already know they are coming into mountains," said Arika, and all of the men's eyes jerked around toward her. "The chief of the Wolf has not been the only one keeping watch on this tribe of despoilers," the Mistress said calmly. "We of the Red Deer have also used our eyes." She tilted her head slightly. "Tell them, Tyr," she said.

One of the young men sitting behind Neihle moved forward slightly, so that the firelight illuminated his face. Tyr said, "As the Mistress said, we too have been keeping watch on this tribe. One moon ago their leader sent a group of horsemen to scout the country into which the River of Gold would take them. We watched them. They went all the way to the Greatfish River." His dark blue gaze rested on Unwar. "They saw the homeplace of the Tribe of the Leopard," he said, "and then they returned to their camp."

Unwar's heavy features looked even more forbidding than usual. "You are certain of this?"

"I am certain," Tyr replied.

"Then they are coming," Unwar said bleakly.

"What exactly do you propose we do?" Haras asked Ronan.

Ronan's reply was succinct. "Combine all our tribes together into one great federation under the leadership of one chief and fight them."

Haras slowly shook his head. "I do not know . . ."

For the first time since he had arrived at the cave, Ronan turned to his mother. "You at least must understand, Mistress. You have been watching this tribe as well as I. This is a hunt, and thus far the tribes of the Kindred have been only the prey. I am saying that it is time that we became the hunters."

Arika looked back at her son. "I am thinking you are right," she said mildly. She turned to the two other chiefs. "The Tribe of the Red Deer has no mind to relinquish its home and its hunting grounds to these unbelievers," she said. "The chief of the Wolf says that it is time to be men. I do not know about men, but I do know that there is not a mother alive who would not fight for her children if they were in danger. I have no wish to see my children carried off to serve as slaves in the tents of these barbarians. I will fight."

Ronan's darkly arrogant face blazed suddenly into a smile, fierce and oddly joyful.

Watching him, Nel felt pain stir in her heart. She thought bitterly, But you did not fight for your child, Mistress. You tried to kill him.

The two male chiefs were grimly silent, unable to shame themselves by once more proposing they try to evade the Horsemasters by hiding. It was Jessl, shaman of the Buffalo, who finally asked, "Who is to be the leader of this federation, then?"

Unwar cleared his throat loudly and said, "I will be glad to put myself and my tribe under the command of Haras. The Tribe of the Buffalo is the largest of all the tribes; its chief should have the preference."

Nel heard an ominous rumble rising behind her. Then Bror's deep voice boomed, "There is only one man who should be the leader of this hunt, and that is Ronan!"

Growls of agreement came from all the men of the Wolf. Nel glanced at Ronan's profile; it was perfectly calm.

Haras bent his head in gracious acknowledgment of Bror's words. "Ronan and the men of the Wolf have done good service to us all in bringing the imminence of danger to our attention. Truly, you have erased any disrepute in which your tribe may formally have been held." He smiled genially. "However, this endeavor needs a leader who will command the unequivocal loyalty of all the members of the Federation. If the Tribe of the Red Deer is to be among our number, then I do not see how Ronan can be the leader."

Arika's face was unreadable. Neihle bent his head a little, as if he were disassociating himself from the entire conversation.

Nel was delighted to hear Berta's liquid voice. "There can be no one else to be the leader but Ronan," Berta declared. She leaned a little forward, bringing her round, olive-tinted face into the light of the fire. "Who else here has led a group of people made up of many tribes and many different ways of worship?" Berta asked. "Who else can be trusted not to favor the ways of his own people over the ways of others? I tell you now"—and here Berta's large brown eyes stared unflinchingly at Arika—"Ronan is a man to honor all beliefs and all ways of worship. To my mind, there is no one else so well fitted to lead the Federation we are speaking of tonight."

Berta withdrew, and over her shoulder Nel cast her a quick, grateful glance.

Neihle's head lifted slightly.

Hamer, shaman of the Leopard, said coldly, "I am thinking you forget what brought the Tribe of the Wolf together in the first place." The shaman glared at the group of people gathered behind Ronan. "You are outcasts," he said, his eyes lingering especially upon Kasar and his rebellious daughter, Beki. "There is not a one of you who could return to the tribes to which you were born. You follow Ronan because you have no choice. I suppose you have in some part redeemed yourselves by your warnings to us, but do not be thinking to take the leadership here!"

"I do not believe what I am hearing" came Bror's thunderous growl.

For the first time, Ronan glanced over his shoulder at his followers.

"I thought it was only the chiefs who were to have the speaking here tonight," Unwar said. "It seems as if the chief of the Tribe of the Wolf has little control over his own people."

Ronan said blandly, "But I do not disagree with what they are saying."

"Then you want the leadership?" Haras asked with genuine incredulity.

"I do not think there is anyone else qualified to take it," Ronan replied.

Silence.

"You are truthful, if arrogant," said Hamer with a chill stare.

"Let us look at the realities," Ronan said. "Do you want to know if I will put myself under anyone else's command? I tell you now that I will. This is not an ultimatum—my interest is in securing the safety of these mountains. But, as Berta pointed out, I am the one among us who has the experience of leading a diverse group of people. The Tribe of the Wolf draws its members from many different peoples and many different ways of worship. I have learned how to get people to work together. This is a skill that will be much needed in the days to come."

"You are not the only man in this company with tact and wisdom, Chief of the Wolf," said Jessl gravely.

Nel opened her mouth to speak, but Bror drowned her out, "You forget, all of you, that we have the horses and are the only ones who know how to tame and ride them."

Haras and Unwar jerked upright and glared at Ronan. "Are you saying that if we do not name you to be our leader, you will withhold from us the use of your horses?"

Ronan's slim black brows had snapped together. "Of course not . . ."

Bror overrode him. "I say this, and hear me well," growled Ronan's rebellious second-in-command. "The Tribe of the Wolf has no need to join in this hunt party. Have you thought of that, my friends? We have a place where no invaders will ever find us. Do you think that we have come here because we long to throw ourselves upon the spears of these Horsemasters? Do you think we have come here out of love for you?"

"Why have you come here, then?" Jessl asked.

"We came because of Ronan," Bror answered uncompromisingly. "We came because he is our chief and he asked us to. But it is Ronan who commands our loyalty, not you, and we will not stand still and let you put someone else in the place that should be his."

Nel bowed her head so that the others should not see the tears brimming in her eyes.

"So," said Haras grimly. "You hold a spear to our hearts."

"No spear," Arika said. Astonishingly, there was humor in her voice. "Only horses." She surveyed the ruffled faces of Haras and Unwar. "There is truth in what the men of the Wolf have said. I have been listening to this discussion, and the chiefs of the Leopard and of the Buffalo have made much talk of 'our spies,' and 'our horses.' In fact, the spies and the horses are not ours. They belong to the Tribe of the Wolf."

For the first time, Neihle entered the discussion. "And the Tribe of the Wolf," he said, "belongs to Ronan."

Haras was astonished. "Will you accept him as your leader?" he asked Arika. "You named him an outlaw, a lone wolf, and cast him forth. Your curse was on him, you said. You sent to tell us all that we would take him into our tribes at our peril. And now are you saying that you will set him up as the leader of this federation, to be the chiefest man of all the Kindred in these mountains?"

Arika did not reply immediately, but asked of Ronan, "Why did you bring all your women with you? If you were so certain you were going into danger, why did you not leave them at home?"

Ronan said ruefully, "They wouldn't stay."

"Of course we wouldn't stay" came Berta's serene voice from behind Nel. "We knew very well that you would need us."

Arika said to Haras, "For the duration of this invasion, the Tribe of the Red Deer will accept Ronan as its chief."

Chapter Twenty-three

After the meeting had broken up, Tyr came across the cave to speak to Ronan and Nel. "I did not think I would be seeing you two again under quite such circumstances as these," he said with a grin.

Ronan's dark face lit with an answering smile, and he put his hands upon Tyr's shoulders in the traditional greeting of the Red Deer. "Good work, Tyr. It was your report that finally put an end to all that foolish talk about hiding."

"Not long after I told the Mistress about your tale of the Horse-masters, she decided it would be wise to keep a watch upon them."

"None of the other tribes seems to have felt such a necessity," Ronan said dryly.

Nel said to Tyr, "Where is Morna?"

The smile abruptly left Tyr's face. "At home," he said. "She is with child. I think the Mistress thought her condition a good excuse to keep her separated from Ronan."

Nel felt as if a hand had closed painfully upon her heart. Morna was with child. Nel said nothing, just concentrated on keeping her face expressionless, on not giving herself away.

"With child?" Ronan said. "Does this mean she is back in favor with the Mistress?"

Tyr shrugged. "I can tell you this. The tribe still thinks of Nel."

A small silence fell. "If that is the case," Ronan said at last, "then I am surprised indeed that Arika agreed to accept me as leader."

Tyr made an impatient gesture with his hand. "The Mistress saw what everyone else saw, with the exception of course of Haras and Unwar. You are the only man who can do it. You were the one who thought to set a watch on this tribe. You were the one who had the idea to train your own horses. You are the one who suggested we form a federation. It was obvious to anyone with eyes that you are the only man for the leadership."

There was the sound of a step, and then a deep voice said, "Ronan." It was Neihle.

Nel pushed her own pain to the back of her heart and stepped closer to her husband. She felt his hand upon the nape of her neck.

"Neihle." Ronan's voice was cool, but Nel could feel the tension in his fingers. This was the man who had been the only father he had ever known. In some ways, Neihle's betrayal had wounded him even more deeply than Arika's.

"I am glad to see you, sister's son," Neihle said. He had made a motion as if to lift his hands and then had dropped them to his sides again. There was a shadowy look on his face, and Nel knew that this meeting was not easy for Neihle either.

Ronan merely nodded, his lips taut. Nel helped them both by remarking pleasantly, "We were surprised to find the Tribe of the Red Deer to be our allies."

"Sa." The shadowy look under Neihle's eyes had darkened further when he realized that Ronan was not going to give him the traditional tribal greeting. "We had actually come to the same conclusions as you, although we did not have the imagination to try to tame our own horses."

"It is not going to be a simple fight," Ronan answered, and Nel was relieved to hear that his voice sounded more normal. She had known it would be easier for him to talk if the subject was the Horsemasters. "We will have to use our knowledge of the mountains against them. To try to fight them face-to-face would be disastrous."

"I have seen them," Neihle said grimly. "I agree."

"I will need to know what numbers of men you have, their ages and their skills."

Neihle nodded. "You will have it."

"Who is to lead the Red Deer men, Uncle?" Ronan asked, the *uncle* coming with reassuring naturalness. "Erek?"

"Not Erek," said Neihle. "Me."

The guards on the horses changed, and the camp settled down for the night. The moon was bright when Ronan sought Nel among the women and said, "Come outside for a little." He added sternly to Leir and Sintra, who had leaped up, panting, tails wagging, ready for a walk, "Not you."

Nel fell into step beside him, and they walked along the great echoing tunnel, past the camp of the men of the Leopard, and out into the cold air. The night was as clear as crystal and very still. Nel shivered inside her fur tunic, and Ronan slipped an arm around her shoulders and drew her close against his side. From the distance came the howl of a wolf, a hunting howl, endlessly drawn-out and eerie.

"Where is Nigak?" Nel asked.

"Hunting," he replied. "Perhaps we just heard him."

They began to walk along the river, listening to the dark water as it rushed restlessly through the quiet, moonlit night. Their bodies moved together in complex unity, his longer stride accommodating to hers with the ease of long practice. She could feel the excitement, the coiled tension of the meeting still in him. For certain he was not yet ready to sleep.

"It is almost impossible to get you to myself these days," he complained.

Nel smiled. It was true that they had had no privacy while moving the tribe from the valley.

"Could you believe Arika?" he asked now. "She supported me!"

"Tyr had the right of it," Nel answered. "She saw that there was no hope of success with either Haras or Unwar as chief."

"But to say that she would fight!" He laughed. "She shamed the men."

"Sa," agreed Nel. "She was certainly a surprise."

"You were right to insist that the women had to come to this meeting. It was Berta who swayed the Mistress, not me."

"I said nothing about the women coming," Nel murmured. "It was Berta."

"You said nothing to me," Ronan corrected, his voice full of amusement. "I am certain you said plenty to Berta."

Nel shot him a look. "You think you are so clever."

"Sa. I do." He kicked at a small moon-silvered stone in his path. "However, now that I have brought all of our women and children out of the valley, I must find a safe place to shelter them. Or have you already thought of that?"

Nel said, "It is not only our own women and children, but those of the Leopard and the Red Deer for whom we must find shelter. They cannot be left where they are now, in the path of the Horsemasters."

"I know." All of the amusement had left his voice.

"The Great Cave is large enough," Nel said.

"Why did I think you would say that?"

"Because you were thinking of the Great Cave too," she retorted.

He laughed, put his hands on both of her shoulders, and swung her around to face him. They were standing now at a little height above the roaring river. "We can see into each other's minds, minnow," he said, bent his head, and kissed her.

Nel pressed against him, her arms sliding around his waist to hold him tight. "I have missed this," he murmured huskily, his lips moving to her temples and then to her hair.

"Ronan," Nel said. "I am afraid."

Still holding her, he backed up a few steps so he could lean his shoulders against a tree. "So am I," he answered soberly.

Nel buried her face in his shoulder and knew that they were speaking of different things. He feared for the tribes; she feared for him.

"These Horsemasters," he was going on, "they make everything I once thought so important seem trivial. When I was cast out of the Tribe of the Red Deer, all I wanted was revenge. I vowed that I would show Arika. I determined that I would be exactly what she thought I was, that I would take the tribe away from her. Now"—Nel felt his shoulder move in a shrug under her cheek—"when the survival of us all is at stake, I see such thoughts for what they were. Small."

The reindeer fur under Nel's cheek was rough and cold, but the arms that held her were warm and strong. She asked, more easily than she had ever thought possible, "Was that why you married me, Ronan? Because through me you hoped to gain control of the Red Deer?"

She felt him stiffen. "Is that what you think?"

She said honestly, "I have always wondered why you stayed away so long."

"Minnow, I don't know why." She shivered and he held her away from him, fumbling for a moment with the front of his tunic until he got it open. Then he drew her against him once more, folding his tunic around the two of them. "Better?" he asked.

She snuggled close. His buckskins were beautifully warm. He was beautifully warm. "Sa," she said.

"I think I did not want to find you changed," he said musingly. "I think I was afraid that a grown-up Nel would no longer be Nel."

Nel tilted her head until her lips found the smooth bare skin of his throat. She tightened her arms about his waist.

He said with a breathless laugh, "If you had not agreed to come away with me, I would have kidnapped you, the way the chief of the Horse kidnapped Alin all those years ago."

"Would you?" Nel murmured. In answer, he bent his head and once more sought her mouth.

A little while later he said huskily, "We can't. It is too cold for you out here."

"Mmm? You were not thinking that way when you made the poor dogs stay home."

He snorted with amusement. "Did I not say you could see into my mind?" He straightened away from the tree. "Let us do this—you keep your tunic on, and I will spread mine on the ground for us."

"All right," Nel said.

The moon watched with pale, detached serenity as he drew her down to lie on the fur-softened earth. Nel could feel the rhythm of his lifeblood beating in his kisses, and she answered with a wildness born of her earlier fear, rejoicing fiercely in the feel of him there within her grasp, so strong, so potent, so filled with life.

The tension and the triumph of the meeting in the cave had awakened Ronan's blood, and now Nel's response ignited the fire of pure desire. He felt he would go mad if he could not have her. She was reaching for him, helping him. He drove, they were together, and the moonlit world dissolved into the oneness of love.

"This is how these invaders fight," Ronan said. "First they gallop their horses into the camp of their victims, spreading fear and confusion. Then they dismount and use their spears on the men, overwhelming the now-scattered defense with their superior numbers and organization.

When all of the men are dead, they collect the women and children, and their chief gives them out to his followers."

Horrified murmurs came from Unwar and Haras. Arika merely nodded, but she looked very pale. The four chiefs, with their seconds-in-command, had gathered in the early morning air to discuss their course of action.

"I think it is clear, then, that in order to turn back these invaders we must show them that we are as good fighters as they are and that they will gain nothing of value here in these mountains," Ronan said. Grim nods came from all the others around the fire.

"I think we should send once more to the tribes on the Atata," Haras said. "The more men who join with us, the better chance we will have."

"I agree," Ronan said. "And I also think that it would be more effective if some men of the Leopard and the Red Deer went as messengers this time."

Unwar turned his heavy-lidded eyes toward Arika and said, "That can be done easily enough."

Arika nodded agreement.

"The next thing we must do," Ronan continued, "is to secure the safety of those of our people who cannot fight: the women, the children, and the old."

"They can shelter at the caves of the Buffalo," Haras said. "If the Horsemasters are coming down the River of Gold, then the territory of the Buffalo will be safe."

"That is a generous offer," Ronan said gravely. "In fact, under the circumstances, it is generous of the Tribe of the Buffalo to be joining with us at all."

Haras lifted his head. "From what I am hearing about the Horsemasters, Ronan, no tribe can count itself safe from them."

Jessl, the shaman, grunted his agreement. "The tribe spoke of this last night." He added proudly, "We can do no more than the Tribe of the Wolf, who are as safely situated as we, and who have chosen to fight."

Ronan gave both of the Buffalo men a look of intense approval, and Haras and Jessl sat a notch taller.

Nel said, "I do not like the idea of leaving our most vulnerable members so defenseless. What if the Horsemasters should decide to send a party of men down the Atata? If all of our fighters are on this side of the pass, there will be no one to protect the women and children except the old men."

Haras rumbled something indistinguishable, and Arika said crisply, "I agree with Nel. Let the nonfighters shelter here at the Great Cave under the protection of the fighting force. If it looks as if the cave is endangered, we can move them."

"The women and children of the Buffalo also?" Haras asked.

"Unless you feel comfortable leaving them at home," Ronan replied. Haras grunted.

"First, then," Ronan said, "we send for all the people of our tribes to gather here at the Great Cave, and we separate out those who can fight from those who cannot."

"Unless we get reinforcements from the other tribes, the number of their men will still be considerably greater than the number of ours," said Neihle.

"You may count on the women of the Red Deer to fight with the men," Arika remarked.

"*What!*" cried Unwar and Haras together.

Arika looked faintly amused. "Not the mothers of young children, of course," she went on, "but our young initiated girls, and those of our women whose children are older. They will be glad to fight." Arika's coldly beautiful face lit with a smile, and for the first time ever Nel saw in the Mistress's face a resemblance to her son. "The women of the Red Deer can handle their weapons," she informed her male counterparts with great satisfaction.

"I have hunted enough times with the girls of the Red Deer to know that that is true," Ronan agreed, his face studiously grave.

"The women of the Wolf can handle their weapons also," Nel put in loyally.

"All of your women appear to be either bearing or nursing children," Arika pointed out. Her voice was calm. "Except you, of course, Nel."

Nel froze still as a deer who is trying to hide its presence from a predator. Ronan did not look at her, but he lifted his hand to give a gentle, comforting tug on her braid. He said to the still-horrified chiefs, "You need not ask your women to fight if you do not choose to."

"Certainly not!" Unwar bristled.

"Our women are not like yours," Haras said to Arika with great courtesy.

"All women are the same," Arika remarked. "It is the chief who makes the difference."

Unwar made a gobbling sound, and Haras frowned into his splendid beard.

"Once we have the tribes assembled," Ronan said calmly, "we will begin to make arrows. Many many arrows. Even the women and the old can help with that."

"Sa." Haras surfaced from his beard. "Arrows."

Hamer, shaman of the Leopard, said, "Arrows are not so deadly as a spear."

"That is true," Ronan replied. "But neither are they so deadly for the user."

"Sa. Sa. That is so." Nods came from all around.

"We cannot afford to lose our own fighters," Neihle said. "If we can hurt the enemy, and not be hurt ourselves, then that is a good strategy. We will make arrows."

"How much time do you think that we have, Ronan?" Jessl asked abruptly.

"I cannot say for certain," Ronan replied. "There are good pastures in the beginning foothills of the mountains, and I hope that the grass there will stop them for a while. They are ever looking for good grazing for their horses."

"Those horses," Neihle said grimly. "They are what has thrown the tribes to the north into such panic. If we only could get rid of the horses!"

"I am hoping to get rid of some of them," Ronan said.

Six pairs of eyes stared at him.

"How?" Arika demanded.

"If our own horsemen ride in amongst their herd and frighten them into a stampede, chances are that the Horsemasters will not recover them all."

Silence fell while all digested this suggestion. Then Neihle said with a smile, "I am thinking that we chose the right leader for this federation."

Even Unwar mumbled his agreement.

Chapter Twenty-four

T he track along the River of Gold wound its way southward, rising and falling, rising and falling, and the thin line of once-distant mountains came ever closer to the advancing Horse-masters. Fenris ordered a halt within the foothills, in a place of soft hills and grassy meadows, and tents were pitched and horses turned out to graze.

The invaders had taken their time since leaving winter quarters, moving at a leisurely pace down the river. Fenris, surveying his present location with satisfaction, decided they would camp in this place until the grazing gave out, and he would send parties of horsemen out to investigate the local tribes.

After he had watched the horse herd turned out, and assigned the guards, Fenris, with Surtur at his side and his other anda following, headed toward the large tent that housed him and his family. He was hungry. The women had been busy gathering plants and berries and digging up roots along the river, and the hunters had come in with a few antelope they had speared. Supper should be ready.

The smell of cooking greeted the kain as he pushed open the flap of his tent, and Fenris saw the big musk ox skull pot simmering on the cookfire. The other tents of the camp were small, housing only a few people, but the tent of the kain was very large, with many skins sewn together and stretched upon long saplings, which the tribe transported by sledge. This tent was the center of the tribe, the hearthplace not only of Fenris but also of his anda, the chief among his men.

"Teala," Fenris roared to his wife as he came in the door, "I am hungry!"

"Sit you down, then, and eat." Teala came forward from the group of household women and gestured him toward the pot. Then she went to collect the bone cups the tribe used to hold their food.

The rest of the anda filed in after Fenris, took their cups from Teala, and dipped them into the pot. Fenris's two eldest sons came into the tent and joined the men. The dogs milled around the tent door, growling and snapping, waiting for their turn. The women sat in their places at the left side of the fire, waiting also for theirs. The children huddled along the edges of the tent, their big hungry eyes fixed on the men, hoping there would be enough left for them.

The men ate in relative silence, dipping their cups again and again into the pot and slurping out the stew until they were filled. Then they handed the cups to the women, who scooped out what was left and divided it among the children and themselves. The bones were tossed to the dogs.

While the women ate, the men talked. Fenris sat in the midst of them, his sons on one side of him, Surtur on the other, listening to the familiar stories about hunting and horses, and watching Siguna. He knew his men thought he was mad to give the girl so much freedom. Bragi, one of the best of the young warriors, wanted her to wife, and Fenris knew it would be a wise match for him to make. Bragi was worth binding to him by ties of kinship. But still Fenris hesitated. Siguna did not like Bragi.

Even Teala thought the girl was too forward. But then Teala had always been jealous of Siguna's mother. Fenris suspected his wife had been secretly glad when Embla had died bearing her second babe. Teala had never seemed to mind the other women who entered her husband's tent; they were captives, after all, and beneath her. But Embla had been one of the tribe . . . and she had been beautiful. Siguna looked like her.

Fenris had been fond of Embla, but he knew that was not the reason he had such a soft place in his heart for Siguna. Siguna was not like her mother. Siguna was like him. It was a thousand pities she had not been born a boy.

He yawned. Outside the sky was growing dark. This time of year the days were long; by the end of them he was weary. Surtur saw his kain's yawn and said, "It is time to be going to our sleeping places."

Fenris nodded and watched as his anda left to go to their own tents and their own women. His sons left also, going to sleep with the other young men under the stars. Within the kain's tent, one of the women began to tend to the fire, while the others settled the small children for the night. Idly Fenris let his eye run among his women, thinking of the coming night. His eyes lit on Kara and stopped.

Kara was from one of the tribes he had conquered last autumn. She was very beautiful, with lustrous black hair and huge dark eyes. He had left her alone over the winter, giving her a chance to get over her grieving. Then, one moon ago, he had taken her to his bed.

The kain had never been a man who liked thrusting himself into dry, stiff-bodied women. He liked them warm, and moist, and receptive, and over the years he had learned the skill of making them so. Little Kara had been well worth waiting for.

"Kara," he said now, and pointed to the place beside him. He saw Teala frown as the black-haired girl rose and slowly crossed the floor. He had chosen Kara too frequently of late to please his wife.

Fenris shrugged. Kara knelt beside him, and he turned to look into the big, dark eyes that were so different from those of his own light-eyed people. He was in a mellow mood, a mood to woo. He grinned at her and said in her ear, "It will be good tonight, little deer. I will make it very good."

He saw with satisfaction how the color rose in her cheeks. He sat watching calmly as the rest of his household settled down, then lay down himself, his arm reaching out for the girl at his side.

Thorn and Mait, together with a small group of men from the Tribe of the Wolf, lay on their stomachs along the rim of trees at the edge of the forest and watched the Horsemasters' camp. Their own horses were securely tied at a little distance behind them, so as not to be either seen or heard by the men upon whom they were spying.

For the last two days, Thorn's eye had been trained upon the slim, silver-haired girl who came and went so quietly about the chief's tent, fetching wood and water and helping to watch over the children. The other women did their work in company with one another, but not this girl. She worked alone. Thorn would have thought she was one of the captive women if she had not been so fair.

She was alone now, heading toward the river with a basket in her hands. As he watched she reached the riverbank, which was steep, climbed down to the water's edge, and began to search among the grasses growing there for those that were palatable. Next, Thorn saw a figure detach itself from the horses that were picketed near the camp and follow the girl toward the river. The man scrambled down the bank, which hid both him and the girl from the view of the camp although not from the view of Thorn, whose spying post was on higher ground.

The girl whirled around when she heard the man coming; then she tossed her head and once more turned her back. As Thorn watched, the man reached for her arm and pulled her toward him, his other hand grabbing at her breast. He tried to throw her to the ground, but she struck at him with her free hand, raking her nails along his cheek. He let go of her for a moment, to clap his hand to his face, and she was off, scrambling up the bank and running like a deer for the safety of the camp. Her basket lay disregarded by the river's edge.

"A gentle suitor," said Kasar disgustedly.

"I am thinking they look to be settling in here for a while," Heno remarked. "The hunting party has been gone for two days now; they are looking for more meat than just this night's supper."

"That is so," said Mait. "And the women unloaded all the sledges."

"It galls me to see so many women of the Kindred toiling under the yoke of these murderers," Kasar said, his young face very grim.

"We should send them Berta," her husband said gloomily. "She would set them to rights in no time."

The rest of the men laughed delightedly.

"Heno, you know the greatest pleasure of your life lies in your battles with Berta," Kasar said.

Heno gave an unwilling grin.

Thorn had not taken his eyes from the silver-haired girl. "Who is she, do you think?" he asked.

"Who is who?"

Thorn glanced at Mait as if he must be mad. "The girl with the hair like moonbeams."

"Ah . . . ," said Kasar. "The girl with the hair like moonbeams." He chuckled. "It sounds to me as if our Thorn is in love."

The hot color flooded into Thorn's face. "It is not so!"

"Draw her picture for us, Thorn," Heno suggested.

"I only wondered who she was!"

"There are many many women in that camp," Kasar pointed out, "yet she is the one you are interested in."

"Leave him alone," Mait said loyally. He turned to Thorn. "She lives in their chief's tent, Thorn," he said with regret. "She is probably one of his women."

"I don't think so," Thorn replied. "That would-be ravisher would never have tried to touch her if she had belonged to the chief."

"That is true," Heno said. "It is clear that this chief is not a one that any of them wants to cross."

Silence fell as the men went back to watching the camp. A group of men came riding in, dragging three dead buffalo on sledges.

"Buffalo!" said Mait with reverence. "I had not realized there were buffalo in this area."

Under the fascinated eyes of the men of the Wolf, the huge carcasses were dumped in the middle of the camp. Women came running, and after a short period, during which the buffalo were obviously being admired, the men were led with ceremony into their tents and presumably attended to by their wives. Other women took the horses to rub them down and lead them off to water. The rest of the women began to work on the buffalo carcasses.

"The women butcher the meat in this tribe!" said Heno in surprise.

"Now there's another job for Berta," Kasar murmured wickedly.

Heno shot him a look from under lowered brows. "Suggest that to her, and she'll butcher *you*."

Mait gave a sharp crack of laughter.

The men of the Wolf went back to their watching. After the carcasses were butchered, a few women took the skins and pegged them out on the ground for scraping. The hides had to be scraped clean of adhering fat and tissue while they were still warm or they became so stiff they were difficult to tan. The scraping of skins was a woman's job in every tribe the men of the Wolf knew of, and the sight of women on their hands and knees working over a hide was familiar. There had been work on hides going on all during the time the men had watched the camp, and the tools the women worked with had looked familiar also: the scraper, which in this tribe was a sharp flat oval stone used with both hands to clean the inner surface of the hide; the flesher made of antler and flint, which was used to plane the hide to just the right thinness; the bone, to abrade the surface of the skin so it would accept the fat and mixture of brains and liver used to tan it; and the shoulder blade, used to soften the hide when it was finished.

While one group of women worked on the initial scraping of the hides, another group processed the meat, cutting much of it into strips to dry in the sun.

There was no sign of the men, who were presumably napping after their great exertions on the hunting grounds.

"I am beginning to think there are some things about this tribe that I like," said Heno.

Mait snorted.

Kasar said, "I am thinking we should watch for another day, and then two of us can return to Ronan and make a report. Do you agree, Heno?"

"Sa," said Heno. "Two to return now and two to return when the Horsemasters begin to move again."

"I will stay," said Thorn quickly.

"That is generous of you, Thorn," Kasar said with a grin.

"I will stay with Thorn," Mait offered.

Heno shook his head. "I do not think it is a good idea to leave two cubs here alone. Either Kasar or I had better stay with Thorn."

Mait scowled. "I am not a child anymore, Heno!"

There was a silence as Heno regarded the face of his wife's brother. "I suppose that is so," he said at last. "I think always of you as the small boy Berta was so frantic about when first I found you. But you are right. You are not that small boy any longer. All right, Thorn and Mait will stay."

The two boys grinned at each other.

"Thank you, Heno," Mait said, and Heno scowled and grunted and fooled no one.

"I have permission from my father to take one of the horses to search in the forest for herbs," Siguna said haughtily to the warrior in charge of the kain's personal horses, which did not run with the rest of the herd but were kept close to the camp, in a roped-in corral.

The two on horse watch were young, friends of her eldest brother, and they looked at her with open admiration.

"Which horse, Siguna?" the one named Skyr asked.

"Buttercup," she answered, pointing to a yellowish mare.

"I will catch her for you," Skyr said.

Siguna watched in silence as Skyr went up to Buttercup with the halter in his hands and slipped it over her nose. He led her out of the corral and asked Siguna, "Shall I put you up?"

Siguna gave him a scornful look, bent her knees, leaped high, and flung her leg over the mare's back. She picked up the reins, clicked to the horse, and, without a backward look, trotted off.

She went for quite a distance, winding her way along a deer track, feeling happier now that she was away from the camp and Teala's incessant scolding. At last she dismounted in a clearing, where there was some grass for Buttercup, and resigned herself to looking for herbs. Fenris would be angry when he learned she had lied to the horse guards, and it would go better for her if she actually did come back with some herbs. Siguna picketed Buttercup by means of a large rock and began to move toward the forest.

Close by, a stallion screamed. Siguna's heart jerked, then began to pound as she whirled to retrace her steps toward Buttercup. There was the sound of crashing branches within the forest, and the stallion screamed again. Then came the sound of hooves.

Siguna reached Buttercup and grabbed her halter. The mare was pulling on her halter and trembling all over.

The drumming hooves were coming closer, and suddenly, to Siguna's utter astonishment, there erupted into the clearing a dark gray horse with a boy on its back. The stallion came to a sliding halt and stared at the mare; the boy, who looked like a startled fawn, stared at Siguna.

"Dhu," the boy said.

The stallion snorted and pawed the ground. The boy patted his arched neck and continued to look at Siguna. "Can you understand what I am saying?" he asked her slowly.

Siguna, who had learned more of the language of her father's captives than anyone else among the Horsemasters, did understand him. She nodded.

"I think, if I let him come up to her and sniff her, it will be all right," the boy said. "He is still only a colt; he probably won't try to do anything."

"I understand you," Siguna answered carefully, "but get off of him first."

The boy slid off his horse's back, murmuring to him all the while. Then, holding the reins tightly, he walked the stallion up to Buttercup. The two began an intensive smelling exchange, accompanied with squeals and little jumps. The boy and girl held their horse's reins and made their own agile leaps to keep out of the way of the excited equine couple. After a short while, however, both horses decided the patches of grass in the clearing looked inviting and lowered their heads to graze side by side. Siguna turned to the boy.

He was only a little older than she, she saw, with floppy brown hair and long-lashed brown eyes. Once again he gave her the impression of a fawn. "You are riding a horse," she said flatly, voicing what was to her the most amazing thing about this whole encounter.

His large eyes grew wary. "Sa," he said. "You speak my language very well."

"I have known some of your people," she replied guardedly.

They looked at each other again.

"Do all of the people in these mountains ride horses?" Siguna asked slowly.

The boy's face was very grave. He did not reply.

"What are you doing here alone?" she asked next.

"I might ask you the same question," he replied.

"I do not understand."

"What are *you* doing here alone?"

"I am gathering herbs," she said.

"You have come a long way from your camp just to gather herbs."

Her eyes narrowed with suspicion. "How do you know where my camp is?"

"I have seen it."

Suddenly, she understood. "You have been watching us, haven't you?" she accused him. "Spying on us?"

His narrow nostrils flared. "Your people have scarcely shown themselves to be friends of my people."

"*Thorn*," called a voice from within the forest.

"Here, Mait!" the boy called back. "Come carefully, there is a mare."

Siguna and the boy stood in silence and listened to the sound of another horse approaching. Acorn raised his head and neighed shrilly to his friend.

"Is it another stallion?" Siguna asked.

"Sa. Another three-year-old. Perhaps it will be all right."

A second boy and horse erupted into the clearing, and things went as before. When all three horses had once more settled down to grazing, Siguna surveyed the boy called Mait. He was darker than the one named Thorn, with very dark brown hair and eyes. His olive-toned cheeks were smooth and beardless.

"What are we going to do about her?" Mait was asking Thorn. "If we send her back to her camp, she will tell them that we have horses."

"I have been thinking of that," Thorn said.

It was the strangest thing, Siguna thought, but she felt no fear. She should be afraid. Even smooth-skinned boys in her tribe were perfectly capable of murdering a girl who got in the way of their plans. But, for some reason, she did not think these boys would hurt her.

"We have seen you come and go about the chief's tent," the one named Thorn said to her. "Who are you?"

"I am his daughter," she answered proudly. Her chin lifted. "My name is Siguna."

There was the faintest glimmer of what looked like relief on Thorn's face. Siguna wondered why.

"I am afraid, Siguna," he said to her, speaking slowly so she would be sure to understand, "that you are going to have to come with us. We won't hurt you, but we cannot set you free to warn your people."

"Perhaps you would promise us to say nothing?" Mait asked hopefully.

Siguna shook her head. "I would never betray my father."

Mait sighed. "I suppose not." He pulled at his lower lip and muttered to Thorn, "What is Ronan going to say when we come in with the Horsemaster chief's daughter?"

"I don't think he will be happy. But he will be even less happy if we let her give us away."

"True. But won't her tribe miss her and come looking for her?"

"This is what we will do," Thorn said. "We will send the mare back with her reins ripped. They will think Siguna has had an accident in the forest. They will look for her, of course, but when they cannot find her, they will assume that she is dead."

Mait nodded solemnly.

"We will have to be very careful to cover the way of our going."

Again Mait nodded. Siguna's crystal gray eyes widened as he added, "We can put her on one of our horses and take turns walking."

"Sa," said the one named Thorn, evidently finding nothing odd in the prospect of walking while a woman rode. "I know we were supposed to remain here until the Horsemasters moved again, but I am thinking the situation has changed."

Siguna, who had followed most of this conversation, realized with growing foreboding that the surveillance on her people had been more or less constant.

"Where are you taking me?" she demanded.

"We are taking you to our own camp," Thorn replied, "and to our own chief."

At those words, and for the first time in this very odd encounter, Siguna was afraid. She assumed the icy expression she always wore to mask her fear and asked, "He will make me one of his women?"

The boys looked horrified. "Of course not!" Thorn said.

"In our tribe, a man has only one woman," Mait explained kindly, "and Ronan is married to Nel. You will be no man's woman, Siguna. It is simply that we wish to keep the fact that we have horses a secret, so we cannot send you back to your father."

"What will you do with me, then?" Siguna asked, truly mystified.

"That will be for Ronan to say" came Mait's reply. He turned to Thorn. "We had better not delay."

"That is so," Thorn said. He took the mare's reins from Siguna and led her apart from the two colts. Then he slashed the braided leather rein with his knife, so it trailed in the dirt, and slapped the mare on her flank to send her on her way. At first she resisted going, particularly when Acorn raised his head and called after her. But Thorn picked up some stones and chased her a little distance along the deer track. When he returned to the clearing, Siguna was sitting on Acorn, with Mait on Frost holding her reins.

Mait grinned. "You can walk first."

Thorn made a face. "Come on," he said. "Let's go."

Chapter Twenty-five

To Siguna's utter stupefaction, the boys let her ride the whole way. It never once seemed to occur to either Thorn or Mait to make her walk. She did not understand it.

She could understand the way they talked about their chief. They were afraid of him, but even more than that, they wanted him to think well of them. That attitude made perfect sense to Siguna; it was the way her father's men regarded him. It was the boys' behavior toward her that she found so odd.

Her first sight of the Great Cave was reassuring. The massive tunnel was impressive, but the large group of people gathered together in the bright sunlight at the tunnel's entrance seemed to be comprised mainly of women and children. It was not until later, when Siguna got a chance to see the arrows that the women were working on so industriously, that her initial complacency died.

All the heads lifted when Siguna and the boys came around the turn and into sight of the cave. Thorn halted the horses at a little distance from the women, and Siguna sat proudly upright and watched warily as a slim, long-legged girl detached herself from the group and approached, two wolflike dogs following at her heels.

"Greetings, Nel," Thorn said gravely when the girl had reached them. "I am glad you are here. We have a little problem."

"So I see," the girl called Nel replied, lifting long green eyes to survey Siguna. "The Horsemasters are on the move again?"

"Na." It was Mait who answered as Thorn slid down from Acorn's back. "But we met this girl in the forest by accident, and she saw us riding the horses. We did not think Ronan would want her to return to her people bearing that particular news."

"She is the daughter of their chief," Thorn put in, flipping Acorn's reins over his head and leading the colt a little forward.

"Dhu," said the girl called Nel. One of the dogs pushed up beside her and nudged her hand with his head. Absently, Nel began to stroke his forehead. The other dog whined, and Mait snapped his fingers. The dog trotted over to Mait, tail wagging, to have its head scratched.

Siguna watched the dogs with wary amazement. The dogs belonging to her tribe were not the sort you patted on the head. In fact, since childhood Siguna had borne a scar on her calf that served her as an eloquent reminder of the ferocity of dogs. She had been only a small girl when the incident had happened, but she remembered well that if her father had not been nearby to pull the dog off her, she would have had far more scars than the single one on her leg.

Nel was still looking at her. "Do you understand our way of speaking?" she asked Siguna, speaking slowly and clearly.

"Sa," Siguna replied gruffly.

Nel straightened up, and the dog she had been petting made its way to Thorn in search of more attention. Siguna stiffened as it came closer to her. Nel saw her reaction and smiled reassuringly. "The dogs won't hurt you."

Siguna stuck her chin in the air. "I am not afraid of dogs," she said, proudly if untruthfully.

Nel said nothing, just continued to look at her. Siguna had the oddest feeling that those extraordinary green eyes were seeing right through into her thoughts. Even more oddly, she didn't resent it.

Finally, Nel said to the boys, "You did the right thing. It is unfortunate that you encountered her, but you were right not to turn her free." She looked again at Siguna. "I fear you are going to have to make your home with us for a while." The tone of her voice was gently rueful.

"So I have been made to understand," Siguna said, her own voice still gruff.

A small boy came running out of the tunnel entrance shouting, "Uncle Mait! Uncle Mait! You're back!" He dashed up and flung his arms around the young man's knees.

Mait laughed and lifted the child to sit on his shoulders. "Sa, I am back, Leam. Where is your mother?"

"There." A small finger pointed in the direction of a woman who was exiting the tunnel at a slower pace than her son. Siguna saw that she had the same smooth dark hair and olive-toned skin as Mait. This must be his sister, she thought.

"What has happened?" the new arrival demanded in a voice that had the same lilting intonation as Mait's.

Once again Siguna heard her presence being explained. Then silence fell, and everyone looked at the slim girl, who seemed to be in charge.

"Tora, will you have someone get me White Foot?" Nel asked. "Thorn and I will take Siguna out to the men's camp. We had better discuss this matter with Ronan."

It did not take them long to get to the valley where the men were camped and the horses were pastured. Siguna, shrewdly checking numbers, was relieved when she saw the small herd of horses. The numbers of men were much greater, greater than any force her father had yet encountered. Yet still, Siguna reckoned, they were but half the number of men who followed Fenris. There was nothing here that should cause her father undue trouble.

"You and Siguna wait here," Nel said to Thorn, and, followed by her two dogs, she cantered down the hill toward one of the massed groups of men in the valley. She rode a little differently from the men of Siguna's tribe, but her balance and control were perfect. She pulled up, and a black-haired man came forward to stand by her horse's side. They spoke together.

"That is Ronan," Thorn said. "Our chief."

Siguna asked curiously, "And is Nel his wife?"

"Sa."

"She is a good rider," said Siguna.

Someone was running for the chief's horse, a big gray stallion, and in a short time both Nel and her husband were cantering toward Siguna and Thorn. Siguna's throat suddenly dried, and her heart began to thud in her chest. Who knew what this chief would do with her?

The horses were approaching the slope, and then they were driving upward, directly at the two who waited on the top of the hill above them. The gray stallion came to a sliding halt in front of Siguna, and she saw with surprise that the chief was young.

"Dhu, Thorn," he said in a distinctly ill-tempered voice, "I told you to keep out of sight."

"I am sorry, Ronan," Thorn replied humbly.

Siguna felt a sudden urge to defend the fawn who had kidnapped her. "I had ridden quite deep into the forest to gather herbs," she heard herself saying.

A pair of cold dark eyes surveyed her skeptically, and their coldness did not lift at the sight of her beautiful face and hair. This Ronan might be younger than her father, Siguna thought, but he was every bit as intimidating.

"Don't glare so at the poor girl," Nel said mildly to her husband. "She is going to have more trouble over this than we are."

Ronan shot his wife an impatient glance. "I do not need the additional worry of a prisoner just now, Nel."

A gray shape came streaking up the path, and Siguna stifled a cry of terror as she recognized a wolf. Her horse, sensing her fear, threw up his head and backed.

"Nigak," Nel said, and the wolf went immediately to stand beside her horse.

Siguna's hands were shaking. Nel gave her a lovely smile. "He can be a little intimidating, I know, but it is only Nigak. He belongs to us and is perfectly safe."

Siguna stared at the wolf out of huge eyes.

"Well, Thorn," she heard the chief saying, "you brought her here, so I am making her your responsibility. Yours and Mait's. You two can nurse her; I do not have either the time or the inclination." Siguna lifted her eyes in time to see him turning his arrogant nose in the direction of his wife. "Nor do you, Nel," he said warningly.

"She cannot sleep in Thorn's tent, Ronan," Nel pointed out.

"She can sleep in the women's camp," Ronan replied. "But Thorn is in charge of her. Thorn and Mait."

"I hear you, Ronan," Thorn said, and Siguna found herself also nodding her head in agreement.

"Nel tells me you left before the Horsemasters moved their camp?" Ronan asked Thorn next.

"Sa," Thorn said in a subdued voice.

"We cannot take a chance of them slipping away. I will send Dai and Tyr to keep watch. Perhaps *they* will have enough sense to keep themselves out of sight."

Thorn hung his head, and Siguna felt a ridiculous pang of sympathy for him.

"Turn the horses loose here, and go on back to the Great Cave," Ronan ordered the boy. "Berta or Fara or someone will feed you."

Thorn nodded.

Ronan wheeled his horse and galloped back to his men. To Siguna's immense relief, the wolf followed him. The dogs, which had effaced themselves as soon as Nigak appeared, came forward again to Nel's side. Siguna gingerly followed the example of the other two and dismounted. She relaxed slightly when the dogs ignored her.

Nel waited while Thorn took the halters from Frost and Acorn. Her own colt rested his chin comfortably on her shoulder, and when Frost and Acorn galloped off to join their fellows, White Foot made no attempt to follow. Siguna found this extraordinary.

As they turned to leave, Siguna noticed something decidedly odd among the formations of men in the valley. She stopped dead. "Are those women I see?" she demanded.

Nel and Thorn followed the direction of her pointing finger. "Sa," Thorn said. "Those are women."

"But they are shooting arrows!"

Silence fell as the three watched a fleet-footed, black-haired girl aim her arrow at a hide that had been stretched upon a pole for a target. The shot went into the dead center of the hide. The girl slowed her steps, stopped, and flung back her head. Siguna was sure she was laughing.

"I do not understand," Siguna said. "Do you have women warriors as well as men?"

"Some of the women who are not mothers of young children are doing weapon training with the men," Thorn answered.

Siguna's eyes sparkled. "But that is wonderful!"

Nel laughed, and Siguna realized how foolish a remark that was for the enemy chief's daughter to be making. To her great relief, the other two let it pass without further comment.

They walked on, and Nel said to Thorn, "I suggest you lodge Siguna with Fara. Now that Eken is busy with her own babe, Fara could use someone to help her look after the twins."

Once again Siguna stopped in her tracks and stared at Nel. "Do your people keep twins?"

Nel's delicate face momentarily appeared to harden. "We do in the Tribe of the Wolf," she said, then continued on, White Foot and the dogs obediently following.

Siguna began to walk also, glancing curiously at Nel's profile. From her other side, Thorn said, "Most of the tribes of the Kindred do not keep twins, but our tribe does. Will you be afraid to stay in the same living space with twins?"

Since early childhood, Siguna had had a policy never to admit she was afraid. She raised her chin. "Of course not."

"Good," Nel said and gave her an approving look.

They were passing two huts that looked as if they had been newly erected against the slope of the hill. A handful of women were sitting in front of one of them, sewing. As she had on the way out, Nel raised a hand in greeting, and the women waved back.

"Surely that is an odd place to build a hut," Siguna remarked.

"Those are the moon huts," Thorn replied.

Siguna looked at him blankly. "Moon huts?"

Nel explained what a moon hut was used for. "You do not have such a custom in your tribe?"

Siguna shook her head.

"Nor do we in my tribe," Nel replied. "Many of our people do, however." She quirked her delicate brows humorously. "At first I thought such a custom was disgraceful, demeaning to the Mother's blood that carries the life of the tribe. However, I soon discovered that the women from the tribes that worship Sky God like the custom. Once a moon it gives them a week away from their husbands and their work, you see."

Privately, Siguna thought the custom sounded wonderful.

They walked for a while in silence. Then Siguna remarked carefully, "It is not just one tribe you have gathered here, then?"

Nel gave her a long green look and did not answer.

"If she is going to live with us, she is certain to find out," Thorn said reasonably.

Nel turned her unnerving gaze on Thorn. Then she sighed. "That is probably true."

Thus given tacit permission, Thorn turned to Siguna. "We are a federation of tribes from all over the mountains," he explained. "We have been following the progress of your people, and we have united to keep them from destroying us, the way they have destroyed the Kindred tribes to our north."

"Name of the Thunderer," Siguna muttered, using her father's favorite oath.

Both of her captors glanced at her, but refrained from asking for a translation.

Siguna was beginning to think that perhaps it was a good thing that she had been captured. She would find out what she could about these adversaries and then try to escape and return to Fenris with the information. If she could do that, she thought, if she could return to her people with such important information, then would her life be different. Then would her father look upon her with pride. He would value her as he did her brothers. A small smile played around the corners of Siguna's lips as she fantasized happy pictures of life in the future.

Siguna settled into the life of the camp with an ease that astonished even herself. Fara was kind, and the chores she asked Siguna to perform were not onerous. The women in the Great Cave worked hard, taking care of children, gathering roots and berries and edible grasses and grains, cooking, keeping their family's clothing in good condition and making new clothes—all things that the women among Siguna's people did. One major difference between Siguna's tribe and this one was that the men of the Kindred took care of the meat. Not only did they bring it in, but they skinned and butchered it. Relieved of this backbreaking job, the women had more time and energy for their other work.

Fara and her friends had been horrified when Siguna told them that the women of her tribe did the butchering.

"Well, what do the men do then?" Beki demanded.

"They are warriors," Siguna answered. "They take care of their horses and their weapons. They hunt."

Berta looked up from the arrowhead she was working on and commented, "The women of your tribe must be fools."

Siguna thought, The women of my tribe are not fools. It is just that they have never learned another way.

Siguna's jobs were to mind the twins, who were lively, charming children, and help with the cooking and the sewing. The women did not ask her to help with the task that was taking up the bulk of their time these days, the making of arrows.

In normal times, Fara said, the tribe's toolmaker would make the arrows. But Ronan had had the toolmakers show the women the skill of arrow making, and that is the chore to which the vast majority of them were now turning their hands.

Some of them worked on arrowheads, which they fashioned with flint tools from the bones of the animals they ate. Others made the arrow shafts, first shaving the wood clean, then passing it over a fire to make it supple, and finally sliding it through the hole of a shaft straightener to make it straight. Finally came the binding of the arrowhead to the shaft with sinew, and the arrow was finished.

Fara had told Siguna that the women had decided it would be ill-done of them to make her work on something that was aimed at the defeat of her own people. How odd, Siguna found herself thinking time and again, that in the camp of my enemies I should be treated with more consideration and courtesy than I ever knew at home.

Either Thorn or Mait was usually at hand, but Siguna soon found herself regarding them as companions rather than as guards. She particularly liked to watch Thorn draw. She had seen such drawings in the caves of some of the tribes her father had conquered, and she found it fascinating to see how a horse could appear on a stone with just a few strokes of Thorn's clever fingers.

It was Thorn who one afternoon told her about the Tribe of the Red Deer, whose girls were the ones Siguna had seen practicing with arrows out at the men's camp. After that, Siguna could not rest until she had a chance to speak to Arika. The women of the Red Deer had chosen to camp at the farthest end of the tunnel, a little distance from the rest of the women of the Kindred, and it took Siguna a few days before she could find an excuse to approach the Mistress.

She spent a mind-shattering afternoon at Arika's feet, hearing things she had never dreamed could be thought, let alone said.

That night, Siguna left her sleeping skins by Fara and the twins, giving the excuse that she had to seek the latrine area. Instead she walked outside the cave, just to be alone and to look at the stars. Her mind had been so stimulated by her conversation with Arika that she knew sleep was impossible, and she found the distant beauty of the stars immensely restful. It was chilly, and she wrapped her fur tunic around herself, leaned against the wall of the cliff, and gazed up at the sky. She had no idea how long she had been there when she heard the low murmur of voices coming nearer. Siguna, who did not want to be disturbed, moved silently to her left, deeper into the shadow of the cliff.

The moonlight picked out the figures of Nel and Ronan. Siguna had not seen the chief since their first meeting, as he and the men largely kept to the valley where their camp was pitched. Tonight, however, he was walking with his wife, his spear in his left hand, his right arm draped across her shoulders, his dark head bent close to hers in absorbed conversation. They were so intent upon each other that Siguna did not think they would notice her.

It was Nigak who gave her away. Siguna froze in terror when she saw the wolf coming straight for her. He stopped when he was but six feet away, his lips drew back, and he growled low in his throat.

"Who is there?" Ronan called sharply.

Siguna was so frightened she could not make a sound. The wolf growled again, and Siguna managed to choke out her name.

"Siguna?" she heard Nel say. "What can she be doing here?"

"Come out," Ronan called. "Nigak won't hurt you."

Siguna was petrified to move closer to the wolf, but she was also petrified that Nigak would attack if she did not do as she was told. Shaking all over, she stepped out into the moonlight.

Ronan had taken his arm away from his wife's shoulder and changed his grip on his spear. When he saw the slim girlish figure of Siguna, his fingers relaxed. "What are you doing skulking around here?" he asked her irritably, signaling for Nigak to return to him.

Siguna was so shaken, both by Nigak and by the danger she had read on Ronan's face, that she told him the truth. "I came out to see the stars."

"The stars?" he repeated blankly.

"Stars," his wife said with amusement. "Those tiny bright fires in the night sky."

"I know what stars are, Nel," he snapped. "What I don't know is why this girl is out in the night, unwatched by anyone. Dhu, she could be heading straight back to her father and we wouldn't know about it until the morning!"

"She wouldn't be so stupid as to try that," Nel said, unruffled by her husband's bad temper.

"I am glad you are so certain of that."

"I am. And Fara is too, or she wouldn't have let Siguna leave her sight."

Ronan looked around. "And where, I would like to know, are Thorn and Mait? I thought I told them they were to be responsible for this girl."

Nel ignored him, looking at Siguna instead and asking sympathetically, "Did something in particular happen today, Siguna, that you felt the need to look at the stars?"

Siguna said, "I spoke today to the Mistress of the Red Deer."

Ronan groaned. Nel punched him lightly on his shoulder and said with mock authority, "Behave."

If one of Fenris's women had dared to speak in such a saucy fashion to him, they would have felt the weight of his hand. Ronan's hand simply moved to rest lightly on the nape of his wife's neck.

"Is it true," Siguna asked Nel slowly, "that you would have been the next Mistress of the Red Deer if you had not married?"

"Who told you that?" Ronan asked sharply. "Arika?"

Siguna shook her head, not wanting to say Thorn's name and perhaps get him into trouble.

Nel answered Siguna with serenity, "Such talk is nothing but speculation."

Nigak yawned, showing all his teeth. Siguna shivered.

"It is growing late and I must be getting back to camp," Ronan said. "Nel, take Siguna into the cave with you and keep her there. I do not like her wandering around by herself." He gave Siguna one of his hawklike stares. "It is not safe."

"Go ahead, Siguna," Nel said softly. "I will be right with you."

Siguna needed no more encouragement to walk toward the safety of the tunnel entrance. Just before she reached it, however, she turned and looked back over her shoulder.

Nel and Ronan stood there in the open, framed by the moonlight. His hands were on her shoulders, and she was looking up into his face, listening to what he was saying. She said something in return, and then, as Siguna watched wonderingly, he bent his head, and his mouth came down on Nel's, and her head tilted back so that her long shining braid fell over the arm that had pulled her so hard against him. Her arms went up to circle his neck.

Siguna turned and went by herself into the cave.

Chapter Twenty-six

*T*he Horsemasters are coming!!!

The words ran through the assembled men of the Federation like wildfire. Dai and Tyr had come galloping in a short while before, shouting for Ronan. Then the news began to spread through the camps. At long last, the enemy was on the trail again.

Ronan immediately moved into action. Over the course of the last few weeks, he had plotted precisely the course he wanted his confrontation with the Horsemasters to take, and his first challenge was to lure them down the river Volp.

He had spoken to Arika about this, for the Volp was the river that flowed through the sacred cave of the Tribe of the Red Deer.

"I want to catch them in the gorge that lies a morning's walk to the north of the cave, Mistress," Ronan had explained. "The men of the Red Deer would often make a great reindeer slaughter there, and it is a good place to trap a large number of men and horses."

Arika had been silent, obviously picturing in her mind the dark, almost sinister gorge that had been cut by the Volp as it rushed through the mountains north of the sacred cave. "Sa," she had said at last. "That is a good place to set a trap."

"They will not get through us, Mistress," Ronan promised. "I could hold the pass that leads out of that gorge with half the number of men that I have. The sacred cave will be safe."

Arika had looked at him for a moment in silence. Then she asked,

"What do you think they will do when they have once seen that we mean to stand against them?"

"I think the first thing they will do is change their ground. That gorge is impossible to cross, and their leader is too smart not to see that. They will go back to the River of Gold. But I am hoping to wound them badly enough at the gorge to somewhat reduce their numbers."

Arika nodded. "And a victory might put heart into the tribes of the Fox and the Bear and induce them to join with us."

"I hope so," Ronan said grimly. "They are fools if they think they are situated too far down the River of Gold for the Horsemasters to find them." He gave Arika a genuinely puzzled look. "I do not understand them. How can they not want to fight?"

Arika had risen. "They do not have the strength of the Mother, as we do," she said. "That is the cause of their fearfulness." And she had walked away, leaving her son staring after her with strained and shadowed eyes.

Ronan knew he could not count on the Horsemasters to choose of their own volition to follow the Volp. In all of their previous scouting expeditions, the Horsemasters had always bypassed the smaller river in favor of continuing down the River of Gold. Ronan had to give the invaders a reason for proceeding along a path they had not previously explored, and he planned to do that by stealing their horses.

In order to accomplish this maneuver, Ronan had handpicked three handfuls of riders from the Tribe of the Wolf.

"I do not want any fighting," he repeated to his chosen raiding party on the night before they left the Great Cave. "We are simply going to gallop into their horse herd and stampede it. We'll carry leather thongs and try to drive some of the horses before us when we return up the Volp, but I do not want anyone putting themselves into a situation where they could be captured." His eyes went from Thorn to Mait to Kasar. "Do you understand?"

The young men all nodded.

"Beki?" Ronan said. "Yoli? Do you understand?"

"Sa, Ronan," said two feminine voices softly. "We understand."

"If we do our job, and scatter their horses, the enemy will not be able to follow us immediately," Ronan said. "They will have to catch their horses first. We should have plenty of time to return to the gorge and get ready for them."

"I am thinking it will not be too difficult," said Beki, her jaunty tip-tilted nose turning toward her husband, Kasar. She grinned. "They can have no idea that we have horses also."

"I do not think they can," Ronan replied gravely. "When they see that we do, I think they will be interested enough in us to follow us. If they do that . . . then we will surprise them at the gorge."

"The biggest problem is going to be that their horses are mares, and ours are stallions," Nel warned.

"You already had us build a big corral to hold whatever mares we may come back with, Nel," Dai pointed out.

"I know. But it is not going to be as easy to handle your horses in the midst of a herd of mares as it usually is," Nel said. "I am just telling you to be prepared."

Solemn nods came from all around the circle.

Ronan said, "I have chosen only the best riders for this job, because the best riders also have the most obedient horses. If there is anyone who does not think he or she can control a stallion under these circumstances, please say so now."

Silence.

"Good," said Ronan. "We will leave tomorrow at dawn."

The Horsemasters made camp for the night not far from the place where a smaller tributary branched off from the wider river they were following. The men pastured the horse herd in a nearby meadow; the women set up the tents and lit the cookfires. He would remain for another day or two in this place, Fenris thought, so the men could do some hunting. Then he would move the tribe once again down the River of Gold, toward the settlement of people his scouts had discovered earlier in the year.

Rich tribes dwelled upon the shores of the River of Gold, the scouts had said. The caves and huts were comfortable, the hunting grounds rich in deer, and there was plenty of grazing for the horses.

Fenris knew that his men were growing restless. They had had no fighting since last summer, and their blood was heating up. They were beginning to fight among themselves; it was more than time for them to redden their spears with the blood of their enemies.

There was a wind blowing off the river, and Fenris hunched his shoulders against it as he walked slowly toward his tent.

He missed Siguna. He had not realized how often his eyes had rested upon her silvery fair head until it was no longer there to gaze upon.

She had been so brave, he thought. And so foolish. A girl who dreamed she could do the things that belonged to a man.

His fault. He had thought that more than once. It was his fault for indulging her, for allowing her to ride horses, for giving her some of the freedom that she was always so wild for. If he had made her live the life she was born to lead, she would be alive now.

Fenris regretted very little in his life, but he regretted that he had not successfully protected Siguna.

He pushed open the flap of his tent and walked in. Silence fell at his entrance, and he lifted his hand. Once more his children began to babble, his women to scold, his anda to boast among themselves. Nothing had changed, he told himself. He was a fool to allow himself to be so sad.

They came at dawn the following morning. A stallion's scream pierced the quiet air of the camp, and Fenris sat bolt upright in his sleeping skins.

"What is it?" gasped Kara, who was once more sharing his bed.

"A stallion has got in with the mares." He was on his feet, pulling on his boots. Outside, he heard the sound of men running. "I will have the hearts of the men on herd duty," Fenris said through his teeth as he ran for the door.

The air outside his tent was gray and cold and smelled of the fear of horses.

"Father!" He turned and saw his second-eldest son running toward him. "Horsemen, Father! They are scattering the mares!"

"Name of the Thunderer!" Fenris began to run toward the corral where his own horses were penned. His stallion, the only stallion kept by the tribe, was going berserk.

There was the sound of thundering hooves behind him, and Fenris whirled around to see a pack of about fifteen of his own horses pounding toward him. In the midst of them, whistling and shouting and swinging a leather thong, was a black-haired man on a gray stallion. The stallion's ears were laid flat back and his head was low and snaking as he slashed at the mares with his bared teeth.

Fenris stared in absolute shock at the man on the stallion's back. The bastard rode as well as he did! The horses were almost on top of him before Fenris took his only option and ducked inside the corral fence, out of the way of the stampeding herd. The mares swept by, and Fenris's shock was multiplied when he saw another horseman bringing up the rear, riding a white-legged stallion and expertly keeping any stragglers from falling behind. Only this horseman was a girl!

"Name of the Thunderer," Fenris said again.

Fenris's stallion, named appropriately Thunder, was frantically screaming after his disappearing mares. The mares in the corral were racing around, trying to keep out of the stallion's way. Fenris ducked back out of the corral before he was trampled. It would be a while before he would be able to catch and halter any of these horses, he thought furiously.

A group of his men were running toward him, and he recognized Surtur in the lead. "Are any of our men mounted?" Fenris shouted.

Surtur came running up. "Vili was grooming his mare and managed to hold on to her. He has ridden after them to see which way they go."

Fenris scowled. "Who was on guard at the horse herd?"

"They came so fast, Kain, that no one had a chance to do anything against them," one of the other men said. "It was not the fault of the men on guard."

"They were not on guard if they let themselves be taken by surprise," Fenris said uncompromisingly. "Who were they?"

Surtur gave him the names.

"Did the thieves drive off all the horses?" Fenris asked next.

"They scattered all the horses, but many of them are still in the vicinity."

"We shall have to get them back, then," Fenris said grimly. "The men will have to go out on foot."

"Aye, Kain."

"When Vili gets back," Fenris said, "send him to me," and he strode off angrily toward his tent.

"They went up the small river, Father," Vili said an hour later, after he had returned to camp and had sought out the kain to report to him. "There were several small groups of them, and they got about six handfuls of our horses."

Fenris was astride one of his own mares, keeping count of the horses as they were brought in. He stared at his son, his thick golden eyebrows drawn together, his eyes as darkly gray as the northern sea from whence his people had come.

"Up the small river," he repeated.

Vili nodded. "I followed them for a short way to make certain."

Fenris stroked his finger lightly up and down the cleft in his chin, something he only did when he was very perturbed. "In the name of the Thunderer, where did these people come from? Our scouts have never seen any sign of a tribe that rides horses."

Vili, who did not have an answer, prudently held his tongue.

"You saw no signs of habitations?" Fenris asked next.

"No, Father. There were many caves in the hillsides, but I saw no sign of life. I did not follow for very long. I thought it was more important to report back to you."

Fenris nodded. "You were right. You did well, my son." He reached down to put a hand on Vili's shoulder. "The only man to keep his horse. I am proud of you."

Vili's fair-skinned face, a thinner, younger, less-handsome version of the kain's, glowed with pride.

"What shall you do, Father?" he ventured to ask.

"Go after them," Fenris replied grimly. "I do not allow anyone to steal my horses and live."

Excitement in the Federation camp rose to fever pitch when Ronan and his raiding party came galloping in, driving before them a milling, whinnying group of mares and foals. Crim immediately ran to open the corral gate, and the riders urged the bewildered, frightened newcomers into the sturdy pen the tribes had built to hold them.

After a bit of a struggle, the mares were inside, and the stallions outside. The riders could finally dismount.

"Dhu!" Thorn said, wiping a hand across his dirty, sweaty brow. "That was not a ride I'll soon forget."

"Nor I." Mait grinned at him, his teeth showing very white in his filthy face. The boys had been riding at the back of the herd, where the dust was thick. "My legs are shaking."

"You did it." The voice was Siguna's. She came up beside them and looked at the familiar mares milling around in the corral. She shivered and wrapped her arms around her shoulders. "My father will be furious."

Ronan was leading his stallion in their direction, and he heard Siguna's comment. "I hope that he is," Ronan said, and then added, "Whoa, Cloud. Whoa, fellow," as his gray stallion suddenly began to plunge and rear. The people near the horse's lashing feet moved back quickly. Ronan jerked once, sharply, on the noseband of the halter and said again, very sternly, "Whoa." The gray rolled his large, brilliant dark eyes and snorted, but his feet remained on the ground. "He is excited by the mares," Ronan said to Siguna, keeping a close hold on the stallion's halter.

Thorn was looking at the gray stallion's splendid, strongly arched face. He had drawn Cloud several times, and he considered one picture in particular, a large one he had painted in the valley cave, among his very best. It was a picture of Ronan and his horse together, standing side by side much as they were now. Thorn had tried to convey the similar lordly look of pride and command that marked both those aquiline faces. He looked now at the stallion face and the man face before him, remembered his picture, and saw a small change he could make.

"They are all excited by the mares," Mait was saying, "but Cloud is reacting more like a stallion than a colt. I saw him driving them, Ronan." Mait gazed at his leader with unfeigned admiration. "I do not know how you stayed on!"

Ronan grinned. "All of those thundering hooves coming behind me, Mait, gave me great encouragement to stay on." Cloud tried to rear again, but Ronan's iron hand held him. "I am going to get him out of here," Ronan said to the trio before him and, clicking his tongue, he began to walk briskly away. Cloud arched his thick muscular neck and followed on prancing feet.

Ronan had estimated it would be at least a day before Fenris would be able to collect his horses and come after the thieves, but the chief of the Wolf was taking no chances. At noon on the day of the raid, he moved his forces out of the Great Cave and westward, toward the valley of the Volp.

The place Ronan had chosen for his ambush was a deep gorge that had been cut by the river between two cave-pierced limestone cliffs. The floor of the gorge was dark with shadows, and the river raced through it as if anxious to leave, roaring loudly up and down the echoing valley.

One of the things Ronan had been doing over the last weeks was separating out the best archers from among the tribes. These were the marksmen that he sent now to climb the steep hillsides on either side of the gorge and hide themselves within the caves that honeycombed the cliffs. With the marksmen went the huge number of arrows the women of the tribes had been so busy making, as well as most of the spears the tribes possessed.

The rest of the men of the Federation would rely solely on their heavy spears. These men Ronan had massed at the head of the pass that led out of the gorge, standing them shoulder to shoulder, their spears pointing forward to form an impenetrable wall of death.

Ronan's advice to his marksmen had been succinct. "Go for the horses first. Once the first animals start to fall, I am thinking panic will set in amongst the rest. Dead horses will clog the gorge, too, and make it more difficult for the rest of them to get out. Then you can aim for the men."

"Sa, sa," the marksmen had replied, and they had gone happily off to their appointed hiding places.

The two other chiefs had been uneasy about the formation in the pass. "It is all very well to say they will not attempt to get through our spear wall, Ronan," Unwar had growled, "but what if they do? They will be on horseback. They can ride us down."

"They cannot ride us down if we stand firm," Ronan had replied patiently. He raised his voice, so he would be sure to be heard by the men around him. "I could hold that pass with just the men of the Wolf if I had to." His voice rang with confidence. "If we hold strong, there is no way that the Horsemasters will be able to break through. We will defeat them." He grinned and turned to address the men. "I wonder how they will like that?"

A roar of voices had been his answer.

And so the tribes took up their positions and waited. The day passed, and the men and girls in the caves settled down for the night, lighting no fires, eating only the dried meat and pieces of fruit they had brought to sustain themselves. The men in the pass did likewise.

Back at the sacred cave of the Red Deer, a morning's walk away,

Nel, Arika, and the shamans of the Buffalo and the Leopard waited also, the necessities for tending the wounded close by their hands.

Night passed and the sun began to rise in the sky. The men of the tribes once more took up their positions. An hour passed, and then another. Then, at long last, the first horsemen appeared on the heights at the northern end of the gorge.

Fenris halted at the sight of the deep and shadowy gorge stretching before him. He held up his hand, and the men behind him halted as well. Fenris narrowed his eyes and scanned the cliffs. No sign of anything living showed anywhere. The river raged in the bottom of the gorge, churning with white. Fenris could hear its roar from here. There was room in the gorge for only three horses to go abreast, Fenris calculated, evaluating the space from the river to the cliff. He raised his eyes. So far as he could see, the exit from the gorge on the far side looked clear.

"Everything looks all right to me," Surtur said from his right side.

"Yes," Fenris said slowly.

"Is anything the matter, Kain?"

Nothing, Fenris thought, except that the hair on the back of his neck was standing on end. He did not trust this gorge. His stallion was quiet, however; nor did any of the mares appear to be objecting to the path in front of them. Fenris turned and looked at the men in line behind him.

He had brought a quarter of his men, a cadre of his finest warriors, on this pursuit of the thieves of his horses. The women and children and extra horses were back at the camp, guarded by enough men to protect them should an attack come in his absence. The kain was not accustomed to thinking about defense, but the raid of two days before had shaken him out of his usual complacency.

"Is anything the matter?" Surtur repeated.

There was nothing he could put his finger on. He could not go back simply because of a feeling . . . "No," he said to Surtur. "Let us go on." He pressed his stallion forward, and the rest of his men followed. The Horsemasters entered the gorge.

Ronan had impressed upon his archers the necessity of waiting until the invaders were three quarters of the way through the gorge before they opened fire. At precisely the three-quarter point, the first arrows began to rain down upon the unprotected heads of the Horsemasters and the vulnerable flanks of their mounts.

Horses screamed. Men shouted.

I knew it! Fenris thought before he began to gallop his stallion forward toward the pass ahead of him. *I knew it was a trap!*

Surtur was riding on one side of him, and Hugin on the other. The three of them raced forward, their heads low against their horses' necks. The screams of wounded horses rent the air.

There was a movement in front of them, and Fenris looked up to see a phalanx of men moving into the pass. Instinctively, Fenris checked his mount. The men in the pass halted and pointed their spears directly forward.

Fenris stared at the tightly massed men. If he galloped Thunder into that wall of spears, he would kill him. There was only room for the horses to hit the men three at a time, and the spearmen were too deep for the weight of three horses to break.

Fenris cursed and slowed his horse even more. He could feel the horses behind him crowding upon Thunder's tail. The stallion lashed out with his heels. Fenris turned to look at the scene behind him.

Many horses were down, clogging the narrow gorge and the way out. Panic, sharp and palpable, was in the air. Fenris wrenched Thunder around. "Go back!" he shouted, waving his fist at the men behind him. "It's a trap! Go back!"

If the men in the pass saw them retreating, Fenris thought desperately, they might charge. That was his only chance, to draw them out of that tight formation and into the gorge. Then he would have a chance of breaking through. His own men began to turn and surge slowly back in the other direction. Swearing and cursing, Fenris looked over his shoulder, to see if the men in the pass had taken the bait.

For one brief, wildly hopeful second, it seemed to the kain that the line of men swayed and began to move forward to give chase. Then a black-haired man stepped forward, faced them, and stretched his spear across the pass, as if he would hold back his men with that alone. The forward movement ceased, the men steadied and held.

Fenris cursed viciously. Whoever their leader was, he was too clever to be lured out of his position of power.

The only thing left for the kain to do was to try to extricate himself and as many of his men as he could from this gorge and the death that was raining down on them. Name of the Thunderer, how many arrows did they have?

"Dismount!" he yelled to the men around him. "Dismount, and let the horses shield you." Then, grim-faced, he took his own advice.

Chapter Twenty-seven

Nel, Arika, and the shamans had only two twisted ankles and one cut leg to treat. The shamans couldn't believe it, particularly when they went up to the gorge and saw the shambles lying within.

Nel didn't go. Ronan had told her not to, and she had followed his advice. It was bad enough listening to the descriptions of those who had been there.

The Horsemasters had left six handfuls of men in the gorge, either dead or too badly wounded to get themselves out. They had left even more horses.

A grim-faced Ronan had given orders that the wounded men and horses were to be dispatched, and all of the bodies were to be stripped of their weapons. The tribes also retrieved as many of their own arrows and spears as they could find, in many cases pulling them out of the dead flesh of their targets. Then the men of the Federation turned their backs on the gorge and left the corpses to the attention of the hyenas.

The approximately one hundred and fifty victorious tribesmen and women did not make the journey back to their camp at the Great Cave that night, but stayed instead near the cave where the Red Deer men traditionally held their initiation rites. Ronan had already sent messengers to relay the news of victory to the waiting women at the Great Cave, and he had previously posted watchers at the Horsemasters' camp, so there was no reason for him not to relax and join wholeheartedly in the victory celebration. But he could not.

He kept looking at the cave and remembering the day of his own initiation. It seemed so long ago. A lifetime ago. He fingered the initiation scars on his upper arm. It was impossible to feel them under the buckskin of his shirt, but he knew they were there.

When he was not looking at the cave, he was looking at the place near the fire where Arika sat. Neihle was on one side of her, but the other side was empty. The heavily pregnant Morna, who for so many years had occupied that place of honor beside her mother, was back at the Great Cave with the other women.

Ronan stared at that empty space. For the whole of his childhood, he had longed to be the one who sat there, had longed to take his place as the Mistress's son. And now, after so many years, after so much bitterness, she seemed disposed to accept him. She had backed his leadership. She had said he was blessed by the Goddess. He did not understand her at all.

He shook his head, as if to clear from it fumes that were clouding his thoughts. A hand touched his shoulder briefly, and he knew, before ever he turned his head, who was there.

"Let us go for a walk," Nel said softly into his ear.

He nodded and got to his feet. The men of the Wolf sitting around him looked up, saw Nel, smiled, and went back to their eating and their stories of the day's adventure. Ronan and Nel slipped away into the forest.

"You looked so serious," Nel said.

"I was thinking that I should be feeling as if I were back at home," he explained. "That cave is the cave where I was initiated. All of my old agemates were sitting around the fires there, and Neihle, who was my mentor. But it seemed as if the boy who grew up in the Tribe of the Red Deer was one person, and I am another."

"You are the same person," Nel said. "But you have journeyed far."

He sighed. "Sa. I suppose that is true."

They walked for a few moments in silence, wrapped in their own thoughts. Then Nel said, "Ronan . . ."

He raised his head alertly, roused from his own reverie by the edgy urgency of her tone. "Sa?"

"Let us go to the sacred cave," she said.

He frowned. "Now?"

"Sa. We are not that far away. We can go there and be back before the morning. No one need know where we have gone."

He halted in a pool of moonlight and looked down. "Why, Nel?"

She would not meet his eyes. He studied her tense, averted face, and abruptly he understood.

He ached for her. He knew how much she wanted a child. If she wanted to lie with him in the sacred cave, he would go with her. But in his heart he did not think it would do any good.

"Do you want to ask the Mother's blessing for a child?" he asked her, his voice very gentle. "Is that it?"

"Sa." Her lovely mouth looked so unhappy. "I think she is angry with me, Ronan. She feels I have deserted her. That is why she will not bless me with a child. I must find a way to placate her, and I thought, perhaps, if you and I went to her sacred place . . ." She lifted her long, beautiful eyes. "Do you see?"

He smoothed his thumbs along her cheekbones. "Sa. I see. But I do not think the Mother is angry with you, minnow. I think the Mother loves you well."

Despairingly she cried, "If that is so, then why will she not give me a child?"

He tilted her face so she would have to look at him, and said soberly, "Hear me, Nel. I do not think you understand how great is the gift the Mother has blessed you with. She has given you the gift of calling animals. Don't you know that if it were not for you, we would never have been able to tame our horses?"

"You would have," she said. "Look at how well all the tribe is doing with them."

"Na." His voice was sharp. "Now we can handle them, but we would not have gotten near them in the first place if it were not for you. I might have been able to take a foal and rear it and tame it as you reared Nigak. But never could I have tamed a herd of yearlings that had been running free. Never. When it comes to handling animals, you are a very great shaman."

She was gazing up at him, trying to understand. "Nel," he said gently, "it is in my heart that for the giving of such a gift, the Mother will require some sacrifice."

Silence. He watched her eyes dilate until they were almost black.

"That is too great a sacrifice," she whispered at last.

"Why?"

She pulled her face away from his grasp and turned away from him. "Because it is a sacrifice for you, also," she said over her shoulder.

He shook his head. "I have you. I do not need children."

She hunched her shoulders. "You are just saying that to make me feel better."

"I am not. *Look at me, Nel.* I mean it. I do not care if we never have children."

Slowly, reluctantly, she turned around. She looked up into his face, and he gazed steadily back. Tears began to well in her eyes when she saw that he was telling her the truth.

"Don't cry, minnow," he said softly. "Please don't cry. You know I can't bear to see you cry." And he held out his arms.

She seemed so small and light-boned as she pressed against him. He smelled the herbs with which she washed her hair. No one else's hair smelled like Nel's. For no one else had he ever felt the gut-wrenching tenderness that he always felt for her. Perhaps he should not have spoken, but he could not bear to see her wearing herself out with longing.

"If you want, I will go to the sacred cave with you," he said. "We will make the sacred marriage in the Mother's own place. But I do not want you to be disappointed if you do not have a child, Nel."

He felt her shudder and try to get herself under control. She slid her arms around his waist and held him tightly. His heart was breaking for her, but he knew that he had spoken the truth. Ronan had long understood that the Goddess gave nothing without exacting some payment in return.

What he had kept hidden from Nel was the fact that, deep down, he was glad she had borne no children. He would keep that secret, he decided, lest she suspect that perhaps his gladness was the very cause of the Mother's anger.

The women of his blood had ever had ill luck with childbearing. Nel's own mother had died. Arika had almost died with Morna and had been able to bear no more. Morna herself was not looking well. Ronan would be very happy to keep Nel safe.

And he was happy, also, to keep her his. He had heard too much of men's grumbling about their enforced continence during the moons of childbearing and early nursing. If he had to do it, he would, but to himself he acknowledged the truth. He liked having his wife to himself. He had the tribe to guide and to rule; he did not need children also.

He touched his mouth to her hair. "You are enough for me, minnow." He added, a little plaintively, "Aren't I enough for you?"

At that, she loosened her grip on him, sniffled twice, and tipped back her head. Her face in the moonlight was silvered all over with tears. "Sa," she said in a husky voice. "You have always been enough for me."

They gazed into each other's eyes. Ronan said, "Do you still want to go to the sacred cave?"

"Sa." The huskiness of Nel's voice was subtly different.

Ronan's face was intent. "I'll tell Bror, so that no one gets nervous and starts to look for us."

Nel nodded.

He lifted a finger and lightly touched her mouth. "I won't be long," he promised and ran back toward the firelight on feet as fleet as wings.

As soon as the men returned to the Great Cave, Siguna sought out Thorn. She wanted to go to the gorge to search for her father. "I cannot leave him there," she insisted. "If he is dead, I must bury him."

"I did not see him fall, Siguna," Thorn kept repeating patiently. "Nor did Mait see him among the dead. Mait was one of those sent to retrieve our weapons, and he did not see the kain. I asked him specifically because I knew you would want to know."

"I must be certain," Siguna said. "He is my father."

She was neither wild nor hysterical. She was perfectly calm and perfectly determined. Thorn, who was equally determined that she not go, did not know what to do with her.

"The scavengers will have been at the corpses for a day and a night," he finally said bluntly. "You do not want to see what is in that gorge, Siguna."

No trace of horror crossed her beautiful face. "It does not matter," she replied. "All that matters is that I assure myself that my father is not there."

Thorn gritted his teeth against his own horror. "Then I will go for you," he said. "I know what the kain looks like. If he is there, and if he is still recognizable, I promise you I will bring him out so you can bury him."

Siguna did not flinch. "You do not understand. I must go myself, Thorn." She repeated, "He is my father."

Thorn glared. "I know he is your father!" They eyed each other. "You are right," Thorn said. "I do not understand. Do you not trust me?"

Siguna made an impatient gesture. "Let us go to see the Mistress," she said.

At those words, Thorn became wary. He had not been overly pleased by the amount of time that his charge was spending in Arika's company of late. Siguna was different after she had been talking to Arika. Thorn had noticed it, and he did not like it. In truth, Thorn was somewhat jealous of the bond that appeared to be forming between Siguna and the Mistress of the Red Deer.

"Why?" he asked now. "What can Arika have to say about this?"

"She will understand why I must go."

"Siguna." Thorn was beginning to get really angry. "Will you please be sensible? There is no reason for you to go to that gorge!"

"No reason that you understand, Thorn," she replied calmly. "I am going to see the Mistress."

"Very well," he snapped. "I will come with you." And the two young people moved off together toward the Red Deer section of the cave.

Arika was giving a voice blessing to one of the tribe's babes, but when she had finished her chant she listened to Siguna's request with no sign of horror or disgust.

"This will be an ugly sight for you" was all she said when Siguna had finished.

"I know that," Siguna replied. Her face was pale and set, her gray eyes wide and dark and dedicated. "But I must see for myself that my father is not lying there, food for the ravens and scavengers of the earth." She lifted her head. "To you he is simply the enemy, but to me he is my father."

Thorn had been silent thus far, but now he said, "Mistress, I have said that I will go to the gorge and search for the kain. It is not necessary for Siguna to undertake this terrible task."

Arika's eyes went back to Siguna. "Do your gods demand this of you?" she asked.

"I do not know overmuch of the gods," Siguna replied honestly. "The women of my tribe do not have a sacred world of their own as do the women of the Red Deer. This is a duty that I have laid upon myself."

"You love your father?"

"I love my father," Siguna said. "But that is not the point."

"You are right," Arika replied. The Mistress's face was very grave. "It is not the point at all." She said to Thorn, "The girl must be allowed to search for her father."

Thorn bit back the rash words that were on his tongue.

Siguna bowed her silvery head. "I thank you, Mistress, for understanding and for granting me this wish."

There was nothing Thorn could do. Arika's word in this matter would not be gainsayed, not even by Ronan. Trying to make the best of it, Thorn said, "She cannot go alone."

The Mistress surveyed him from his head to his toes. Thorn set his teeth and refused to be intimidated. Arika finally said, "Then you may accompany her."

"But I must look myself!" Siguna said sharply. "I cannot give this task to any eyes but my own."

"You shall be the one to look," Arika promised. "Go now, my daughter. There is no more time for you to waste."

After the two young people had disappeared around the curve in the tunnel, Arika turned to one of the matriarchs who had heard the exchange. "There is a girl who understands the sacredness of duty," the Mistress said thoughtfully.

"So I was thinking," the matriarch replied.

"Such a girl will find no room to breathe in the tribes that follow Sky God."

"The boy seems very interested," the matriarch commented. "If he seeks to marry her, she will have to go to his tribe."

"He is more interested in her than she is in him," Arika responded dismissively.

The matriarch sighed. "It is unfortunate that the same could not have been said about Nel and Ronan."

Arika's face closed. "Come," she said sharply. "It is time to check the wounded."

Cloud picked his own surefooted way down the rocky path between the hills while the man on his back reviewed in his mind the sequence of his action against the Horsemasters.

I need to determine what was successful for us and how I can use that success for the next time, Ronan thought.

He recognized with regret that surprise would never again be the same devastating factor it had been in the gorge. The chief of the Horsemasters would never let them be caught in a trap like that again.

He was clever, this Fenris. He had almost succeeded in luring Ronan's men into breaking ranks. If he had done that . . . Ronan's mouth set grimly as he thought about what might have happened if his men had left their nearly invincible formation and begun to pour down into the gorge.

The marksmen on the cliffs would have been immobilized. The enemy horsemen would have had a good chance of breaking through the strung-out defenders and gaining the pass. If Ronan had not kept his men out of that gorge, the ravens would be feasting on more than the Horsemasters this day.

Fenris had understood all of this. Ronan had seen the expression of bitter disappointment on the kain's face when he had realized that the spearmen were going to hold. It had been the strangest feeling, but for the briefest of moments, Ronan had felt an affinity with the chief of the enemy forces. He had known exactly what Fenris was feeling.

Cloud had reached the bottom of the mountain path, and Ronan turned him in the direction of the men's camp. It was very quiet in the hills today, he thought, glancing around. All of the scavengers were occupied elsewhere.

That shoulder-to-shoulder, spear-forward formation had worked extremely well, Ronan decided, shifting his own spear from his right hand to his left. It had turned back the horses. What he had to do now was figure out how he could continue to make such a formation work when he did not have the narrow chasm of a gorge to contain the enemy.

Cloud suddenly snorted and threw up his head. Ronan roused himself from his preoccupation, looked ahead, and saw the solitary woman waiting for him on the edge of the track. Instinctively, he braced his back, and Cloud's stride checked. It was Morna.

The two of them had dwelled within sight of each other for over a moon now, but never had they been in the same company. Ronan had yet to speak one word to his sister, nor had she spoken to him. They had both comported themselves as if the other were invisible, a tactic that had been aided and abetted by the rest of the men and women of their tribes. All knew what a weight of accusation and bitterness lay between Morna and Ronan, and all preferred to pretend that they did not.

For one brief and terrible moment, it seemed to Ronan as if time had rolled back. He was a young boy again, and Morna had come to lure him into an unspeakable sin. Cloud, reacting to the sudden rigidity of his rider, pawed the ground and began to sidle.

Then time rolled forward once more, and Ronan saw the swollen, child-heavy body of his sister. He touched Cloud with his heels and went forward to meet her.

"You," he said, in unconscious echo of his words five years before. "What are you doing here?"

She smiled at him mockingly. "I have not come for what you may think, Ronan." She placed a thin, white hand upon her great belly. "This is somewhat in my way these days."

He kept his seat on Cloud and watched her warily. "You should not have ventured so far alone. You are too near your time."

"I know I am near my time," she said. "I have felt death on the wind these last two days."

His brows drew together. "The only death on the wind has been the deaths of the Horsemasters. You are weary, Morna. That is all it is."

"Na." She shook her head and her loose red-gold hair floated around her shoulders. Even now, with fatigue imprinted in every line of her face, with shadows staining her eyes and thinness hollowing her cheeks, even now, she was beautiful. "I have known I was doomed since first I began to carry this child," she said. She shrugged. "It is the Mother's punishment on me. I know that as well."

She frightened him. She frightened him because he found himself believing her.

"Punishment for what you did to me?" he asked, his voice sounding like a croak.

Her eyes flashed in their old way. "You deserved what I did to you," she said. "Na, this is for something else."

He had no intention of asking her what that something else might be.

"I will die," she continued with eerie matter-of-factness, "but my child will live. It will be a boy and my mother will not want him. So, Ronan, I am going to leave him to you and Nel."

Ronan went absolutely rigid.

Morna's face lit with an enchanting smile. "I should not have told you, I know. I should have left it until there was nothing you could do about it. But I so much wanted to see your face."

Ronan found his voice. "Nel cannot nurse a child," he said harshly.

"Someone else can nurse him for her. But I will name Nel to be his mother." She put her hand on her side and leaned a little forward. "Once she takes my child in her arms, you will never get him away from her, Ronan."

He stared at her and saw Morna recoil from what she read in his eyes. Then she recovered herself, and once again she smiled mockingly. "Won't you like that, Ronan? Seeing my son at your hearthfire every night? Watching your beloved Nel holding him close to her heart?"

He felt frozen. His limbs wouldn't move. He did not think he would ever be able to get off of Cloud again. He said stiffly, "The child's father may have somewhat to say about your plans."

"Ronan." Her face brimmed with malicious joy. "Do you think anyone knows who this child's father is?"

He closed his fist upon Cloud's mane, to keep from lifting his spear against her.

"You hate me," Morna said. "Good. Because I hate you."

"Why?" It was the one thing he had never understood, why she should hate him so. "Why? Morna. Why do you hate me?"

She answered simply, "Because I wanted you and you did not want me."

There was nothing he could answer. He drew a long, shuddering breath and pressed Cloud forward, past the pollution that was his sister and his sister's unborn child.

Chapter Twenty-eight

One week after Ronan's meeting with Morna, she gave birth to her son. Ronan had said nothing to Nel about his conversation with his sister. He had been sickened and appalled by it, but for the first time in his life, he was afraid that Nel would not see things the same way he did. Morna had found a weapon that would strike at the very heart of his life, his relationship with Nel, and he did not know what he was going to do.

All during that week of waiting, Ronan told himself that Morna had been wrong. All women so near to giving birth feared they would die, he thought. He was a fool to so upset himself over the words of a sick, malevolent woman. There was certainly enough for him to worry about without borrowing trouble from Morna!

There had been a baby born shortly after the tribes had gathered at the Great Cave, and Morna's was the second. The women took her out to the moon hut for privacy, and after a full night and day of hard labor, it was clear that this childbirth was not going as smoothly as it should.

Arika stayed with her daughter, saying prayers to the Mother and making all the ceremonials that were supposed to ease the baby's way out of its mother's body and into the world. But hour after hour went by, and still the baby would not come.

Morna was suffering terribly. Her screams did not reach very far beyond the moon hut, but there was a pall over the whole encampment as they waited for news. Everyone knew it was going on too long.

As the day dragged by, Ronan's heart grew heavier and heavier. Morna had foreseen the truth, he thought bleakly. She would die and leave behind a child for him to rear.

Won't you like that, Ronan? Seeing my son at your hearthfire every night? Watching your beloved Nel holding him close to her heart?

It was very late in the afternoon when at last Berta came out to the men's encampment to tell him the news: Morna was dead and had left her son to the care of Nel and Ronan.

Every atom of Nel's being yearned toward that baby. When Arika had placed Morna's child in her arms, joy had leaped like wildfire in Nel's heart. She had been ashamed of that joy, but she could not contain it. Her arms had curled around the tiny, warm bundle, and she had looked down into the small, perfect face of Morna's son.

"One of the women of the Red Deer has nursed him already," Arika said. "You will have to find one of the women of your tribe to nurse him as you obviously cannot do it yourself."

Nel looked into Arika's ravaged face, and pity nudged at the joy in her heart. She said, "Will you sit and have some tea, Mistress? You look exhausted."

Arika let out a long shuddering sigh. "Sa," she said. "I will have some tea with you, Nel."

Beki said softly to Nel, "Let me take the babe for you, Nel, while you speak to the Mistress. I will put him to sleep beside Eken's little one."

Nel did not want to part with the baby, but she looked at Arika's face, then turned to transfer carefully the precious bundle into Beki's arms. The rest of the women melted away, leaving the two alone by the fire. "She knew she was going to die," Arika said. "She told me when the pains were first beginning that she would not live to see her son." Arika bowed her head. She looked beaten. She looked old. "It is the only time I have ever seen the Goddess in Morna, when she told me she was going to die."

Nel's sensitive mouth curved downward with reflected pain.

Arika lifted her head. "She told me she was going to die and that she wanted you to have her child."

Nel nodded gravely. "I am the only woman left of her Mother's

Line, and Ronan is her only brother. Of course she would name us to take her child."

Arika looked steadily into Nel's eyes. "That may be true, but that is not why Morna named you. Don't you understand, Nel?" There was a pause as Arika's eyes bored into Nel's. "She did it to punish Ronan," Arika said.

Now the pain in Nel's heart was not a mere reflection of Arika's. "Ah . . . ," Nel's hand went to her throat, "I had not thought . . ."

In truth, all she had been thinking, all she had been feeling, was the baby.

"I brought the child to you because I promised Morna I would do so," Arika said. "But it is up to you and Ronan, whether or not you will keep him."

"Ronan will not mind," Nel managed to stammer.

"On the contrary"—Arika's voice was harsh—"I am thinking that he will mind very much."

Nel bent her head.

"I can find someone else in the tribe who will take him," Arika said. "I will not expose him, Nel. You need have no fear of that."

Nel shuddered.

When Arika next spoke her tone was more gentle. "You have never conceived?"

Nel shook her head. With downcast eyes, she told Arika of her own belief that she had offended the Mother. Then she repeated what Ronan had told her.

"Ronan said that?" Arika asked in a strange voice.

"Sa," Nel said.

"He surprises me," his mother said. "He continually surprises me." She looked at Nel's half-hidden face. "Perhaps he will surprise me again and say that you may keep the child."

At that, Nel threw up her head. "It is not enough that he says the child may stay for my sake. He must accept it also." Nel's eyes glittered. "Both Ronan and I know what it is to grow up in a place where you are not wanted, and it is no good. I would never do that to a child. Never!"

Arika was very pale. She put down her half-drunk tea. "You must discuss it with him, then, and let me know." Moving slowly, like an old woman, she lumbered to her feet. "I must go now and see about burying my daughter," she said, turned, and walked wearily away.

Ronan sent his men to their supper, but he himself did not remain in camp to eat. He felt the men watching him as he walked out of the valley, Nigak at his heels. Berta's news had reached every ear by now, and he knew the men were wondering what he was going to do about Morna's child.

He had taken the track that led to the Great Cave, but once he was out of view of the valley he veered off of it and cut south toward the cliffs. He was not yet ready to face Nel.

What am I going to do?

Berta had told him that Nel had taken the baby. Well, that was no surprise. He had known all along that Nel would take the baby. She had tried valiantly to hide from him her disappointment when her moon blood had begun to flow a few days after they had been together in the sacred cave, but he had seen the pain in her eyes.

If he told her that he could never accept Morna's child into his heart, she would understand. She would give the baby up. More than anyone, Nel understood how wrong it would be to leave a child where it was not wanted.

But he had seen the pain in her eyes.

What am I going to do?

He checked at the sight of a solitary feminine figure walking toward him along the base of the cliff. For a moment, sheer panic held him frozen. Nigak whined. Then Ronan saw that the girl's hair was silver-blond, not red-gold, and his heart began to slow to its normal beat.

It was Fenris's daughter. Siguna. He frowned. She should not be out here alone. He strode forward, Nigak pacing watchfully at his heels.

Siguna saw Ronan at almost the exact moment he saw her, and she halted against the cliff, her wary eyes on Nigak. She had learned to be fairly comfortable with Nel's dogs, but the wolf still frightened her.

"What are you doing out here alone?" Ronan said.

To Siguna's relief, Nigak went right by her and began to sniff along the bottom of the cliff. "Where are Thorn and Mait?" Ronan demanded next, and she raised her eyes to see him scowling at her.

"Back at the Great Cave," Siguna said. "I wanted to be alone."

His frown deepened. "You have too much of a liking for being alone."

Siguna drew a deep slow breath and steadied herself. She didn't know why, but there was something about Ronan that always seemed to unnerve her. She answered him in an even tone. "These last days have not been very easy for me, and Thorn and Mait were kind enough to understand."

She could see him remember why she might not have found the general rejoicing in camp very enjoyable. He passed a hand across his brow as if to rub away the scowl and said in a milder voice, "I am sorry, Siguna." He dropped his hand. "But there are dangerous animals about; it is not safe for you to wander so far from camp."

She thought that he looked weary. It came to her then that neither was Ronan in his usual place. Had he too been in search of solitude?

She asked tentatively, "Is something wrong?"

A raven swooped by overhead, its wingbeats making a hissing *shhou, shhou* in the heavy stillness. A picture of what the ravens had been doing last week flitted through Siguna's mind, and she shuddered. As if from a distance, she heard Ronan's voice saying, "Is it possible that you have not heard?"

She shook her head, forcing herself to concentrate on his words. "I have heard nothing."

"I thought everyone must have heard." He too was watching the raven, his dark eyes narrowed against the sun, bitterness in the hard lines of his mouth. "It is Morna," he said. "She died in childbirth and left her son to my care and Nel's."

Siguna's breath hissed in her throat.

The bitterness edging Ronan's mouth deepened. "Sa. It is hard to believe, is it not?"

Slowly, Siguna seated herself upon a large rock that was jutting out from the cliffside. She knew what lay between Ronan and his sister; she had not been two weeks with the Tribe of the Wolf before she had heard that tale. She was also well aware of Nel's barrenness and the sorrow it had caused her. She said now, looking up into Ronan's wintry face, "I did not know."

He grunted. "Well, now you understand why I too have been avoiding going home."

She was deeply surprised that he was speaking to her in such wise. Slowly it came to her that this confidence sharing was his way of apologizing for having forgotten her own sorrow.

"Will Nel take the child?" she asked softly, ready to drop the subject instantly if that was what he wished.

He braced his right hand against the wall of the cliff and bent his head to look at her. "What do you think?"

Siguna replied honestly, "I do not think it will matter to her whose babe this may be—she will love it anyway."

His face was utterly bleak. "That is what I think too."

Siguna averted her eyes from that unguarded face, resting them instead on the hand he had braced against the cliff wall. It was a thinner hand than her father's, but the forearm that was exposed by Ronan's rolled-up sleeve was hard-muscled and deeply tanned.

Ronan said, "She wants a child, and when a woman has a longing like that in her heart, there is nothing a man can say or do that will change it."

Siguna tore her eyes away from that strangely exciting hand. She said something about how hard it was for a man to accept another man's child.

He shook his head, signifying that was not it. "I am his mother's brother," he said. "In the Tribe of the Red Deer, it is the mother's brother who is a child's closest male relative. I have obligations to this child. I know that. But . . ." Here his voice broke off. His face was even bleaker than it had been.

He was looking for help, Siguna thought suddenly. That was why he was discussing this with her. He was seeking for a way to make this child acceptable to him.

Suddenly, fiercely, desperately, Siguna wanted to help him. She made herself draw a long, settling breath before she asked, "Then why not take him, Ronan?"

His nostrils flared. "The answer to that should be obvious, I think. This is Morna's child." The way he said his sister's name indicated the depth of his revulsion.

Siguna regarded the dark, arrogant face that was so clearly outlined against the cobalt blue sky. "Is it that you are afraid the child will be like Morna?"

He nodded his raven head.

Two red deer, a buck and a doe, suddenly appeared between the cliffs that guarded the path to the south. As Siguna gazed at them, they noticed Nigak and bounded away, disappearing as suddenly as they had come.

It was a sign, Siguna thought. The deer were a sign from the Mother. Suddenly she was sure that it was the Goddess's doing that she and Ronan had come together on the cliff path this day.

For the first time in her life, Siguna closed her eyes and prayed: *Mother, help me. If you have truly sent this man to me, then give me the right words to say.*

Siguna opened her eyes. She looked at Ronan. She said, "We have bred horses in my tribe for many generations, Ronan, and any one of us would tell you that, no matter how wild the stallion or mare, if the foal is gentled young, then he is yours. The color, the speed, the temperament, all these may come from the parents; but the spirit belongs to the one who tames it. I am thinking that this is true for children as well as for foals."

Ronan was silent for a long time. Finally he said, "I do not know." He looked suddenly very uncertain and very young. He repeated, "I do not know."

Siguna's heart went out to him. Her hands longed to go out to him as well, and, feeling their movement, she clasped them together in her lap. She made her voice very cool in order to mask her emotion. "What would Nigak have been like if he had been left to his own mother to rear?" she asked. "He would have been the same wolf in blood and bone, but his spirit would be utterly different."

They both turned to look at Nigak as he sniffed his way along the cliff, checking for the scent of another male wolf. Ronan answered slowly, his eyes still on Nigak, "That is so."

Another silence fell between them. Nigak raised a hind leg and left his own scent on the lower part of the cliff.

Siguna smiled, as if something that had been eluding her had suddenly fallen into place. "You took twins into your tribe, Ronan, when no one else would. Why did you do that?"

His dark eyes were puzzled, as if he did not understand the change of subject. He shrugged and said, "It is simply that I do not believe that babies can be evil."

He fell silent as he heard his own words.

This time the silence went on for a very long time. High on the cliffs Siguna could see several ibex. A male with sharp horns was reclining on the top of a flat boulder. As she watched, his head sank slowly under the weight of his horns until his nose touched the rock; then it jerked up, only to begin to descend again.

Siguna's voice seemed to come from a place deep inside her, a place she had never before plumbed. "Do you think that any living thing could be touched by Nel and not learn to be gentle?"

The softest sound, as of a breath being slowly released, floated in the air. Was it Ronan? Or was it something else? Siguna looked around and was caught by a pair of dark eyes.

"You have a wisdom that is beyond your years, Siguna," he said.

She gave him a beautiful smile.

His expression altered, and Siguna abruptly found herself confronting the hard, intent, hunting look of the sexual male. It was a look Siguna was all too familiar with. It was a look she both feared and hated. Usually.

"How old are you?" Ronan asked.

She tried to answer, reminded herself to breathe, and managed to stutter, "Th-three-handful years."

That dark gaze flicked lightly, speculatively, along the swell of her breasts. Siguna's pulses began to beat faster, but she was not afraid.

"That is old to be yet a maiden."

She raised her chin. "How do you know I am yet a maiden?"

He smiled, as if he found her question amusing. "Were you promised to a man of your tribe?"

She shook her head in violent denial.

Both the hunting look and the amusement were in his eyes now, and Siguna realized with astonishment that she wanted him to touch her.

He reached to pick up his spear. "Come," he said. "I will walk with you back to the Great Cave."

She stood up from her rock and found her eyes looking directly at the pulse that beat in the strong brown column of his throat. She was breathing rapidly and her legs felt unsteady.

What is the matter with me? she thought.

He said in a soft, dark voice, "I find it hard to believe that there was no man in your tribe who was special to you."

She answered, stupidly, betrayingly, "The men of my tribe are not like you."

There was a catastrophic silence, and then he grinned. "They most certainly are not. Heno says the men of your tribe need an introduction to Berta."

She realized, with dizzying relief, that he had misunderstood her. She stared at that intoxicating smile and managed to croak, "I am thinking Heno is right."

"A man who does not value a woman is a fool," Ronan said, and the hunting look was back in his eyes. His voice deepened. "I promise you, little one, that if you choose to make your home with us, there will be many men more than happy to value you."

But they will not be you.

As soon as the words formed in Siguna's mind, she panicked. What was she thinking?

Ronan called to Nigak and turned his steps toward home. As she fell in beside him, he said in his usual voice, "I am glad I met you today, Siguna, but don't come out alone again. I don't say this because I don't trust you, I say it because it is not safe."

"Nel goes about alone," Siguna said defensively.

"Nel is never alone," Ronan replied. "If she doesn't have Nigak, she has the dogs. Lately even White Foot has taken to following her around like a lost puppy." He was trying to sound aggrieved, but Siguna's sharp ears caught the unmistakable note of tenderness beneath the surface exasperation.

Siguna realized with a mixture of sorrow and relief that she would always be safe from Ronan. He might look with appreciation at an attractive woman, but it was Nel who held his heart.

Siguna had never met a man like Ronan before. He could be as ruthless as Fenris ever was; she had seen that when she had waded through the stinking corpses in the Volp gorge. He was a leader who exacted the same obedience from his men that her father did. Yet he was not really like her father at all.

A man who does not value a woman is a fool.

Siguna had not been thinking of Nigak alone when she had told Ronan that nothing could be touched by Nel and not learn to be gentle.

Chapter Twenty-nine

The baby slept, and when he woke Eken fed him. Nel had left the Great Cave shortly after her conversation with Arika, and as the daylight slowly waned, she still had not returned. The women of the tribe put their children down to sleep and gathered around the hearth in the cave chamber they had taken for their own.

"It will be a cruelty if Ronan won't let her keep the babe," Beki said defiantly.

The women of the Wolf looked at each other, and it was Fara who finally responded. "More than anyone, I have reason to know how tolerant Ronan can be in regard to children." Her sweet face was deeply troubled. "But, Beki, I do not think it is fair to expect him to accept Morna's child at his hearth."

Berta said heavily, "He is the child's mother's brother."

Tora said, "It is hard for me to believe that such a one as Morna was once considered the Chosen One of the Mother." Her level brown gaze turned to her sister. "Morna has done this to break Ronan's marriage."

Berta sighed.

"That will not happen!" said Yoli. "You heard what Nel said to the Mistress, Tora. She said that if Ronan could not bring himself to accept the child, she would send the baby back to Arika. Nel will not let Morna destroy her marriage."

Beki said flatly, "I do not care what Nel may have said. I do know this: if Ronan makes her give up the child, she will never forgive him."

Heavy silence blanketed the chamber.

"I am afraid that Beki is right," Berta said at last. "There is nothing in the world more powerful than a woman's yearning for a child. It is put into her heart by the Mother, and no man can stand in its way."

"It does not help that in the Tribe of the Red Deer there are a number of children who look exactly like Ronan," Fara said sadly.

Yoli sighed.

"No one would make a better mother than Nel!" Beki said passionately. "It is so unfair that she has not had a child."

Eken, who had nursed the orphan along with her own daughter, said now, "He is a beautiful baby. Perhaps once Ronan sees him . . ."

Tora was shaking her head. "Men do not feel the same about these things as women do."

No one contradicted her.

In the sudden silence, a step could be heard outside the chamber opening. Then the shadow of a man was in the doorway, ducking his head to keep from hitting it on the stone arch. He straightened and looked at the group of women staring back at him. It was Ronan.

"Where is Nel?" he asked, when once he had ascertained that she was not present.

"We don't know," Berta replied. "She talked to Arika shortly after . . ." She waved her hand in lieu of finishing the sentence, then added, "We have not seen her since."

Ronan's face looked tired and bleak. "Where is the baby?" he asked next.

"Next door, sleeping with the other children," Eken answered. "I nursed him after I nursed my Melie."

"Will you get him for me?" Ronan asked her.

"Sa." Eken scrambled to her feet. "Of course, Ronan. Of course I will get him for you." She shot a quick glance at Fara before disappearing into the adjoining chamber, where all the children were sleeping.

Fara asked gently, "Would you like us to leave you alone, Ronan?"

He stared at her as if he had not understood. But then he nodded. "Sa. That would be . . . good."

The women quietly got to their feet and melted toward the door as Ronan came further into the chamber. He was standing by the hearth, his hands clasped behind his back, his head bent, when Eken came back into the room, the baby in her arms. She hesitated a moment and then walked up to him. "Here he is," she said, extending her arms a little so that he could see.

Ronan looked down.

He was indeed a beautiful baby. His small face was perfectly formed, the skin pink, not the angry red of most newborns. His fuzzy hair was brown, and the eyes that blinked sleepily up at Ronan were a soft and misty gray.

"He does not look like Morna," Ronan said. His face was an unreadable mask.

"Na." Eken was having a hard time talking around the lump in her throat. "He looks like himself."

Ronan continued to stare at the baby with that masklike look on his face. Eken continued to hold the baby out to him as if it were an offering. The lightest of sounds came from the arched door opening, and then Nel was with them in the room.

Nel had just spent what were perhaps the most emotionally exhausting hours of her life, and she looked it. When at last she walked into the room and saw Ronan and the baby, she still did not know what she was going to say. She had spent hours and hours trying to resolve the conflict, and her thoughts were still going around in circles.

Fine words she had said to Arika earlier, words that had wounded, words that had been meant to wound. "Ronan and I know what it is to grow up in a place where you are not wanted," she had said, and Arika had been vanquished.

Fine words, but Nel knew that this baby was not unwanted. No baby in the world was more wanted than this one was.

Part of her said that eventually Ronan would come to accept the child as his own. Surely, she told herself over and over, surely she would be able to make him understand that this child had been given to them by the Mother. It was what she herself felt. Strongly. Surely she would be able to convey this conviction to Ronan.

But the objective, rational part of her said that she was being unfair, that she was laying too great a burden on her husband in asking him to take this child of his sister's. She feared that if she forced Ronan to keep the child against his own instincts, she was risking the poisoning of the most precious thing in the world to her, her marriage.

Nothing, she thought, was worth that risk.

And then she came into the cave and saw Ronan and the baby. Without uttering a single word, Eken walked up to her, deposited the baby in her arms, and went out the door. Ronan and Nel were left alone, staring at each other across the bundle in Nel's arms.

Ronan spoke first. "He does not look like Morna."

Nel looked down into the drowsy baby face. She drew a deep, shuddering breath. "Ronan," she said. "Ronan . . ."

Slowly Ronan crossed the space that lay between them, stopped, and then he too looked down. The baby yawned, showing an impressive expanse of pink gums.

"Morna told me a week ago that she was going to do this," he said.

Nel tore her eyes away from the baby. "You never told me that!"

He shook his head. "It was an ugly scene."

"Ronan." She was holding on to the baby as if she were drowning and he was her only chance to keep afloat. "I will not try to tell you anything good about Morna. She did this for revenge, I can see that well enough. But . . . sometimes . . . sometimes good can come out of evil, Ronan. I have been thinking, you and I made the sacred marriage together in the Mother's holy place, and I begged her for a baby. And now . . . so soon after . . . this baby has been placed in my arms." She drew in a deep, ragged breath. "Do you not think that perhaps it is the Mother's wish that we take him?"

Ronan looked at Nel's face, looked at the stain of bluish shadow under her eyes. She seemed to him now just as small and as defenseless as the baby in her arms. His eyes went once more to the baby. It did not look at all like Morna.

I do not believe that babies can be evil. He had said that, and it was true.

He heard himself saying firmly, "I think you are right, minnow."

Nel gazed up at him, not daring to believe what she had just heard. He was suddenly angry that this should mean so much to her. It made him feel that he had been pushed out of the center of her life. "I am not a monster," he said. "Did you think I was going to rip him out of your arms?"

She shook her head vehemently. He could see her fighting back tears. That made him feel like a monster in truth, and he reached forward to put his arms around her. To do that, he had to put his arms around the baby as well.

Nel leaned against him and began to sob, deep, wracking, wrenching sobs. She cried so hard he was afraid she was going to drop the baby, so Ronan took him from her. Then the baby began to cry.

"Dhu," said Ronan. "If you keep this up, Nel, I warn you I will change my mind."

At that she laughed. It was a husky, quivery, watery sound, but definitely a laugh. "Give him to me," she said. As soon as she took him, the baby stopped crying.

"You seem to have the same touch with babies that you have with horses and wolves," Ronan said.

Nel's smile was wet but radiant. She lifted her face and pressed a kiss along his jawbone. "I love you so much," she said. "There is not another man in the world like you."

Ronan looked at his tiny rival. "Just see that you remember that," he said, and he was only partly joking.

The day after their devastating defeat in the gorge, Fenris gathered his anda around his hearth. These were his captains, the warriors whom he had given command over the other horsemen of the tribe. The day before yesterday they had numbered eight. Today their number was six.

As the somber-faced men took their places around the hearth in the kain's tent, they were joined by two new faces: Vili, the kain's eldest son, and Bragi, his friend. The boys seated themselves in the places left empty by those who had died in the gorge, lowered their eyes deferentially, and waited.

Fenris rested his big hands on his knees. "So," he said, "it seems we have an enemy."

Growls came from six throats.

"Cowards," Surtur spat out. "They are afraid to come out and fight like men."

"That is so," grunted another man.

The kain disagreed. "It was a clever trap," he said coldly. "Cleverly thought out and cleverly executed." His wintry gray eyes circled the faces of the men before him. "It has been many years since we have been opposed by force, but these mountainmen are obviously ready to fight to keep us out of their hunting grounds."

"They surprised us once," Surtur growled. "They will not surprise us like that again."

The rest of the men began to talk all together. Only Fenris and the boys were silent. At last the voices ran down, and faces turned once more toward the kain.

In the silence, Fenris took up his spear and stabbed it deeply into the bare earth beside him. The men looked with fierce anticipation at the quivering shaft. This was what they had been waiting for. The spear was the sign that the kain was about to speak words of war.

Fenris said, "I have lost six handfuls of my finest warriors, and I say to you now that I will avenge them. I have called upon the Thunderer, and he has answered me."

A deep murmur came from the men.

Fenris spoke again. "I will take these mountains, my brothers. I will descend like lightning upon the land of my foes, and to you will go their fairest women and their highest-stepping horses. The beasts of their hunting grounds will fall upon your spears, and their children will serve at the doors of your tents."

This time it was a roar that arose from the throats of the listening men, and Vili's teeth gleamed in a great white grin.

It was Surtur who made the ritual response for the anda. "You are our kain, and wherever you lead, we shall follow. If ever we should fail you, it is for you to abandon us and cast us out, solitary, to the forsaken earth." This was the tie that bound together kain and warrior in the tribe of the Horsemasters, and a reverent silence fell around the fire as the men cherished the words in their hearts. From the edges of the tent could be heard the soft murmurs of women shushing children: "Be quiet, my child, be quiet. Your father is meeting with his anda. You must be quiet."

"I wonder how they learned to tame horses," Vili murmured at last.

Fenris said, "How they got the horses is not important. What is important is that they have them." He set his mouth in a way that made the cleft in his chin more pronounced. "I have said that I will go after these mountainmen, and I will. But no more will I ride like a blind man into mountains that I do not know."

The faces of the men were somber. They nodded.

Fenris said, "We shall continue along this River of Gold as we had planned. Our scouts have gone before us and we know the land is open.

There are tribes dwelling upon this river. Horseless tribes. My scouts have seen them."

"That is so," spoke up Skoggi, who was the chief of the scouts.

"We will attack these tribes," Fenris said.

Pleased grunts greeted this remark, and then an expectant silence.

"We will make such a slaughter that the mountains will run red with blood," Fenris promised.

Grins.

"I will make these mountainmen come to me," Fenris said, "and then I will cut them to pieces."

A noisy group of children were playing in the small clearing near the Great Cave that had been alotted to them by the adults. Thorn had been told that Siguna was minding the children, and he had come in search of her.

The happy scene in the clearing betrayed no signs of the imminent conflict facing the adults of the gathered tribes. At the one side of the clearing, a group of children were taking turns using the swing that Neihle had made for them. He had done this by lashing a vine first to the ends of half a log, and then to the sturdy lower branch of a birch tree that had edged into the clearing from the surrounding forest.

Another group, mainly boys with a few of the Red Deer girls mixed in, were playing a game with hoops made of peeled wood and small spears. It was a game Thorn remembered well, and he watched the children with a smile of faint nostalgia.

The game was simple in concept, more difficult in execution. One child would roll a series of hoops one after the other across a length of ground, and as they passed, another child had to hurl the spears through them in such a way that the spear stuck into the ground with the hoop spinning on it. As the hoops were rolled with full force, they bounced high and erratically, but even so, Thorn was pleased to note that the children with the spears did not often miss.

He turned away from the game and saw Siguna walking toward him, the sun glinting on her silvery hair. As Thorn watched her approach, he felt a familiar ache in the region of his heart. She was so beautiful, he thought. He wanted desperately to draw her picture, but there was little chance for solitude these days. Nor did he want to draw her face on the walls of the Great Cave. He wanted her in his own special cave in the valley; he wanted her among the pictures he had made of the rest of the tribe. In truth, it was more than Siguna's picture he wanted. When this conflict was over, he wanted to bring her home with him.

She gave him a fleeting smile as she came up to him. "What are you doing here, Thorn?"

"Looking for you," he replied. The hours they had spent in the gorge had been grisly in the extreme, and though Siguna had persisted stoically in her search, Thorn knew that the experience had been devastating for her. It certainly had been devastating for him, and he had neither known nor cared about any of the men who had been transformed by death and scavengers into such horrifying carrion.

He looked now into Siguna's eyes and was relieved to see that the shadow that had been there for the last few days appeared to have lifted. He smiled at her. "I have never seen Nel so happy," he remarked easily.

"Sa," Siguna agreed.

"Ronan is the only man I know who would have allowed her to keep that babe," he said next. "No one thought that he would."

Siguna regarded him curiously. "What would you have done, Thorn?" she asked.

Thorn stared at her in surprise.

"Would you have let her keep the babe?" Siguna persisted.

"Well . . ." Thorn ran his fingers through his brown forelock, pushing it off his forehead. "I suppose I would have," he said.

Siguna smiled. "I thought so."

Thorn looked wistfully into her lovely face. He wanted very much to tell her how he felt about her, but he knew that this was not the time for such words.

"Aiiiyee!" The high-pitched shriek rose above the quieter babble of peacefully playing children. Both Thorn and Siguna whirled around to see what was happening.

A group of boys had collected handfuls of acorns from the forest floor and were throwing them at each other. As Thorn watched, one of the boys advanced boldly on the enemy, flinging his acorns with deadly accuracy. The returning missiles bounced harmlessly off the reindeerskin vest that he was holding out in front of him.

"Dhu," Siguna exclaimed and started forward to halt the battle.

"Wait." Thorn's hand shot out to grab her arm.

She halted, surprised by the strength of his grip, and looked at him angrily. "Someone may lose an eye, Thorn! I must stop them."

He did not seem to hear her. He was staring at the boy with the vest, an expression of intense concentration on his face. At last, slowly, his fingers opened, and he released her.

After Siguna had halted the fight and gotten the boys involved in a more peaceful activity, she returned to where Thorn was standing. "Why did you try to keep me from stopping the fight?" she asked him curiously.

"It was nothing." He looked at her, but his expression was abstracted. "I must go, Siguna."

"Where?" she demanded.

"I need to talk to Ronan." Without further comment, he turned and strode away.

Ronan sat staring thoughtfully at the spear in his hand. He had sat thus for the last few nights, and neither Bror nor Crim, who shared his tent, had dared to ask him what he was thinking.

It had been a half-moon since the battle at the Volp gorge, and word had come to the tribes that the Horsemasters had packed up their camp and were once more traveling down the River of Gold. Ronan had responded to this news by announcing that he would move the men of the Federation to the Red Deer homesite on the Greatfish River within the next few days.

In the meantime, he sat and looked at the spear. At last Bror could stand the suspense no longer. "What do you see in that spear, Ronan, that you should regard it with such fascination for two straight nights?"

Ronan did not lift his eyes from the weapon in his hand. "It is not one of our own spears. It is one we took from the bodies of the Horsemasters in the gorge."

"Sa," Bror said patiently. "I can see that."

Finally Ronan focused his brilliant dark gaze on his friend. "How do you see that?"

Bror blinked. "The wooden shaft is not so long as is the shaft of our spears."

Ronan grunted and held the spear out to Bror, who was sitting across from him by their small hearth. "What else is different?"

Bror regarded the spear thoughtfully, then lifted it to a throwing position. "It is lighter," he said.

Ronan gave a pleased smile. "Sa. It is shorter, and it is lighter. All of their spears are like that, Bror. We took enough of them from the gorge for me to be certain that they are all alike."

"I am thinking they make them like that because they go on horseback," Crim said. "A longer, heavier spear would make it harder to keep one's balance."

"Exactly." Now Ronan was grinning.

Bror put down the spear. "All right," he said resignedly. "We give up. What does it mean?"

"It means that our spears, being longer and stronger, will wound the enemy before theirs can wound us," Ronan said.

The two men stared at him in dumbfounded silence. "Ronan," Crim finally said, his voice carefully reasonable, "it is true that that would be an advantage if men on foot were fighting men on foot. But they will be on horseback. And we do not have enough horses to counter the numbers they can bring against us."

"We turned back their horses in the gorge," Ronan said.

Bror slammed his hand against the ground. "That was because of the gorge!"

"That is so. But there is no reason we cannot use the same tactics again. True, we will never have so perfect a location as the gorge, but there are several places along the Greatfish where an oncoming host might be halted. We would have to spread our line much wider than we did in the gorge, of course." He narrowed his eyes. "Picture it, lines of spearmen several deep, shoulder to shoulder, holding the line at the place where the Red Deer valley would open out behind them."

"It is not possible," Crim said.

"The Horsemasters would have to attack uphill," Ronan pointed out.

From outside the tent they could hear the distant voices of the men on firewatch talking.

"It does not matter. Men on foot cannot stand against horses," Crim said.

"I think we can hold out for long enough. Remember, Fenris does not know our numbers. If we can hold on for long enough, I think he will turn back."

Silence fell as the men contemplated the picture Ronan had painted with his words. A sudden roar of laughter came from the men on firewatch.

"They could use javelins and arrows against us before they attacked," Bror said.

Ronan smiled with genuine pleasure. "Thorn has come up with a defense against that."

Bror and Crim stared at him in amazed expectation.

"He has designed something to protect our men against enemy weapons."

"What?" Bror demanded.

"It would look like this." Ronan picked up a rock and sketched a rectangular shape in the dirt. "We can make them of wood and attach some kind of a hand grip on the inside. Do you see? A man would hold it before him, so, and it would keep him from being struck by his enemy's weapons."

"Dhu," Crim breathed. "I do see."

"This was Thorn's idea?" Bror said.

Ronan grinned. "It came to him while he was watching a group of boys pelting each other with acorns."

Bror grunted.

"These ideas will take time to put into practice," Crim said. "The men will need to practice keeping their formation. We will have to make these shields."

Ronan raised his head. "I know."

"Do you think the Horsemasters will allow us the time?"

"If they don't," Ronan said, "we shall have to distract them."

Chapter Thirty

"Do you want to bring some of the mares with you?" Nel asked. "There are two handfuls of them who are trained to be ridden." It was a hot summer afternoon, and Nel had gone out to the men's camp to see Ronan. They had ridden into the next valley, picketed their horses, and found a comfortable spot for themselves on the thick grass.

"I would have to build a corral for them and keep them separated from the stallions. It's not worth the trouble, Nel, for only two handfuls of horses."

Nel sighed. "I suppose that is true."

Ronan was lying on his back in the grass, his hands behind his head, his eyes narrowed against the brilliant summer sky. "I'm sure you can make use of the mares here," he said in a voice that sounded almost sleepy. "Use them as packhorses to send us the shields that the women are making."

Nel, who was sitting cross-legged next to him, nodded. "I have been thinking I would have Siguna show me how her tribe uses horses to pull. Besides the shields, we will have to be sending you greens and grain and fruit. Men have little skill in gathering, and you must have something to eat besides meat."

"Mmmm," Ronan said. His eyes had closed.

Nel looked down into his relaxed face with a mixture of tenderness and annoyance. On the one hand, she worried that he was driving himself too hard. On the other hand, she had not sought him out just to watch him sleep.

She said, "You are outnumbered by these Horsemasters. Siguna says there are more than two of them to every one of us."

His lashes lifted. "I know that, Nel."

Nel bit her lip. A long strand of silky hair, loosened from her braid, had fallen across her face. She blew it back, and Ronan smiled faintly. He crossed an arm over his eyes to shade them and asked, "What is the matter, minnow? You did not come out here just to tell me things I already know."

Nel said with great determination, "I want to come with you, Ronan."

For a long moment he did not answer. Then he sat up. "You can't. I am not even taking the women of the Red Deer this time."

"Arika is going."

"Arika is the chief of her tribe. She is different. Besides"—and he shot her a dark, sideways look—"Arika does not have a baby to take care of."

"I would not bring Culen," Nel replied promptly. "He can stay with Eken."

There was a surprised silence. Then Ronan shook his head. "You are speaking foolishly, Nel. You do not really want to leave Culen, and there is nothing you can do for me if you come."

She leaned toward him. "I can take care of the horses. They will not listen to anyone else as well as they listen to me."

As they both knew, this was unarguably true. He said, "There is little to be done with the horses. And, with Arika gone, I need you to be in charge here to see to the shields and the food."

"Berta can do that."

"Berta will not be able to handle the mares."

"Siguna and Beki can handle the mares."

He closed his eyes. "Nel. You cannot come. It is impossible."

She did not answer. He opened his eyes again and looked at her. The summer sun had tinted her skin to a pale golden hue, with just the faintest flush of rose over the cheekbones. Her lower lip was chapped from the way she chewed on it when she was worried. The loose strand of hair had slipped once more over her forehead and looked in danger of becoming entangled in the sweep of her eyelashes. He raised his hand and smoothed the lock back gently.

"I had a dream last night, Ronan," she said in a low voice. "A terrible dream." Her long eyes, gray with distress, lifted and clung to his face.

He set his heart against that look. "You cannot come," he repeated. "As I told the girls of the Red Deer, I want none of our women within the reach of these rapists. If I bring you, then Haras will have the right to bring his wife, and Unwar his. Then the wives will want to bring their children. Then they will need more women to help with the children . . ." He shook his head emphatically. "Na, Nel. You cannot come."

As he spoke, Nel's eyes had been slowly changing from gray to the deep, glittering green that signaled anger. She said, "I see now that the Mistress was right."

"Right about what?" The words were out before he could consider their wisdom.

"Right about the arrogance of men when they come into power."

His mouth thinned. "Did she mention also the unfairness of women?"

They glared at each other.

"You did not even ask me about my dream," Nel said.

Ronan took a hard hold upon his temper, reminding himself that he had not brought Nel to this secluded valley to argue with her. To gain time, he pulled up a single strand of long grass and squinted at it. "It is just that I am not in the mood to hear a sad tale about how you saw me lying dead somewhere in a pool of blood." He put the long grass leaf in his mouth and began to chew on it.

His words did not soothe Nel at all. In fact, they incensed her. "You're annoyed at me because you think I am paying too much attention to Culen and not enough to you. That is the true reason you are making these speeches about women and children being in your way."

There was enough truth in this remark to infuriate Ronan. He jerked the grass out of his mouth. "You ungrateful little brat," he growled.

"And I'll have you know that I did *not* see you lying dead in a pool of blood," Nel snapped. Her eyes were flashing, her cheeks flying flags of hectic color. The loose strand of hair slipped over her forehead again, and she lifted her hand to brush it away. Her buckskin sleeves were rolled in the summer heat, and Ronan could see the faint scar on the inside of her fragile wrist.

As he stared at that delicate, blue-veined wrist, his ill temper vanished. What a fool I am, he thought wryly. "Minnow," he said, giving her one of his most beguiling smiles. He reached, and his own hard, calloused fingers closed around her wrist. "I don't want to fight with you."

Nel shot him a still-angry, distrustful look.

He was moving his thumb up and down on her wrist. "What did you dream, if it was not about me lying dead in a pool of blood?" he asked soothingly.

"I wish you would stop talking about lying dead in a pool of blood! It can't be lucky, Ronan."

The skin of her wrist was so smooth, so incredibly soft. He raised his other hand and again brushed the loose hair away from her brow. He sniffed the familiar fragrance that was her hair. Her head was tilted back now, her long cat eyes gazing up at him. "You are lucky for me, Nel," he said and bent his head to her mouth.

He felt her arms come around him, and then she was clinging close, her whole body cleaving to his. "You are so unafraid," she whispered, when his mouth had left hers to move to the hollow of her throat. "Don't you see? That is why I am afraid for you, because you are so unafraid for yourself."

"Don't be afraid, Nel," he murmured. He was drawing her down to lie beside him on the warm summer grass. "It does no good."

She heaved a great shuddering sigh. "I know," she said. "I know."

Shortly after Ronan moved the men and the horses away from the Great Cave, Nel pastured the mares and foals in a nearby valley. "This trying to keep both male and female horse herds just does not work," she said to Siguna ruefully as the two young women stood together in the bright sunlight watching the horses sample their new grazing.

"That is why my people keep only mares," Siguna said. "We have just one stallion, and that is Thunder, who belongs to my father. Of course, we occasionally lose some of our mares to another stallion's harem"—Siguna smiled—"but my father keeps guards with the herd always, and that does not happen as often as you might think."

Nel sighed. "I have often thought how much easier horsekeeping would be if we could only have mares instead of stallions."

"Why don't you?" Siguna asked curiously. And Nel told her about Impero and the Valley of the Wolf.

"Do you mean you have had these horses tamed for only two years!" Siguna said when Nel had finished.

"Sa."

Siguna stared at Nel. "Do you realize how amazing that is?"

Nel shrugged. "That is what Ronan says. Myself, I do not think it is so amazing. Animals have such a great-hearted generosity, Siguna. If you are kind to them, they will do almost anything for you."

"Animals certainly give their hearts to you, Nel," Siguna returned with a smile, "but that is not necessarily true for everyone else." She bent her mind to Nel's problem. "The only thing you can do is kill the stallion who is presently in the valley and replace him with one of your own," she advised. "A stallion who has been tamed will let you handle his mares."

"I have thought of that." Nel bent her head and scuffed her moccasin around in the grass. "I'm sure Ronan has thought of that, too. Cloud would be a perfect replacement for Impero."

Siguna smiled. "So there is the solution to your problem."

Nel gazed out at the peaceful scene before her and shook her head. "Why not?"

Still looking at the mares and foals, and not at Siguna, Nel said, "The valley was Impero's home before it was ours. If we did that to him, then we should be as bad as your father."

Siguna's breath caught audibly.

Nel turned her head. Her face was somber. "It is true, Siguna. I am sorry to have to say such a thing about your father, but it is true."

"He . . ." Siguna tried to find words to explain. "He is not bad, Nel. It is just that the men of my tribe know no other way."

"They revere nothing," Nel said flatly.

"Na," Siguna agreed sadly. "They do not."

"Do you wish to return to them?"

Siguna gave her a startled look. "Do you mean now?"

"You cannot return now. But someday . . . when all of this is over . . . will you wish to return?"

Siguna thought of the scheme she had made when first she had come to this camp as a captive. She would discover their plans, she had thought, and then return to her father and be a heroine. Slowly she shook her head. "I do not want to return, Nel. I have learned a little about reverence, and I do not want to return."

Nel put an arm around Siguna's shoulders and gave her a brief hug. "It is in my heart that the Mother put it into your mind to go wandering in the forest the day that Thorn and Mait found you, Siguna."

"I have been thinking that also," Siguna confessed.

Two long-legged foals galloped off across the pasture, one chasing the other. Nel smiled.

"Do you think the Tribe of the Wolf would take me in?" Siguna asked.

"Of course. But I am thinking that the Mistress has already marked you for her own," Nel said.

Siguna's crystal eyes grew very wide.

"You cannot be so surprised," Nel said. "She has given you a very large amount of her time."

Siguna was obviously flustered. "I have had many questions, and she is very kind."

"Arika is not kind," Nel said positively. "If it were offered, would you like to join the Tribe of the Red Deer, Siguna?"

The great gray eyes grew luminous. "Sa," Siguna said.

Nel said, "Talk to the Mistress."

Fenris sent scouts out again before moving the main body of his camp, and they returned with the news that the Tribe of the Leopard had evacuated their homesite on the Greatfish River.

Fenris's thick blond brows drew together in a scowl. Nothing was going as it should of late.

"Perhaps the tribe simply moved to another location for the summer months," Surtur said from his place at the kain's side.

"Perhaps," Fenris grunted. "Or perhaps they are part of that group of mountainmen who attacked us."

The scout who had come to make the report said now eagerly, "We found some tribes dwelling farther down the River of Gold, Kain. They looked to be fully as rich as the first one."

Fenris's brow smoothed slightly. "You saw these tribes?"

The scout nodded emphatically. "We saw them. We thought at first of following the other river east, but it seemed to be leading into higher hills, and we feared we might find ourselves in the midst of another trap."

Fenris's scowl returned, as it did at any mention of the defeat in the gorge.

The scout continued hastily, "So we returned to the River of Gold and followed it south. It leads into very high mountains, but before the mountains rise, we found two tribes. We were very careful, Kain. They did not know we were there."

"When did you see them?" Fenris asked.

"Early yesterday. We galloped all the way back."

"Good," Fenris said and nodded approvingly. He looked around the circle of his anda. "I do not want to give *these* tribes time to disappear," he said. "We ride tomorrow at dawn. Pass the word to the men."

Grins came from all his men as they obediently rose to their feet. "Tomorrow at dawn," they said. "We will be ready."

The following morning, the Horsemasters galloped out of camp. They rode south for all the day, riding hard down the fertile plain that stretched on either side of the River of Gold. By nightfall, the horsemen were within striking distance of the Tribe of the Bear.

They would wait for the following day, Fenris decided. Dawn was one of his favorite times for attack, as he could be fairly certain of catching most members of a tribe still within their huts at dawn. So, as the light faded, the Horsemasters picketed their horses and settled down for the night, ready to be up and away in the early morning.

The shaman of the Bear was an old man, and he slept lightly, especially toward dawn. On this particular day, as he lay in his sleeping skins waiting patiently for the morning, the murmur of distant hooves from down the valley came to his ears.

Reindeer? Reindeer should not be in the valley at this time of year. They should be in the mountains.

The drumming sound was coming closer. What could it be?

From out of nowhere, a picture of Ronan's sternly warning face floated before the shaman's eyes.

The Horsemasters, he thought. *It is the Horsemasters.*

The old man staggered to his feet and, without even stopping to put on his moccasins, rushed out his door and ran for the chief's hut. "Wake up! Wake up!" he shouted as he ran. "The Horsemasters are coming!"

He reached the chief's hut and plunged into the darkness within. "The earth is trembling like thunder!" he cried. "Get up, Sanje! The Horsemasters are coming!"

The chief, who had been sleeping naked with his wife in their sleeping skins, leaped to his feet. For a moment he stood still and listened. The earth was indeed resonating with the drumming of oncoming hooves.

"Wake the tribe!" he said to the shaman. "I am coming!" And he reached frantically for his clothing.

The shaman ran back outside, his breath wheezing in his old lungs. There were men carrying spears running out of the men's cave in response to his earlier call. The grayish yellow light of early morning streaked the sky. Women and children were coming out of the huts now, the children crying with fear. The shaman collapsed next to the men's cave, his old legs trembling so hard they would hold him no longer. The chief came rushing past him, shouting to the women to get back inside the huts.

The shaman looked toward the river. He looked up the valley.

They came out of the morning mist, falling upon the Tribe of the Bear in a storm of terror and death. The shaman felt his breath come short, felt a sharp pain knife through his chest. His last conscious thought was *We should have listened to Ronan.*

Chapter Thirty-one

The day after he and his men had pillaged the homesite of the Tribe of the Bear, Fenris and the Horsemasters rode south and did the same thing to the Tribe of the Fox.

"No point in giving them any time to prepare a defense," he said to Surtur as they conferred together once the main part of the attack on the Tribe of the Bear was finished. "A number of these people escaped into the forest, and they may try to warn the tribe to the south."

Surtur grunted in acknowledgment.

The two men stood, reins in hand, and looked in silence around the devastated camp of the Bear. The bodies of men littered the ground. From within the huts came the sound of wailing children and weeping women.

"Have one of the huts stripped of its goods and pile the bodies in it," Fenris said to his second-in-command.

"Hugin is already seeing to that, Kain."

Fenris nodded. Over the years, he had found that the most efficient way to get rid of the slain was to pile them in a hut, along with as much wood as readily could be found, and set fire to it. If he left the corpses to the hyenas and the ravens, then he would not be able to use the tribe's campsite. And indeed, as he watched, some of his men were beginning the business of stripping the bodies of the slain. Hugin stood by the hut chosen for the cremation and watched with hawk eyes to see that everything taken from the bodies was piled in one heap for the kain to distribute as he saw fit.

"I will leave some of the men here tomorrow, to guard the captives, and the rest of us will ride out again at dawn," Fenris said.

"Good," Surtur said.

Fenris's stallion pawed restlessly, and the kain lifted a hand and stroked its soft nose. "Tell the men that I will give out the booty of both camps together."

"What about the women?" Surtur asked. "Our own women are not with us, and the men will be hot to lie with a woman after the excitement of the day."

"Mmm." The stallion began to rub his head against Fenris's thigh, and the kain braced himself against the heavy pushes. "There are not enough women to go around all the men."

"The men do not mind sharing."

Fenris had found the place the stallion wanted scratched, and the horse was standing quietly, eyes half closed, as the kain attended to him. "I will not give the women out permanently, then," Fenris said. "We will wait until we have the women of both tribes together. Those men who want a woman for tonight may choose one, but it will be just for the night."

Surtur nodded. "Will you choose first, Kain?"

Fenris smiled ruefully. "I am too old a bull for rutting after fighting, Surtur. I will leave the women to the younger men tonight."

Surtur's eyes flashed. "You are not old, Kain!"

The stallion, distracted by the sight of a mare being walked nearby, raised his head and snorted. Fenris ran a dirty hand through his thick, blond hair. "I do not know, Surtur," he said with a weariness that surprised even himself. "I do not know."

The men and women of the Bear who had managed to escape the massacre of their tribe did not in fact head south and west to the Tribe of the Fox, but north and east, to find Ronan. They had fled in scattered groups, and it was in scattered groups that they came straggling into the campsite of the Red Deer beginning two days later.

The men of the Federation were appalled, but not surprised.

One of the first refugees to come in was a man who was married to

Rilik's wife's cousin. "We warned you," Rilik said to Altin, his relation by marriage. "Three times since the Federation was formed did Ronan send to tell the Tribe of the Bear that you were not safe. You would not listen, and now see what has befallen you."

The grim-faced Altin replied, "Sanje thought we were close enough to the Altas to be safe. He was certain the Horsemasters would choose to go down the Greatfish River rather than come south toward the Altas."

"They did go down the Greatfish," Rilik returned. "But the Tribe of the Leopard had evacuated its homesite. That is why the Horsemasters chose you instead."

"Dhu," said the husband of Rilik's wife's cousin despairingly. "It was horrible, Rilik! They came with the dawn. There was no chance even to organize a fight! The only chance was to flee into the forest, which we did. It was our good fortune that I awoke with the shaman's first warning, and our hut was one of those farthest from the center of the camp. Mara and the babe and I were able to get up the hillside and into the forest just as the horsemen attacked."

Thorn, who had been sitting beside his father listening to this tale, now asked quietly, "What of the Tribe of the Fox? Did anyone who escaped try to get south to warn them?"

"I had my wife and child to see to," Altin returned, but he looked a little ashamed. "Perhaps some of the other men set out to give a warning."

To do them justice, it turned out that two of the men of the Bear had indeed attempted to sound the alarm to the Tribe of the Fox. But the men of the Bear were on foot, and they arrived too late.

This the men of the Federation learned from the survivors of the Tribe of the Fox massacre, who also found their way to the Red Deer campsite.

Ronan sent the women on to the Great Cave to be dealt with by Nel. Then, a week later, when he was certain that all the survivors had made it into camp, Ronan called a meeting of the chiefs.

"What fools they were," said Unwar, chief of the Leopard tribe, as the four of them met in the men's cave to discuss what to do about the refugees.

"Less than three handfuls of men of the Bear escaped, and even fewer from the Tribe of the Fox." Haras's voice and face were heavy with genuine sorrow.

"Scarcely any women and children got free," Arika remarked coldly.

Unwar turned his heavy-lidded eyes toward the Mistress. "At least the women and children are not dead," he pointed out. "The men are."

In the hazy glow of light from the cave opening, the Mistress's face managed to look both austere and ruthless. "Rape is an ugly thing," she said. "Some of the women may well have preferred death."

Haras said, "I do not doubt you, Arika."

A shadow flitted through the hazy sunshine; it was Nigak, searching for Ronan. Ronan waited until the wolf had snapped playfully at his nose and settled down at his side before he said, "This chief of the Horsemasters is a very clever man. One of the reasons I called this meeting is to consider what he is likely to do next."

"What would a wolf do next?" Haras asked ironically.

Arika said, "What would *you* do next, Ronan, if you were the chief of the Horsemasters?"

Ronan looked at his mother thoughtfully, but then he answered, "The first thing I would do would be to bring up the rest of my tribe. There is good summer grazing in the high pastures of the Tribe of the Fox. The game is abundant and there is plenty of grass for the horse herd. It is an ideal location for a summer camp."

"Sa?" Haras prompted. "And then what would you do?"

"Before leaf fall," Ronan said, "I would plan to destroy my enemies."

Two ravens circled overhead, and Unwar made a sign to ward off evil with his thumb and his forefinger. "How would you do it?" he grunted.

"I'd return to the Greatfish. We are obviously sheltering to the south and the east of the River of Gold."

"You think they will come down the Greatfish?" said Haras.

"Sa," said Ronan. "I do."

Silence.

"I think you are right," Haras said at last.

Arika nodded in agreement.

Unwar's flat features looked even more forbidding than usual. "Well then," he said, "they will find us ready for them."

"They still outnumber us badly," Haras said. "I am thinking it is time to send again to the Tribe of the Squirrel. Perhaps now they will comprehend their danger."

"I was thinking the same thing," Ronan agreed. "Perhaps you might send two of your nirum, Haras. The words of men of the Buffalo will carry weight with the Tribe of the Squirrel, I think."

Haras nodded agreement. "I will send Megar," he said. "Megar's sister's daughter is married to a son of the chief of the Tribe of the Squirrel."

Everyone nodded their approval of this arrangement.

Ronan put his hand upon Nigak's head. "Now, what of the men of the Fox and the Bear?" he asked. "With whom shall they fight?"

In all of their training drills, Ronan had been scrupulous about keeping the men of each tribe together. In this way, neighbor would be fighting next to neighbor, and friend next to friend, giving each warrior the greatest incentive to be faithful and do his best.

"You have the smallest number of men in your tribe, Ronan," Haras said generously. "Let them fight with the men of the Wolf."

Unwar and Arika nodded their agreement.

Ronan said slowly, "You are right in that it makes sense to combine the refugees with the men of the Wolf for fighting purposes. But I am thinking that we should allow them to choose a leader of their own, to sit on the chief's council with us."

This suggestion was not popular with Unwar. "These men are lucky they had a place to run to," he growled. "I see no reason to give them a voice in our councils."

Haras said curiously, "Why should you want to do this, Ronan?"

"They are broken men," Ronan replied. "They need to feel that they are not just hangers-on, that they are truly part of the Federation. Letting them name a leader, and I mean only one leader to represent both tribes, will give them a sense of . . ." He broke off as if searching for a word.

"Worth," Haras said quietly.

"Sa." Ronan gave Haras an approving smile. "Worth."

The chief of the Buffalo looked pleased with himself and turned his leonine head toward Unwar. "I think Ronan is right," he said.

"Oh, very well," the Leopard chief agreed ungraciously. "What does it matter to me, after all?"

Arika said nothing, but she waited in the cave until the two other chiefs had departed to return to their men. Ronan looked at her as he turned from the cave opening, where he had been exchanging a last word with Haras, and raised an inquiring eyebrow.

"Whom do you think the men of the Fox and the Bear will name to be their chief?" Arika asked her son.

Ronan shrugged. "I do not know, Mistress."

"Matti, I would guess," Arika said.

Below the arched bridge of his nose, Ronan's narrow nostrils flared just slightly. Arika smiled.

"Perhaps," Ronan said.

Matti was the eldest son of the chief of the Tribe of the Fox, and it had become known in the last few days that he had urged his father to join the Federation. The only reason Matti had not died in the fighting was that he had not been there; he had been hunting with a few of his agemates in the mountains.

"An ardent youngster like Matti will be inclined to agree with anything you suggest," Arika said.

Ronan's face became very still. He said nothing.

"You are a very clever young man," Arika said softly. She began to walk toward the doorway. "I have always thought so." She went right by Ronan, the top of her head passing just below his nose, and serenely walked away.

Ronan had been right when he had said that Fenris would send for the remainder of his tribe, that the homesite of the Tribe of the Fox, nestled in the foothills of the Altas, was a perfect summer camp for the Horsemasters. The women and children, the horses and sledges, and the herd of mares and foals came down the River of Gold at a much slower pace than the warriors had and settled into the comfortable valley that had once been home to the Tribe of the Fox.

The women and children of the tribes of the Bear and the Fox took their places in the tents of the Horsemasters.

"Why don't you rebel?" Mira, a daughter of the chief of the Fox, asked one of the women of the Kindred who had dwelled for a year in the kain's tent. "There are many women in this camp, more women than men. If the women rose up in rebellion, what could the men do against us?"

"Kill our children" came the simple, devastating answer.

Mira's eyes dilated until they were almost purely black. "They would not do such a thing."

"They would. They did. There was a woman once who took up a spear against the man to whom she had been given. She killed him. In answer, the men of the tribe killed her, her sisters, and all of their children. They wiped her blood from the face of the earth."

Mira was horrified. "Fenris did this?" she asked hoarsely.

Kara shook her head. "It was before Fenris became the kain. It was his father who ordered the killing."

"Dhu," Mira breathed, making a sign with her fingers. "They are evil evil men." She shuddered. "And he has forced you to sleep with him?"

Kara flushed. "Fenris is not an evil man," she said. "It is hard to explain this, I know, considering the terrible things that he has done. But I do not think he is an evil man."

Mira was looking at her as if she were mad.

"He follows a savage god," Kara said slowly. "It is the god who tells him to do these terrible things."

"Every time I look at him," Mira said coldly, "I see the dead bodies of my father and my brothers."

"I understand. I used to see that also," Kara said.

"But now you do not?"

"I am alive, Mira, as you are alive. We must make the best of what we have been given."

Mira's breath was coming short and hard. "I think you are as bad as he is," she said bitterly, turned, walked to the edge of the large tent, and sat with her back turned to Kara.

Kara slowly went to the tent door and ducked out. Her eyes searched the large campsite until they found the figure she had been looking for, and then they stopped.

She told herself that she did not blame Mira for what she was thinking. Sometimes Kara even thought the same things about herself. But it was not so simple as that, she thought now. Fenris was not so simple as that.

He was standing in a circle of men, watching two of the younger men wrestle in the center. There was a great deal of laughing and shouting going on. As Kara watched, one of Fenris's many children came running up to him and tugged on his hand. The kain laughed and bent to swing the little boy up onto his shoulder so he could watch the wrestling.

Kara looked at the broad shoulder upon which the child sat with such security, looked at the big hand protectively encircling the fragile childish arm, looked at the back of the shapely blond head.

Surely, she thought, surely such a man would never be able to order the death of a woman and all her children.

But she was afraid that he could.

She had long since forgotten what her first husband looked like, had long since forgotten the unpleasant and painful invasion of her body that had been their mating. All of that had been buried irrevocably by the new sensations she had learned in the arms of Fenris.

He could be so tender. That was the thing that had caught her, that under all the brutality there could be such heart-stopping tenderness. She would catch him looking at her sometimes with such warmth in his gray eyes that her whole body would flush with the desire to be with him. In these last heady months, when only she had been summoned to share his sleeping place, she had almost managed to forget what he was.

But then there had been this new massacre, with the men of the Bear and the Fox lying dead, and their widows and orphans forced into the tents and beds of the murderers.

Mira was right, Kara thought. She was a traitor to her race and to her gods.

The wrestling match was over, and Fenris was turning away. He swung the little boy down from his shoulder and turned to say something to Surtur, who was, as always, by his side. His face flashed open into a smile.

Kara heaved a ragged sigh, turned, and went back into the tent.

Chapter Thirty-two

I t took Nel a day and a half to get the sledges from the Great Cave to the men's campsite on the Greatfish River. She used the mares that Siguna told her had been trained to pull, and Siguna showed her exactly how to fashion and attach the harness that attached the sledge to the horse.

Three of the sledges contained the shields that the women had been working on for weeks, and one sledge contained baskets of fruits and berries the women had gathered to supplement the diet of meat which their menfolk, left to themselves, would primarily exist upon. Nel and Siguna and Beki and Yoli led the mares for most of the way, and the sledges were followed by a number of other women who wished to visit their husbands.

Ronan had kept men continually stationed at the Great Cave to bring in meat for the women, periodically changing them to give as many men as possible time with their wives. It was those wives whose husbands had not yet had hunting duty that Nel had designated to accompany the sledges on this particular journey.

Nel herself had not seen Ronan since he had moved the men away from the Great Cave over a moon ago. He had sent her messages by the revolving hunters, but he himself had not felt able to leave the campsite on the Greatfish. So it was with an eager heart that Nel led her sweet-faced brown mare along the path that she knew would open any moment into the homesite of the Red Deer.

Here was the last turn, she thought. The mare, seeming to sense Nel's excitement, walked more quickly. Around this curve. Now!

Dhu. Nel stopped in her tracks, and the train of people and horses behind her stopped as abruptly to keep from running into her sledge.

Advancing toward Nel and her supply train was a moving wall of spears.

The men in the front line saw her first and checked, still retaining their line formation. With well-drilled balance and discipline, the men behind adjusted their steps and halted also.

A familiar voice, edged with a familiar temper, snapped, "Why are you stopping?"

"It's Nel," a man shouted. "Ronan, Nel is here with the shields!"

The men whose wives had not accompanied Nel vacated the huts and tents for the night and left them to the more fortunate husbands, who wasted no time in making up for too long a separation.

"It is a good thing the weather is pleasant," Ronan murmured to Nel as they lay together in his sleeping skins in the tent that he usually shared with Bror and Crim. "If it had been raining, the men might not have been so accommodating about sleeping outside."

"The weather is always pleasant in summer," Nel returned tranquilly, her head comfortably pillowed on Ronan's shoulder. "And the wives I brought with me belong to the men who have not yet had a turn on hunting duty. Fair is fair, after all."

"I am not complaining, minnow," Ronan said, and she could hear the smile in his voice. "Believe me, I am not complaining."

One of the dogs, both of whom were sleeping in the doorway, yipped in his sleep. "In fact," Ronan said, "it was far easier to get rid of Bror and Crim than it is to get rid of these dogs of yours!"

"They don't go hunting at night, like Nigak does."

"That doesn't mean they have to insist on sleeping with you!"

"They keep me company when you are gone."

Ronan sighed.

Nel asked, "The shields are all right?"

"The shields are all right."

"No further news about the Horsemasters?"

"So far as I know, they are still at the homesite of the Tribe of the Fox. I have men watching them, of course."

"And what of the Tribe of the Squirrel?"

"There is good news from the Tribe of the Squirrel. These last two attacks apparently convinced them that no place is safe. They will join with us."

"Ronan! That is wonderful news. The Tribe of the Squirrel is quite large, is it not? That should mean many more fighting men for you."

She felt his chest rise and fall with a deep, controlled breath. "It should, but there is a problem. They hold one of their most sacred yearly ceremonies at the full of the moon, and they will not march to join us until after the ceremony is completed."

The moon was not yet halfway to its first quarter. "Oh," said Nel, dismayed. "That is stupid."

"Very stupid." Ronan's voice was bitter. "But there is nothing I can do about it. When the first two messengers came back with that news, I sent more men to try to convince the chief to change his mind. No use. The Tribe of the Squirrel won't move until after its ceremony."

"It probably won't matter," Nel said. "It sounds as if the Horsemasters are very comfortable where they are. They probably won't move themselves until after the summer weather is finished and the higher altitudes start to grow cold."

"I hope so, Nel. Dhu, I hope so."

"I have missed you so much," she murmured, deftly changing the subject to one more pleasing to both of them. She raised herself to rain feather-light kisses all along his smoothly shaven cheek and jawbone. She had taken her hair out of its braid earlier, and it streamed forward over his throat and bare shoulders, a mantle of palest brown.

He lay motionless on his back and let her kiss him. The single stone lamp on the floor behind his head threw its muted light upward, illuminating Nel's face, and he said softly, "You are very beautiful, Nel. Motherhood becomes you."

She stilled. Their faces were very close, and they looked gravely into each other's eyes. Except for a perfunctory initial inquiry, it was the first time he had mentioned the baby.

"Always in my heart there has been this one empty place," she said to those familiar, those beloved dark eyes. "Now it is empty no longer."

"I am glad." His face was very serious. "I have been thinking about this, Nel." A flash of humor came and went in his grave eyes. "That is, when I have not been thinking about the Horsemasters." He reached up and closed his fingers around her wrist. "And I know that I can be a father to Culen. It may take me a little time to grow accustomed to him, but it will be all right. You don't have to worry anymore." He moved his thumb up and down on her wrist. "It will be all right."

The eyes looking back into his were very green. "I won't cry," she said at last in an unsteady voice, "because I know how you hate it. But I want to."

"Nel," he said, "you can do better things for me than cry." And he levered her downward until she was once more lying beside him on the furs.

She sniffled. "Of course I can." A spark of indignation colored her voice. "In fact, I already have."

"Once?" Now he was the one to sound indignant. He raised himself on his elbow and stared down into her face. "You came all this way, for once?"

She smiled up at him. "I thought you were tired."

He spent a good part of the night demonstrating that he was not.

Siguna's night was different from the other women's, but in its own way, it was exciting. Arika was in an unusually garrulous mood, and she and Siguna sat up by the light of the stone lamp and talked for hours. The Mistress was particularly interested in the details of Siguna's life with the Horsemasters.

"He is a terrible man, your father," Arika commented when Siguna had finished an anecdote. "Hard and merciless. Yet you care for him."

"I suppose he is those things," Siguna said unwillingly. She rested her chin upon her updrawn knees. "But he can be more tender than any woman. He was so to me, often. Perhaps it was because my mother died, and in his own way he tried to make that up to me, but he let me do things that none of the other girls were allowed to do. And he wouldn't let Teala pick on me." She smiled. "Once, when I fell and cut my leg badly and had a fever"—she ran her forefinger up and down the place on her calf where the old scar was—"he even let me sleep next to him, and he told me funny stories to cheer me up."

Arika said, "Perhaps he favored you because he saw that you were like him."

"Na," Siguna said, misunderstanding. "I am said to look just like my mother." She ran her finger once more over the place on her leg where the scar was. "Do you know," she said thoughtfully, "I have sometimes thought that if my father had been reared in the ways of the Red Deer, he would have been like Ronan?"

Arika reached out and carefully repositioned the single stone lamp. She said, "And I have sometimes thought that Ronan could be like your father."

The eyes of the two women, old and young, met and held.

"But he is not," Siguna said.

"He is not," Arika agreed. "That he is not, I attribute principally to Nel."

Siguna smiled a little sadly. "I have never seen a man so entwined with one woman as Ronan is with Nel."

Arika's eyebrows lifted in a gesture that was purely ironic. "I think I can safely say that at one time or another Ronan was 'entwined' with every unmarried girl in his age group. He was not always so exclusively attached to Nel."

For some reason, Siguna suddenly remembered the sounds that would come from her father's sleeping space when he lay with one of his women. Then she remembered the way Ronan had once looked at her, and her stomach fluttered.

Arika was going on, "Although I will admit that Nel influenced him even when she was yet a child. In taking care of her, he learned tenderness."

Siguna bent her head, afraid of what Arika might read on her face. When the Mistress changed the subject, Siguna was at once both relieved and sorry.

"Why did you ride into the forest on the day that you were captured?" Arika asked.

Siguna gathered her thoughts. "I don't know. I just felt that I had to get away from the other women." She frowned in an effort of memory. "I felt . . . suffocated."

"What led your steps along that particular path?"

"I don't remember. I think I just let my mare wander."

Arika smiled, as if satisfied by the response.

Silence fell in the Mistress's hut. Arika made no movement toward her sleeping place, however, so Siguna said tentatively, "May I ask you a question, Mistress?"

"Sa."

"How does the Tribe of the Red Deer differ from the other tribes that follow the Mother?"

Arika settled herself more comfortably on her buffalo rug. "Mother-right reigns in all the lands of the Goddess," she explained, "but only the Tribe of the Red Deer has a woman chief."

"I do not think I understand what you mean by mother-right," Siguna said. "I know that Berta comes from a tribe that is ruled by a male chief, but I do not understand how a tribe that is ruled by a man can be said to follow mother-right."

"Mother-right means that the blood of a family, as well as its goods, is passed on from mother to daughter, not, as in your tribe and in the tribes that follow Sky God, from father to son," Arika said, thus neatly explaining the system of living that would one day be called matrilineal.

"You mean a family's belongings . . . the household goods . . . the tools . . . the *horses* even . . . belong to the women?" Siguna asked incredulously.

The Mistress smiled faintly at the look on Siguna's face. "Surely, this is only sensible if you want to keep an inheritance within the family," she said reasonably. "Motherhood is certain; fatherhood is not."

Siguna blinked.

"In the tribes of the Goddess," Arika continued, "it is the woman who is head of the family. A mother will share her home with her daughters, her daughters' husbands, and her daughters' children. And it is the mother, the matriarch, who will have the final word in all family affairs."

Siguna thought of the men of her tribe and could not imagine them consenting to live in such a way. She said, "But what of the sons?"

"When a son marries, he goes to live in his wife's home with his wife's family."

"And the men of the Goddess consent to do this?"

"Why should they not? The authority of the mother is as natural to them as the authority of the father is to your people."

A little silence fell as Siguna digested this idea. Then she asked, "But even under the law of mother-right, you said most tribes are ruled by a chief?"

"Sa."

"Why is that, I wonder?" Siguna asked.

"I have often wondered that myself," Arika confessed. "I had a long discussion recently with Berta, and she said that it was because so much of a woman's life is spent in the bearing and nursing of children. When the cares of the immediate family are so physically demanding, it is difficult for a woman to take upon her shoulders the rule of the entire tribe as well."

"It is certainly true that men spend less time and effort on children than women do," Siguna said, half-humorously, half-ruefully. She clasped her hands around her knees and looked at Arika's lamplit face. "But the Tribe of the Red Deer is different."

"Sa. For as long as people remember, the Tribe of the Red Deer has been ruled by a woman."

"Why is that, Mistress?"

"I do not know. Perhaps somewhere in the past a matriarch decided she would not marry, that she would take the rule into her own hands, and it has remained that way ever since."

"Is it a law that the Mistress may not marry?"

Arika gave Siguna a sharp look. "Why do you ask that?"

Siguna looked with grave attention at the tips of her moccasins. "I had heard somewhere that Nel was to be the next Mistress, but that she gave up her chance when she married Ronan."

Silence.

"I think it is true that Nel is beloved of the Mother," Arika said at last. "But she does not have it in her to be the Mistress."

"Why?" Siguna asked.

"It is as you said earlier. She is too entwined with Ronan. The tribe would never come first with her."

"I see," Siguna said slowly.

"The Tribe of the Red Deer is very close to the Mother," Arika said. "I feel that deeply. And the Mistress of the tribe is the closest of all. The Mistress can have no husband to divide her loyalties or to divert her power into his own hands." Arika's hand lifted instinctively to touch the pendant she wore always around her neck. "This is why it is so important to me to preserve our matriarchy. Something unique and sacred will be lost if ever the Red Deer comes to be ruled by a man."

"Even if that man himself worships the Goddess?" Siguna asked.

Arika's reddish brown eyes glowed in the light of the stone lamp. "Even if that man were the son of the Mistress herself." A beat of silence. "Even if that man were Ronan."

Arika's finger continued to caress the ivory pendant upon which was drawn the great-bellied shape of a woman about to give birth. "I am not young any longer," she said, "and I have lost both my daughter and Nel. At night I lie awake and wonder who is to succeed me."

"You have a son," Siguna said softly. "It is in my heart that Nel would come back if Ronan could come with her."

Arika shook her head. "Ronan is a man whose nature demands that he take the lead." She smiled a little bitterly and admitted, "He is too much like me. If Nel became the Mistress, Ronan would rule the tribe. And I do not want that."

Siguna was watching the ivory pendant that lay against Arika's breast. "Is there no other woman of your blood you can call upon, Mistress?"

Arika laced her fingers together and regarded them thoughtfully. "I have been thinking of late that the next Mistress does not necessarily have to be of my blood," she said. "Years ago, when Alin, the Chosen One, was seduced away from us by the chief of the Horse, the Mistress chose a girl of different blood to rule after her. That girl was Elen, who was my mother."

Arika paused, and Siguna nodded to show that she was following.

"I have been thinking," said Arika, "that to make up for Alin's loss, the Mother has sent us you."

Siguna's eyes stretched wide. *"Me?"*

"It was the Mother's call you heard the day that you rode into the forest," Arika said with sublime certainty. "Have you not felt that?"

"Sa," Siguna whispered. "I have felt that."

"You have your father's strength in you, Siguna; and you have some of his ruthlessness, too. That is good. The Mistress must sometimes be pitiless when she carries out what is her duty. You understand this. You understand the sacredness of duty. I saw that when you undertook to search the bodies in the gorge."

"But I am not a member of your tribe!"

"You could be," Arika said, "if you wished to be." A beat of silence. "Do you, Siguna?"

"Sa." Once again the answer was but a whisper. "I want to very much."

Arika smiled as if she were not surprised.

———

Siguna thought she would never fall asleep, so many thoughts were teeming in her brain. She finally drifted off, only to be awakened shortly after dawn by the sound of raised voices.

Arika had awakened even before she had; Siguna saw her figure at the hut's door. "Come," she said over her shoulder to Siguna, "it looks as if Tyr has brought in one of your father's men."

Fully awake by now, Siguna scrambled to her feet, found her moccasins, and followed Arika out the door.

There was a small group of men standing in front of the tent Siguna knew belonged to Ronan. Siguna recognized Tyr and two other men of the Red Deer, but the one her eyes flew to was the defiant young man who was standing in the midst of the other three, with his hands bound behind his back. It was her brother, Vili. With a startled cry, Siguna ran forward, calling his name.

"Siguna!" Vili was more surprised to see her than she was to see him. "We thought you were dead!"

"No," she answered him in their own tongue. "I was captured while I was out in the forest. What happened to you? Why are you here?"

"Father sent me to scout along this river. Like you, I was captured." Vili cursed and sent a furious look toward Tyr. "They were watching for us."

"You weren't alone?"

Vili shook the blond head that was so like their father's. "No. Luckily, Bragi got away."

The three men of the Red Deer had been listening in uncomprehending silence to this conversation, and now Tyr looked toward the tent in front of which they were standing and said, with obvious relief, "Ronan! Look what we found in the forest."

Siguna's head snapped around in time to see Ronan straightening up from the tent opening. He was not wearing his headband, and his black hair streamed around his face. He was shoeless and shirtless, wearing only buckskin trousers that had obviously been pulled on in a hurry. He pushed his fingers through the loose hair on his forehead and surveyed Vili from head to toe. He spoke to Siguna without looking at her. "You know him?"

"Sa. He is my brother."

"It's obvious he was sent here to spy on us." Ronan's eyes had never left Vili. "Was he alone?"

When Siguna didn't answer, Tyr did. "We didn't see any others, but I doubt it."

At last Ronan turned his head to look at Siguna. She stared back, her face suddenly stricken, and said nothing. After a moment he said, "Never mind, I know the answer already. Your father would never have sent him alone." He ran his fingers through his hair again, thrusting it back off his face, and turned to say something else to Tyr.

Siguna stared at Ronan, at the tangled black hair that was clinging to the strong, tanned neck, at the smoothly muscled shoulders and upper arms, at the wide chest, the flat stomach and narrow hips. Deep inside her, something rippled.

"Who is he?" Vili asked her urgently, inclining his head toward Ronan.

"Their kain," Siguna replied. Then, when Ronan looked at her inquiringly, she said, "He wanted to know who you were. I said you were the chief."

There was the soft rustling sound of door skins being pushed back again, and then Nel was with them. She had taken more time to dress than her husband; only her unbraided hair betrayed her hurry. Ronan said to her, "It's Siguna's brother. Tyr caught him scouting us."

The beautiful flush of rose in Nel's cheeks disappeared. Ronan slipped his hand under the silken fall of her hair and rested it reassuringly on her nape. The two large wolfdogs came padding out of the hut to stand by her side.

"Was he alone?" Nel asked her husband.

"He won't say, but of course he wasn't alone."

"We searched the forest for any others," Tyr said, "but if they were on horseback like this one . . ." He shrugged.

"Where is his horse?" Nel asked.

Tyr said, "Unfortunately, we had to spear the horse in order to capture the man."

A little silence fell. Then Ronan said bleakly, "So, now he will know where to find us."

Siguna understood immediately that the "he" referred to her father.

"Do you want to send some of your own men to ride after the others?" Tyr asked.

"When did you capture this one? This morning?"

"Last night. We searched for any others until it was dark."

"It is too late, then," Ronan said. "They have too much of a start."

All this while, Vili had been standing perfectly still, straight-backed, with defiance on his face, his hands tied behind his back.

Nel said, "The poor boy looks exhausted."

Vili turned his eyes in her direction, seeming to guess that she was speaking of him. He looked at the two dogs who guarded her side, and Siguna said immediately, "The dogs are as tame as Father's old mare, Vili."

"Vili?" Nel said. "Is that your brother's name, Siguna?"

"Sa."

"Please remember, he is not our guest, Nel," Ronan said sternly. "He is our prisoner. I do not want him let loose to return to his father with further descriptions of our camp and our numbers."

"I understand that, Ronan," Nel said. "But that doesn't mean we can't feed the boy. After all, he is Siguna's brother."

Siguna smiled a little at Nel's typical kindness. However, when she looked at Ronan he was wearing what Mait and Thorn had called his "black look." He was obviously unhappy with this new development.

Arika spoke for the first time. "If they have scouted the river, that means they will know the terrain."

Ronan's scowl got even blacker.

"We had better call the other chiefs," said the Mistress, "and discuss the situation." Then, as Ronan did not move, she added tartly, "Tyr and Siguna are perfectly capable of seeing to the boy, Ronan. Get yourself dressed!"

Everyone stared at Arika in astonishment. She had sounded exactly like a mother.

Chapter Thirty-three

Within the hour, the Federation chiefs had gathered in what, in more ordinary times, would be the Red Deer tribe's men's cave. They sat on deerskin rugs, in a circle around the unlit hearth, and their faces were somber.

"The situation is thus," Ronan said. "By tomorrow, Fenris will know the location of our camp and the numbers of our men. We must expect him to attack in a very short time."

"We can retreat to the Red Deer summer camp," Arika said.

"That is a good idea," Unwar agreed. "That will give us the delay we need until the men of the Squirrel come. Without them, we are outnumbered two-to-one."

"Not to mention that the enemy are all horsed," said Haras.

Matti, the young man who had been chosen to represent the remnants of the tribes of the Fox and the Bear, listened with bright eyes and a grave face and said nothing.

"I particularly did not want him to know our numbers," Ronan said bitterly. "That is why I posted men to intercept his scouts."

"Perhaps the boy was alone after all," Unwar said.

"He is the chief's son," Haras said. "Would you send your son alone on such a mission?"

Unwar grunted, then shrugged in acknowledgment of Haras's point.

Ronan repeated, "I think Fenris will move quickly. He will not want to give us a chance to change our ground."

"The Mistress is right," said Unwar. "We should retreat to the Red Deer summer camp."

"If we do that, we will be leaving the women and children in the Great Cave unprotected," Haras protested.

"Move the women and children too," Arika suggested.

Ronan said slowly, "I have been thinking . . ."

All the faces turned to him.

Ronan laced his hands upon his knee and frowned thoughtfully at his intersecting fingers. "All this time my plan has been to fool the Horsemasters into thinking that we are larger in number than we actually are," he said. "This Fenris is too clever a chief to risk his men in what he perceives to be a losing fight. There is no reason for him to do so, not when he can find easier prey elsewhere." His frown deepened. "However, now we must assume that Fenris knows our numbers. He will not be turned back as easily as I had hoped, and so our strategy must be changed."

"Changed to what?" a grim-faced Haras asked.

Ronan glanced up from his hands. "The most effective weapon we have is surprise. Surprise is what won us the victory in the gorge. It is in my heart that we must rely on surprise once more."

"How?" said Arika tersely.

Ronan went back to the contemplation of his fingers. "Even on horseback, they cannot move from the homesite of the Fox to the Greatfish River in one day. They will have to make an overnight camp somewhere along the way, and I am thinking a likely place is that great crescent-shaped meadow that lies below the Greatfish." He shot a look at the Leopard chief. "Do you know the place I mean, Unwar?"

Unwar grunted agreement. "It would be a good place for them to make camp. The river is there for water, and the meadow will give them plenty of grass for their horses."

"The mountains come right up to the edge of the meadow," Ronan explained, his gaze going now from one face to the next. "And the mountains are covered with beech and pine trees. We could conceal all our forces in those mountains, and the Horsemasters would never know."

"What are you suggesting, Ronan?" Haras asked uneasily.

"I think we should attack them while they are encamped along the River of Gold," Ronan said.

"Attack?" said Haras.

"You are mad!" said Unwar.

"Why?" said Arika.

Matti was silent.

Haras leaned forward. "Ronan," he said in measured tones, "think of what you are saying. These Horsemasters are seasoned fighters. They have pillaged and destroyed an untold number of tribes to the north. Now they are coming after us. They seriously outnumber us. The men of the Squirrel have promised assistance; surely you must agree that wisdom tells us to wait until they can reach us before we take action."

"Haras speaks true," Unwar said. "I will agree that your leadership until now has been effective, Ronan, but this proposal of yours is mad! The mountains are our one protection. To descend from the mountains means to be trampled down by the enemy's horses or cut to pieces by their spears."

"And if that happens," Haras said, "think what it will mean to our women and children."

A heavy silence fell as the chiefs contemplated that ugly picture. The summer sun slanted in the cave opening, and a patch of sunlight danced upon the crown of Ronan's head.

Once again, Arika asked her son, "Why?"

"I think it is the way to win," he answered simply. He narrowed his eyes. "Picture how it will be. We will attack by moonlight, when they are sleeping. The most important part of this plan is that they won't have a chance to get to their horses, and on foot we are the better fighters. Our spears are heavier and longer, and we have the shields. Our men are in good heart—they remember the victory in the gorge. They have been training hard, and they have confidence in each other."

From somewhere outside the cave, a horse's whinny sounded. Ronan said firmly, "I think our formation will hold together. I think we can win."

Matti, his fierce young face lit with joy, spoke his first words of the meeting. "I agree."

"I do not. I think we should retreat to the Red Deer summer camp and await the men of the Squirrel," Unwar growled.

"Can you tell me what is to prevent the Horsemasters from following on our heels to summer camp?" Ronan asked. "I doubt they will give us enough time for the men of the Squirrel to join with us."

Unwar scowled, and Arika said, "Whatever we decide to do, we must do it quickly. It would be fatal for us to be caught here now."

The four men all agreed with that.

Arika looked around the circle of faces. "There are a handful of us, so whatever course of action three of us choose must be the decision of the council."

They all looked at Ronan. "I think we should attack while the Horsemasters are still on the River of Gold," he said, his face set and stern.

Matti spoke up quickly, "I agree with Ronan."

Unwar came next in the circle. "I think we should move to summer camp and wait for the men of the Squirrel."

Everyone looked at Haras. "I am sorry, Ronan," the Buffalo chief said, "but I agree with Unwar."

Ronan bowed his head. His hair shone panther black in its small patch of sun. "So then," he said expressionlessly, "we are two against two."

All but Ronan looked at Arika.

"Mistress," said Haras with great gravity, "it seems that yours will be the deciding voice in this matter."

Arika was staring with trancelike concentration at the top of Ronan's head and did not seem to realize she had been addressed. "My dream . . ." she murmured softly. "Dhu, it is just like my dream."

The men were silent, not wishing to disturb her trance. Ronan sat like a stone, his head bathed in sunlight.

Finally, when at last she was seen to take a deep breath, Haras asked quietly, "Did you see something we should know about, Mistress?"

Arika was clearly shaken. Ronan, who knew the dream was somehow connected to him, raised his head slowly and looked at his mother out of somber eyes.

Arika met his gaze, then drew another long, uneven breath. But her voice, when finally she spoke, was clear and sharp as an icicle. "What I saw tells me that if we follow Ronan, we shall win," she said, her eyes still locked with those of her son. "I think we should attack."

Siguna and Tyr took Vili to what used to be the women's cave. Tyr posted a guard, and Siguna went to get her brother something to eat. When she returned, she found Vili sitting inside the cave alone, his young face looking white and strained. He accepted gratefully the hot tea and fruit she handed him.

Siguna sat in silence and watched while he ate and drank. Vili's presence brought her father so much nearer, she thought with a twist of pain. They had the same hair, the same eyes, even the same dent in their chins.

"How is Father?" Siguna asked as soon as Vili showed signs of completing his meal.

"He is well." Vili wiped his mouth with the back of his hand and contemplated his sister somberly. "He thinks you are dead, you know."

"I told you. I was made captive. There was no way I could send him word."

"He grieved for you," Vili said. "He always favored you, and he grieved sorely at your loss."

Siguna heard and recognized the faint note of jealousy in Vili's voice. Vili was Teala's son and had heard all his life the tale of how unfairly Fenris favored Siguna. "I am sorry for that," she said now softly and bowed her head. "I did not want to grieve him."

Vili finished his tea. "Perhaps it is just as well that he thinks you dead," he said calmly. "It would be worse for him to have to think of you being raped by these mountainmen."

"No one has raped me!"

Vili stared at her in open disbelief.

"It is true," Siguna said in a more moderate tone. "These people do not treat women the way the men of our tribe do. Here a woman is . . . respected. Honored, even."

"The women of our tribe are respected and honored," Vili said indignantly. "My mother has ever had the ordering of the kain's tent in her hands!"

"What of the women who have been forced into service against their wills?" Siguna countered.

"Oh, those," said her brother with a shrug. "They are only captives."

The voices of the guards on duty outside the cave drifted in. They were talking casually about a boar hunt they had both been on.

Siguna said, "Well, I am only a captive, but I have been treated with the same respect that the men of the Kindred give to their own women."

Vili's eyes narrowed. "You sound as if you like living here."

Siguna said defiantly, "I do."

Vili's mouth set, and for a moment he looked uncannily like his father. "Then you are in truth dead to us," he said brutally. He turned his face away from her. "Get out."

Siguna got to her feet, looked once more at her brother's averted face, and walked out the door.

Vili spent the rest of the morning waiting for them to come for him. They would want information from him about his father's intentions, and when they discovered he would not give it, they would kill him. Vili could think of no other reason to account for his still being alive.

The morning went by. No one came. Nothing happened. There seemed to be a great deal of activity in the camp, and finally Vili went to the opening of the cave and looked out.

The two men with spears who stood on guard just outside looked at him, said something to each other, and gestured him back a few steps. He backed up obediently, and they let him be, regarding him expressionlessly out of steady, watchful eyes.

A drill of some sort was going on down by the river. Vili squinted into the sun, trying to make out what it was that the men were holding before them. Was it some new kind of weapon?

Whatever it was, clearly these mountainmen were intending to fight. That was good news, Vili thought. They had less than half the number of men his father had, and scarcely any horses. Fenris would learn the lay of the land here from Bragi, so there would be no more nasty surprises like the one they had pulled in the gorge.

A very pretty girl brought Vili his lunch, but even though Vili tried speaking to her in the spattering of her language he had picked up from his father's captives, she only smiled and shook her head and ducked back out of the cave.

After he ate, Vili began to pace. This uncertainty was terrible! It had been a mistake to send Siguna away. At least she might have answered some of his questions. He sat down and stared at the empty hearthplace. The guard outside his door was changing every couple of hours, so there was little chance that the men would lose their vigilance. The afternoon advanced, and Vili, who had lain awake all the previous night, went to sleep.

The sun was hanging low in the sky when Vili finally awoke. The first face he saw when he opened his eyes was Siguna's, and relief flashed in his eyes. He made a movement to sit up and then saw that she was accompanied by the black-haired man who was their chief. The two were speaking together in the tongue of the Kindred. Vili sent up a prayer to the Thunderer for strength and prepared to meet his fate.

Siguna noticed that he was awake. "Here is the leader of the mountainmen, Vili," she said. "He has just been saying to me that if you were not my brother, he would surely kill you."

A spark of hope ignited in Vili's heart and he sat up. "He is not going to kill me?"

Siguna shook her head. "It is true that we have never been great friends, Vili, but you are my brother. I have asked for your life, and he has given it to me."

Vili's eyes narrowed. "He is your man?"

"No."

A huge wolf walked into the cave. Vili froze. The wolf walked up to the man, who dropped a hand to caress its head. The man said something to Siguna. Vili caught the word for *escape*.

"Ronan says that if you try to escape, the wolf will get you," Siguna relayed to Vili. "The men of the tribe will be leaving this place on the morrow, and the women will keep guard on you."

The man called Ronan next said something about dogs.

"There are also his wife's two wolfdogs," Siguna translated.

Vili slowly got to his feet. Standing, he was not quite as tall as the black-haired chief. Keeping a wary eye on the wolf, he asked Siguna, "Where are they going?"

"That is none of your concern."

Vili's gray eyes flicked from the wolf to his sister. "Are you one of the women who are to guard me?"

"No," Siguna said. "I will neither hold you nor will I free you, brother. But you will remain here until the struggle between your tribe and ours is finished."

Vili registered that *ours* with shock. No matter what he had accused her of, he had never doubted that she would help him if it was within her power. "How can you so betray our father?" he asked incredulously. "He was ever so good to you."

Siguna went very pale. The black-haired chief said something to her in a sharp voice. She shot him a very revealing look, then shook her head and said to Vili, "You would not understand."

But Vili thought he did understand, and he stared with a mixture of anger and curiosity at the mountainmen's chief. He had a wife, Siguna had said, and for certain he had borne all the signs of a man who has been busy in bed when he stepped forth from his hut early this morning. But obviously Siguna fancied him. Siguna, who had never shown the least inclination toward any of the men of her own tribe, who had spurned even Bragi, fancied this black-haired, hawk-nosed man who stood beside her now.

"No one has raped me," she had said to him this morning. Perhaps not, Vili thought now cynically, but the bastard has most certainly treated her to more than just the respect and honor she was babbling on about earlier.

The chief was watching him, his eyes narrowed, and the thought came to Vili that he looked fully as dangerous as that wolf at his side. For the first time, Vili felt a pang of doubt about the coming struggle.

"What were those weapons I saw the men down by the river carrying?" he asked Siguna abruptly.

"Weapons?" she asked in confusion. "They were spears, Vili."

"The other weapons," he explained. "The ones like this." And he sketched the shape of a shield in the air.

"Oh," said Siguna, and she looked at the chief named Ronan. The chief smiled, and a chill ran up and down Vili's spine. The black head shook in a negative. Siguna said, "That is none of your concern."

He would have to get away, Vili thought. He would have to chance the wolf and the dogs and get away. The women didn't matter. You could put a spear into a woman's hand, but you couldn't teach her to throw it.

"Ronan has sent for the girls of the Red Deer to come and guard you," his sister said.

"The girls of the Red Deer?"

"The Red Deer is a tribe headed by a woman chief," Siguna said with relish, "and all of the girls are trained in weaponry. Do you remember the fight in the gorge?"

Vili nodded grimly. He most certainly remembered the fight in the gorge.

"Many of the arrow shooters that day were girls of the Red Deer," Siguna said.

Vili said, "I don't believe you."

Siguna grinned. "Wait," she said, "and see."

Thorn was standing with Vili's guards when Siguna and Ronan came out of the cave. Ronan shot one look at the boy's face and excused himself to Siguna, saying he had to go and check his men.

Siguna stayed where Ronan had left her and watched Thorn as he approached. He still retained the fawnlike look she had remarked when first they met, but since the fight in the gorge, his large, long-lashed eyes had lost some of their innocence. "How is your brother?" he asked as he stopped before her.

"Relieved, I think," she replied. "He expected to be killed."

Thorn nodded, and side by side, they began to walk in silence toward the camp. At last Thorn said, "I wish there was a place where I could talk to you alone!"

Siguna regarded him out of the corners of her eyes. She was not unaware of Thorn's interest in her. And she liked him. She liked him more than any other boy she had ever known. She considered him her friend. But she did not feel for him what she suspected he wanted her to feel.

He was looking at her wistfully. There was going to be a battle, Siguna thought. Men would die. There would be no harm in giving him a few moments of her time. "We could walk along the river for a little," she suggested.

His face lit in reply.

They made their way along the shore, and once they had rounded the bend and were out of sight of the camp, they stopped. Siguna turned to Thorn and encountered a look on his smooth, youthful face that startled her. It was the same hard, intent look that she had seen most recently on Ronan's face, that time they had been alone together in the hills.

It did not frighten her to see such a look on Thorn's face, but neither was her breathing coming faster nor her heart hammering in her chest.

"Siguna," Thorn said. His own voice sounded decidedly breathless. "I love you."

She drew a long, slow, even breath and said nothing.

"I have been holding my tongue," he went on. "I know that we have taken away your freedom. I know that your loyalties are torn. I know that I should not be saying this to you now. But . . ." Here he bit his lip and fell silent, obviously not wanting to pressure her further by stating the obvious: *But I might never have the chance again.*

It would be wrong of her to give him false hope, Siguna thought. Best to get all clear between them now. She opened her lips to tell him about her talk with Arika and stopped when she saw a shadow fall across Thorn's face.

It was late in the day, and the two of them were standing in the slanting, orange rays of the dying sun. Siguna looked up. The sky was cloudless and there was no sign of a bird. Yet she had distinctly seen a shadow cross Thorn's face. Fear struck her heart as she realized what it was that she had seen.

"I won't press you for an answer now," Thorn was saying softly. "But when all of this is over, will you think about marrying me?"

Siguna could not reply.

"You would love the Valley of the Wolf," Thorn was going on. "I know you would." He looked at her anxiously.

Siguna heard herself answering in an oddly hollow voice, "I will think about it."

Thorn's face blazed with radiance. He raised his right hand and hesitantly ran a caressing finger along her cheek. Siguna stepped closer to him, lifted her mouth, and felt his lips come down on hers. Pain knifed through her at their gentle touch, and she put her arms around his waist and held to him fiercely.

"Why are you crying?" he asked in quick concern when at last she dropped her arms and pulled away. His own eyes were bright with happiness.

She shook her head as if to clear it. "I am crying because you are going away," she said.

He smiled and took her hand in his. "I will be back," he said lightheartedly. "Never fear, Siguna. And when I return, you will give me your answer."

She raised his hand to her cheek and did not answer.

Chapter Thirty-four

"We will conceal ourselves in the mountains, then fall upon these outlanders like an avalanche in the spring," Ronan had told the assembled tribes in the morning. "And like the avalanche, we will sweep them away!"

The men of the Federation roared back their approval.

All during the day, Ronan labored to drill his men in the use of the new shields as well as to organize the march to the River of Gold. The tribes were to leave with the morrow's dawn, but Ronan did not come to his own bed until long after darkfall.

Crim and Bror had once more offered to give up their places in the hut they shared with Ronan, and Nel sat alone before the small fire she had made to ward off the evening chill, waiting. The scene in the hut was peaceful: Leir and Sintra snoozed comfortably by the door, the small flames of the fire flickered, and the stone lamp shed its warm glow on the unrolled sleeping skins. But there was no peace in Nel's heart.

It is here, she thought over and over again. It is finally here. Ronan will leave me tomorrow to go out and fight the Horsemasters. He will leave me, and he may not come back. Ever. He may not come back.

I cannot bear it, she thought. If Ronan should die, I cannot bear it.

Worst of all was her own helplessness in this. She could not go with him. She could not stop him—knew it would be wrong to stop him even if she could.

But . . . never to see Ronan again . . . "I cannot bear it," she whispered into the still and unresponsive air.

The minutes went by. Nel had just put another small branch on the fire when the dogs raised their heads. The door skins were pushed up, and Ronan came in alone. The dogs, relieved not to see Nigak, lowered their noses to their paws once more.

Nel, who had sworn not to burden Ronan with her own fears, managed a smile. She said lightly, "You have had a busy day."

"Sa." He dropped to the rug beside her and rubbed his forehead in a gesture of fatigue. "Very busy. But I think all is ready now for us to leave."

Nel looked at him and knew a desperate need to throw herself into his arms, to cling there and weep her heart out. To hold him and never to let him go.

He said, "It is a great nuisance that the scout Tyr captured turned out to be Siguna's brother. To be frank, if he were anyone else I would simply get rid of him. But I can hardly do that to Siguna's brother."

It took a moment for Nel to focus her mind on his words. She frowned. "You wouldn't just 'get rid' of someone else either," she objected.

He raised a well-defined black brow. "I wouldn't?"

She shook her head. "That is the difference between the Horsemasters and us. If we behaved like them, then we would be as bad as they are."

Ronan raised his other eyebrow and seemed to be considering his reply. "Perhaps you are right," he temporized.

Nel said firmly, "You would never do such a thing."

Ronan did not look as if he agreed with her. "If he tries to get away, Nel, you cannot be tenderhearted," he warned. "I cannot afford to have him warning Fenris!"

"I understand that, Ronan. If we have to put a spear into him to hold him, we will."

Ronan smiled faintly. "Someday remind me to ask you how that differs from simply killing the man out of hand." Nel opened her lips to answer him, but he raised a hand to forestall her. "I am leaving four of our men to guard Vili until the women of the Red Deer get here."

"That is not necessary, Ronan," Nel objected. "You have too few men as it is. Those of us who are here can easily take care of Vili."

Ronan shook his head. "I am leaving horses for the men," he explained. "Horsed men will be able to catch up with us before we reach the River of Gold." He lifted his left hand and brushed her cheek with gentle fingers. "For all your fine words, Nel, I do not think you could kill a man. And you are the only woman present who has been trained to throw a spear."

That gentle touch almost undid her. She lowered her eyes, swallowed, and said in a low voice, "What men will you leave?"

"Dai, Okal, Kasar, and Lemo."

She nodded without raising her head.

"Beki and Yoli left for the Great Cave before midday, and they will ride hard. The women of the Red Deer should be here by darkfall tomorrow."

Once more, Nel nodded.

"Nel," Ronan said in a slightly different tone, "if we should lose this fight, you must gather the tribe's women and get back to the valley."

Nel's throat went dry.

Ronan went on, "If the Federation should lose, what men are left will do what they can to protect the women and children at the Great Cave. But I want the women of the Wolf to go back to the valley."

Nel clasped her hands around her knees.

"Are you hearing me, Nel?" Ronan asked. "Collect our women from the Great Cave and keep to the forest, the way we did when you ran away with me. You remember the way."

Nel said nothing.

"You will be safe in the valley." Then, when she still did not speak, he said, "Nel, you must promise me that you will do this."

I can't, she thought. If you are dead, then I want to die too.

"I owe it to my men to do what is in my power to keep their wives and children safe. If I am not there to do it myself, then you must do it for me."

Very, very slightly, Nel shook her head.

There was a silence.

"Minnow," he said very gently, "I cannot go out to fight with an easy mind if there is fear in my heart for you. Promise me you will go back to the valley."

She struggled to compose her face. At last, she said, "I hear you," and raised her eyes.

His face looked tense and worried as well as tired. The worry, she
knew, was for her. He was right, she thought suddenly. She could not
send him off with a divided heart. She held her voice steady. "I will
get our women and children to safety, Ronan. I promise."

Slowly his face relaxed. Then slowly he raised his hands and cupped
her cheeks between his long, hard fingers. His calluses were rough
against her skin. He bent his head and put his mouth upon hers.

Save him for me, Mother, Nel prayed as her eyes closed and her
body swayed toward him. Do not let him die. Save him.

She reached out, slid her arms around his body under his arms,
and held to him tightly, her face still upturned to his. After a moment
he leaned forward and, without breaking their embrace, laid her back
upon their bedplace.

His lovemaking was fierce, a blazing affirmation of life and love
performed in the chill shadow of death. After he had fallen asleep, Nel
lay awake, cradling jealously in her arms the warm, living flesh that
tomorrow might be cold and still.

I cannot live without you, she cried in her heart. Ronan, I cannot.
I cannot.

There was nothing she could do.

Ronan had said she was incapable of killing a man. He was wrong.
If she had Fenris here right now, within reach of her spear, she would
run him through without thought or mercy.

Save him for me, Mother. Do not let him die.

There was nothing she could do.

At dawn the following morning, the men of the Federation marched
out of the homesite of the Red Deer and moved down the Greatfish
River in the direction of the River of Gold. Their destination for the
night was the homeplace of the Tribe of the Leopard. From there on
the following day they would cut west into the mountains that overlooked the valley of the River of Gold.

The day's march went well, and the tribes reached the homesite of
the Leopard before darkfall. They ate their supper and rolled up in their
sleeping skins for the night. The only disturbance that occurred during
the night was the arrival of Okal, Dai, Kasar, and Lemo. They reported
to Ronan that a contingent of women of the Red Deer had arrived just
after midday to take over the guard on Vili.

The men of the Federation were on the move again by dawn, and by midday they had reached the place where the mountains sloped down to the valley of the River of Gold.

Before them stretched a large crescent-shaped meadow, intersected in the middle by the river. Opposite, on the far side of the meadow and the river, the rugged limestone mountains rose again, thickly studded with trees of pine and birch.

The men of the tribes set up their camp, and Ronan posted a watch on the valley. From their vantage point, the men of the Federation would be able to see the Horsemasters coming downriver long before they had reached the meadow.

The day advanced and still there was no sign of the enemy. The men unrolled their sleeping skins but made no fires. They ate dried meat and fruit washed down with cold water, not tea, and went to sleep.

The moon was almost full. In a few days, the men of the Squirrel would have their ceremony and then be free to come to the aid of the Federation.

Too late, Ronan thought bitterly, as he gazed up at the bright moon. Whether or not there was likely to be a Tribe of the Squirrel ever to hold that ceremony again would depend upon what happened upon this meadow below within the next day or so. For Ronan was in no doubt that the whole future of the mountain tribes hung upon the coming fight.

What to do about the horses? This was the problem that worried Ronan most. He was confident that if he spread his line wide enough, his men could stand their ground against the Horsemasters if the enemy were forced to fight on foot. But if even a small group of them got to their horses and got behind the Federation lines, then there would be real trouble.

Like a shadowy wraith, Nigak threaded his way among the sleeping men to the place where Ronan lay. The wolf had wanted to accompany Ronan, and Nel had insisted that he be allowed to. As Nigak settled down beside him, Ronan's thoughts turned to his wife. She had promised she would go back to the valley, and he knew he could rely on Nel to keep a promise. The Mother would look after Nel, he thought. Even if the worst happened, and he and all the men perished in this coming fight, Nel and the women could survive in the valley. They could hunt the animals that dwelled within the valley walls if they had to.

His mind reverted to the source of its unrest. What to do about the horses?

Suddenly, he heard Nel's voice in his mind: *Stallions!* she had said to him once, with a mixture of impatience and amusement. *They are surely the most possessive creatures who ever lived.*

When had she said that? He thought, and then he remembered: They had been watching Impero as he herded his mares jealously away from one of his exiled yearling sons who had gotten too close to the herd. Nel had made that remark as she watched the great white stallion nipping ruthlessly at the heels of a mare, most probably the colt's mother, who wanted to approach him.

Ronan opened his eyes and stared once more up at the moon. He thought of Impero. He thought of Cloud's instinctive herding behavior during the one raid they had made on Fenris's mares.

That is it, Ronan thought. The Horsemasters' herd ran free. All he needed to do was set his young stallions loose upon the herd of mares, and they would do his work for him.

After a few more moments, Ronan closed his eyes on the moon and went to sleep.

It was late afternoon the following day when Ronan got the first report that the Horsemasters were coming down the river. Lying encamped in the mountains, the Federation men were able to watch as the huge mass of men and horses came cantering onto the meadow below. Ronan picked Fenris out almost immediately; he was riding in the forefront of his men, a man on either side of him and a smaller group spread out behind. To Ronan's profound relief, the kain turned his horse toward the river, halted and dismounted. The rest of the Horsemasters followed him, and soon the entire mass of men was dismounted as well. Horses were rubbed down. Packhorses began to be unpacked and some tents to be set up. The horse herd was turned loose to drink from the river and graze on the rich meadow grass. Cookfires were lit. The Horsemasters were making camp for the night.

It helped Ronan enormously that Fenris was indeed going to stop for the night on the meadow. If he had not, then Ronan would have altered his plans, but this was best. The Federation forces were already in position here, and as long as they exerted reasonable caution, there was little chance of their presence being noticed.

Ronan's plan was to attack during the night, when he could count on the Horsemasters being asleep. The day had been clear, and the moon was bright enough to light what needed to be lit for such a venture.

He met with the tribal leaders over their cold suppers.

"We shall have to draw the tribes up into a long line in order to prevent the enemy from getting around behind us," Ronan said. "That is the thing we must absolutely avoid, giving them the chance to encircle us."

The faces of the chiefs were grim. Neihle, who was leading the Red Deer men in place of the Mistress, was the one to ask: "What of their horses? If even a few of them reach the horses and get behind us, then we are likely to have panic among our men."

"I have been thinking of that," Ronan said. Then he told them what he had decided to do. "Thorn and Mait can drive our stallions into the herd of mares," he elaborated. "Six handfuls of stallions will be more than enough to create chaos in the herd, I am thinking. No man will be able to get close enough to catch a mount."

Unwar and Haras grinned.

"Good thinking," Neihle said tersely.

Young Matti simply nodded his head.

"I have been thinking that I will form our line into the shape of a flying eagle," Ronan said next. "I want more men in the wings than in the center. If the center cannot hold, it will not be as dangerous as if the wings are broken. The enemy will not be able easily to come behind us from the center, but if the wings are not strong enough we will not be able to contain them."

There was silence as all the men tried to picture in their minds the formation Ronan had just described.

"Where will each tribe be?" Haras asked.

"The left wing will be the men of the Buffalo, under Haras; the right wing the men of the Leopard under Unwar." Ronan turned to Neihle. "Uncle, I would like to split the men of the Red Deer and put half in one wing and half in the other."

Neihle nodded gravely.

"You will command the Red Deer men who are fighting in the left wing," Ronan said. He hesitated infinitesimally. "And I will command the Red Deer men in the right."

Unwar made a sharp sound of surprise.

Neihle and Ronan were looking at each other. "The men of the Red Deer will be proud to follow you," Neihle said at last, slowly and deliberately.

Nigak raised his nose from Ronan's thigh and pricked his ears forward, as if in acknowledgment of a tribute.

"And the center?" Haras asked.

"The men of the Wolf, led by Bror, and the men of the Fox and the Bear, led by Matti."

Unwar chewed reflectively on his dried deer meat, then nodded his approval. His heavy-lidded eyes looked around the faces of his fellow chiefs. "We are all of us fighting for our homes, for our wives and for our children," he said. "Perhaps this is not the place I would have chosen to make our stand, but we are here. This night we will win or we will die; there is no middle way."

Ronan looked at the Leopard chief in surprise. He had not expected such a sentiment from Unwar.

"Unwar speaks true," Haras said and bowed his noble head.

A bird called in the silence, a high clear trilling sound in the dying day.

"Get some sleep," Ronan advised them all. "We will move out in four hours' time."

Chapter Thirty-five

Moonlight bathed the world in a glimmer of silvery luminescence. In the nighttime silence, nearly two hundred men lifted their spears and their shields and fell in behind their leaders. Then, still in silence, they began slowly to descend the tree-strewn hill that sloped to the meadow whereupon the Horsemasters lay sleeping in their camp.

Fenris had built big fires to ward off any predators that might be seeking to drink from the river during the night, and Ronan was certain there were men posted to keep watch on both the fires and the surrounding meadow. But no outcry came from the camp. No sentry had seen the men creeping so carefully down the hillside.

When they were almost to level ground, the men of the tribes formed up behind their leaders in the battle positions they had been given. When the quick and silent disposition was finished, the left and the right wings were each four lines deeper than was the center, which was composed only of the men of the Wolf under Bror and the remnants of the Fox and the Bear tribes under Matti.

"I am giving you the toughest job," Ronan had said to Bror back at camp when he apprised Bror of his plans. "I am asking you to hold the center, and I am not giving you enough men to do it."

Bror thought of those words now, as he took his place in the front line and looked over his shoulder at the men to his rear. His eyes fell upon Heno, who was directly behind him. Heno grinned and lifted his spear slightly. Bror smiled back and turned around to face forward once more, his heart suddenly swollen with love for these men who formed the fellowship known as the Tribe of the Wolf.

Still nothing stirred in the camp by the river, eerily lit by the leaping fires. Silence enveloped the world. Bror did not know how Thorn and Mait were keeping the horses so quiet, but they were. Then, from the farthest end of the right wing, Ronan's voice rang out. *"Now!"*

Bror started to move forward at a steady trot, and out of the sides of his eyes, he saw the men beside him move forward with him. Behind him the rest of the men would be scrambling down the last of the hillside and falling into their places in the line.

It was a quarter of a mile to the Horsemasters' camp. They were halfway there when the thunder of horse hooves from farther down the valley told Bror that Thorn and Mait had made their move.

Shouts were coming now from the Horsemasters' camp, and the firelight showed men scrambling out of sleeping skins and grabbing their spears. Still the tribes came on at a slow and steady pace. Ronan wanted them to stay together, not to separate and go searching among the camp for victims. "Give them a chance to come to us," he had said to the gathered men earlier in the night. "Let them throw themselves upon our line. Do not be betrayed into breaking!"

Bror could see now that the Horsemasters were hastily forming up into a band to oppose them. From his place in the front line, he could hear a deep voice shouting what must be orders. Then the first bunch of the enemy was running forward, spears forward, straight at the advancing line of tribesmen.

"Steady!" Bror called to his men and kept his shield in place, his spear level. He saw the man who was coming toward him and braced himself for the encounter.

The first wave of the defending Horsemasters hit into the Federation line with a shock and went down. Bror kicked at the dead body under his foot. The man's spear had bounced right off his shield. Bror grinned.

Suddenly, the night was split with the screams of a stallion. Next came a cacophony of wild whinnies and thundering hooves. No need to worry about them getting to their horses, Bror thought with glee. The horses are gone.

Another wave hit the Federation line, and then another, and the tribes held strong.

The same deep voice made itself heard, even over the noise of the horses, and the men of the Horsemasters began to form into a more organized grouping. Again they came on, and this time each man Bror killed was followed by another. They were gaining more and more in number, and the weight of the onslaught was forcing Bror back. He looked in desperation at both of the Federation wings and saw that they were holding. It was only the undermanned center that was being pushed back.

"Hold!" Bror shouted to the men around him. "Hold!" Two men down from him, he saw Dai manage a step forward. Then Okal was at Dai's side. Bror surged forward himself, and the men of the Wolf came after him.

The Horsemasters were far greater in number, but their shorter spears and lack of shields gave them a vulnerability the men of the tribes did not possess. Nor had they been trained to keep an even front and act with a regular movement, as the Federation men had been. They were incredibly brave, rushing forward again and again in desperate groups, striving to force a lane into the Federation line and break it. But the tribes were feeling their superiority, and even though the relentless attacks told upon their inferior numbers, the sight of the slaughter they had already done gave them the courage to keep on.

The fight went on in the moonlit valley.

Bror wasn't sure when it happened, but all of a sudden he realized that the center was under heavier pressure. It seemed as if the enemy at last had perceived the weakness in Ronan's disposition and was attacking it.

Furiously, the Horsemasters hurled themselves again and again into the center. Bror's arm and wrist and shoulder ached from the blows he was taking upon his shield. Next to him, he saw Cree go down. The man who had felled him bent swiftly and picked up Cree's shield. Then he came after Bror.

Bror parried the spear blows with his shield, but he could not retaliate as effectively as he had previously, for now the enemy had a shield also. Bror glanced up briefly into his enemy's implacable face and recognized Fenris.

"Dhu," he muttered under his breath.

Fenris shouted something to his men and, with a mighty blow, forced Bror to step back. Bror felt the line behind him starting to give.

"Hold!" he cried furiously.

But at last the weakness of the center was being exploited. Fenris shoved past Bror, and then another man followed behind the kain. The Horsemasters had breeched the line.

"Run," Bror heard Dai screaming at him. "Run for the hill, Bror. We can regroup there!"

Realizing there was no longer a line for him to hold together, Bror followed Dai's instructions and ran.

As soon as he reached the shelter of the trees on the mountain, Bror turned. Most of the men had reached the hill before him and were waiting to see if the Horsemasters would follow. Bror hoped desperately that they would.

It soon became clear, however, that Fenris was not going to be lured into a pursuit. He had got a wedge of his men in between Ronan's two wings and was clearly going to try to exploit the divided ranks of the enemy.

The outcome would depend upon how successful the tribes had been up until now, Bror thought despairingly, as he yelled for his men to form up again. Had they killed enough of Fenris's men?

"Should we charge again?" Matti asked eagerly.

"Wait," Bror said. "Wait and see first where Ronan will need us the most."

The men of the center waited tensely, Bror watching to see if the Horsemasters were still strong enough to attempt a flanking movement around one of the wings.

Nothing happened. Fenris appeared to have concentrated all of his remaining forces in the center. They were fighting on two sides, but there were enough of them to hold their position. The battle raged on, neither side appearing to have enough power to strike the killing blow.

Then, as Bror watched, the far end of the tribes' right wing detached itself and swung around in orderly formation toward the back of the center.

Ronan was outflanking the Horsemasters!

With a broad grin splitting his dirty, bloody face, Bror roared to his men to follow and ran forward to join with his chief.

The shock of the new attack from behind was what finally broke the Horsemasters. Many of the men, seeing the tribesmen running from the mountains, did not realize that Ronan's center had broken and thought it was a new force entering the fight. In fear and confusion, the Horsemasters turned and ran.

Many of the tribesmen were hot to follow, but Ronan's voice, miraculously audible over all the tumult, ordered them to stay. Within a few minutes, quiet had fallen on the body-strewn plain. The battle was over. Bror thought with stunned incredulity: *We won.*

As the sun slowly rose in the eastern sky, the cleanup after the battle continued. The Federation dead and wounded had already been collected, the totals being an incredible thirty-one wounded and eighteen dead. The bodies still strewn all over the plain belonged to the Horsemasters.

It was Dai who brought Ronan the word that they had found Fenris. "He's alive," Dai reported. "He took a blow on the head and has a wound in his shoulder. Apparently, when one of his men saw him go down, he flung his own body over the kain's to protect him. He was successful. At any rate, Fenris is alive and the other man is dead."

"How badly is he hurt?" Ronan asked.

"I think it was the knock on the head that felled him. The shoulder wound does not look that serious." Dai rocked back on his heels and exhaled slowly. "Shall we put him with the others?"

Ronan had given orders that the injured Horsemasters were to be separated from the dead. This was unlike what he had done in the gorge, when the injured had been killed where they lay. His men clearly preferred the killing.

Slowly, Ronan nodded his head. "And see that his shoulder gets some attention, Dai. I would like to speak to him before we do anything else."

Dai looked as if he were going to say something; then he just shrugged his shoulders and walked away.

By dawn all of the Federation men had been accounted for, except Thorn and Mait.

"They were on horseback to drive the stallions," Ronan said when their absence was reported to him. "I wouldn't be surprised if they got caught in the middle of the herd's stampede. They will make their way back here, never fear."

"I hope you are right," Rilik, Thorn's father, said with a worried frown. "I hope he wasn't thrown and trampled."

"Not Thorn," Ronan said with confidence. "That boy can ride anything."

Rilik smiled, but the worry still lurked in his eyes.

The sun was a bright yellow ball in a bright blue sky when finally Ronan sought out Fenris. Siguna's father. His enemy.

The wounded Horsemasters had been put together under the shelter of some small trees that grew at the edge of the meadow where it met with the mountain. The number of the wounded, Ronan had been told, was forty-eight. The dead numbered over two hundred. Ronan's plan had been effective indeed.

As Ronan approached the prisoners, the kain was sitting up, his back against a tree and his head slumped forward. The shoulder of his buckskin shirt was stained with dried blood. He looked to be asleep. Ronan paused and considered for a moment the figure before him.

This was the man responsible for the deaths of untold numbers of Kindred men. This was the man who had enslaved untold numbers of Kindred women. It was a strange feeling to have him like this, wounded and vulnerable and very much at Ronan's mercy. I should hate him, Ronan told himself, as he took a few more steps forward. This is a man I should hate.

"Fenris," he said clearly. There was no response. He said the name again, and the disordered blond head moved. The kain lifted his head slowly, as if it hurt, and saw Ronan. He said something in a language Ronan did not know.

"Can you understand me at all?" Ronan asked in the tongue of the Kindred.

The other man nodded, then winced at the movement. He ran his tongue around his lips as if they were too dry. "I understand . . . a little," he said in a deep voice that had lost but little of its strength. The kain's eyes were dark gray in color, Ronan saw, not pale like his daughter's. "Who . . . you?" Fenris asked.

Ronan answered. "I am the leader . . . the kain . . . of these men."

Fenris squinted at him as if trying to get him into focus. Ronan could see that there was a great bruise on the kain's left temple. His head must be pounding like a shaman's drum, Ronan thought. He had taken a blow like that once, and the headache had lasted for days.

"You want . . . what?" Fenris asked.

Ronan stared into the other man's face. In spite of pain, in spite of injury, in spite of defeat, Fenris yet managed to look authoritative. And Ronan realized that he had no answer to the kain's question. He did not know what he wanted from Fenris. He just knew he wanted something.

He said, because he did not know what else to say, "Your daughter is safe."

Fenris frowned, not understanding.

"Siguna," Ronan said. "Siguna is safe. She is with us."

Awareness slowly dawned in the kain's eyes. "Siguna? Siguna is live?"

Ronan nodded. "My men took her from the forest. She is safe."

A flash of something Ronan could have sworn was joy flickered across Fenris's face. Then his mouth set. "She your woman?"

"Na!" For some reason he couldn't define, it was very important to Ronan that Fenris know Siguna was safe and untouched.

"She is no man's woman," he said. "She is safe." Then, as Fenris still looked at him uncomprehendingly, Ronan put his hands behind his back. "No man has touched her," he said. "It is not our way."

"No man touch," Fenris repeated, and his mouth softened fractionally. "Is good Siguna is live." He moved his head to look at the men around him, and his face tightened with pain. "You kill us," he said simply.

"You killed my people," Ronan returned, his voice harsh. "You killed many many men."

Fenris said, "Sa."

"Why?"

Fenris sighed, and his gray eyes lifted to meet Ronan's. "I do not know," he said. He looked genuinely puzzled, but whether it was by Ronan's question or by his own lack of an answer, Ronan did not know.

Looking back into the kain's eyes, Ronan recognized finally that there was a strange bond between this man and himself. He had always felt it in his heart; now for the first time, he admitted it in his mind.

I cannot kill him, Ronan thought. I don't know why, but I cannot kill him.

His black brows were drawn together, as if he could feel Fenris's pain in his own head. He said, "We will not kill you."

The kain looked skeptical, but then, as he continued to regard Ronan, his face slowly changed. "Is true?" he asked with wonder.

"Is true."

Fenris was silent, evidently trying to make sense of this amazing news. He gazed out at the body-strewn plain, the remnant of his defeat. "Dead men," he said, gesturing. "Burn."

Ronan was horrified. The tribes of the Kindred always buried their dead with reverence. "Fire?" he said, wanting to make sure he had understood correctly.

"Sa. Too many dead. Dangerous. Burn." The kain, Ronan realized with a mixture of amazement and unwilling respect, was giving orders. Once more Fenris ran his tongue around his cracked lips.

"I will send a man with water," Ronan said abruptly, turned on his heel, and departed.

Fenris was right, Ronan thought as he traversed the plain. There were too many dead Horsemasters to bury. Nor could he leave them lying here much longer, or the plain would be crawling with predators. He would do as the kain suggested and burn them.

He lifted his head as he made the decision, and it was then that he saw the boy and horse in the distance, coming slowly down the river. He raised his hand to shade his eyes from the morning glare. One boy leading one horse. Sunlight glinted off smooth dark hair. Mait.

Ronan felt his heart plummet. Where was Thorn? His legs moved forward, and then he broke into a run.

As the distance between him and Mait closed, Ronan saw for the first time that Mait was not walking because his horse was lame. He was walking because the horse was bearing another burden. Unconsciously, Ronan's steps slowed. He did not want to see what he was afraid he would find upon Frost's back.

Mait noticed the oncoming chief for the first time and halted. As Ronan came up to him, he saw that the boy's face was streaked with tears. He looked to the horse and saw the slender body lying across its back, legs and arms dangling on opposite sides. Saw the tangled mop of brown hair.

He felt as if someone had punched him in the stomach.

"What happened?" he asked Mait hoarsely. "Did he fall?"

"Na," Mait said. "We got caught up in the stampede, but the both of us stayed on. It happened after we had managed to separate our horses from the others and were coming back." Mait raised a fist to scrub at his eyes, a childish gesture that was unbearably poignant. "We were coming through the forest above the river. Thorn was going first." He swallowed audibly. "One of the fleeing Horsemasters must have seen us and lain in wait. He leaped out at Thorn, pushed him off Acorn, and mounted him. Thorn tried to grab for Acorn's halter, and the man . . . the man . . ." Mait began to sob.

Ronan reached an arm around Mait and pressed the boy's face into his shoulder. "He ran Thorn through with his spear," Mait sobbed. "He ran him through and galloped away. I jumped off Frost and ran to him, but . . . but . . . oh, Ronan, he was dead!"

Ronan continued to hold Mait as he stared with dry and burning eyes at the limp and slender body slung over the horse. One of the reasons he had chosen Thorn to drive the horses was to keep him out of the fighting. And instead, he had sent the boy to his death.

I am so clever, he thought with corrosive bitterness. And in my cleverness I have killed Thorn.

Mait seemed to be getting himself under control, and Ronan dropped his arm. "If only he had let the man have Acorn," Mait said miserably. "If only he had not grabbed for the halter!"

Ronan nodded. Then he picked up Frost's reins. "Come," he said to Mait. "We will have to find Rilik."

Chapter Thirty-six

The bulk of the Federation women waited at the Great Cave for news of the fight, but the small group who had been at the Red Deer camp when the men marched off remained there. They had been augmented by only nine young women from the Tribe of the Red Deer, whose job it was to make certain that Vili did not get free to return to his father.

Vili was incredulous when he discovered that he was to be left in the guardianship of women, unbound. But it was so. The men actually mounted their horses and rode out of camp, leaving him the freedom of his arms and his legs. They were mad, Vili thought, but he was certainly not fool enough to express that view out loud.

He became even more confounded by the men's actions when he saw the women who were to guard him. They were young girls of Siguna's age! The men had brought the girls to the cave, showed them Vili, and then left. That black-haired chief would have his men's hearts when he discovered what they had done, Vili thought.

The first shift on guard duty was composed of three of the girls, all of whom were carrying spears and javelins set into spearthrowers. It was afternoon. He would wait until the dark, Vili decided. He would have to chance the wolf and the dogs, but these girls would be no problem at all.

He stood in the recess of the cave door and watched them. They were pretty girls, he thought, girls who would be much better employed at work in a man's tent than left unsupervised to play with a man's weapons. What fools these tribesmen must be!

One of the girls, a long-legged, black-haired beauty, noticed him watching them. She made some comment to the other girls, who laughed.

Their laughter did not at all upset Vili. He was too busy running his eyes up and down the black-haired girl's body. He felt his phallus begin to rise. He would relish a chance to show that one what kind of weapon a real man could wield, he thought. He walked slowly to the cave entrance and leaned his shoulder against the rocky archway, his eyes boldly raking the girl's body.

The three girls had turned to face him when he moved into the archway. He realized suddenly that all three of them were holding their spears.

"Back," the black-haired girl said firmly, gesturing with her free hand to illustrate her command.

He grinned. "I like here," he said in their language.

"Back," the girl said again, and when still he did not move, she began to come forward. He crossed his arms casually, his right shoulder still leaned against the archway, his eyes on the spear. If she came close enough, he would grab it . . .

"Aieeh!" He clapped his hand to his upper left arm and stared at the girl. The spear had moved so quickly he had not had time to react.

"Back," she said once again. He could feel the warm blood welling beneath his fingers. Slowly, his eyes on the girl's perfectly calm face, Vili backed into the cave.

Scowling furiously, he pulled his shirt over his head and stared at his arm. It was not a serious wound, he saw. But it hurt! He set his jaw and glared at the cave opening. She'll pay for this, he vowed. He had nothing else to use to stop the bleeding, so he balled up his shirt and used that.

A short time later, Siguna entered the cave carrying more water and some deerskin cloths. "How is your arm, Vili?" she asked.

He was bare to the waist, as his bloody shirt was now unwearable. "It hurts," he answered furiously. "And I am cold."

"I'll find you another shirt once I have taken care of the wound," Siguna promised. She put her small pot of water down on a rock. "Come over here, into the light from the door."

Vili did not want the black-haired girl to see how effectively she
had hurt him, but he knew the wound needed attention or it might go
sour. He stalked over to where his sister stood and let her look at his
arm.

"It's not that bad," Siguna said. "I'll wash it out and pack it with
the herbs Nel gave me and it should heal very well."

"What kind of women are those girls?" Vili demanded. "She attacked
me! I was standing there perfectly quietly, and she attacked me."

"Lara said she told you to get back into the cave and you wouldn't
go," Siguna said. Her head was bent as she worked on the wound, and
he gritted his teeth so he wouldn't give that girl . . . Lara . . . the
satisfaction of seeing him wince. "I told you about the girls of the Red
Deer, Vili. They can handle their weapons. They hunt like men. Do
not underestimate them, or you will get hurt again." She had finished
washing the wound, and now she began to press herbs into it.

Vili was silent until she had finished; then he said haughtily, "She
caught me off guard."

Siguna wrapped a piece of deerskin around his upper arm and began
to fasten it with two thongs.

"Siguna," Vili said, and now his voice was low and urgent. "What
is happening?"

Siguna finished knotting the last thong. "I can't tell you, Vili," she
said.

"These mountainmen did not run away. They were preparing for
a fight; I could see that very well."

Siguna looked up, sighed, then nodded her head. Vili scowled at
her. "He will not catch my father in another trap like that gorge. Bragi
and I scouted all the land along the river."

"I know."

"Siguna." He dropped his voice even further. "You must help me
to get away."

Her gray eyes were unhappy. "I can't."

"Why not? There is nothing I can tell my father that Bragi has not
already told him," Vili said reasonably.

"There is always the chance that Bragi has not made it back to
Father."

Vili snorted. "He was riding Firewind. Of course he will make it
back."

"He could have an accident," Siguna argued.

"Don't talk like a fool," he said impatiently.

The sound of girls' laughter came from without the cave's opening, and both Vili and Siguna fell silent, listening.

"I can't, Vili," Siguna said regretfully. "You know too much. You know that the tribes have left this campsite. You know they are in the mood to fight. I cannot set you free to bring that news to my father."

There was a white line around his mouth. "That black-haired chief must be a stallion indeed, to have brought you to such a state of submission," he said brutally.

Instinctively, Siguna swung her arm, and her hand smashed against Vili's cheek. A loud resounding *crack* echoed through the cave. "You know nothing about him!" she said through her teeth. Her breath was coming fast, and her hands were balled into fists at her sides.

He reacted instinctively, his arm shooting out to grab her shoulder, his fist coming up to retaliate.

There was the rush of feet in the doorway and a warning shout. Vili's head jerked around toward the cave opening.

"Do not touch her." The girl spoke the words slowly and clearly enough for Vili to understand. Her spear was pointing at him steadily.

For a moment, Vili hesitated. He could use Siguna to cover himself, he thought. He might even get away. But even before the thought had finished, his fingers were relaxing on her shoulder. What would his father say if he learned Vili had bought his freedom at the price of his sister's life? He stepped back and let Siguna go.

She backed away from him a few steps, but then she stopped and raised her head. He kept his face impassive. She said, surprisingly, "I am sorry, Vili."

The girl with the spear kept watch until Siguna was safely out of the cave. It was the black-haired girl again. Vili stood still, waiting for her to leave as well. Instead she stood there, her eyes going over his naked torso as boldly as his had gone over her body earlier.

Vili's arm was throbbing. He was more worried than he wanted to admit about his father and his tribe. He had just been wounded by one girl and struck by another. He had had enough.

"You want sex?" he said, using the word for mating he had learned from the Kindred women he had bedded. He gestured crudely. "Come. I give it you."

To his astonishment, the girl did not stalk away. Instead she smiled and made some reply, using words he did not understand. He scowled and shook his head. Her smile deepened. She was amazingly pretty. She said slowly, "Are you good?"

His jaw dropped.

"You look good," she said, her eyes going unashamedly over his chest and his shoulders before they dropped to his waist and below.

What kind of women were these?

She laughed delightedly at the look on his face, flicked her tongue enticingly around her lips, and departed. Slowly.

A few minutes later, another girl came to the cave door and tossed in a shirt. Vili put it on and lay down, determined to sleep.

One day went by, and then another and another. It was almost suppertime on the fourth day when Kasar and Dai came riding into the Red Deer camp with news of the fight.

"We won" were Kasar's first words as he jumped off his horse only to have Beki immediately cast herself into his arms.

Eken was back at the Great Cave, so Dai had less distraction and was able to impart to Nel and the other women who had come running a more detailed story of what had happened on the plain by the River of Gold two nights before.

There were loud exclamations of relief from everyone as he concluded his tale.

It was Nel who finally asked, "Whom did we lose, Dai?"

A tense silence fell as all the women stared at Dai, willing him not to say the name of their man.

Dai began first with the tribes other than his own. "From the tribe of the Leopard," he said gravely, and began to name names.

After the list from the other tribes had been concluded, and one wailing woman had been borne away, Nel said again steadily, "And the Tribe of the Wolf?"

Dai's face was very stern as he looked around the small circle of women who were left. "We are a small tribe," he said, "and so we are bound to feel each death more deeply."

"Who?" Nel asked again, a little less steadily than before.

"Cree and Mitlik are dead," Dai said. "Okal and Heno were

wounded, but the shamans think they will recover." He looked at one young face in particular and said gently, "I am so sorry, Yoli."

Her hand went to her mouth. "Not Lemo?"

Very, very gently, he said, "Sa."

"Not dead? Dai, tell me he is not dead!"

"I wish I could tell you that," Dai said wretchedly. "Dhu, how I wish I could tell you that!"

Yoli made a small animal-like sound, and seemed to sag. Beki rushed to put an arm around her waist to support her. "Not Lemo," Yoli said piteously. "It can't be true. Not Lemo."

"Beki," Nel said quietly, "take Yoli back to her hut and get her some tea."

Beki nodded. "Come along, Yoli," she murmured coaxingly. "Come along with me and let me take care of you." As if in a daze, Yoli let herself be led away.

"There is more," Kasar said grimly when the two women were out of hearing. He looked now at Siguna. "We have lost Thorn also."

There was a sharp cry of anguish, but it came from Nel. Siguna had bowed her head, but she said nothing. She had been prepared to hear such words, had known she was saying farewell to Thorn when she had kissed him by the river after seeing his death shadowed upon his face. Now she stared dry-eyed at the earth and listened as Kasar told them how it had happened.

A heavy silence fell upon the small group, the happy news of victory effectively overshadowed by the grim toll of the dead.

"We have lost more men than any other tribe," Berta said.

"The Tribe of the Wolf was in the center, and the center was where there were the most deaths," Dai replied.

One of the tired horses began to toss his head up and down, and Nel reached up to catch his halter and rub his nose.

Siguna's voice spoke tentatively into the silence. "My father?" she asked. "Do you know what happened to my father?"

They looked at her with hostile eyes.

"He is alive," Dai said. "Hurt, but alive. Ronan made us collect the Horsemasters wounded this time, and he was among them." Clearly, this was not a decision with which Dai agreed.

Siguna bent her head.

"Evidently you got some of the horses back," Nel said to the two men, her hand still upon Dai's horse's nose.

"Sa. We had Mait's horse, of course, and Ronan had kept back three others. We spent a whole day searching for our stallions and the scattered mares. Ronan sent Kasar and me on after we had collected the first batch. The men were still out searching for more of the horses when we left to bring the news to you."

"You have been riding long and hard," Nel said quietly. "Come and we will get you some food."

Siguna remained where she was while the rest of the group moved off toward the huts; then she herself began to walk quickly toward the cave where Vili was being held. The girls of the Red Deer were congregated outside in a group, talking together in low tones, and she walked past them without a word and went directly into the cave.

Vili was sitting cross-legged on the floor, idly throwing small stones into a circle he had scratched in the dirt. His head jerked up as Siguna came in.

"We lost," she said. "But Father is still alive."

A shifting array of expressions passed over her brother's face. Then he said, "I don't believe it. We outnumber them two to one. It isn't possible for us to have lost."

Siguna went to sit beside him on the floor. "This is how it happened," she said, and she related the story she had heard from Dai.

"Name of the Thunderer," Vili said when she had finished. "Is Father one of those who got away?"

Siguna shook her head. "Dai said he was one of the injured they carried from the field."

Vili's eyes strayed toward the circle in the dirt and the stones with which he had been amusing himself. His lips set hard. "They have him, then."

"Yes."

"How badly is he hurt?"

"I don't know. Dai did not say. He had just given out the names of their dead and was in no mood to answer questions about Father."

Neither of them appeared to notice how Siguna's allegiance had shifted with the news of the battle's outcome.

"How many of our men died?"

"More than two hundred, they said."

"That is more than half of us!" Vili said incredulously.

"Yes."

Vili, true child of his tribe, asked next, "What will happen to our horses?"

"I do not know. Dai and Kasar said Ronan was trying to collect as many of them as he could."

Silence fell as the two of them stared, unseeing, at the stones within the circle.

"He killed all the wounded we left in the gorge," Vili said next. "Why didn't he do that this time?"

"I don't know."

Vili's breath was coming hard. "I cannot bear to think of Father in the hands of his enemies!" he said fiercely, smashing his right fist into the palm of his left hand over and over.

"Ronan won't hurt him," Siguna said.

Vili flashed her a scornful look.

"See how you have been treated," she pointed out. "These are not people of violence."

Vili's scorn for her ignorance increased. "Two hundred dead, and you say these are not people of violence?"

"We forced the fight on them," Siguna said stubbornly. "You know that is true, Vili."

Vili's jaw was jutting out, making the dent in his chin very noticeable. He frowned and began to finger the cleft, an unconscious imitation of Fenris's own gesture when he was worried, and tears suddenly welled up in Siguna's eyes. "I cannot bear to think of Father lying hurt and helpless either," she whispered brokenly. She began to sob harshly, in the manner of one who is not accustomed to tears.

Vili turned to her, his face twisted with pain. Then, abruptly, he reached his right arm out and drew her close against his side. Siguna turned her head, buried her face in her brother's shoulder, and cried. After a minute, Vili rested his forehead on the top of her head and let his own tears slip slowly into her soft and silvery hair.

Brother and sister were sitting together in somber silence half an hour later, their shoulders touching, their heads bent, when Arika entered the cave.

Both blond heads lifted at the same time, and the relationship that could not be perceived in their features was immediately evident in the identical movement of those heads.

"Mistress!" Siguna said with surprise. She did not move away from her brother.

Arika saw immediately that she was in danger of losing Siguna. She let her eyes linger only briefly on the handsome boy who was staring at her out of narrowed gray eyes, and then she said to Siguna what she had come to say. "I have spoken to Dai, and he tells me that Fenris was not badly hurt. He has a shoulder wound, but evidently what felled him was a blow to the head. One of your men was found lying across your father's unconscious body, quite evidently protecting him."

"Surtur," Siguna said immediately. "It must have been Surtur." She turned and relayed Arika's message to Vili.

Even in the dimness of the unlit cave, Arika could see the flush of color that came into the boy's downy gold cheeks. He said something, and Siguna nodded.

"Was Surtur . . . the man who protected my father . . . was he alive?"

Arika shook her head.

Brother and sister looked at each other. It was Vili who spoke next. "What you do now?"

"I don't know." Arika looked at Siguna. "I don't know what Ronan's plans are, and I am thinking it would be wise of me to discover them. I am going to join the men at the River of Gold. Would you and your brother like to come with me?"

Chapter Thirty-seven

I n the end, Siguna and Vili left camp the following day escorted by Nel and Kasar. All four of them were riding the mares Nel had used so short a time ago to transport the shields. Arika had decided to follow after them on foot, with the Red Deer girls who had been guarding Vili as her escort.

"I have hopes of Siguna," Arika had said to Nel after her brief session in the cave with Siguna and Vili. "It is necessary, however, that she see her father."

Nel had not pushed the Mistress for a more extensive explanation, as Arika's wishes in this case echoed Nel's own. Instead, Nel had ridden out of the Red Deer camp with Kasar and her two charges at the first light of dawn the following day.

Vili was impressed by the riding ability of the two women who accompanied him. He had known Siguna could ride, of course, but he had never quite admitted to himself just how well she could manage a horse. And the other one, the one named Nel . . .

"You ride good," he said to her grudgingly after he had followed her in a swift gallop across an open pasture.

She gave him a friendly smile. "Your mares feel different from our horses," she said. "It takes some getting used to."

Vili understood only some of her words, and he glanced to Siguna for help. She translated.

He immediately looked interested. Nothing could catch Vili's attention like a discussion of horses. "How different?" he demanded.

"Your horses' shapes are different," Nel said. "Here"—and she pointed to the line of her mare's shoulder—"and here"—she pointed to the legs. "Legs are short."

"Short?" He did not like what he was hearing.

"Compared to ours"—this Nel returned tranquilly. "You will see. I will show you our stallions when we reach my husband's camp."

Siguna translated.

Vili nodded. "I see," he said. He curled his lip. "Short. Huh."

Nel smiled.

The sun was sinking toward the rim of the world when Nel and her party arrived at the edge of the valley and gazed out at the broad meadow through which the River of Gold flowed peacefully on its long journey to the sea. There was a large camp spread out upon the river's bank, and farther up the valley a herd of horses grazed in the light of the westering sun.

"Our horses," Vili said involuntarily.

"Where are our men?" Siguna asked Kasar urgently.

Kasar shaded his eyes as he looked into the sun. "In the camp with our men, I think. Come." Kasar pushed his mare forward to the edge of the hill. "We shall soon see."

Ronan and Fenris had been talking for some time, and both were finding the language barrier that divided them frustrating and time-consuming. Because of it they were only able to communicate in simple words and thoughts, and they were trying to come to terms about the future of Fenris's tribe—a subject that was most definitely not simple.

They heard Siguna's voice first, calling a word that Ronan did not know. He saw Fenris's head lift at its sound, saw the look that came over the kain's face. Fenris got to his feet just in time to catch his daughter in his arms.

Siguna was saying the same word over and over and over again as she clung to Fenris. The word, Ronan realized, must be *Father*.

Ronan was just beginning to reflect with pleasure that now Siguna was here he would have someone to translate between him and Fenris, when the figure of a young man stepped forward also, saying the same word.

The kain looked over Siguna's head. "Vili," he said, and held out his hand. The boy crushed his father's fingers to his forehead in a gesture that managed to suggest both homage and love and said something Ronan did not understand.

Ronan thought: How did Vili get here? He frowned, turned, and saw his wife walking toward him, followed as usual by her dogs. The rush of joy and wonder he always felt when he saw her surged through his heart. His frown was replaced by a smile, and he called, "Have you come to make sure I'm not mishandling your horses?"

"Sa," she returned. A few more paces and she had almost reached him. "Why else would I be here?" Without slowing her steps at all, she walked into his embrace.

It was Siguna who broke the family tableau first, pulling back slightly to stare up into Fenris's face. "Are you all right?" she asked fiercely, her eyes on the great multihued bruise that adorned his right temple.

"I am well," he answered. He looked from his daughter's face to that of his son. "You have heard? We were beaten."

"I have heard," Vili replied somberly.

"This is what is left." Fenris gestured to the men clustered behind him on the riverbank.

"It is hard to believe," Vili said. "So many men dead." His gaze returned to the kain. "What of your anda, Father?"

Fenris answered his son's unspoken question. "Bragi survived. He took some wounds, but the medicine men say he will recover."

Vili's face lightened slightly.

"They surprised us," Fenris said. His eyes moved to Ronan. "He is clever, that black-haired one. He attacked at night. He surprised me."

"But what is going to happen now, Father?" Siguna asked. "What is Ronan going to do with you?"

"We were just discussing that when you arrived," Fenris said. "You always were quick with their language, Siguna. It is good you are here. You can help us to understand each other."

Still within the protective circle of her father's arm, Siguna looked to Ronan. "My father wants me to translate between you."

Ronan nodded. "I had the same thought myself when I saw you. We have been talking for half the afternoon and have made scant progress."

"You are not going to kill him!" Siguna said quickly.

Ronan's face was impassive. "If I were going to kill him, Siguna, I would hardly need to discuss the matter with him."

Siguna said with dignity, "I will be happy to help with your discussion."

"Thank you."

Nel said firmly, "I think we should eat before you begin to discuss anything."

Ronan slipped his hand under her braid and rested it on the nape of her neck. "Did you bring some cooking herbs?" he asked hopefully.

She smiled up at him and shook her head. "I brought medicine herbs."

He sighed.

Listening to the exchange between Ronan and Nel, Siguna felt as if a great weight had rolled off of her chest. Ronan was going to make a bargain with her father. There was not going to be a slaughter. Fenris would be safe. She gave a tremulous smile and asked, trying to emulate the lightness of their tones, "Who is cooking for my father?"

"The same men who are cooking for us," Ronan replied gloomily. "Ask him how he likes the food."

Siguna turned to Fenris, her face bright with relief and joy. "Ronan wants to know how you like the food, Father."

The kain looked astonished. "How I like the food?"

"Yes. He is missing the hand of a woman in his food."

Fenris suddenly grinned. "He speaks true," he said to his daughter. He looked at Ronan and nodded. "The hand of a woman is noticeably missing," he said.

"There has to be something growing along the river we can use to season their food," Nel said to Siguna. "Come along with me, and we'll look."

"All right," Siguna agreed. She turned to Fenris. "Nel and I are going to look for some herbs for your food. I shall be back soon."

Fenris looked from his daughter to Nel to Ronan, then back again to his daughter. He shook his head in bewilderment. "That is good," he said. He looked again at Ronan.

Ronan said, "We talk. After." He made a gesture as of eating. All the amusement had fled from his face. It was perfectly sober.

Fenris nodded. "Sa," he said in Kindred speech. "We talk."

———

Nel said to Ronan, "What are you going to do with them?"

They had finished eating and were walking slowly along the river in the direction of the herd of mares. He did not answer her question but said instead, "The men think I am mad not to have slain them all. I had a fight with the chiefs over it. Neihle stood by me, and finally Haras did also."

She slipped her hand into his and curled her fingers around his thumb.

"I told them that the fight in the gorge was different," he said. "I had no choice there. We were still in danger. I could not afford to take prisoners, and it was kinder to kill the wounded than to let them be eaten alive by hyenas. But this time . . . this time we finished them."

Nel's only reply was briefly to lift his hand to her cheek.

"I kept thinking of what you said to me when we took Vili," he said in a sudden rush. " 'If we act as they do, then we are as bad as they are,' you said." His brows were knit as if in pain. "It is in my heart that you were right, Nel. If I kill all of these men, then I am no better than they were when they destroyed the tribes of the Fox and the Bear."

The river was red in the light of the setting sun. On the opposite side a small herd of deer had come to the water to drink. On their side of the river, a few ravens were circling over a large pile of stones. Ronan said, his eyes on the stones, "We burned their dead and buried what was left. I had the stones heaped up to keep the predators from digging up the grave."

Nel let out her breath. "How will the dead find their way to the underworld if they have been burned?"

"Fenris told me to do it. They were his men."

They walked for a while in silence. Then Nel said, "They are strange people,"

"Sa."

Nel asked once more, "What are you going to do with them?"

"I have been thinking I will send them back to the north, Nel, and make them settle there. There is no reason why they cannot lead a life such as ours, a life where they hunt animals and not men."

"Back to the frozen tundra?" Nel asked incredulously.

The sky to the west was streaked with red and black; against it Ronan's profile was outlined in sharp relief. "Na," he said. "I was thinking of the land near where the River of Gold flows to the sea. It was Kindred

land, I know, but there are few men of the Kindred left there now. It
is good hunting territory, minnow. The Tribe of the Owl lived a good
life there until the Horsemasters came ravaging through."

Nel nodded slowly. "There is only one problem. How can you be
certain they will stay there? How can you be certain they will not start
off on another journey of destruction the moment your back is turned?"

An utterly implacable look came over Ronan's aquiline profile. He
said, "I will keep their horses."

Nel halted. Her fingers tightened on his thumb, turning him so he
had to face her. The red sky rose behind his head like a halo. "Keep
their horses?" she repeated.

"Think, Nel," he said. "It is the horse that gave this group of men
their mobility. It is the horse that gave them their chief weapon of terror.
Take away their horses, and they become like any other tribe."

There was a breeze blowing off the river, and it ruffled through his
black hair, blowing a few strands forward across his cheek. Nel said,
"They can tame new horses, Ronan. They have the skill of it."

"Perhaps. But it will take them a very long time to catch wild horses
and tame them. They will not have the valley, like we did."

There was a thoughtful silence. "That is so," she said. She nodded
twice, then repeated slowly, "That is so."

In a single harmonious movement, they turned and began to retrace
their steps toward the camp. "What of their women?" Nel asked after
they had gone a little way.

"The captive Kindred women will stay with us. They will be welcome within any of our tribes, or, if they have family in any northern
tribes that are still intact, they can return there."

Nel smiled up at him. "It is a good plan," she said. "I have been
thinking and thinking ever since I heard of the captives of what we
could possibly do with them, and you have found the answer. You
always do."

"I must get Fenris to agree, of course."

Nel said, "He will have no choice."

It did not take the kain long to come to the same conclusion as Nel,
and he agreed to Ronan's terms.

"They will keep our horses?" Vili asked in horror when he learned of the terms of the agreement the following morning. "But without our horses we will be just like anybody else!"

"That is precisely what he wants," Fenris said wearily to his son. "He does not want to give us a chance to ride over his land any longer."

"Father!" Vili's gray eyes glittered. "All we have to do is pretend to go north. Then can we double around and steal back our horses from them."

"Ronan has already thought of that, Vili. He is sending men to escort us."

"He expects us to walk the entire length of the river?"

"Yes."

"It will be winter before we reach the country he is speaking of!"

Fenris shrugged. After a minute, he added, "He is also taking back our captive women."

Vili snarled, "This is outrageous."

The kain lifted a shaggy blond eyebrow. "It is an amazement to me that we are alive, Vili. Think you more on that, my son. If this Ronan were a man like me, we would all have been fed to the flames some days since."

Vili scowled, encountered his father's steady gaze, and dropped his eyes. When he raised them again he saw to his astonishment that Siguna was approaching them, and Arika was at her side.

"Name of the Thunderer," he muttered, "what is *she* doing here?"

"Father," Siguna said as soon as she had reached their side, "here is the Mistress of the Tribe of the Red Deer, who wishes to meet you."

Fenris gave his daughter a questioning look. "Mistress? What is a Mistress?"

"The Red Deer has a woman chief," Siguna said. "That is what she is called. Mistress."

Fenris said nothing, merely turned inscrutable gray eyes toward Arika's face. She met his gaze unflinchingly and remarked, "So this is your father, Siguna."

Fenris continued to regard the woman before him. Arika's aging skin could not completely mask the beauty of the sharp bones beneath, and her gaze was utterly ruthless. Very slowly, Fenris began to smile. "A woman chief," he said softly.

Siguna opened her lips to translate the remark, but he put his hand

upon her arm to halt her. He addressed himself directly to Arika. "You
are kain?"

Arika inclined her head. "Sa. I am kain."

Fenris looked at his daughter. "Truly," he said, "these people will
never cease to amaze me."

Vili stood by the river and gazed with burning eyes at the herd of
horses grazing at the far end of the meadow. As he watched, a rider on
a gray horse came out from beneath the shadow of the mountains and
galloped toward the herd. It was Ronan, riding his young stallion.

The horse was magnificent, Vili had to admit that—taller than their
own horses, with a long flowing mane, not the short, stubby one common to the horses Vili was familiar with.

The stallion was growing excited as he approached the mares, but
Ronan was managing to keep him to a direct, steady, forward gallop.

Name of the Thunderer, Vili thought, that was a horse!

A girl's voice sounded from behind him, and Vili swung around to
find the black-haired girl of the Red Deer standing there. He saw immediately that she was unarmed and alone.

They stared at each other, Vili noticing with surprise that her eyes
were not brown, as he had always thought, but dark blue. He gestured
to her hand and asked sarcastically, "Where spear?"

She shrugged. "I do not need it."

She was very beautiful, he thought, and his young male body immediately roused. It had been a long time since he had lain with a
woman. His eyes narrowed, and he looked at her speculatively. Why
had she sought him out?

She smiled at him with perfect frankness. "You look good," she
said. She looked him up and down. "You show me how good."

He blinked. Had he misunderstood? She held out her hand.
"Come," she said. "I will take you."

Vili never hesitated. He grasped her hand in his and let her lead
him away from the camp and toward the sloping side of the mountain.
Her hand was callused like a boy's. He heard someone behind them
shout, and she turned and called something back. When she faced
forward again, she was laughing.

They progressed steadily toward the shelter of the mountain and the
trees. Vili could feel the blood pulsing in his veins. The thought flitted

across his mind that perhaps she had hidden a weapon somewhere and was going to kill him.

He didn't care, so long as he could have her first.

They had reached the lower slope of the mountain. She dropped his hand and began to climb, following the path taken by the descending men several nights before. Vili followed.

A quarter of the way up the slope, sheltered by pines and fully leaved birches, was a small glade where the hill leveled off briefly. The black-haired girl turned to him. "My name is Lara," she said.

He pointed to his chest. "Vili."

"You are very," and she used a word he did not know. He frowned.

"Handsome," she repeated. He shrugged impatiently, still not understanding. He was not interested in talking. He grasped her arm, pulling her toward him. She came willingly, raising her hands to draw his mouth down to hers.

As Vili kissed her, he ran his hands up and down her body. She rubbed against him. He groaned and with one swift movement threw her to the ground, immediately plunging after her himself. Straddling her, a knee on either side of her hips, he began to rip off his trousers.

"Na, na, na, na," Lara said. She was a little breathless from hitting the ground so suddenly, but her blue eyes were very bright. He stared at her as she lay there beneath him. What did she mean, na? She was mad if she thought he'd stop now.

"Slow," she said to him. "It is better. Like this." She untied the thongs of her shirt, reached up for his hand and slid it under so it touched her naked breast. His fingers closed, and he felt her nipple stand up against his palm. She smiled. "Sa," she said huskily. "Good." Completely unafraid, she beckoned him to lie beside her, and, to his own amazement, he obeyed.

The next hour was a revelation to Vili. He had never dreamed that there could be so much more to mating than the simple act! Nor that such prolonged agony could be the source of such aching pleasure.

He could not wait long the first time, but the second time went on and on and on. Lara had skills Vili determined he would teach henceforth to every woman he ever lay with. And he himself found a pleasure he had never known before, when he saw that Lara was as hot and excited from his touch as he was from hers. He had not known women could feel that way. It was a decided improvement, he thought, over the brief and solitary pleasure he had known in all his previous encounters.

When it was over at last, and Vili lay on his back staring up into the blue sky, he thought of his father's women, and how they would look if the kain should chance to glance their way. Vili had always thought it was because his father was as strong as a stallion. After today, he suspected that it was something else.

Chapter Thirty-eight

There was utter chaos among the women left behind in the Horsemasters' camp when they learned of the defeat of their men. The first news had been brought by some of the Horsemasters who had managed to escape from the battlefield unharmed. Complete defeat: that was the word they carried. Three quarters of their men left dead or dying on the field. No one knew what the mountainmen would do with the men they had taken prisoners.

The women did not know what to do. Wives and mothers were frantic about the safety of their husbands and their sons. Captive women felt a spark of hope that the possibility of freedom might loom in their futures now that their captors were dead or defeated. But no one knew what to do.

Two days after his discussion with Fenris, Ronan collected a handful of mounted men, and Siguna and rode south along the River of Gold to the Horsemasters' camp to explain to the waiting women just what had been decided in regard to their future.

Kara gathered with the rest of the women and children in the wide open space along the river and listened to Siguna as she stood on the top of a sledge calling out the names of the men who had survived the fight and were being held captive by the mountainmen. The first name she had given was that of Fenris, and after hearing that, Kara stopped listening.

The list rolled on, with women shrieking with joy as they heard the name of a husband or a son. When the names were finished, a heavy silence fell. Those who had not heard the names they longed for stood like frozen statues.

"Not everyone who is unnamed is dead," Siguna said into that frozen hush. "Some escaped from the fight, but I do not have those names to give you."

At that, a woman near Kara began to weep audibly. Someone shushed her, and silence fell once more.

"What is to happen to our men who are still living? What is to happen to us?" It was Teala, Fenris's wife and Vili's mother, who called out the questions all were waiting to have answered.

"The leader of the mountainmen will tell you that," Siguna said, and she motioned to the black-haired man who had been standing near her on the ground. At her signal, he leaped with easy grace to join Fenris's daughter on the top of the sledge.

"Fenris and I have come to an agreement," he said in the language of the Kindred. He spoke with an unfamiliar accent, but Kara had no trouble understanding him. Siguna translated what he was saying so the women of the Horsemasters would be able to understand also.

Kara listened to his words with ever-increasing amazement and relief. There would be no massacre. There would be no further enslaving of women. Simply, the whole tribe of invaders would be pushed back to the north and deprived of their horses to ensure that they remained there.

"I know that there are large numbers of captive Kindred women among you," the black-haired man was saying. "Unfortunately, many of you come from tribes that no longer exist. Those of you who have parents or relatives in other tribes will be free to rejoin them. If there are some of you who wish to take husbands and make your homes with the tribes of these mountains, know you will be welcome." He paused and his face suddenly became very stern. "Whatever you may decide," he said, "know this: the women of the Kindred will no longer be forced to serve in the tents of the men who murdered their fathers and their husbands."

Silence fell. Siguna did not bother to translate the last sentence.

When they realized that the leader was done speaking, feminine voices speaking the language of the Kindred began to be heard.

"I shall return to my parents and the Tribe of the Horse," the woman behind Kara said excitedly.

"And I to the Tribe of the Marten," said someone else.

"Both my husband's and my father's tribe were destroyed," said a third woman bitterly. "I suppose I shall stay here in the mountains."

"What of our children?" a voice called out. "Many of us have had children by the men of this tribe. Will our children be welcome along with us?"

"A child belongs to its mother," the black-haired man replied in some surprise. "Of course your children will be welcome."

Kara rested her hand on her slightly rounded belly. She had known for over a moon now that she had a babe on the way.

If she returned to her father, he would marry her off to another man like her first husband. For the first time in many many moons, Kara thought of that husband. He had not been a bad man, she thought. He had never murdered anyone, never knowingly done harm to anyone. He had not been like Fenris.

He had been a better man than Fenris, she told herself. Any of the men of the Kindred were better men than the kain. If the victory had gone to the Horsemasters, there would have been a massacre. I must remember that, Kara thought. She drove her nails into her palms and inhaled unsteadily.

"So you will be leaving us soon." Kara turned to look into Teala's face. The kain's wife did not look as pleased at the prospect as Kara would have expected her to. Teala had never been actively unkind to her husband's favorite, but Kara knew that the woman resented her as she did not seem to resent the other women who dwelled in the kain's tent.

Kara said, "Yes. I will be leaving."

Teala's blue eyes regarded her bleakly. The breeze from the river blew the short fringe of hair on her forehead. "I had a great fear in my heart, but all will be well for the tribe so long as he is alive." Her mouth pinched together as if she felt a sudden pain. "It will be hard for him," she said. "Very hard."

For the first time, Kara noticed the strands of gray that threaded through Teala's coronet of blond braids. She noticed also that the kain's wife's face was thinner than it had been and sallow. She frowned and asked with quick concern, "Are you well, Teala?"

Teala gave her a narrow, measured look and did not answer. Instead she said, "It was no surprise to me to see Siguna. That is the kind of girl you are never easily rid of."

Kara said softly, "The kain must have been glad to see her. He always had a fondness for her."

"She won't stay with him," Teala said. "Not that one. He will be left to face this alone . . ." Abruptly, Fenris's wife turned and moved off.

Later, as the women gathered their most basic belongings and loaded them onto the handful of sledges they were being allowed, Kara asked one of the steppe women who had been with Fenris for a very long time if Teala was well.

"No," the brief answer came. "She has been sick for some time. I do not think she will live to see our new home."

Kara made a sound of sorrow.

"Her son lives," the other woman said bitterly. "I would give up my life too, if only I could say the same."

Kara thought of the eager young face of the kain's second son and felt the weight of his mother's sorrow.

The men harnessed the mares they had ridden to the loaded sledges and set off with the women and children up the River of Gold. It was a slower trip by foot, and two days passed before they reached the meadow where the Federation tribes were camped with their captives.

At Ronan's signal, the caravan halted along the river. The figure of a man detached itself from the crowded men's camp and began to approach. Kara's heart leaped in her breast when she saw it was Fenris. He halted at a little distance from the train of women and waited for the black-haired chief, who was moving to join him.

Kara stared at the kain greedily, reassuring herself that he was indeed alive and well. He seemed to be carrying one arm a little more stiffly than usual, but otherwise he looked perfectly normal. As Kara watched, the two men met and spoke to each other. Then the kain turned and signaled toward the camp he had just left. Immediately men began to stream toward the train of women.

Kara, who had no husband or son to greet and exclaim over, withdrew to the edge of the caravan to be out of the way. Fenris and Ronan stood side by side and watched as husbands and sons and fathers were reunited with wives and mothers and children. Kara did not watch the reunions, however. Instead, she watched Fenris.

He was looking at Teala and Vili, his face a calm, inscrutable mask. She saw when his eyes left his wife and his son and began to search slowly among the crowd of Kindred women. When his eyes found her she was ready.

They looked at each other across the distance. His face never changed. Then, still slowly, his eyes moved on.

It was men of the Kindred who separated out the women of their race, smiling and speaking gently to the pack of former captives whom they were taking in their charge.

"Most of us are from tribes far to the north of these mountains," one girl said when they were all collected together in a separate camp. "How will we get back to our families?"

A lovely, brown-haired girl with unusual green eyes answered gently, "We will send riders to all of the tribes of the Kindred with the news of your rescue and ask them to send men to the Great Cave to escort you home."

"Home!" one of the girls said on a heartfelt sigh. "I can scarce believe it has happened at last!"

The day waned, the sun set, and the women and children settled down to sleep. On the morrow, the depleted tribe of Horsemasters would begin its trip north, escorted by an armed and mounted contingent of Federation men, who would make certain they reached their destination.

Kara did not sleep at all. She was haunted by the face of Fenris as it had been this afternoon. Calm. Resigned. Marked with lines of pain that Kara knew were not set there by physical discomfort. He had lost huge numbers of his men. He had lost two of his own sons. He would lose more of his children, as their mothers chose to leave him to return to their own tribes. For some reason, the picture of Fenris watching a wrestling match with one of his little boys perched on his shoulders kept flashing into her mind.

He will be left to face this alone.

These men who had taken them in charge were very kind, Kara told herself again and again. She must remember that, think of that.

They were giving the women their choice, something that was unheard of in Fenris's world.

Kara arose at dawn and moved through the thin valley mist toward the river's edge where the caravan of Horsemasters was assembled, ready to depart. Ronan had allowed them the temporary use of horses to pull the sledges, and a few of the smallest children and the more seriously wounded men rode on the sledges with the tents and household belongings. Ten armed and mounted men, led by a huge man Kara heard Ronan address as Bror, prepared to escort the beaten tribe.

Fenris was on foot with the rest of his men. Kara felt a pain in her heart to see him so. Fenris without his horse! How would he bear it?

They were beginning to move forward when Fenris turned and saw her. She stood, not breathing, not thinking, only looking at him. Just then the last of the mist lifted, and the sun rising over the top of the mountain struck bright sparks from his shaggy blond hair. She saw his gray eyes crinkle slowly at the corners in the way she loved. She saw him smile, saw him lift a hand. His lips moved, formed a word. "Come."

She took one step, and then one more. Then she was running. He had opened his arms and she was in them, held tightly against him, back where she wanted to be.

Arika could feel the mood in the Federation camp change almost as soon as the Horsemasters were out of sight around the bend in the river. Things here were finished; it was time to move beyond the battle, time for all the tribes to return home.

However, when she mentioned to Neihle that the Red Deer men ought to begin preparing to leave the valley, her brother gave her a strange look. "The men have been talking, Arika," he said, "and there is something we would like to discuss with you."

Arika grew immediately wary. "What is it?"

Neihle lifted both his hands. "Let a few of us go apart from the other tribes. This is something that concerns the Red Deer only."

"Very well," Arika said crisply. "Where?"

"This way," Neihle said, and for the first time Arika saw the group of Red Deer men gathered in the grass near the base of the hill. Slowly she walked beside her brother, and despite her calm face, her heart was filled with apprehension. The apprehension did not lessen when she saw that it was not just the young men who awaited her, but a representative group of older men as well. In fact, and her eyes surveyed the solemn male faces once more, it seemed as if all the age-set leaders were here. Her apprehension deepened.

"Greetings, Mistress," the men murmured respectfully as she arrived in their midst.

Arika nodded coldly.

"Sit down, please," Neihle said, and one of the men spread a deer-skin robe on the grass for her. They had come prepared, Arika thought grimly. She sat.

The men looked to Neihle. "Mistress," he said. His face and his voice were grave. He was sitting across the circle from her, and he met her gaze now and held it. "The men of the Red Deer wish to invite Ronan to rejoin the tribe."

Her thin nostrils quivered faintly. She had known it had to do with Ronan. "Why?" she asked.

"If Ronan returns to us, then Nel will return also, and it is our wish to have Nel as Mistress after you are gone."

Arika was not fooled by Neihle's soft, reasonable voice. Her eyes narrowed. Her own voice was icy. "It is not the business of the men of the tribe to name the next Mistress."

Neihle's gaze shifted slightly. Arika knew she could control her brother; she always had. She looked to the other men.

Tyr said firmly, "We want Nel to be our Mistress, this is true. But we also want Ronan to be our chief. Thus is it done in all the other tribes who follow the Mother: the husband of the Mistress is the chief. And thus do we desire it to be done in the Tribe of the Red Deer."

It was her greatest fear, spoken out loud by Ronan's closest friend. Arika stiffened her back, drew the mantle of her authority about her, and prepared to fight. "Who are you to say what shall or what shall not be done in the Tribe of the Red Deer? I am the Mistress, the voice of the Mother. I am the one to speak for the tribe."

This time Tyr's dark blue eyes did not falter. "We are the men of the tribe, Mistress," he answered. "We are the fighters. We are the hunters. We want one of our own kind to lead us, and the one that we want is Ronan."

She had always feared that one day the men would try to assert their power. It was why she had put aside her son and why, finally, she had banished him. And she realized now, with bitter despair, that it had all been for nothing.

"Na," she said nevertheless.

"We let you drive him out once," Tyr said. "We knew, all of us, that Morna lied." He leaned a little forward, compelling her attention. "*You* knew that Morna lied, Mistress. Yet still you drove him out. And to our shame, we let you do it. But no more. Ronan is a man of the Red Deer. He is a man for the tribe to be proud of, and we say that he shall take his rightful place among us."

There was an acrid taste in Arika's mouth.

"You are no longer young, Mistress," Erek said persuasively. "There must be someone to take your place when you are gone. Nel is the great-granddaughter of Elen. Who could be better than she?"

Arika opened her mouth to suggest Siguna and then closed it again. In the mood they were in, the worst thing she could do was to suggest the name of an outsider. "There are many girls of the Red Deer who could take my place," she said instead.

"There are none like Nel," said Neihle.

Of course, it was not Nel she was objecting to. They all knew that.

There were geese swimming on the river. Arika watched them, small black dots on the golden water, identifiable to her only by the honking sounds they made. Her eyes were not what once they had been, she thought. It was true. She was growing old.

Ronan had won. The men were trying to distract her with talk of Nel, but Arika knew what would happen. Ronan would take over the tribe, and Nel would let him do it.

"When did you discuss this with Ronan?" she asked bitterly. Implied, even if not said, was the added thought: Behind my back.

Tyr did not look at all ashamed. "We haven't."

It was a moment before Arika understood. "You haven't discussed this with him?"

"We wished to speak with you first, Arika," Neihle said.

"That is kind of you," she replied with icy courtesy. Her brother at least had the grace to look ashamed. "When were you planning to speak to Ronan?" she added.

They looked at each other.

"Get him," she ordered Tyr. Let them do it now, she thought. In my presence. Let it be as difficult for them as it can be.

After a moment's hesitation, in which he again exchanged glances with the other men, Tyr arose and began to walk in the direction of the main camp.

Ronan, too, had been making plans for the future. In fact, he and Unwar were just concluding a discussion when Tyr approached and requested Ronan's presence.

"Of course," Ronan agreed courteously if somewhat abstractedly, his mind still on the conversation he had just finished. He nodded to the chief of the Leopard and turned toward Tyr.

"We will need Nel also," Tyr said.

That caught Ronan's attention. He looked at Tyr, a line between his slender black brows. "Do you want to tell me what this is about?" he asked pleasantly.

Tyr shook his head. "You will know very shortly."

"Nel is with the captive women," Ronan said.

"Wait here," Tyr said, "and I will get her."

Ronan folded his arms across his chest, balanced himself on slightly spread feet, and looked at the flock of geese on the river. His mind turned to his conversation with Unwar. It had gone even better than he had hoped. Then he began to think of his plans for the future.

A dog yipped in pain. Ronan turned to see Sintra looking up indignantly at Nel.

"She walked right under my feet!" Tyr was exclaiming. "I didn't see her."

Nel gave the dog's head a brisk pat and continued to walk on. "She's always trying to get next to me, Tyr, and she's slowed down because of the puppies she's carrying. I'm sorry. I should have told you to look out for her."

"Those fool dogs," Ronan said as they all came up to him, Sintra pressed close to Nel's knees. "Nigak has far too much intelligence, not to mention dignity, to get himself stepped on."

"That is true," Nel said fairly. Behind Tyr's back, she gave Ronan a questioning look. He shrugged to indicate his own ignorance, and the two of them obligingly fell into step with Tyr.

Ronan felt a shock of deep surprise when he saw that Arika was with the men. He glanced quickly at Nel and saw that she was frowning.

What's afoot here? he thought.

The men of the Red Deer were seated in a circle, and they indicated the place they had made for Ronan and Nel. Mystified as well as faintly uneasy, Ronan sat down and looked at Arika.

But it was Neihle, not Arika, who began to speak. He had to repeat himself twice before Ronan understood.

Dhu, he thought. He stared in stunned amazement at the male faces around him. They were faces he knew well. Faces he had grown up with. His eyes came to Arika and stopped.

She looked back at him, her head held proudly, her eyes glitteringly bright. It was the moment of her defeat, and both of them knew it. She had never looked more like a chief.

The geese were rising from the river now. The whole sky was whirring and wheeling with them, and the sound of their *keer-onks* echoed down the valley.

He heard himself asking, "What of my people from the Tribe of the Wolf?"

"I have no doubt that they will be welcomed back into their former tribes," Neihle said. "After all, it is largely because of the Tribe of the Wolf that these mountains were saved from destruction."

"Those of your people who worship the Goddess can come to us," Erek added generously.

Silence fell. The geese were winging their way up the river now, honking and yulking to each other in the way of their kind. Ronan watched them disappear in the direction of the devastated home camps of the tribes of the Fox and the Bear.

"Well?" said Tyr.

Ronan turned to Nel, who was sitting so quietly by his side. What shall I do? he asked her with his eyes. What do you want me to do?

She returned his look gravely, then rested one slender hand upon his knee. He understood from its light pressure that she was leaving the decision up to him.

This was what he had always wanted, to be chief of the Red Deer. Even as a boy, deep in the innermost recesses of his heart, he had wanted it. When he had left home, a pariah, an exile, he had sworn to come back as the chief. It had even been part of the reason he had married Nel, because through her he had hoped to win his heart's desire.

How ironic that now it was being offered to him, he no longer cared. More—he no longer wanted it. He realized, with a great lift of his heart, that at long last he was free of his mother.

He covered the slim fingers on his knee with his own warm hand. He said, "I have already decided not to take the Tribe of the Wolf back to the valley. There is not room enough there for additional people, and what is left of the tribes of the Fox and the Bear are going to join with us. We will occupy the old homesites of those two tribes. I have made certain that this is acceptable to the Tribe of the Leopard, which will be our nearest neighbor. Unwar has extended his welcome."

There was absolute silence. Even the noise of the geese had faded. Nel's fingers turned and laced themselves with his.

"You will not come back to us?" Neihle said at last.

"Na, Uncle. I already have a tribe that depends upon me. I cannot abandon them now."

Silence fell again. Then Arika said, "I am proud of you, my son."

Ronan smiled with genuine amusement. "I am certain that you are, Mother," he said. "I am certain that you are."

EPILOGUE

One year later

They stood shoulder to shoulder at the place where the ravine widened to give access to the valley. The scene before them was brilliantly illuminated by the bright afternoon sun: the mirror-calm lake; the thick, lush, snow-fed grass, ablaze with flowers; the enclosing walls, with flowers growing in all the tiny crevices. In the distance beyond the walls loomed the snowy peaks of the Altas, shimmering white bridges between heaven and earth.

Nigak pushed past Ronan and cantered out onto the grass. Then, flattening out and running like the wind, he streaked away down the valley.

Nel laughed softly. "He is home."

"Mama," piped a small clear voice from the cradleboard slung upon Ronan's back. "Igak!"

"He'll be back, Culen," Nel said. "Nigak always comes back."

"The huts don't look as if they have been touched," Ronan murmured, and Nel followed his gaze. In unison they started forward, each leading a horse and followed by Sintra and Leir.

White Foot whinnied excitedly as he recognized where he was. The horse herd was halfway down the valley, but Nel could see how Impero's head lifted at the sound of that whinny.

"I had almost forgotten how beautiful it is," she murmured.

"The most beautiful place in the world," he said.

Nel sighed.

They went to their old hut, and Nel unwrapped Culen from his cradleboard and set him on his feet. A group of the men of the Wolf had come to the valley last autumn to collect some of the belongings that the tribe had left behind, but neither Ronan nor Nel had been back since they had left to go and fight the Horsemasters over one year before.

Culen toddled around the hut. He had already been walking for two moons and was quite steady on his feet. Sintra and Leir followed him, sniffing nostalgically at remembered smells.

Ronan collected the old water pot that was still in the hut and went to get water from the lake.

Nel untied the sleeping skins that had been fastened to the horses' backs and spread them on the hut floor, first removing the cooking utensils that were wrapped inside them. As soon as Culen saw the cookpot, he came running. "Hungy. Hungy."

"I know, love. I know. Mama will cook soon."

Outside, they could hear Ronan giving water to the horses.

"Tirsty," Culen said, and went determinedly to the door. He called, "Dada, I tirsty."

"Come down to the lake with me, then, and we'll get you a drink," Ronan answered. Culen rushed off.

Left alone, Nel regarded the remaining fruits and grains she had stored in the cookpot. Ronan was going to have to get them something to eat, she thought. Perhaps a fish from the lake. Fish was easy for Culen to chew.

Most Kindred children had nothing but mother's milk until they were almost three years of age, but Nel had begun to feed Culen real food as soon as he had a few teeth. She had found that, if she mashed his fruits and chewed his meats for him, he could eat just fine. In fact, she thought it was good for him. He was larger than most children his age and had begun to walk and talk at an early age.

She went to the door of the hut and looked out. Ronan had lifted Culen to his shoulders, and the little boy was riding proudly, surveying the scene before him like a chief. Nel smiled mistily to see them so.

I am glad that we decided to do this, she thought. It is good to be by ourselves for a little. When we are at home, it is so hard just to be by ourselves.

She repeated her thought to Ronan later that evening, after Culen had been put to sleep and the two of them had gone outside so Ronan could build a watch fire.

"I know," he answered. He left the blazing fire and came over to where she was standing near the hut. As they stood together watching the fire, he said, "The bigger the tribe gets, the more of our time it seems to take up."

"I miss the days in the valley," she said softly. She laughed. "Remember the fuss over the horse-calling ceremony?"

"Mmmm." He sounded amused.

"Life was simpler then," she said.

"We could never have kept the number of horses we have now if we had stayed in the valley," he pointed out. "You know that. You were the one who was always complaining about the difficulty of keeping stallions."

"I know. Horsekeeping is certainly much easier now that we have the Horsemasters' mares with just Cloud to lead them. Nor does Cloud seem to mind White Foot and Frost, the way Impero would."

"He would mind them if we set them loose to join the herd, but as long as we keep them separate in their own corral, they are safe."

"The other tribes appear to be faring well with the horses we gave to them."

"They are learning," Ronan said.

Nel rested her cheek against his shoulder. "The valley brings back so many memories of Thorn," she said.

She felt him stiffen. She knew he felt responsible for Thorn's death. This last year she had tried and tried to tell him he was foolish to blame himself, but he would not listen. Finally, she had come to understand that it was precisely this very ruthlessness in holding himself accountable that made Ronan such a fine chief.

"He has left a gap in the tribe," Ronan said. "It is still there."

"Sa."

Despite the fire, the night air was cool, and she pressed closer to his warmth.

"Come inside, Nel," he said in a low voice.

Inside, the light from the single stone lamp showed them Culen sleeping peacefully, nestled between Sintra and Leir.

Ronan smiled. "I sometimes fear that Culen will grow up thinking he is a dog himself."

Nel chuckled.

It was warmer within the hut, and the air smelled faintly of the fish that Nel had grilled earlier. She sat down on her sleeping skins and began to undo the braid in her hair. Ronan went to the water pot and ladled himself a drink. She watched as he tipped his head back, watched the working of the muscles in his strong brown throat as he swallowed. He finished his drink, stripped his buckskin shirt over his head, and went to hang it on the wall.

For all of her earlier complaints, Nel thought, it had been a happy year for them both. The wound of rejection Ronan had carried in his heart ever since his expulsion from the Tribe of the Red Deer had finally healed. He could meet his mother now with no more emotion than he showed to Haras or any of the other chiefs. He had done so, in fact, at the last Spring Gathering.

And for her, the wound of childlessness had healed also. She had Culen now. Ironically, Morna's hate-filled legacy had proved a means of strengthening Ronan's marriage instead of destroying it. Every time Nel saw her husband pluck Culen from amongst the dogs and lift the shrieking and delighted baby to his shoulders, joy and gratitude surged through her heart.

Ronan had finished undressing and was coming toward her now on bare and silent feet. Nel shook out her hair and untied the thongs at the neck of her shirt.

"You are slow tonight, minnow," he said, and kneeling in front of her, he finished the job of undressing her himself.

They stretched out together on the sleeping skins, and as he kissed her, his fingers gently caressed her breasts. The familiar ache of passion began to build, and when his tongue slipped in between her lips she opened her mouth against his, sinking under his touch, yielding her body utterly to his caresses.

"Nel." His voice sounded like a growl. His mouth was all over her now, and she was quivering and quivering, reaching for him, seeking him, needing him.

"Come inside me, Ronan," she whispered. "Now. Come now."

The time for gentleness was over, and when he drove into her hard, filling her full, she closed around him, holding to him, moving with him in the most ancient of all mankind's rituals.

The following day, accompanied by Culen, Nigak, and the dogs, they walked up the valley to the cave that Thorn had made his own.

After the brightness of the day, it was very dark inside, and Ronan lit both of the stone lamps they had brought with them. Nigak and the dogs curled up outside in the sunshine, and Culen, after peering distrustfully into the damp darkness, announced that he would stay with the animals.

Nel hesitated. "He will be all right, Nel," Ronan said. "There are no real predators in the valley, certainly nothing that Nigak cannot handle."

"All right," Nel relented, and the two of them lifted their lamps and entered the cave together.

It was a small cave, nothing like the tremendously deep sacred cave of Thorn's Buffalo tribe. This cave had only two chambers: a small outer room and a larger inner chamber, and it was in the inner room that Thorn had done his work.

Ronan felt his breath catch as he realized what it was that surrounded him on the walls: scenes of the valley, drawn in black pitch and colored in ocher. There was an ibex pawing with a foreleg, to sweep the snow away from its forage; there a sheep, peacefully reclining, its eyes mere slits of satisfaction as it chewed its cud. And horses. Everywhere on the wall there were horses.

"Look," Nel said, "there is White Foot! And Acorn!"

"Sa, and here is Impero, standing guard over the mares."

After a while they moved slowly on, circling the cave to their left, and as they moved they realized that while Thorn had devoted the right wall to the valley animals, the back wall had been devoted to something else.

"Ronan," Nel said. "Look how he has drawn Berta."

Without a doubt it was Berta, with her smooth dark hair and her large brown eyes. It was a picture of her head and shoulders only, and Thorn had caught the secret smile that so often played upon her lips.

Thorn had been true to his word, Ronan saw, and had only drawn those members of the tribe who had not objected. "Here you are, Nel," he said.

"Sa."

Slowly they moved along until they came to the end of the back wall; then they turned to look at the wall to their left. The other walls had been uneven, and Thorn had placed his pictures according to the contours of the rock. But the left wall was very smooth, and as Ronan lifted his stone lamp he realized that it contained only one very large painting.

"Oh . . ." It was Nel's soft breath as she came to stand beside him and saw what was there.

It was a painting of Ronan and Cloud, a painting of their two faces, the stallion's positioned just above the man's, as if he were standing at the man's shoulder. Together, they seemed to be watching something that was out of reach of the painting.

Ronan looked at Cloud's face. Arched, regal, and masculine, the eyes wide-set and large, the edges of the thin flaring nostrils dilated in faint alarm, his horse might almost be breathing, so real did he seem. Ronan felt tears sting behind his eyes.

Thorn, he thought. *Thorn.*

"You look alike," Nel was saying wonderingly. "Why did I never see that before? You and Cloud look alike."

Ronan tried to swallow around the lump in his throat. He glanced at his own picture. "Are you saying I look like a horse, minnow?"

"Your expressions are the same," Nel said. "Look. Surely you can see for yourself what Thorn has done."

"Sa," he said after a moment. "We look like arrogant bullies, the both of us."

He felt her arm come around his waist. He never had to tell Nel what he was feeling; she knew.

"He should not have died," Ronan said harshly.

"What he did in this cave will remain," Nel said. "Long after you and I are dead, Ronan. Long after the Tribe of the Wolf is but a memory, this cave, and what Thorn did here, will remain."

He thought about that, thought about what might happen, many many years hence, when strange people might come into this cave and see these pictures upon the walls.

"He drew for the joy of it," Ronan said. "He did not do it for a hunting ceremony, or for any other reason save the pure joy of it."

"It is in my heart that you can see that in the pictures."

A small voice came from the outer chamber. "Mama?"

"Dhu," said Nel, and she moved hastily toward the doorway. "I am coming, Culen. Stay where you are, please."

"Where Dada?" Ronan heard the child say next.

"He is coming too."

With one last look at the picture upon the wall, Ronan turned away and moved to rejoin his family.